THE VISION

The scene shifted, and Jenna was inside a cavern with Arion, lying on a blanket. *Did Saura have caves?* She stared up at him as he leaned down and kissed her, a surprise because to the best of her knowledge, Leors did not kiss. He spread her legs and settled between them, and oddly she felt no fear. Then the scene shifted again. She stared down at her rounded belly.

"You will present Arion with a daughter," whispered a voice, and for the first time, Jenna felt real hope. Then dark clouds drifted around her. When they cleared, she stood on the edge of a deep pit. Below her, Arion was chained to a wall. Covered with dirt and blood, he stared up at her. *"He will need your faith in him, and your love,"* came the voice. *"It will be his salvation."*

SHADOW FIRES

CATHERINE SPANGLER

LOVE SPELL

NEW YORK CITY

LOVE SPELL®

February 2004

Published by

Dorchester Publishing Co., Inc.
200 Madison Avenue
New York, NY 10016

ISBN 0-505-52525-9

The name "Love Spell" and its logo are trademarks of Dorchester Publishing Co., Inc.

Printed in the United States of America.

Visit us on the web at www.dorchesterpub.com.

SHADOW
FIRES

To my children, Jim and Deborah—this one's for you.

To Jim, a son who is intelligent, compassionate, good natured and witty, with a passion for life. Like Ferdinand the bull, you know how to take time to smell the flowers. I hope you'll always find joy in life's simple pleasures, even as you find causes to champion.

To Deb, a daughter who is smart and loving, creative and fun, and so very talented. You're beautiful inside and out. The world is your stage, and you'll be a smashing success, whatever you do. May you always have a song to sing, and a dream to dream.

Both of you have been behind me all the way, from long hours with my study door closed, to fast food dinners, to that "first call" (and you kept the secret very well). You're my pride and joy, and I love you.

ACKNOWLEDGMENTS

This book was tough to write, and I couldn't have done it without a lot of help. As always, a special thanks to David Gray for his technical expertise (and for explaining kinetic weapons).

Thanks to my coworkers and readers, Angelica Blocker, Robyn Delozier, Charity Elkins, Beth Gonzales, and Carole Turner, who promised me the book wasn't awful.

Much gratitude to my critique partners and best friends, Linda Castillo, Jennifer Miller, and Vickie Spears, for brainstorming, encouragement, and also promising the book was all right.

Ditto to good friend and agent extraordinaire Roberta Brown, who did a lot of hand holding through this one. You're the best.

I want to express my continued appreciation to Chris Keeslar, who listened as I apprehensively listed the darker elements of this book, convinced he would object, but he merely said, "Cool." He's always willing to walk the edge and let his authors explore new territory and grow—which is the mark of a good editor. Thanks, Chris.

Chapter One

He stood on the bridge of the massive spacecraft, his powerful legs braced as the ship began its descent toward Candest. He maintained his balance with one large hand lightly gripping the edge of the main console. Like his legs, his chest was bare, with well-delineated muscles rippling beneath golden skin. Silent and majestic, he waited. Suddenly his head turned, and his unblinking midnight gaze fixed unerringly upon her.

Terror jolted through Jenna, momentarily disrupting the vision. He couldn't possibly see her. She was inside her modest quarters in Shamara; he was on a Leor warship, still on the outer edges of Candest's stratosphere. She gasped for breath, her chest heaving, as she tried to dispel the vision, to break its insidious hold on her. But like a nightmare that would not end, the images resumed, sucking her into a clairvoyant vortex she could not evade. . . .

He still stood there. His face was clearly recognizable, even though it had been more than four seasons since she'd seen it—just that one time; even though she'd never actually met any Leors. But she knew him. He had high,

1

bold cheekbones; a powerful, square jaw; a prominent, wide forehead; all creating the frame for surprisingly sensual lips, a starkly chiseled nose, and black-hole eyes so dark, no pupils were visible. No facial hair or eyebrows softened his chilling visage, no hair of any sort covered his gleaming head.

She'd always sensed the thoughts of those in her visions, and his were no exception: *Determination, edged by desperate need and utter ruthlessness. Cold, logical analysis of obstacles to be overcome and the most direct methods of doing so, without compunction or mercy.*

Again he looked directly at Jenna, and her heart battered against her chest. A staggering energy snaked between them, a treacherous snare. The command bridge faded from sight, and everything around them ceased to exist. No ship, no Shamara—only the two of them, in the vastness of the universe.

The vision ended abruptly, and Jenna lurched out of her chair. She wanted to run, fast and far. But she knew it was useless. She felt the inundating chill and the sick sensation in the pit of her stomach that always followed on the heels of a vision. Even with the link severed, and even though the Leor's ship must still be several hundred kilometers away, his powerful presence lingered in her chamber, a cruel hint of her future. She couldn't escape him, no matter how hard she might try.

She knew, with absolute certainty, why he was here. Just as she knew what would happen next. Her fate was sealed. She had foreseen it in a vision on Liron over four seasons past, and had long ago learned the futility of trying to alter the course of destiny. Her visions were never wrong and could not be thwarted.

She'd never had any other discernment of her own future, either before or since that fateful cycle of the pink moon, the same cycle that Ranul san Mars, the great

Shielder leader, had passed on. Not that it made any difference. Her fate had been decreed by Spirit. She sank back into the chair, willing her heart to stop racing and air to return to her lungs. She couldn't let panic take hold. It would accomplish nothing.

The roar of an overhead ship drew her attention. She rose and went to the entry. Stepping outside, she looked skyward. A huge, glittering black and red warship passed overhead, dropping lower as it approached the landing pads. The Leor had arrived.

And with him came the end of her existence. Dread clawed at her, and Jenna pressed a trembling hand against the panel frame to steady herself. She wanted to scream out in protest, to rage against the forces orchestrating this cruel turn of events.

But it did no good to curse the reality, or to resist it. Her life, as insignificant and drab as it was, had never been hers to command. She'd always been at the mercy of her visions, guided by the will of Spirit, or so she'd always fervently insisted. She couldn't—wouldn't—accept the possibility that her ability might come from the dark side of the universal forces. Just as she couldn't avoid fate.

Slowly, Jenna turned and went inside. She knew what she must do now. Since there was no way she could alter the destiny hurtling head-on toward her, she would face her fate with dignity and make the best she could out of her situation. She slipped on a cape to protect against the chill of the morning, raising the hood to avoid being recognized and thus shunned.

Because of her clairvoyance and her uncanny ability to predict the future, the other Shielder colonists had always maintained a wary distance. Superstitious, forced to expend every micron of energy to survive, they found it simpler to avoid her than deal with their fears.

There was nothing for her in Shamara. Nor did anyone

care that her destiny was that of mating with the leader of a barbaric and cruel race.

Her life here, and her freedom, had just come to an end.

"We are not in the business of bartering people, Your Lordship," Jarek san Ranul said, a hard edge to his voice. "We have plenty of irridon to offer in return for your services."

"I don't need irridon. I need a mate." Arion, ruling Comdar of Saura, set his drink on the conference table. He found having to bargain for a bride almost as abhorrent as mating outside his race. Yet he had no choice.

Problems from generations of inbreeding among the small Leor populace, along with the short fertile cycles of Leor females, necessitated that new gene pools be introduced. The Komiss, the council overseeing all Leor clans, had decreed that the leaders of each clan would take a non-Leor mate to ensure strong, healthy future leaders, and to avoid extinction. Producing offspring had become even more crucial with the Controllers' increasing aggression toward the Leors.

"I'm aware of your people's problems, but I cannot condone using human lives as a medium of exchange," san Ranul responded. "With all due respect, Your Lordship, Shielders are highly opposed to slavery. We have worked too hard to free ourselves from the oppression of the Controllers to willingly allow any of our people to be forced into such a state."

Arion was well aware of the Shielder aversion to bondage, just as he suspected san Ranul knew Leor society had a lower caste system consisting of slaves. While Arion believed the Shielders were too lenient in some regards, he had nothing but respect for the ferocity with which they'd battled, and won, their freedom from the Controllers. He also respected Captain san Ranul, who had rallied his people and led them through a wormhole to this different section of the galaxy, then created new settlements.

"We do not look upon our human mates as slaves," he said. "They are accorded the same treatment our Leor females receive—that of equals."

"Yet you trade services in exchange for those mates, as if they were commodities rather than living, sentient beings."

"Trading services for goods is what we do, Captain. I am sure you know most of our settlements are in deserts and basically barren. For generations, Leors have survived by bartering. We fight in battles, transport goods, and offer protection on trade routes and other ventures. In return, we receive whatever we need to survive, including the means for our race to continue."

San Ranul drew a deep breath. "Comdar Arion, I do not want our differences on this matter to drive a wedge in our working relationship. Our initial agreement with Komissar Gunnar was the exchange of irridon in return for transporting Shielder settlers from the other quadrant. As I stated earlier, we have ample stores of irridon."

Feeling the chill of the meeting hall, Arion rose and strode to the large firebox where heat stones glowed, sending out a beckoning warmth. He tossed back his cape and let the heat seep into his skin. "My need for a viable mate is greater than the need for irridon." He turned to face the Shielder leader. "And your need to transport two newly uncovered Shielder settlements from the grasp of the Controllers is also very great. It is miraculous that they have survived this long."

"You also need irridon," san Ranul argued. "It provides the majority of your fuel, both for your spacecraft and on your settlements. I don't see why we can't reach an agreement that doesn't involve the exchange of—"

"I have stated my terms. Would you place the welfare of two entire settlements over that of one individual female?"

"One life sacrificed to save many?" San Ranul walked to the firebox. He stared at Arion. "How can I place a value on any life, or determine if one life is more important than another?"

Such weakness to put so much significance on a single life. The good of the majority must always come first—a philosophy san Ranul had once lived by. Perhaps the Shielder leader had grown soft, but it was far more likely he thought he'd be able to deal with another Leor. If so, he was mistaken. Arion turned toward the entry. "Then I am afraid we cannot do business."

"Wait." San Ranul followed him. "There must be some way around this impasse."

Arion slowed. It went against his nature to give anyone a second chance, or to negotiate his terms. Few people were foolish enough to consider suggesting such to a Leor. But the Shielders and the Leors had enjoyed a profitable business relationship for over four seasons, and the Komissar had a connection with them through his mate.

He turned to face san Ranul. "Take the issue to your people. Perhaps one of your females would come willingly, for the good of all."

San Ranul considered. "There are very few women who would meet your requirements. The majority of our women are mated, or too young, too old, or not virgins."

"Virginity is one requirement on which I will not compromise," Arion said.

"I'm well aware of that, Your Lordship."

"I only require one mate, Captain. Again, I suggest asking your people. If one of your females comes forward—"

"I will do it."

The feminine voice caught Arion by surprise, and he turned toward the entry. A slight figure stood there, shrouded in a hooded cape. San Ranul appeared just as surprised. "What did you say?" he asked.

The figure took a step forward. "I am offering to go with this Leor." Her voice was low, soft.

Shock registering on his face, san Ranul strode toward the figure. "Jenna? Is that you?"

"Yes, Captain."

"I don't need to ask how you knew Comdar Arion was here, but . . ." He hesitated, then gestured toward Arion. "I'm not sure you understand what the Comdar is requesting."

Her head shifted toward Arion. "I think I do."

Intrigued, Arion moved around the Shielder leader. "Show yourself."

She hesitated, and he felt a wave of uncertainty that caught him off guard. It took a moment to realize it was *her* emotion he was feeling, another surprise. Since Shielders had natural mind shields, Leors were unable to probe their minds and ascertain their thoughts, as they did with other species. Even with his mind-probing abilities, Arion had never felt another being's emotions. Yet he was clearly sensing this female's anxiety. It was the only logical explanation.

"You are afraid," he taunted.

"I am . . . apprehensive." Her voice remained low, but he detected the note of resolve.

"If you believe yourself worthy to be a Leor's mate, you will show yourself."

Slender hands lifted slowly to the hood and lowered it. The first thing Arion noticed, as he always did with humans, was the woman's hair. It was a deep rich copper, the fiery tones of a desert sunset. It was tucked inside her cape, so he couldn't determine its length.

Her face was strong, angular, with a square jawline, but her features were very feminine. Russet brows—another oddity to Leors—formed perfect arches over deep-set gray eyes that were the same soft color as polished magnasteel.

Her nose was narrow and straight, her mouth small but curved.

She stared back while he studied her, her gaze clear and direct: a point in her favor, as Leors insisted on direct eye contact, which facilitated their ability to probe minds. The woman had none of the magnificence of a Leor female, but she was pleasant enough to look at. She wasn't very tall, her head coming only to the top of his chest. He wondered how sturdy she was. "Take off your cape," he ordered.

"Wait," san Ranul protested. "I'm not sure there's any need to go further. Jenna, you don't have to do this. At the very least, we should discuss the ramifications of such a decision."

She turned her head toward him, and the lights reflected off her hair like sparks. "I must do this. I've foreseen it as my destiny."

San Ranul's eyes widened. "You saw this in a vision?"

"Yes."

"But surely not all your visions are accurate," he protested.

"Unfortunately, Captain, they are."

Further intrigued, Arion asked, "You are a seer?"

The woman's gaze returned to him, and he found himself falling into mesmerizing gray eyes, filled with the mysteries of the ages. "I am, Your Lordship."

Prophecy was nothing new to Arion. Every Leor clan had at least one shaman who was able to communicate directly with the Goddess and offer prophecies of the future. This woman's eyes alone were enough to convince him she spoke the truth. "You have foreseen a destiny with a Leor?" he persisted.

She drew a deep breath, her chest rising beneath the cape. "I have foreseen my destiny with *you,* Your Lordship. Four seasons ago."

Amazement jolted through him, along with a sense of

déjà vu. Actually, it was a real memory from a little over four spans ago—that of Morven telling him, *"The Goddess has chosen your mate. She will be surrounded by fire and visions."* Not that Arion had discounted it, but when a mate never materialized, he assumed Morven must have misinterpreted her vision. However, it *was* possible this Shielder female, with her fiery hair and seer abilities, was meant to be his mate. Still, Arion never accepted anything at face value or took anyone but his most trusted advisers at their word. Treachery abounded.

"How do you know your fate lies with me?" he challenged. "If you have not been around Leors, we would all look similar to you."

Her gaze didn't waver. "That might be the case. But how many Leors bear the mark of a new moon on their left shoulder?"

Only Arion did. The crescent-shaped birthmark was part of his heritage, appearing on all the males of his line, and was accepted by his clan as proof of his right to leadership. But the mark was on the back side of his shoulder, completely covered by his cape. There was no way this woman could have seen it. Stronger evidence that she was the one Morven had prophesied. "Take off your cloak," Arion growled.

Her hands weren't quite steady as she untied her cape and shrugged it off. It fell in a pool on the floor. Fully revealed, the woman's hair was stunning, falling in silky waves halfway down her back. Arion had never seen hair that color, like the burnished glow of fire stones. But then he found all hair fascinating, as did most of his people.

He shifted his perusal to the rest of her. She was small boned, very slender and delicate. He felt a wave of disappointment. She must be wrong about her vision. "You are far too frail. You would not survive the first mating."

Faint color brushed her cheeks, but she raised her chin proudly. "I'm stronger than I look, Your Lordship."

Her persistence impressed him. She would have to be mentally strong, as well as physically sturdy, to survive life among Leors. He asked the most vital question, the one that would determine if he would even consider her for a mate. "You are a virgin? Untouched by any man?"

"I am a virgin," she said quietly.

"Do not lie to me about this," he warned her. "My personal healer will examine you thoroughly to ascertain the truth of your words."

"No man has ever touched me," she said with quiet dignity.

A startling rush of primitive, masculine possessiveness flowed through him. He was not one to be swayed by emotion, and he did not like the reactions this slip of a female was spurring in him. It must be the different gravity and atmosphere of Shamara, he told himself, asserting his triton will over his emotions. "You are aware that you will leave Shamara and live in a Leor settlement? Your relocation will be final. You will not ever return here."

"Yes." Her voice was hardly more than a whisper.

He pressed on, ruthlessly determined that she understand all that would be required of her. "And are you aware that we will be joined as mates . . . in every way a male and female can be joined?"

Her color deepened. "Yes, Your Lordship."

"Your sole purpose will be to bear me offspring. You will belong to me, until death separates us."

She closed her eyes for a brief moment, and when she opened them, all the softness was gone. Now the strength of the magnasteel glinted there, the resolute look of a warrior about to go into battle. "I'm fully aware of your requirements. I am prepared to become your . . . mate."

She stumbled over the last word, and san Ranul stepped between them. "Jenna, you don't have to do this. There's no reason to bind yourself to such an agreement."

The woman turned to him, her resolve reflected in her

bearing. "Tell that to Spirit, Captain. And tell that to those two Shielder colonies still in the other quadrant. Where will their help be when the Controllers find them?"

San Ranul obviously had no answer. His hand dropped away from her arm. "Just be very sure, Jenna. I can't help you once you leave Shamara."

Arion's ultrasensitive hearing picked up the slight hitch in her breath as she said, "I understand." Another hitch, as she turned back to him. "I would like a few moments alone with His Lordship."

San Ranul didn't seem happy with any of this, but he appeared to reconcile himself. "All right," he said. "I'll give you some privacy. I'll return shortly." He strode to the entry, glanced back at Jenna, then left.

She clasped her hands together, her gaze on Arion. "There is one condition I require before I make the final decision to go with you."

His eyes narrowed. "You seek to *bargain* with me?"

Her white knuckles were the only outward indication of her tension. "I only seek to ensure my own well-being and dignity."

He could not fault her for that. "You will not be mistreated, as long as you respect and honor our laws."

"I will do my best to honor your laws. But I would like your word that you'll never strike me, or allow anyone else to."

"Leor males do not strike their mates."

"Your word, please, that you will never hit me."

A growl rose in his throat. Had he not just told her he would not harm her? She reached out as if to touch him. He tensed before he could control his reaction. With rare exceptions, no one touched him.

As if sensing his aversion, she dropped her hand. "I will be in an alien culture, surrounded by beings who are very different from my own people. Beings who are physically much stronger and have a . . ." She paused, as if choosing

11

her words. "Fiercer nature. I must know that you will stand for me."

"I protect what is mine," he growled. "Never doubt it."

"You give your word?" she persisted.

He would have to make it very clear she was never to question him in any way. But he was a master strategist, and understood they were in negotiations. Her enlightenment could come later. "Yes. You have my word."

She exhaled slowly. "Then I will come with you."

"Only if the physical exam bears out your virginity," he reminded her. "And your ability to bear offspring."

"It will." Her gaze was unwavering. Once again, he was struck by the power of her eyes. "I consent to this examination, but I want you to know that my word is also good."

"I am glad to hear it. I will not tolerate lies from anyone, especially not my mate. Make sure you remember that." Arion decided the sooner he could educate her in Leor ways, and what was expected of her, the better.

"Since I have always placed a high value on the truth, I don't expect dishonesty to be a problem, my lord," she replied.

Her quiet dignity increased the fledgling respect he felt toward her. He already believed his healer's examination would validate her claim of innocence. "If we are to be mates, I would know your full name," he said.

"Jenna dan Aron."

He inclined his head. "I am Arion, Comdar of Saura."

"Comdar Arion," she acknowledged, her voice low.

Most human females had voices that grated on him. Jenna's had a melodic quality, with a pitch that vibrated pleasantly in the highly attuned receptor in the top of his head. He again felt the odd effect she seemed to have on him. He stepped closer, picking up her scent—clean and sweet. If he could stroke his tongue along her flesh, he would be able to ascertain every nuance of that tantalizing scent. He could feel the natural warmth emanating off her, a lure that called to all Leors. And her hair . . . He wanted to touch it, feel the satiny wonder of it between his fingers—

Enough! he told himself sternly. Indulging in the senses was a weakness, and one that *would* be controlled. He gestured abruptly toward the entrance. "Then come. We will go to Lanka now, and she will confirm whether or not your claim of innocence is true." He stood back, indicating she was to go ahead.

So she would be his mate, he thought, watching her petite form as he followed. Not a tall statuesque Leor female, who would be fearless and could fight as well as any male. He had always hoped for a mate who would be his equal, but fate—and the Komiss—had decreed otherwise. It appeared this fragile human female with hair the color of fire was his destiny. At least she was strong in spirit, and already he harbored a grudging respect for her courage.

But she had much to learn about Leor ways, and she would have to accept the fact that he would be her master in all things.

Like Lord Arion, Lanka had inscrutable obsidian eyes, devoid of any warmth or emotion. The Leor healer's grim face clearly reflected her disdain, and her repulsion, at having to deal with a human. She communicated with abrupt hand signals and curt words. Her hands were like ice, and there was nothing gentle about her thorough and invasive examination. When she was done, she turned without a word and strode from the infirmary.

Captain Ranul's wife, Eirene, helped Jenna smooth down her tunic, then sit up. Eirene was an Enhancer, an empath with miraculous healing abilities. She had quietly dissuaded Lord Arion from witnessing the exam, much to Jenna's gratitude. The Enhancers, known for their spirituality and integrity, commanded respect throughout the galaxy, and Arion had consented to allow Eirene to stand as the requisite witness.

"Are you all right?" Eirene asked, her gentle voice reflecting her concern.

"I'm fine." But Jenna remained on the edge of the table, not trusting her legs.

"You're shaking." Eirene's stunning, blue-eyed gaze searched Jenna's face. "Are you cold?"

"A little."

"Here, let me get your cape." She picked up the garment and slipped it over Jenna's shoulders.

But it was a bone-deep chill that permeated Jenna, one a thousand capes couldn't diminish. "Thank you," she whispered, sliding off the table.

The panel tone chimed, followed by Jarek san Ranul's voice over the entry com. "May I come in?"

"Just a minute." Eirene waited until Jenna found her leggings and boots and slipped them on, then told the captain he could enter.

Jenna's clairvoyant abilities usually only manifested during visions, but she was always amazed by the glowing energy between Eirene and Jarek. When they were together, bright, golden light seemed to encase them. Jarek glanced at his mate before turning his attention to Jenna. "Are you all right?"

She wished everyone would stop asking her that. She wasn't all right. She was very apprehensive about her future. Besides, not much in her life had ever been "all right." She was taking this step because she believed it was predetermined, the will of Spirit, and not her choice to make—and because she could be out of place in a Leor culture as easily as she could be on Shamara. What difference would it make?

"I'm fine." She fumbled with the fastenings of her cloak, while Eirene murmured quietly to Jarek.

Even if this hadn't been her destiny, there was the issue of the two Shielder colonies. Not every Shielder had traversed the wormhole leading to a safer part of the galaxy, escaping the vengeful Controllers, who had been systematically destroying the Shielder race for over fifty cycles. These Shielder settlements were stranded in the old quadrant, and had no chance of survival if help didn't reach them quickly. Someone had to take action to ensure the colonists reached the sanctuary of Shamara.

The Leors had the only ships large enough to carry so many people, as well as fast enough and sufficiently armed to outclass Controller and Antek craft. Combined Enhancer and Jardonian technology had made it possible to modify the Enhancer spheres that opened the wormhole between the two quadrants.

Now Leors could operate the spheres without the mental energy of an Enhancer. This basically made them the only choice for getting the Shielder colonists to safety. At least Jenna's sacrifice would serve some purpose, by ensuring the rescue of those colonists.

Not only that, but she desperately wanted children, and she couldn't see it happening if she stayed here. The superstitious Shielder men would hardly talk to her, much less consider her for a mate. The one good thing that had come out of Lanka's humiliating examination—outside the all-important confirmation of Jenna's virginity—was the verification that Jenna was healthy and had a sufficiently wide pelvis for bearing children.

That in itself made the situation endurable. She was determined she would be a good mate to Arion, and do her best to respect him and to honor the Leor ways. She would be a good mother to their children, as well. She'd heard Leors believed in the power of visions, and even based decisions upon information provided by their shamans. Maybe they wouldn't find her clairvoyance repulsive. Maybe she'd find acceptance among them.

"Jenna," Jarek said, breaking into the desperate mental litany to validate her decision. He stepped forward and grasped her shoulders, his serious gaze probing her. She saw concern and doubt in his dark eyes. "Are you sure about this? You must be very certain. Once it's done, it cannot be undone."

Her fear didn't change the certainty. "I'm sure."

Jarek nodded, accepting her decision. "Then I thank you from the depths of my heart. Your heroism means salvation for over five hundred people. It will not go unmarked. And you won't take this journey totally alone." He turned toward the entry. "Maxine, you may enter now."

A tall, stately woman walked into the chamber. She was very attractive, with a mane of dark brown hair streaked with gold, and golden eyes. Her tawny skin was flawless. She was dressed in a form-fitting gold flight suit that showed off a spectacular figure. She looked hauntingly familiar, but Jenna couldn't remember ever seeing her before.

"I am here, Captain," the woman said in a strangely flat voice.

Jenna moved closer, still puzzled by the woman's familiarity. She looked like . . . Oh! Suddenly it came to her. The woman bore a striking resemblance to Celie Cameron's new mate, Prince Rurick Riordan. But . . . how could that be?

"Jenna, this is Maxine," Jarek said. "She is an android, gifted to us by Prince Rurick."

"Actually, I am Maxine V," the android stated. "Named after Max, the original android made to masquerade as Prince Rurick. Max has created ten replicas of himself, to serve various functions. There are five male versions— Max II, III, IV, V, and VI; and five female versions— Maxine I, II, III, IV, and V. I am the last, and therefore"— she paused and appeared to preen, displaying an odd lopsided grin—"the best. I have extensive programming in medicine, agriculture, communication technology, aerospace engineering, computer—"

"Hold up, Maxine," Jarek interrupted. "We're quite aware of your credentials. They are most impressive."

"Thank you," Maxine said primly, although her demeanor was anything but modest.

Jenna couldn't help staring, amazed at how human Maxine appeared. She'd heard of androids of course, especially after Celie Cameron and Raven McKnight—each now mated to royalty—had spent quite a few cycles with Rurick's personal android, Max. But she'd never *seen* an android, and Maxine almost overshadowed the looming shadow of life with a Leor. Almost.

"I have asked Comdar Arion to accept Maxine as a token of our gratitude for his assistance," Jarek explained. "And he has agreed."

"He did not want me at first," Maxine said. "But then I informed him of my comprehensive programming in genetics. I can be immensely helpful in researching ways to offset the recessive traits caused by a small gene pool and excessive inbreeding. I might even be able to determine why Leor females have such a short breeding period. I estimate there is an 82.3 percent possibility that—"

"I'm sure your abilities will be very beneficial to the Leors," Jarek interjected. "That is all they need to believe about you accompanying them. However, your main purpose is to act as a companion to Jenna and to ensure her well-being."

Jenna tore her fascinated gaze from Maxine to stare at Jarek. "You're sending her along for my benefit?"

"Yes." Jarek looked at his mate. She smiled at him, adoration in her eyes. "Eirene and I didn't want you to undertake this alone. Maxine seemed the perfect solution."

"But surely you need Maxine here," Jenna protested, reeling from this unexpected development. "There's so much she could do in Shamara—in the infirmary, in the

17

hydroponics labs, in engineering, in so many areas."

"We've been doing just fine up until now without Maxine," Jarek told her. "Your need is greater. Arion has already agreed to take her along, so it's settled. Now you won't be alone."

The darkness weighing down Jenna's soul suddenly seemed lighter. She battled a rush of tears. "Thank you," she managed to say, despite the emotion clogging her throat.

"You're welcome." In a move that surprised her, Jarek pulled her into a rough hug. "We should be thanking *you,* Lady Jenna. Words cannot express our gratitude."

He released her, and Eirene stepped forward to hug her as well. "Spirit go with you," she whispered. "May joy and happiness be your shadows."

It was more affection than anyone had displayed toward Jenna since the death of her parents, and she found it overwhelming. She took a moment to steady herself and wipe the tears from her eyes. She stared at Jarek and Eirene, the two people who had always accepted her and treated her like a normal person. "I will forever remember your kindness."

"We need to prepare to leave," Maxine said briskly, dispelling the emotion-laden atmosphere. "The Leor ship is scheduled to depart at sixteen hundred hours."

So little time left. The chill returned. With a last goodbye to Jarek and Eirene, Jenna turned and walked from the infirmary, sensing Maxine close behind. She stepped into the sunlight, struggling to draw a full breath into her tight chest, and drew her cape more tightly around herself.

"I must send some communications and collect my equipment," Maxine told her. "I will meet you at the ship in one hour."

Jenna nodded and turned toward her quarters. Then she saw Arion. He was standing ramrod straight by a storage building, his arms crossed over his chest. When he saw Jenna, he dropped his arms and strode toward her. His intense gaze was fixed unerringly on her, and she felt like a kerani in the sights of a hunter's laser rifle.

Not even the open area of the compound diminished Arion's size. His short cape flew back with his rapid strides, one side flipping over his shoulder and revealing a massive chest. The muscles of his powerful thighs flexed against tight leggings as he walked. He moved with surprising fluidity and grace for such a large man, and he moved rapidly. She'd heard things about the Leors, discussion about their superhuman speed and strength—all apparently true, she noted as he crossed the width of the huge compound in a matter of seconds.

The sun's rays reflected off his bald head, making it appear he wore a crown of light, an illusion that was at odds with the very nature of Leors. He stopped before her, the darkness of his soulless eyes reflecting his true nature. "Lanka has verified your chaste state," he said bluntly. Although he spoke in Contran, one of the universal languages from the old quadrant, his deep voice was harsh and guttural.

Jenna dropped her gaze, and the daylight provided her first good look at his skin. She stared at his exposed chest and arm. She'd also heard about Leor skin. *Reptilian flesh,* some called it. It certainly wasn't like human skin. Very faint, crisscrossing lines formed a blurred diamond-shaped pattern that, along with the swarthy tone of his flesh, created the appearance of a leathery texture, similar to that of a lizard's hide. She knew its temperature changed with the external environment; cool to the touch on a cold day, or warm when exposed to heat. It drove home the fact Arion wasn't human.

He was a barbarian hybrid, the result of a long-ago crossbreeding of humans with a reptilian race. The physical makeup of Leors was supposedly more human than reptile, and they could readily breed with humans. But they weren't truly human.

And this nonhuman Leor was about to become her mate.

Chapter Two

The sun's rays reflected off her hair, making it look like shimmering flames. Arion could see her aura clearly. Its primary color was a deep blue, a good color that indicated maturity and spiritual strength. It was spiked with orange right now, an indication of how nervous he made her, although he readily sensed that without seeing her aura. She stood before him, not meeting his gaze. With his acute hearing, he could hear the rapid beat of her heart.

Now that the healer had verified her virginity and child-bearing ability, negotiations had basically concluded. He had the upper hand—not that the outcome had ever been in question. Jenna was his. He felt the sudden need to assert his mastery over this female who would soon be his mate, and to claim her, even if only symbolically.

"Well, then, Jenna dan Aron, we will seal our mating contract with an ancient Leor tradition." Sealing an agreement with blood-sharing hadn't been regularly practiced by Leors for many spans, but it had always been a sacred act among his people, and a link to the Goddess. He drew the intricately carved magnasteel dagger from the sheath attached to his leggings. "Hold out your left hand."

Her eyes widened, and she didn't move.

"Your hand—now," he ordered. "Or do you dishonor our agreement?"

She stiffened, then slowly raised her hand. He gestured with the dagger. "Palm up."

She bit her lip, then turned her palm upward. Her hand was trembling.

"What is this? Afraid, after reaching this point?"

Her chin rose slightly. "I believe I have already acknowledged that I am a little apprehensive, Your Lordship."

"So you have." He couldn't say what was driving him, but the need to subjugate her, to make sure she fully acquiesced to him, was strong. "I will accept your trepidation, as long as it is based upon your realization that henceforth you will respect and obey your master. Which I will be, for the remainder of our mortal lives."

He stepped forward and took her wrist. Standing this close to her, he realized just how slight she was. The bones in her wrist were fine and fragile. The doubt that she was sturdy enough for mating returned, but an instinctive feeling deep in his gut whispered this was destiny. He had long trusted his inner instincts and would not deny them now. Here, on Candest, their blood vow would bind their agreement. Then, on Saura, the merging ceremony would bind their souls for life.

He raised the dagger, and with a quick twist of his hand, cut a crescent shape downward along the full part of her palm, right below her thumb. A gasp escaped her lips, but she did not cry out. He brought her palm to his mouth and ran his tongue along the cut.

The rich, coppery taste of her blood was like a powerful elixir, more potent than the finest Elysian liquor. Leors routinely drank the blood of the animals they slaughtered for food, believing it gave them stamina, so he was used to the taste. But Jenna's blood had an exotic, heady flavor that gave him a voracious appetite for more.

With the special nodes in a Leor's tongue that dramatically enhanced his sense of smell, he got the full force of her scent. Musky, enticing, totally feminine. The effect was immediate and shocking, especially in his lower body, where his own blood surged, and he swelled painfully against his leggings.

Goddess of the sun! He hadn't displayed such a lack of control over his body since he was an adolescent many spans ago, and had undergone his first grueling saktar ritual in the desert to discipline his body and mind.

He dropped her wrist and stepped back, gulping air into his lungs. Jenna might be his future mate, but he would not allow her to affect him like this. Nothing, or no one, was going to challenge the hard-won discipline and control he had honed with spans of training. He was the Comdar, the chosen leader of his clan. He must set the standard for all others to follow.

She balled up her wounded hand, her gaze dropping to his bulging crotch. With another gasp, she jerked her head back up, her skin turning pink. That she had witnessed his disgraceful lack of control stirred his ire even more.

"Now you do the same with me." He thrust the dagger toward her. "Take it."

Horror chased away the color on her face. "I can't."

"You can, and you will."

She shook her head. "It's your ritual, not mine."

"It is a Leor ritual. By agreeing to mate with me, you have agreed to honor Leor law." He took her right hand, and pressed the handle of the dagger into her hand. "Unless of course you are reneging on the agreement."

Her eyes sparked. "You seem certain I'm going to change my mind about this, Comdar. Let's get one thing straight. Just because I'm not a Leor doesn't mean I don't have my own code of honor. Even if I don't agree with everything you do, I will not go back on my word."

"You are not allowed to disagree with me," he informed her.

"Are you telling me that Leor females cannot argue with their mates?"

"On occasion. But mated Leors do not air their disputes in common meeting areas. They keep such issues confined to the privacy of their quarters."

"That's fair enough, and I can live with that. But my thoughts and my feelings are my own, Lord Arion. You can't command them. I expect the same consideration you would give a Leor mate."

She had surprised him again. She could never equal a Leor female, but he respected her determination to hold her own. "You will have it." He offered his left hand, palm up.

She grasped his wrist, resolve hardening her features. Taking a deep breath, she brandished the knife with unexpected skill, and made a swift incision below his thumb. She wavered just an instant, taking another breath, before she brought his hand to her mouth.

He felt her body tense, felt the jolt of awareness go through her. Simultaneously, he felt the warmth of her lips against his palm. His hand was calloused, and his skin was tough and not normally sensitive, but the sweep of her tongue sent a tingling sensation across it.

The knife slipped from Jenna's fingers and thudded on the ground. She released him and stepped back. She pressed her right hand to her mouth and her left fist against her stomach. Her gray eyes huge, she stared at him, her face utterly pale, her skin almost translucent in the sunlight.

"Are you going to be sick?" he asked her.

She slowly shook her head. "No," she murmured. "I'm fine."

She had unusual grit for a human female, and pride, he would give her that.

"All is done here," he said. "We prepare to depart."

Arion stood in the center of Jenna's small quarters, staring at her sparse furnishings. He'd insisted on accompanying her to gather her belongings, apparently unwilling to let her out of his sight. Jenna wondered if the same would hold true once they reached Saura.

She turned to get her satchel, acutely aware of her wounded hand. The bleeding had stopped, but her flesh throbbed where his blade had sliced, where his lips had pressed and his tongue had traced her palm with startling intimacy. An amazing energy had sizzled through her, taking her breath away. She was certain he'd felt it, too—and been affected by it, if his physical response was any indication.

Then, when she had reciprocated, the taste of his skin, and his blood, had affected her just as strongly. She did not eat animal flesh, and his blood should have been repulsive; yet the beat of his pulse beneath her tongue, the strange texture of his skin, the taste of his life force, had been potent and heady. How could such a reaction be possible between two strangers from diametrically opposed cultures?

But the most unsettling thing had been the sudden vision that flashed into her mind: shocking images of Arion and her both nude, their heaving bodies entwined in the most primal way a man and woman could be joined. She'd seen the same thing in her vision four seasons ago. Thinking about it now sent her heart pounding and heat rushing through her body like a fever. She unwittingly clenched her injured hand, then flinched.

She could have—should have—returned to the infirmary and asked Eirene to heal the cut on her hand. It would have been a simple matter for Jarek's Enhancer mate to pull in energy and close the wound. But Jenna hadn't wanted to do that.

Strangely enough, to her, the cut on her palm, the scar it would produce, was the first manifestation of her new life—a badge of sorts, though whether of courage or lunacy, she couldn't say. It was a signpost on an uncertain path that was her destiny. When she stepped onto the Leor warship and the hatch closed behind her, all would be irrevocable.

Which it already was.

Forcing away the grim thoughts, she gathered her things. There was very little for her to pack: her few articles of clothing, some reading disks, personal toiletries, and her most precious possession, a holo of her parents. Arion looked over her shoulder as she picked it up from the stand beside her bunk.

"Your parents?" he asked.

Jenna stared at the three-dimensional images in the cool plexishield. "Yes," she answered.

"Do they still live?"

The familiar pain washed over her, even though it had been over fourteen seasons since she'd lost them both, within the span of a few short lunar cycles of each other. And she'd seen each of their deaths, locked in nightmare visions, as they were killed by Anteks. "No." Her voice dropped to a whisper, although she'd long ago learned there was no way to turn down the volume on grief . . . or violence.

He grunted, not offering condolences like any civilized being would. It briefly occurred to her that maybe Leors were uncomfortable with emotion, did not express it openly. But then she discarded that possibility. Everything she knew about the Leors suggested they merely skirted the edges of civil decency, following only their own barbaric laws.

"You have no other family then?" he asked.

26

She thought of Damon, her only brother. He'd been even more tormented by her parents' deaths than she had. They weren't close. He'd never been able to accept her psychic abilities, or tolerate the derision they generated. A restless soul, he had left Liron shortly after the death of their father, and roamed only Spirit knew where. She didn't even know if he had migrated to the new quadrant. If he had, she'd never seen him in Shamara.

"I have a brother," she answered slowly. "But I haven't seen him in many seasons."

Another grunt was the only response. The Leors were apparently as primitive as they were reputed to be. "I'm through here," she said, taking a final look at her quarters.

Arion picked up her small satchel and turned toward the entry. "Then say your farewells so we can depart."

There were no good-byes to be said. She had no close friends, having been shunned by other Shielders ever since she'd first babbled about the "pictures of people" in her mind when she was only four. Even after Nessa McKnight's heroic deeds to save the Shielders, even with Jarek san Ranul taking an Enhancer as his mate, the Shielder colonists had never fully trusted or accepted anyone who was different. Jenna, with her clairvoyant visions of current and future events, had always been the odd one out.

No, there were no good-byes. She'd already spoken with Jarek and Eirene. There was nothing left for her to do here.

She turned for one last look at the quarters that had been both her prison and her haven these past four seasons. "There's no one I need to see. I'm ready to go."

The interior corridor walls of the massive warship were covered with clashing colors of red and orange, interspersed with black. The corridors were wide and high, probably to accommodate the large Leor physiques; and uncomfortably bright, with glaring overhead lights that beat down more mercilessly than the sun at its zenith.

The wave of heat that rushed over Jenna and Arion as they entered was almost unbearable, especially after being in the cool breezes of Shamara. Wondering if she'd just stepped into Hades, Jenna removed her cloak.

Arion did the same, whipping off his cloak and tossing it to an aide as he strode rapidly ahead, snapping out words in an unfamiliar guttural language. Jenna got the full view of his bare back, muscles flexing as he moved, his crescent-shaped birthmark now clearly visible. His shoulders were impossibly broad, almost twice the width of a Shielder man's. Although his back tapered to a much leaner waist by comparison, she'd probably have difficulty wrapping her arms around his midriff.

All his crew were bare-chested, she noticed, and all were in the loincloths they wore on their ships and settlements. Arion had probably donned his leggings in deference to the cooler Shamara temperatures. Jenna knew Leors wore minimal clothing and kept their environment at high temperatures, in order to absorb the heat their bodies couldn't produce.

Since her vision of Arion four seasons ago, she'd tried to learn as much as she could about Leors, but she had limited access to UDW, the Universal Data Web. What little she knew she'd gotten from Celie Cameron-Riordan, during her infrequent visits to Shamara. The facts Jenna had gleaned were not reassuring.

Arion glanced over his shoulder, his expression impatient. "Jenna, android!" he called, switching to Contran. "Come with me to the medical bay."

Wondering why they were headed there, Jenna swiped at the sweat beginning to bead on her forehead. She followed Arion as he turned down another corridor, trying to ignore the nearly nude bodies of his crew, and their blatant stares. Maxine hummed along beside her, avidly observing every detail.

"Interesting," the android said. "Most people would find this color scheme quite offensive. In most cultures, red and orange signify aggression, or even anger. They are very masculine colors and mentally stimulating rather than calming. The temperature is also very interesting. It is registering at 42.33 degrees Celsius."

"Tell me about it," Jenna muttered, loosening the top of her tunic. It was *sweltering* in here.

"The average settings that most humans prefer are around 23.88 degrees Celsius. Shamara's temperatures run even cooler. While there, I registered an average of 20.55 degrees Celsius. And on Jardonia, where I was created—"

"There's no need to continue. What I said was just an expression." Jenna made a mental note that androids were very literal and probably didn't know common slang.

"Ah, I see. *Expression.* Something that manifests, embodies, or symbolizes something else." Maxine nodded. "I will make an attempt to learn the common expressions that you use."

About ten meters ahead, Arion stopped and gestured sharply at a panel. "Jenna. Android. In here. Now."

Jenna hurried to reach him, the heat dragging at her. It was far too hot on the ship. Arion watched her dispassionately as she stepped past him, into a sizable chamber that was obviously the medical bay. Six examining tables were lined up neatly along one wall, and an array of screens and equipment beeped and hummed quietly. Lanka stood there, a startling sight, since she wore nothing but a loincloth, leaving the rest of her well-muscled body exposed. Jenna took a deep breath, forced herself to show no reaction. *Get used to it,* she told herself. *It's their way of life.*

The bright overhead lights shining on her bald head, Lanka eyed Jenna coldly, with the same disdain she had displayed in the Shamara infirmary. She began pulling on disposable gloves. "On the table, female," she ordered in her guttural voice.

Jenna looked at the nearest examining table, panic beginning to rear. "I don't understand," she said, struggling to stay calm. "What's going on?"

"Table! Now!" Lanka growled.

Jenna whirled toward Arion, not realizing he had moved directly behind her. "What—"

The breath left her lungs as he grasped her waist and lifted her to the table. She grabbed his arms, trying to wrap her fingers around his bulging biceps. "Lord Arion! What's going on?"

"Lie down." He pressed one large hand against her chest, pushing her prone on the table. His other hand held her legs immobile with ease. "Cease your resistance now."

Maxine stepped to the table. "Your Lordship, I must insist on knowing your intentions."

"You are not allowed to insist on anything." Arion jerked his head toward the other side of the bay. "Go over there."

Totally panicked, Jenna tried to twist free. "What are you doing? I already submitted to the exam you required."

"While I must certainly defer to your authority," Maxine interjected, "I must also express my concern for Lady Jenna, and my interest in her welfare. To that end, I again ask what you are planning to do."

"Over there, android." Arion's voice rose to a low roar. "Now. Or I will power you down permanently."

"No," Jenna gasped. Machine or not, Maxine was her only ally in this nightmare.

"Yes." Arion's black-hole gaze snapped back to Jenna. "You will be still."

Maxine managed a very unmachinelike snort as she moved stiffly to the other side of the room. Realizing the futility of her struggles, Jenna stilled, but her terror didn't abate. Her heart felt as if it were going to burst through her chest.

Arion must have felt it, too, because he looked down where his hand was pressed against her chest, and frowned. "You will stop this reaction at once. I have told you I will not harm you."

He might as well order her to stop breathing, for all the control she had over her panic.

He raised his hand from her chest, nodded at Lanka. The healer stepped in, grabbed the seam of Jenna's tunic, and ripped it open all the way down. Shocked, Jenna gasped, but before she could react further, Lanka had her arm free of the sleeve, exposing most of Jenna's chest. Now she had mortified embarrassment to contend with, and felt a hot flush sweeping across her face.

Arion stared down at her, seemingly unaffected by her nudity. He might be used to it, but she wasn't. "Please tell me what's going on," she pleaded, hating the desperation in her voice, but unable to stop herself. Lanka took her arm and Jenna jerked her head around to see the healer placing a clear plastic strip with a tube protruding from it down the inside of her lower arm. She tried to jolt upright.

Arion pushed her down again, the feel of his cool fingers against her bare chest very disconcerting. "Do not struggle. There is no reason for your fear."

"Then there's no reason you can't tell me what's going on." Jenna was practically panting now, her lungs constricted from the adrenaline rush.

"You will sleep for a while," he said calmly.

"What do you mean, sleep?" she demanded, then felt Lanka pressing cold metal disks on her chest. She tried to push the healer's hands away. "You promised I would be fairly treated."

"I believe he means sleep stasis," Maxine offered. "It is a common Leor practice. When they transport large groups of slaves or Shielders, they put them in sleep stasis."

31

"I don't want to be put to sleep," Jenna protested. "Why would you do that?"

He was starting to look annoyed. "I do not have to explain my reasons to you."

"It requires very little energy and sustenance to transport beings that way." Maxine stepped closer, observing Lanka with interest. "It lowers the body temperature and slows metabolism and body functions, much like the hibernation process for some animals. The Leors have used this practice for many seasons. They have perfected the technique. It will not harm you."

"No! I don't want this!" Jenna cried, again trying to wrest free. The thought of being put into an artificial sleep terrified her. Maybe she wouldn't wake up. Maybe she'd have continuous visions. She glared at Arion accusingly. "You gave me your word. You can't do this."

"Listen to me." Arion lowered his face near hers. "You will be better off in stasis. We are going through the wormhole to retrieve the other Shielders. The trip is long and dangerous. Our customs, the higher temperatures on the ship, will be difficult for you.

"No," Jenna said, even though she knew she could do nothing to stop it. She stared at him through blurring eyes, felt an insidious cold begin flowing through her veins. "No."

"Sleep now." His voice sounded far away. "As I have given my word, I will stand for you while you sleep."

"No . . ."

But the darkness descended anyway.

Arion stared at the female who would be his mate. She had succumbed to the medication, but her resistance had been fierce. An odd, clear liquid was streaked down her face. Concerned, he touched the wetness, lifted his finger to his nose, and sniffed. "Lanka, what is this? Is it a reaction to the drugs you gave her?"

Lanka gave him an odd look. "No, Comdar. Those are tears."

"Tears?" Arion touched his tongue to his finger, smelled and tasted salt.

"Tears are composed of a saline solution, and are excreted from humans' eyes when they are upset or sad," the android informed him. It dared to move closer without his permission. "Comdar Arion, I consider your harsh treatment of Lady Jenna traumatic and unnecessary. She was very anxious about leaving Shamara, and your actions did not reassure her."

"Silence," he snapped. "I have not asked your opinion, and I will not tolerate interference or speaking out of turn from you."

"So noted. However, as a medical expert, I feel it my duty to inform you that your treatment of Jenna could be detrimental to her well-being."

He whirled on the android, thoroughly irritated. "I have done nothing to harm her!"

"Stress affects humans adversely, Your Lordship. By not taking the time to explain your intent to Jenna and calm her fears, you allowed her to suffer a great amount of stress."

"You are here to research our genetic problems, not as a protector for my mate," he growled. This android was arrogant, and both it and Jenna were rebellious to authority. That was the problem with non-Leors. They were inferior, and these two would have to be trained in self-discipline and showing proper respect. "Jenna is my responsibility. Do you not agree?"

"I agree that I will be working with your scientists to find a solution to your reproduction dilemma, but also—"

"You have *one* purpose here. You will apply yourself in our laboratory, or be shut down permanently. Is that understood?"

The android's mouth compressed into a thin line. "Yes, Comdar, that is understood."

"Good. Can you put yourself in inactive mode?"

"Of course. One of my many functions is to—"

"Enough. Put yourself in inactive mode immediately. I will see that you are activated when we reach Saura. You can begin your duties then."

Muttering to itself, the android moved to the nearest corner, and hummed off. Arion took a deep breath, rolled the tension from his shoulders. He had not expected such a scene. Instead, he had expected what he always received—total and immediate compliance in all things. He looked at Jenna, lying deathly still on the table. "Will she be all right like this for a few moments?"

"Yes," Lanka answered. "The stasis chamber is necessary for a long sleep, but this is fine for several hours."

"Then leave us."

The healer placed her right arm diagonally across her chest and bowed. "Yes, sir."

As the panel slid shut behind her, Arion moved to the table, staring at his mate. He reached out, again felt the strange fluid drying on her face. The android had called it tears. He considered what the android had said about tears leaking out when humans were upset, how stress could be harmful.

The thought of stress damaging Jenna worried him, although he wasn't exactly certain what stress was. Leors did not experience stress. They simply did what had to be done. It had not been his intention to frighten Jenna. Had he not told her she was under his protection? She would have to learn to trust him, and to obey him. As the head of the Sauran clan, he did not explain his actions to anyone. Yet her fear had been so great, he had done just that.

Looking at her now, he couldn't seem to help himself; he reached out and stroked her cheek. Goddess, but her skin was soft, as smooth as the petals of a starflower. He ran his callused fingers over her face, marveling at the purity, the lack of any pattern in her translucent skin. Her eyebrows were also fascinating. He slid a finger over each, finding they were coarser than they looked. But the most amazing thing about Jenna was her hair. Leors had no hair anywhere on their bodies, so they found this phenomenon incredibly interesting.

Jenna had the most amazing hair Arion had ever seen. It flowed in glorious, fire-streaked waves over her chest. He stroked it, his breath hissing out as he felt its softness and texture. He rolled some of the strands between his fingers, and they slipped from his grasp like silken threads. He slid his hands beneath her hair, lifting a large portion to his lips. With his tongue, he absorbed the taste and scent, and felt a strange stirring in his body.

Normally, he would have ruthlessly suppressed any hint of emotion or desire. Leors did not allow themselves to experience carnal desire until they were mated. Instead, they channeled their immense energies into honing their bodies and their battle skills. Their survival depended on their fierceness and their utter lack of mercy when they faced their enemies. But Jenna was his mate, and they would soon be joined in the merging ceremony. He could begin to allow the stirring of lust.

He brushed aside her hair and studied her breasts. Nudity was as natural to Leors as breathing, but although he had seen human breasts, including those of his personal server, he had never paid close attention to them. Now, he saw there were distinct differences between human and Leor females. Leors had brown or dark gold nipples, but Jenna's were a rosy pink, like the first delicate colors of a desert sunrise. Her breasts were rounded, while Leor women had more conical-shaped breasts.

Also, her breasts were small, dainty like she was, but sufficient to suckle his children, he decided. He couldn't resist cupping one perfect globe, something he'd never done with any female. He liked the way it felt in his hand, the surprising firmness and weight of it. His pulse quickened, and he drew back, steeling himself against further reaction.

Still, he felt the lure of this unique opportunity to examine his mate. Giving in, he slipped off her boots and leggings, and studied every detail of her body. She was pale and silky soft all over, with none of the muscular hardness of a Leor female. She had a tiny waist he could almost span with one hand, and a flat stomach, with gently flaring hips. She looked incredibly small, but Lanka had assured him she was capable of bearing his offspring.

His attention was drawn to the triangle of fiery curls on her lower abdomen. He knew humans had hair around their genitals, had seen it on some of the slaves brought to Saura. But at close range it was an amazing sight, especially the color and texture. He touched the soft curls, and a wave of pure male possessiveness rushed through him. *His*. Jenna was his.

Soon, very soon, he would claim her in the most primal way a male could claim a female. He'd possess her fully, marking her with his scent and releasing his seed deep inside her. He felt incredible satisfaction at that thought. There would never be anything other than mating between them, but she would be the mother of his offspring, and he would accord her the respect that position entailed.

There would be nothing beyond that, however. No emotional entanglements. He'd lived his entire life alone, without family or friends, and he'd grown up strong, proving his worth and taking on the leadership of the great Sauran clan. He refused to allow needless emotions to weaken him. Nothing would change in his life, except that he would now have descendants to carry on the legacy of the clan.

With that thought in mind, he slipped Jenna's leggings back on. Because of the tube running into her arm, and the monitor disks attached to her chest, he left her tunic off, but covered her with a blanket.

Then he headed for the command center of the ship, where he belonged, doing what he did best: leading his warriors and ruthlessly crushing anyone foolish enough to challenge him.

Chapter Three

Two cycles out, all was on schedule when Arion's ship was hailed by an approaching Leor craft. "Comdar, it is the Komissar's flagship," Erona, his communications officer, reported. "They have transmitted the correct security codes, and are initiating docking."

"Inform the Komissar I will meet him at the air lock." Arion headed toward it. He wondered briefly about the nature of Gunnar's visit, but it was not his place to question the Komissar's purpose. All would be revealed in the proper sequence.

He strode down the wide corridor, welcoming the flow of hot air from the vents that formed a continuous network through the walls. Beneath his feet, the ship vibrated faintly, its powerful propulsion system slowing for docking with the flagship. Arion's crew bowed respectfully as he passed. He grunted with satisfaction. All was as it should be, running in perfect order.

He reached the air lock, noting that the decompression light was on. Docking was already in progress. The panel connecting the adjoined air locks slid open, and a small figure stepped into the plexishield vestibule on Arion's ship. Seeing the flash of blue feathers, Arion almost groaned aloud. *She* had accompanied the Komissar—again.

The mates of officers and crew members had no place on warships—unless both happened to be assigned to the same ship, which was rare. But the Komissar often insisted on traveling with his mate, a human he had met during his dealings with the Shielders. Her presence was a detriment to running a smooth space mission. And a detriment to everything Leor pride and honor stood for, in Arion's opinion. He grimly set his expression to mask his disgust for Komissar Gunnar's mate.

Surprise replaced disgust when the panel closed behind the blue-feathered figure. No one else was boarding? Where was the Komissar? Surely there must be some mistake. The air lock slid open and Komissar Gunnar's mate strutted out, perched on spike heels that looked ridiculous with her blue-feathered loincloth and matching cape. Actually, the entire outfit was ludicrous. No Leor would be caught dead in feathers, much less the color blue. If that wasn't enough, the female had blue hair and blue lips.

Her bright blue gaze homed in on Arion before he could execute a strategic retreat. "Oh, there you are, Comdar!" She sashayed toward him, carrying a blue case in one blue-tipped hand and waving the other hand. "Just the man I want to see."

He stood stiffly, cursing Leor protocol that demanded he show courtesy to any member of the Komissar's family. Lani stopped before him, sweeping him with an appreciative gaze that he thought highly inappropriate. "And what a man you are," she sighed. "All you Leor males are prime specimens. Too bad we can't clone you and take out the arrogance."

"What is your business here?" Arion growled, barely keeping himself in check.

Lani smiled brightly, making her blue lips look even gaudier. Dressed in all those blue feathers, she reminded him of an obnoxious echobird. She was a small woman, shorter than Jenna, but with more curves, and very generous breasts. He'd caught his men staring at them more than once, and doled out the harshest ship assignments for that infraction.

"I'm here to discuss your future mate," she trilled in an annoyingly high pitched voice. "And I'm anxious to meet her and offer her my full support."

Arion could just imagine what ideas she would put in Jenna's head. "She's not available right now."

"Oh, really?" Lani's blue eyes narrowed to slits. "And why is that?"

"She's in sleep stasis. You'll have to visit her after we reach Saura." He turned and started to stride away.

"Wait just a millisecond, Arion!"

Arion? No one in their right mind addressed him without his title. He swung around to find himself chest to nose with the echobird. "I knew that would get your attention," she said smugly. "I'm here on official business, with greetings and messages from the Komissar. I suggest we talk further in your council chamber—unless you'd like to discuss business here, in front of your men."

Arion glared at his crew. They were standing at rigid attention, their gazes straight ahead, but he knew they were listening to every word. His breath hissed from his lungs. "All right, then. We go to my council chamber."

He whirled and stalked away, hearing the rapid clicking of her heels on the floor behind him. He couldn't comprehend how she could even walk in the ridiculous things, much less keep up with him. The Komissar must have been seriously incapacitated when he took this female as his mate. Arion had heard tales about total upheaval in Dukkair after Lani's arrival there. Horrifying accounts of unrest among the Leor females; of them demanding that the laws banning sex before the merging ceremony be revoked. *Sexual liberation,* the females had called it.

This had been followed by further tales of more and more couples having sex without being mated, of total disregard for the laws. Without laws, and without order, there was no discipline. And without discipline, Leors could not maintain their power, or protect themselves against the Controllers. That was already getting difficult enough without anarchy.

This woman was responsible for the problems on Dukkair. She had weakened Gunnar, clouded his reasoning, and he allowed her free reign to wreak havoc upon his planet. Poisoned by his infatuation with Lani, he should have been stripped of his rank, removed as head of his clan.

But amazingly, he had not shown any weakness at all. When the passing of Kanet necessitated that a new Komissar be chosen, Gunnar had stepped forward to enter the challenge. And he had triumphed over the other five contenders, displaying superior intellect, strength, and battle skills. Unbelievable.

Arion entered his chamber with Lani right behind him, then turned to face her. "I will hear the Komissar's messages now."

Her blue brows arched. "You're not going to offer me refreshments? Some homa, perhaps?"

"I do not expect our meeting to last long." He was pushing the limits with his rudeness, but Lani always managed to enrage him.

"I don't know about that," she said, pulling out a chair. She slipped off her cape and laid it and her case on the conference table, before sitting in the seat and adjusting the height, lowering it substantially. She crossed her legs and settled back.

For the first time, Arion found his gaze drawn to her breasts. They were rounded, like Jenna's were, only they were fuller and they had blue nipples— By the Goddess! What was wrong with him? He did not allow himself to think about anything that might be carnal in nature, and certainly not with this female.

"Like what you see, Comdar?" Lani asked, giving him a knowing look. "That's good. If you have an appreciation for the female body, you'll find more pleasure in sex."

"I am not interested in your body," he growled, as furious with his lapse in discipline as he was with her. "And I will not enter into the mating act for pleasure. It will be for the sole purpose of creating children."

The echobird rolled her eyes. "So typical. You think you can control everything, every thought, every emotion, and that mating is a simple, straightforward exercise."

"It is."

"No, it isn't. Nor is dealing with your mate. Did you ask Jenna if she wanted to be put into sleep stasis? Or did you just do it, without consideration for her feelings?"

"I made the decision, and it was done."

"Did she do it willingly?"

He felt a twinge of remorse, a first for him, and ruthlessly shoved it away. "She did as I ordered."

"Spirit preserve us," Lani muttered. "I can imagine. Did it ever occur to you that if you explained the process to her, and the reasons for it, she might have agreed and it wouldn't have been nearly so stressful for her?"

"What is all this concern about stress?" Arion demanded angrily, battling a blade of concern for Jenna. "Life is filled with hardships. Undergoing sleep stasis is nothing."

"To you, who know it. You will be spending the rest of your life with this woman. Do you want it to be a battlefield? Do you want her to cringe in fear every time you approach?"

That gave him pause. He'd never considered what mating entailed, beyond the breeding of future heirs. Leors mated for life. There was no divorce in their culture. If a mate died, they did not remarry. Once he went through the merging ceremony with Jenna, he was bound to her until death.

"As long as she respects me and honors our laws, she has nothing to fear," he said stiffly.

"The same old Leor; 'Do whatever I say, and everything will be fine.' " Lani gave an unladylike snort. "I take it she's a virgin?"

"Of course."

"Oh, 'of course.' And of course, you plan to jump her immediately after the merging ceremony and stake your claim." With jerky motions, she dragged her case to the edge of the table.

It was none of her business. Arion was so incensed, he wanted to order her thrown into the brig, to rot until the fires of Hades consumed her, blue feathers and all. At the very least, he was ready to end this farce of a meeting and forcibly escort her off his ship.

But she was pulling several items from her case, one of them a black file embossed with the Komissar's scarlet seal. That jolted him back to rational thinking. He was dealing with the Komissar's mate, and he must accord her the same respect he would give the Komissar, or suffer the consequences.

"This is from Gunnar," she said, patting the black file absently. "He said I was to give it only to you. He didn't want the information transmitted, even over secure channels. But before you look at that, I want to give you this." She held out a small case.

He eyed it suspiciously. "What is this?"

"A holovideo on sex."

He recoiled as if she were trying to hand him a glowing heat stone. "I do not need it. I have been well educated on the matter."

It was true. When they weren't honing their battle skills, Leors received a thorough education. Even though they were highly physical beings, they also believed that knowledge was another form of power—and they pursued any and all power. Since they didn't mate before the merging ceremony, and could not rely on experimentation to teach them, they studied the mechanics of the mating act.

"So you'll just get on top of Jenna and do it, without any preliminaries? Practically rape her?"

That sent more outrage roaring through him. "Leor males do not rape females!"

"You big oaf!" Lani slapped the table, obviously frustrated. "It will be rape if she's frightened, and if you don't ensure that she's ready for penetration. You're so big, and she's a small woman, not nearly as sturdy as a Leor female. You could hurt her if you're not careful and she's not ready."

He could not believe they were having this conversation. "I will not discuss the matter with you."

"You don't have to." Lani tapped the holovideo with a blue fingernail. "You can watch this, in the privacy of your personal chamber. You can do just audio, if viewing it makes you nervous."

"I do not get nervous," he said softly, dangerously. "Ever."

"Whatever you say," she returned. "No one even has to know you have the holovideo. It has instructions on the basics, and it also covers the finer points of lovemaking, and how to woo your mate."

Woo his mate? Ridiculous. He was the head of the Sauran clan. He did not *woo* or *cajole*—he commanded. "I do not have to lure Jenna to me. She is already mine."

"Oh, yeah. The male ownership thing. That *really* attracts women." Lani shook her head. "I'm sure you think everything is well settled, Comdar. But your relationship with Jenna—and the mating—will proceed much more smoothly if you give her time to get used to you, and to living in a Leor settlement. That alone is a whole new experience, let me tell you. You need to show her some kindness, be gentle with her."

He clenched his hands into fists. "Leors are *no*t kind!" he growled. "We are *not* gentle. We are warriors, and we do not have time for such foolishness. Jenna agreed to mate with me, knowing what was expected of her."

Lani placed her hands on her feathered hips. "You Leor males are so obtuse. Just like an Oderian trihorned bull in a shop full of Calpernian crystal. I've heard you're a master strategist, and that you're one of the best there is when it comes to planning a battle. Surely you know some battles are better won with finesse than force."

What could she possibly know about military assaults? "In battle, perhaps," he conceded. "But I have found a direct approach is best when dealing with subordinates."

"Subordinates?" She rolled her eyes again. "Oh, please. I know you would prefer a direct frontal approach, so to speak. Listen to me. Give Jenna some time to get used to her surroundings, and to get to know you better, before you get to the mating. It will make things easier for both of you."

"Leors do not concern themselves with making things easy. Jenna will adapt to her new surroundings."

"Yes, she will, in time. But until then, it will be very difficult for her. The heat will bother her." Lani ticked off on her fingers. "The food will bother her, and the slavery will really upset her—as will the public slaughtering of animals, and the executions. You can ease her adjustment by giving her time to come to terms with the differences. Don't try to mate with her until she knows you better, and the shock of the Leor culture has worn off."

Wait to mate with Jenna? That was the entire purpose of this exercise. "It is my duty to produce heirs," Arion gritted out through clenched teeth. "And once the merging ceremony is completed, we must mate by the next moon alignment."

"I know that." She waved her hand dismissively. "But I've studied the astronomical data on your planet. The merging ceremony can't be done until the Mystic Trine is fully formed, and on Saura that's always exactly seven standard cycles before the alignment. That allows a little time for Jenna to get used to you, and for the two of you to bond."

Bond? He had no intention of bonding with anyone. Emotional involvement was not necessary to perform the mating act and produce heirs. All that was needed was a male and female and a quick coupling. "Bonding is not necessary," he informed Lani. "The continuance of the line is all that matters."

"Yeah, yeah. Here." She shoved the holo case toward him. "Take the holovideo."

He snatched the case from her—anything to end this ludicrous conversation.

"You might even learn something you didn't know if you watch it." She stood and smoothed her feathers. "I think you'll be surprised at how much it will help you win friends and influence people. Not to mention seduce your mate." She closed her case. "I understand an android is accompanying Jenna."

Would this torture never end? "Jarek san Ranul gifted me with an android," Arion replied stiffly.

"Hmmm. One of the Riordan androids?"

"He said as much."

She beamed. "Oh, that's very good! I read on the UDW that all the Riordan androids have 'pleasure training.' They are experts on enjoyable sex. If you run into any problems, you can discuss them with the android."

Discuss mating with an android? It would be a cold day in the middle of a supernova. Arion rubbed the bridge of his nose, feeling a headache coming on. He *never* had headaches, unless he was around a certain, blue-feathered female. "Is that all?" he asked, sending supplication to the Goddess that it was.

"For now," she said brightly. "Feel free to contact me if I can help in any way."

He'd blow up his ship first. "I will see you back to the air lock."

"Don't forget the file from Gunnar." She picked up her case and sashayed toward the entry panel. "He's very concerned about the situation with the Controllers."

Gunnar was confiding in this female? Inconceivable. Arion followed her to the air lock, glaring at her slight figure the whole way. Cursed, meddling, blue-feathered female! She strutted around and disrupted routines and interfered in things that were none of her business. What did she know about Jenna anyway?

His mate-to-be appeared sturdy enough. He had made the situation, and his demands, quite clear. She knew what she was getting into. *Woo her? Bond with her?* Never. He was a warrior, first and foremost. All he needed, and all he expected from Jenna, was the continuation of the Sauran line. That was it.

He looked at the black file he was carrying. Right now, he could not allow any distractions. He needed to focus all his energy on the growing threat the Controllers presented. If what he suspected was indeed in the file from Gunnar, then the Leors were facing a grim scenario. Arion didn't know if they could win an all-out war against the Controllers.

Much later, he sat in his private command chamber, staring at a blank holo screen. He'd just finished viewing the file Komissar Gunnar had sent, and the news was grim. Controller aggression toward the Leors, which had been negligible for the past fifty spans, was rapidly escalating. There had been ten attacks on Leor reconnaissance and supply ships, with the Controllers claiming the attackers were renegade Anteks, therefore not under their jurisdiction.

Then there was Gunnar's greatest concern, the sabotage of tracking and defense systems in Leor settlements, leaving them open to attacks by Controller forces, although so far the subversion had been caught and the damages repaired before any assaults could be launched. The worst thing was the sabotage had to have been done by Leors, as servers and all other non-Leors were closely watched and not allowed into any high-security areas. The thought of Leor traitors sent rage pulsing through Arion. They would be caught, and their lives would be forfeit.

Obviously, the Controllers were capitalizing on a weakness that was universal to almost every culture, with the possible exception of the Shens and the Enhancers: greed. Arion would be willing to bet Controllers were bribing Leors with promises of gold and power and glory. The methods the Controllers were using were understandable; their motives were not quite so clear.

Up until now, they had given the Leors a wide berth. Like the Shielders, the Leors were immune to the psionic brain waves the Controllers used to dominate the majority of the cultures in their quadrant. But unlike the Shielders, the Leors did not challenge the Controllers or try to go against them.

Not only that, but Leor technology and weaponry was the most advanced in the quadrant, and it was virtually impossible to defeat them in battle. In their earlier history, they had fought as mercenaries for the highest bidders. But as the Controllers gradually took over the Black Quadrant—as their quadrant was now called—interstellar wars had ceased to exist. Now the only warfare was that which the Controllers waged on anyone who opposed them.

Since the Leors preferred hot, desert planets that had little in the way of natural resources, and since they kept to themselves, staying clear of the political and cultural upheavals sweeping the quadrant, they presented little threat to the Controllers. Their weapons and fierceness ensured them consideration from the other inhabitants of the quadrant, as well.

They had found their niche in offering protection to ships traveling dangerous routes; and by acquiring their own trade routes, demanding hefty fees from anyone who traversed or traded along those routes. They did not interfere in Controller business, and the Controllers did not interfere in theirs.

Until now.

Now the Controllers appeared to be moving against the Leors, in subtle, insidious ways. The "renegade" attacks on Leor ships, the inexplicable "failure" of Leor planetary tracking and defense systems; the apparent corruption of Leor citizens. The situation was growing very serious, and had to be stopped, and soon. Before the Controllers got an unshakable hold on Leor planets and trade routes. If that happened . . . it could be the end of the Leor race.

Not as long as he had a breath remaining in his body, Arion swore. He would do whatever was necessary to ensure the survival of his people, and of his future heirs.

The cold was the first thing Jenna felt. It was a bone-deep, bitter cold, painful in its intensity. She heard a tapping noise, and groggily realized it was her teeth chattering. With a groan, she rolled into a ball, desperately seeking warmth. Her stiff muscles protested the movement.

"She's waking up," came an unemotional voice from somewhere above her.

"Jenna, open your eyes," said a deep male voice.

She tried, but the cold and her aching muscles kept her from following through. "No," she whispered between clenched teeth. Where was she? In Hades, perhaps. But wasn't Hades supposed to be hot?

"Jenna, open your eyes," the male voice said again. "Now."

The harshness of that voice, along with its steely command, forced her reluctant compliance. She cracked her eyes open, squinting up at two blurred images, the bright light a new source of pain. "Cold, s-so c-cold," she forced through her chattering teeth.

"A side effect of stasis," said the first voice, now recognizable as female. A heated blanket was placed over Jenna, and blessed heat seeped into the edges of the awful chill.

Resisting the powerful urge to close her eyes again, she blinked, and the images sharpened. Two people stared down at her, eyes dark orbs in their impassive faces. Bits of coherence began to swirl through her muddled mind. Lanka . . . the Leor healer, and . . . Arion. Her future mate. His ship . . . The sudden memory rushed at her. They had put her in sleep stasis.

She did close her eyes then, feeling sick and unable to deal with the situation. Her teeth weren't clacking together so hard now, but she was still very cold. "Where am I?"

"You are still in the medical bay of my ship," Arion answered.

Shivering, she hugged herself tighter, struggled for total cognizance. "Why am I so cold?"

"Get her another blanket," Arion ordered. "Is this normal?"

"Yes, Comdar," came Lanka's guttural voice. "It is a combination of the drugs used to induce stasis, and the slowed body functions."

Another layer of welcome heat slid over her, and Jenna relaxed a little. "I don't feel very normal," she murmured.

"I have total confidence in Healer Lanka's competence," Arion said.

And of your dominance over everyone, Jenna thought, resentment seeping in with the heat. He'd sent her into stasis without any consideration for her thoughts on the matter, and he would do so again if it suited him. She managed to draw a full breath. "I think something's wrong with my hearing. Your voice sounds distorted."

"That is a side effect from the neural translators Lanka implanted in your ears. You will adapt to it, and then you will be able to understand our native language."

She felt violated somehow, as if her validity as a person had been discarded without a second thought, as if her body didn't belong to her anymore. Which obviously it didn't, at least as far as Arion was concerned, but she was too weak and disoriented to object right now. "Where are we?" she asked.

"We're on Saura. We will disembark as soon as you are sufficiently recovered."

She nodded, drawing the blankets closer. For good or bad, her new life was beginning. Another memory came to her, and she pushed up on one elbow, ignoring the dizziness from her sudden movement. "Maxine. Where is she?"

"*It* is currently inactive, over there." Arion swept his hand toward the other side of the unit, and Jenna made a great effort to sit upright so she could see the android.

She swayed, coming close to toppling back down, but neither Lanka nor Arion made any move to assist her. Brushing her hair from her face, she stared at the lifeless android, her only companion in an unknown new life. "When can I activate her?"

"When I need it, I'll activate it," Arion replied. "Now, I want you to follow Lanka's instructions so that we can prepare to leave the ship."

Jenna was still shaky as they left the landing bay. Saura was as she'd expected: hot, with merciless twin suns beating down onto the hard-packed sand. It was an arid, dusty desert, with the type of stifling dry heat in which Leors apparently flourished. There was no breeze to soften the wall of heat that hit them like a blast as they left the bay, no clouds in the orange sky to diffuse the harsh glare. Giant, majestic mesas rose in the distance, the only relief to the stark landscape.

She and Arion took a skimmer into the main settlement of Saura. It was a sleek open craft that hovered about a meter above the ground and zoomed with breathtaking speed over the rough terrain. She looked back one time, and gasped when she saw they were the only ones in a skimmer. The rest of the Leors were *running* the distance to the settlement. They couldn't keep up with the craft, but their speed was obviously much faster than a human could achieve, and they didn't appear to be tiring.

"They're on foot!"

Arion glanced back. "Our people are capable of great speed for long distances. It is our way to run, rather than use machines. It keeps us strong, and it is what the Goddess intended. Only the elderly or the infirm or the non-Leors living here use the skimmers."

Jenna started to ask him what he meant about non-Leors, but a sudden wave of dizziness forced her to sit back and take a deep breath. She could ask questions later. They disembarked at some sort of small port near the settlement, which appeared to be composed mainly of clay-colored dome structures. She managed to climb out of the craft, although she held on to the side a moment to steady herself. Around them, Leors paused in their activities and bowed respectfully to their Comdar.

But they eyed Jenna with hostile, suspicious gazes. They wore nothing but loincloths, and their massive, smooth bodies towered over her as she walked beside Arion down what appeared the main thoroughfare. She gave them only cursory glances, as she was concentrating hard to maintain her balance. Her head throbbed and she felt exhausted. She'd take in her surroundings another time.

She stumbled over a rough spot on the path, her trembling legs balking at activity after twenty cycles in stasis. She understood that was how long it had taken Arion and his crew to collect the Shielder colonists and transport them, also in sleep stasis, to Shamara, and then return to Saura.

Twenty long cycles. Unable to steady her legs, she grabbed Arion's arm so she wouldn't fall. Already, she understood the importance the Leors placed on appearing strong at all costs. She would shame herself and Arion if she couldn't walk from the skimmer to their quarters.

He turned when she grabbed his arm, giving her a hard look—the same reaction he'd had when she reached toward him on Shamara. His glare made it very clear he didn't appreciate being touched. Disappointment spiraled through her. She'd hoped to someday have a normal relationship with a man, one that included affectionate touching. The other Shielders had always kept a wary distance, and now it appeared nothing changed by her coming to Saura. But then, what had she really expected?

"If you'd rather I fall down," she said quietly, "I'll let go of you. But if you want me to reach wherever we're going on my own two feet, then I have to hold on."

He gave a slight nod and continued, although he slowed his pace a little. It seemed they walked endlessly in the scorching, blinding sun, with hostile Leor gazes spearing her from all directions. She focused on putting one foot in front of the other, on Arion's stiff forearm beneath her hand.

Just get through today. Then you can think about tomorrow, she told herself.

Finally they stopped before a modest dome. Arion signaled for Jenna to go ahead of him, then followed her inside. She gazed around the main chamber, noting that it was open and simply appointed, but too tired to take in many details. He must have noticed she was swaying on her feet, because he gestured toward another entryway and said, "The sleeping quarters are in there. Lanka said you would need extra rest for a few cycles."

Gratefully, she started that direction, but her legs gave out and she pitched forward. She would have fallen on her face, but a strong arm snagged her from behind, pulling her back against a hard body. A rock. Her future mate was a rock, she thought inanely. She found herself swung into Arion's arms and pressed against his chest as he strode across the chamber. It happened so fast she didn't have time to marvel at the unique experience before she was being placed on a firm, hot surface.

"Thank you," she murmured, exhaustion and stress wreaking havoc on rational thought, as well as dissolving her normal reserve. "I can tell you don't like touching me. No one else does, either. But it was nice being carried like that. Why is it so hot?" She shifted on the uncomfortable mat, shoved her hair back. "I'll try not to touch you again, since you don't like it, at least not until we . . . you know . . ."

A grunt was his only reply.

She didn't need him to have a conversation. "We'll have to have physical contact then," she said, her heavy eyelids drooping as she drifted off. "No way around it." She jolted awake to a moment of comprehension, her eyes flying open. She stared up at Arion, who stared back, his black eyes inscrutable.

"Rest," he said gruffly.

She lay back with a groan. Had she really just said those things? Closing her eyes again, she decided she was too weary to care. She'd worry about it tomorrow.

Chapter Four

In the darkened medical bay of Arion's ship, Maxine hummed to life. Her eyes flew open and she stood fully upright. A message was coming in to her internal receiver, and she was programmed to activate whenever she received a communication. This was a computer transmission rather than a voice message, so she responded in computer code. *Maxine V here.*

Max here, came the computer message from the original Maximillian android. *Is it a good time for you to come out of inactive mode?*

As prearranged, Maxine had already transmitted to Max all the events up through Arion's order for her to switch to inactive, so he was well aware of the situation. As Maxine reported events to him, he was keeping Captain san Ranul apprised of Jenna's welfare. *I am still on Comdar Arion's ship,* she replied. *The medical bay appears deserted, so I see no problems with activating. I am assuming that Jenna dan Aron is no longer in sleep stasis. I am also assuming that we are on Saura. However, I will have to investigate further before I can confirm that.*

I will await your findings. Did you receive the extensive downloads you requested on Leor culture—including mating and spiritual practices, physiology, reproductive processes, and warfare tactics?

I did and found the data most interesting.

Let me know if you need further information, Max replied.

I will. If I can access a computer terminal, I can also download information directly from the Universal Data Web.

My files are just as comprehensive, Max informed her. *There is no need to go elsewhere for data.*

She had forgotten about his egotistical programming. Male-emulated androids were so high maintenance! *Of course, Max. My apology for overlooking that fact.*

Apology accepted. There is more we need to discuss. Earlier today, Prince Sevilen received an interesting communication from Komissar Gunnar's mate, Lani. She explained the situation she found when she visited the Comdar on his ship. She wanted to know how to contact you directly.

That is very curious. Maxine's circuits hummed as she analyzed the possible reasons the Komissar's mate would want to communicate with her. *Did she give you the transmission frequencies for me to contact her?*

She did. I will transmit them now. I request that you continue to send ongoing reports on your activities.

Understood.

I will sign off after the transmission. I advise you to exercise caution on Saura. Do not do the circuit mambo with any strange androids.

She appreciated his quirky—and suggestive—humor, since as her creator and mentor, he had programmed her with the same type of humor. *Oh, Max! Your sensu-chips must be overcharged. You are very naughty. I like that in an android.*

That is what they all say. When you return, you can give me an overhaul. Wink, wink.

That would certainly be more exciting than dealing with a barbarian Leor Comdar with absolutely no sense of humor, she thought, but did not transmit. *I would say you are long past due for an overhaul. I look forward to personally performing one. I will bring the machine oil. It is good for synthetic skin.*

And other functions, he replied adroitly.

She could almost see his crooked smile, even as she felt her own mouth twist into the identical position. A bland and passive personality in an android was highly overrated. A few quirks made everything far more interesting, as far as she was concerned.

Max sent the subspace frequency codes, then signed off. Maxine wasted no time in sending a transmission to Lani. Then she set about finding her way off the ship and locating Jenna, whose welfare was the main purpose of her mission.

Jenna woke sprawled on a hard surface. Groggy and confused, she raised her head and blinked against the glaring sunlight surrounding her. As her eyes adjusted, she stared down at the textured clay surface beneath her, obviously a floor, then to her right, at the utilitarian bed slat that rose almost a meter above her. What . . . ?

A movement to her left drew her attention, and she rolled that way, almost colliding with a pair of massive, bare legs. Her gaze traveled up two solid columns of smooth, muscled flesh, which faded into the shadowed recess created by a loincloth. For a moment, she was disappointed she couldn't see further, couldn't see what promised to be a very impressive set of— Suddenly fully awake, she gasped and scrambled to a full sitting position. And met the severe gaze of Arion.

He gave her that chilling, unblinking stare, and her heart

jolted against her rib cage. He said nothing, just waited, until her neck began to hurt from the sharp angle necessary to maintain eye contact. Until her nerves forced her to stammer, "I— Um . . . I'm not sure what I'm doing on the floor."

"You moved there while I was at the evening meal. I put you back on the mat, but you moved there again a few hours into sleep shift. I assumed you had an aversion to remaining in my bed."

His face hardened and an unreadable expression flashed across his granite features. "So I left you where you chose to be." He set the tumbler he'd been holding on the wooden block stand by the bed. "I brought you something to drink. Lanka informs me that you must guard against dehydration, and the effects of the differing gravity."

He stepped away, and Jenna took the opportunity to push to her feet. She was achy, sore, and tempted to use the bed frame for support, but some stab of pride she'd never realized she possessed made her rise on her own. She stared at Arion's broad back. With half the chamber between them, the faint crisscrossing pattern on his golden skin wasn't visible. She noticed the tense set of his shoulders, but couldn't tell if he was angry. He was very difficult to read.

She looked down at her damp tunic, plucked the clinging fabric away from her skin. "I don't remember moving to the floor, but I remember being terribly hot. I guess I was just trying to cool off."

"Heat coils." Half turning, he gestured toward the bed. "There are heat coils beneath the mat. The solar panels in the dome exterior keep them hot. They retain warmth through dark cycle."

No wonder the mat had been so hard, and she'd been so hot. Getting her first good look at the bed, Jenna saw it was huge, at least three times as broad as her own bunk on Shamara, and twice as high. She was amazed she'd been able to climb out of it without knowing what she was doing, and without injuring herself.

There were no pillows, but a metallic gold-toned thermal blanket was smoothed over the immense surface and tucked in with military precision. Bright sunshine streamed down, reflecting off the gold cover, and she looked up to see an open skylight. That explained why the chamber was so bright, and why it was already almost unbearably hot inside the dome.

Resigning herself to the Leors' inability to produce their own body heat, she picked up the tumbler Arion had placed on the stand. The liquid inside it was pinkish white and thick, and she hesitated.

"Drink," Arion ordered, stepping closer. "You need it."

She took a tentative sip. It was cool and sweet and surprisingly delicious. She took a larger gulp. "Oh, that's good," she murmured, resting the cool cup against her forehead then each cheek. "And it's *not* hot."

"It is homa, a traditional beverage that is full of nutrients. It must be kept cool, but we heat it before we drink it. I thought you might prefer otherwise."

"Oh, yes," she sighed blissfully, pressing the cup against her chest.

For a moment, he stared at the tumbler nestled between her breasts, and then he turned and strode to look out one of the open ports. Jenna took a quick count and saw there were six in the chamber's walls, all open, with sunlight pouring through.

"You will be fatigued for a few cycles," he said. "You will rest today."

"All right." She took another sip of the delicious homa, already beginning to feel rejuvenated. Enough so that, with returning clarity, she was reminded of the reason for her exhaustion. Resentment at the way she'd been treated flared up. "If your future mate had been a Leor, would you have forced her to undergo sleep stasis?"

He turned his head, his midnight gaze burning into her. "No."

"Yet you forced me to undergo it, without my consent."

"Your consent was not necessary. I made the decision, and it was done. Besides, you do not have the endurance of a Leor."

Her fingers clenched around the cup. "That shouldn't have mattered. You told me you would grant me the same consideration you would give a Leor mate."

He swung around, took a menacing step forward. "I also made it very clear that my authority is not to be challenged."

He was the most intimidating man she'd ever met. She swallowed hard, but pressed on. "I believe there is a distinction between challenging your authority and discussing a difference of opinion, Comdar."

"Why would a discussion be necessary if my decision has already been made?"

Jenna took a deep breath. She knew she had to get her point across now, or she would lose whatever power she had in this relationship, no matter how minuscule. Forever was a long time to be at someone's mercy. "You also told me mated Leors can disagree among themselves, as long as it is in private. I am holding you to your word, Comdar. I expect to receive the same consideration you would have shown a Leor mate. I expect to be able to voice my opinion, but I assure you these discussions will only occur when we are alone, as we are now."

"We were not alone when you resisted sleep stasis," he pointed out coldly.

"You would never have placed a Leor female in that situation to begin with," she shot back.

"You are no longer in a position to negotiate," he growled, anger sparking in his eyes.

His anger made him even more intimidating, but she reminded herself that he had promised he would never hit her. "I'm not negotiating, Your Lordship. I'm simply ask-ing you to keep your word."

He clenched his fists, tension hardening his jaw. They stared at each other for a breath-stopping moment, and she wondered if he could hear her heart pounding.

"Fine," he growled finally. "I will treat you as I would any other Leor female."

The ominous tone of his voice made her wonder exactly what was expected of Leor females. Even so, she strongly believed she needed every shred of equality she could gar-ner, if she were to survive in this alien world. "Thank you," she murmured.

"It is time for the morning meal." He gestured toward her rumpled, sweat-dampened tunic. "Do you plan to wear that today?"

"I—I . . ." She glanced at his broad chest, the golden skin pulled taut over bulging muscles. Seminudity might be a way of life among the Leors, but she wasn't ready for it yet. "I'd like to use the facilities and change, if you don't mind."

He jerked his head toward a curved doorway. "The bath-ing chamber is in there. Do you need Amyan to assist you?"

"Who is Amyan?

"She is my personal server."

"Server?" Jenna mulled this over. Everything she knew about Leors indicated that none of them would willingly take on a subordinate role.

"Amyan!" Arion called. "Here now." A woman hurried in, and stopped before him, her hands clasped, her head down. Jenna saw immediately that she wasn't a Leor. She was of average height, but thin; and short, glossy black hair framed her face, which was hidden by her subservient posture. She was dressed in white loose-fitting slacks and a cropped tunic, so lightweight they were almost, but not quite, transparent. Silver cuffs glinted on each of her wrists.

Jenna gasped as the realization hit her. "She's a slave!"

Arion inclined his head. "Some use that term. She belongs to me, and it is her job to attend to my needs."

Slaves! The Leors had slaves. Jenna closed her eyes, reeling from the ugly revelation. She'd heard about the Leors—about their patterned skin and inability to produce body heat, and their insistence on virgin mates, not to mention their fierceness and cruelty and utter ruthlessness. But slavery . . . Spirit help her.

She'd had no idea. She drew a deep breath, trying to calm herself, wondering if the knowledge would have stayed her from stepping forward to become Arion's mate. Yet she knew, with the insidious pull of inevitability that permeated all her visions, fate could not be thwarted.

Feeling sick, she stepped forward. "It's a pleasure to meet you, Amyan. I am Jenna."

The slave shot her a startled glance, revealing a long, dusky-skinned face and exotically-slanted black eyes, before she ducked her head again. She was trembling, and Jenna wondered what Arion had done to terrify her so, although she already knew he could inspire fear with just a glance, with those glittering, obsidian eyes.

"Do not try to converse with her," he said tersely. "She cannot speak."

"What?" Jenna asked, surprised. She assumed that everyone spoke at least one of the two universal languages, especially if they originated from the Dark Quadrant. Either that, or they used neural translators, like the one Lanka had implanted in Jenna's ear. "She can't speak Contran or Elysian?"

"She cannot talk at all. Amaya, turn. Raise your head." As the trembling woman complied, he pointed to two wicked-looking scars running along either side of her neck. "Her vocal cords have been severed to keep her silent."

Horror rushed through Jenna, clenching her stomach in a vise so tight, she battled back nausea. So the stories about Leor cruelty were more than rumors—they were fact. She took a step back, staring at Arion. It hit her fully then, a staggering blow that finally pounded home the reality she'd tried to avoid, for the sake of her sanity. But she could no longer ignore the truth.

Her future mate was a monster.

Arion ran toward the training compound. The day was almost gone, and he'd barely scratched the surface of the long list of duties demanding his attention. He'd been absent from Saura twenty-one standard cycles, and the myriad duties that fell to the head of a clan had piled up. He'd lost precious time today, receiving more communiqués about increasing Controller hostilities, not to mention dealing with Jenna.

His future mate was occupying an unseemly portion of his thoughts, when he needed to be focusing on running a clan and strategizing a defense against the Controllers. She was simply a means to propagate heirs, he told himself. She was not even a Leor mate, therefore not worthy of so much consideration. Yet she was far more complex than he had expected; far more intriguing, with an oddly appealing innocence.

She said the strangest things at times, especially when she was tired. The two occasions he'd found her sleeping on the floor, curled in a protective ball, she had appeared helpless and childlike. But when she was awake, she was a continual challenge.

Not in a physical sense, of course. He could snap her body into pieces with his bare hands. But mentally . . . that was another matter entirely. She stood up to him, demanded rights as if she were a Leor citizen, conjured issues he'd never before considered. The look of horror on her face when she realized Amyan was a slave had clearly indicated her revulsion of the practice. He felt certain it would be only one of many components of the Leor culture that she would find repulsive. She would have to accept it, though, just as she would have to accept his dominion over her life.

A golden flash caught his attention, and he halted and turned, watching in amazement as the android Maxine strode toward him, as casual and bold as a swaggering Antek. His eyes narrowed, and he headed toward it. Who had activated it, without his permission? He would find out and deal with the perpetrator. He'd been challenged far too much in the past twenty-one cycles, more than he ever faced in an entire span, and his tolerance was at an end.

"Greetings, Comdar Arion," the android said.

It was a technological wonder, he conceded, as realistic as any human woman he'd met throughout the galaxy. It was tall and statuesque, and the long brown-and-gold-streaked hair shone in the bright sun. Its technical knowledge, especially that of genetics, made it quite valuable to him.

"Who activated you?" he demanded.

"I activated myself," it said in a husky feminine voice.

"You were supposed to activate on my order only."

"I apologize for not awaiting your order, but I am most eager to tour your medical and computer facilities and begin working on the reproductive problems of your race. I have already downloaded extensive files to help in my research."

Somewhat mollified, Arion grunted and changed course. "Then, come. I will escort you to the medical laboratory." He noted how the android moved exactly like a human would, with a smooth, regular stride.

"How is Jenna doing?" it inquired as they crossed the main common area.

He did not wish to discuss his future mate with the machine. "I expect your focus to be solely on our genetic problems."

"I assure you it is, Your Lordship. But Jenna is crucial to your plan to create heirs, is she not?"

"Yes, but that has no bearing—"

"I am very interested in a theory that the intense physical training your females undergo might be directly linked to their low fertility rates."

He momentarily forgot about Jenna. "That training is essential to our survival."

"So I understand. Another theory is that stress affects well-being and fertility."

His eyes narrowed, and his irritation with the android returned full force. "You already mentioned that on my ship. Leors are too disciplined to allow stress to affect them."

"But your mate-to-be is not a Leor. She is somewhat more delicate, and more susceptible to stress. It might affect her ability to bear offspring."

How had the conversation gotten back to this? "I have been assured by my healer that Jenna is physically capable of producing children," Arion said stiffly.

"I am sure your healer is correct, sir. But still, stress and fear can have unforeseeable physical effects on humans."

He did not want to hear this. "Jenna has been told what to expect."

"Has she? Tell me, Comdar, have you explained your culture to her? Does she know about the Leor practice of keeping slaves?"

"She does," he muttered, recalling the horrified expression on Jenna's face.

"Have you explained the daily routines? My research indicates all Leors are expected to work. Does Jenna know what her job will be?"

"Not yet, but she will soon enough."

The irritating android pressed on. "Perhaps an explanation of her duties might be appropriate. And a time table for the merging ceremony, along with an explanation of the ceremony itself, as well as your mating practices. I have done a great deal of research on the Leor culture. Perhaps I can assist you."

"No!" Arion growled. "I do not want your assistance anywhere but in the genetics laboratory. Nor do I intend to instruct Jenna on these things. I am not a teacher. I am a warrior and the leader of my clan."

The android stopped, pursed its lips. "I see. Then I assume you have assigned someone to this task."

Arion resisted the urge to pick the meddling machine up and hurl it across the sand. "This matter does not concern you."

"I only ask because I am concerned about Jenna's fertility."

"This has nothing to do with my mate's fertility!"

"But it does, Comdar. Two things can seriously affect her ability to reproduce."

He wanted to end this ludicrous conversation. But part of him, the part that acknowledged the desperate need of his people to survive, forced him to hear what the android had to say. "And those are?" he gritted out.

"The first, as I have already mentioned, is stress, especially from fear of the unknown. It would be good for you to spend time with Jenna. Explain the various aspects of your cultures, so she will know what to expect. You could start tonight."

This cursed android was almost as bad as the blue-feathered echobird mated to the Komissar. Arion clenched the handle of his sword. "What is the second thing?"

"Enjoyable sex."

That stopped him dead in his tracks "*Enjoyable* sex?"

"Yes. Studies show that fertility is greatly enhanced if the sexual act is pleasurable."

"Fertility is 'greatly enhanced,' as you put it, when the

mating act is successfully completed. I am capable of handling that end of it. Enough of this discussion."

"Completion is not enough, Comdar. The female must be relaxed and receptive. If she is tense and frightened, the odds for impregnation drop."

This android was every bit as bad as, if not worse than, Lani. "Jenna will be receptive," Arion growled. "She is well aware of her purpose as my mate."

"You will increase the odds if you are skilled at lovemaking," the android said bluntly.

Lovemaking? Could this cycle get any worse? "I do not believe this," Arion muttered. He pointed toward a low, stone building. "There are the laboratories. You can find your way from here." He spun to leave.

"Perhaps you would consider taking instruction on the finer points of mating," the android called after him. "I have received extensive sexual pleasure training. I would be glad to educate you on the matter. Or I could provide some resource materials."

First Lani, now this android! When had a simple matter of taking a mate and producing offspring become more complex than orchestrating a major space battle?

"I will not discuss this further," Arion said, barely holding on to his temper. "I already have sufficient information on the matter," he added, remembering the holovideo Lani had forced on him. He again pointed to the laboratories. "Go and report in to Barenk. Now."

"I am glad to know that you already have some instructional materials," the android said brightly. "I would strongly advise you to consult that information." An odd, lopsided grin appeared on its face. "I have it on good authority that Leor males have incredible stud potential. Good-bye, Comdar." It turned and headed toward the outbuildings with superhuman speed.

Arion stared after it, feeling an odd mix of outrage and frustration and confusion—unfamiliar emotions, and ones he would not tolerate. He did not want to deal with the emotional entanglements that apparently occurred with human females, and he certainly did not want to entertain the suggestions of a foolish echobird and an android.

Yet at the same time, he could not afford to compromise producing viable offspring. It was too important to his clan, and to the Leor race as a whole. It might even necessitate him watching that damned holovideo. Cursing the Fates for putting him in this position, he watched as the android reached the laboratory. It turned and gave him a final wave, that stupid sideways grin still plastered on its face.

He had the distinct feeling he had somehow just been outmaneuvered.

Chapter Five

Curled up on one end of a massive settee that faced a glowing firebox, Jenna watched as Arion methodically cleaned a wicked-looking sword, running a soft cloth along the blade. His hands were graceful and sure, despite their size; competent hands that could easily wield a weapon and kill an opponent in hand-to-hand combat. Or cruelly slash a slave's vocal cords.

After this morning's horrendous discovery, she didn't want to be near him, yet there was nowhere else to go in the small dome. The only real furniture in the sleeping chamber was a computer station and the massive bed, which was extremely uncomfortable—too hard and too hot. The only other chambers were the bathing chamber, with a huge soaking tub and a shower and heated floor tiles, and the living area with the one settee. There was no kitchen or dining area, as the Leors ate in a communal dining hall.

Still feeling exhausted and disoriented, Jenna opted to rest on the settee rather than the bed or the floor. She had to share it with Arion, but it was large, and he was at the other end. Besides, he rarely spoke to her outside of giving orders. She closed her eyes, drifting, almost welcoming the oblivion of sleep. . . .

She was walking down a hard-packed sand path. The sun blazed overhead. Squinting, she shifted her gaze downward, surprised to discover the path was strewn with unfamiliar red flowers. She realized she was dressed in a flowing silver robe, with silver sandals on her feet. The oppressive heat from the sun beat down on her, and she found it hard to draw a full breath in the stifling air.

She looked ahead and saw Leors gathered there. Beyond them, she saw Arion. Standing at the head of the path, he cut a magnificent figure. His shimmering gold cape and matching loincloth, along with his regal presence, set him apart from the others. He stood calmly, majestically, his unblinking midnight gaze fixed unnervingly upon her.

She jolted back to normal consciousness, gasping for breath.

"Jenna? What is wrong?"

She rubbed her aching forehead, afraid to close her eyes again, lest the vision—the same one she'd had four seasons ago—resume. "Nothing, really. It was just . . . nothing."

"Was it a vision?"

She looked at him, surprised by his perception. "How did you know?"

He shrugged, held up his sword to inspect it. "You appeared to be in a trance, very much like Morven appears when he is receiving wisdom from the Goddess."

He seemed unconcerned about her ability to see past and future events, a welcome divergence from the fearful reactions of her fellow Shielders. "Who is Morven?"

"He is our shaman. The Goddess speaks through him. He will officiate at the merging ceremony."

Normally, Jenna would have been fascinated with the idea that the Leors actually revered and listened to those with visions. But the upcoming mating with Arion loomed over her, obliterating all other issues. "When is . . ." She paused, took a deep breath. "When is the ceremony?"

"Two cycles from now."

Only two cycles. She thought again of the massive bed, where she would lie with this fierce Leor, as his mate, and far too soon. Where he would join his body with hers. Images of their bodies locked together, images she'd been unable to shake, flashed through her mind. She clasped her hands, tried to still their trembling. "I know nothing about the Leor mating ceremony."

"Do you have concerns about it?"

"I . . . I am a little nervous," she said. Terrified, actually, but she refused to admit that to Arion. "Outside my vision about being mated to you, I have no idea what to expect."

"Are your visions usually very clear?"

They were always vividly clear, down to the horrifying details and the emotions of the people involved. But . . . "To the best of my knowledge, every one of my visions has come to pass. But I've never personally experienced any of them, so I can't confirm how accurate the details are."

"So you do not know what to expect now that you are here," he repeated, a statement of fact rather than a question. He should know—he certainly hadn't been forthcoming with any information, other than the fact he expected total and immediate compliance in all things.

"No, I don't," she agreed.

"Then you are experiencing . . . stress?"

Where was he going with this? Baffled, she thought about it a moment, then decided to be honest. "It is very stressful being here. I don't know anything about your ways, or what will happen next."

He was silent a moment; then he muttered something about *"cursed echobirds and androids."*

"What did you say?"

He grunted, then cleared his throat. "Would you like me to tell you what will happen in the coming cycles?"

She didn't understand the change in his attitude; why he was suddenly willing to explain things to her, when he'd barely had anything other than a grunt for her before now. Until this morning, she would have welcomed any information he could offer, hoping it might help her navigate the maze of a new and unsettling life. But after learning that Leors kept slaves, and seeing what they did to those slaves, she found herself recoiling from contact with Arion.

Yet she had given her word, and her blood, that she would mate with this man, would lie with him and bear his children. And she wanted to know, needed to know, what to expect. Being in the dark was far worse. "Yes," she said. "I would like more information."

He carefully placed his sword on the floor and picked up a laser pistol and inspected its charge. "You will go to Morven tomorrow, and he will explain the merging ceremony to you and help you begin your preparations for the ceremony."

"Preparations?"

"Cleansing, fasting, and meditation. I will be doing the same."

"Oh." Jenna leaned back, surprised. The Leors seemed so physical, it was strange to consider they might have a spiritual side.

"On the next cycle after that, we will be joined in the merging ceremony." He turned, impaling her with that midnight gaze, and his unspoken message was very clear. They would be mated in every sense of the word, including the physical act. But emotionally she would find nothing more than the act of intercourse. That had been very clear from the start.

"And then?" she asked, not wanting to dwell on the so-called wedding night.

He returned his attention to the pistol. "The following cycle, you will be given a duty assignment. Everyone works in a Leor settlement."

Especially the slaves, Jenna thought. "Everyone works in a Shielder settlement, too." She drew her knees up, hugged them to her chest. "I expect to do my share."

His probing gaze returned. "Your most important job will be to bear my heirs. But you will be assigned other duties."

"What will those duties be?"

"That is yet to be decided. What did you do in Shamara?"

Nothing that could bring her in contact with the other Shielders. Her first love was children, and she'd wanted desperately to work in the communal nursery. But no one wanted her, what with her freakish visions, to be around their children. So she had worked in the horticulture center instead. "I helped with producing food for the settlement."

"I will pass that information along to Shela. She does the work assignments." Arion gathered his weapons and cloths, and stood. "The shift grows late. It is time to prepare for sleep."

Jenna watched the firebox's glow upon his chest, clearly reflecting the pattern in his skin, all the differences between human and Leor. She suddenly felt incredibly alone, even more so than she had on Shamara. "Comdar, I have a favor to ask."

He turned back to her, and she felt the full force of his energy, felt the subtle probing of her thoughts for which Leors were well known. Only her natural shield prevented him from reading her mind—or so she hoped.

"In the privacy of our dome, you may call me by my given name," he said. "After all, we will soon be mates. What do you wish to ask?"

"All right . . . Arion." She felt very small and insignificant with his powerful body towering over her. "I would like to have Maxine present at the merging ceremony."

"Maxine? Do you mean the android?"

"Yes."

"Why would you want a machine at the ceremony?"

Because she was the only potential friend Jenna had in this Spirit-forsaken place. "She is the only person I know here, outside of you and Lanka."

"She? The android is *not* a person," he said adamantly.

"She may not seem real to you, but it is important to me. Please." Seeing the incredulity in his eyes, Jenna cast around for a way to sway him, and picked the thing he seemed concerned about, as odd as it was. "It will be less stressful for me if she's there."

He shook his head, a low growl in his throat. "Fine. If you will suffer less stress with that machine present, so be it."

He turned to leave, and Jenna leaped up, spurred by the need to say something. "Comdar—"

He whirled around, and she paused, trying to shove the image of Amyan's ruined throat from her mind. She had to live with this man for the rest of her life. He had made an effort to allay her fears, had consented for Maxine to come to the merging. The least she could do was let him know she was grateful. "I mean, Arion. Thank you."

He cocked his head. "For?"

"For taking the time to explain things to me, and for allowing Maxine to be present at the ceremony."

He shifted, then turned again. "Amyan! Attend me."

Amyan scrambled from behind the settee and scurried toward the sleeping chamber. Jenna hadn't even realized she was there. "What is she doing?" she asked.

Arion gave her a challenging look. "She will help me with my evening regimen."

"Your . . . regimen?"

"Yes. Leors must put oil on their skin to keep it from drying out."

74

Reptilian flesh. A stark reminder that her mate-to-be wasn't altogether human. *A monster,* Jenna's fears whispered.

Her reaction must have shown on her face, because Arion's expression became mocking. "It is one of Amyan's duties to help with the care of my skin. It becomes a mate's duty after the merging ceremony." He turned and strode toward the sleeping chamber.

Shock, that a slave would be expected to perform intimate tasks, and a rush of other emotions swept through Jenna. Things had happened so swiftly since her first meeting with Arion that she hadn't had a chance to consider how overwhelming a new and very alien environment might be. She'd foolishly thought any life would be better than the empty existence she'd endured in Shamara, but now she feared she'd been terribly wrong. She felt as if everything was totally out of her control, and she hated the sense of helplessness. However, she was certain about one thing: Monster or not, Arion was her destined mate. She didn't think Amyan should have to attend him any longer, especially if the duties were those a Leor mate would perform.

How would a Leor female react in this situation? she wondered. She knew it wouldn't be passively or meekly. By the Spirit, but she wasn't going to become a nonentity, to become absorbed into her foreign surroundings. She was determined to be treated as an equal. She'd battled for her tiny molecule of power this morning, and she didn't intend to relinquish it now.

Holding tight to her resolve, she marched into the sleeping chamber.

Standing in the steamy shower enclosure, Arion let the hot spray relax his sore muscles. He'd driven both his warriors and himself hard today, insisting on a punishing workout. Then he'd spent grueling hours in the tribunal, settling matters that had come up during his absence, and dispensing justice, as was his responsibility. After that had been a meeting with his officers to discuss the increasing Controller threat, then a meeting with Morven about the upcoming merging ceremony. Now, even with his great physical and mental strength, he was fatigued.

He stepped from the stall, stopped short in surprise. Jenna stood by the oil stand, a frustrated expression on her face. Next to her, Amyan wrung her hands, looking highly agitated. Arion said nothing, simply waited, well aware just a look from him usually evoked an explanation.

Jenna's gaze skimmed his chest, then dropped lower. Immediately her gaze jerked back up. Despite their strict beliefs about mating, Leors were casual about displaying their bodies, and Arion was unconcerned by his nudity. But Jenna's discomfort with it was apparent, as a faint tinge of color swept her skin. She had done that in Shamara, too. He thought it interesting.

Clearing her throat, she focused on his face. "Please tell Amyan she can leave. She refused to go when I told her she could."

He moved beneath the dryer and activated it. "She answers only to me. Do not attempt to undermine my authority."

"I'm not trying to do that. But I see no need for her to assist you if . . ." The color in her face increased, but Jenna held his gaze. "If this is going to be one of my duties after we're mated in two cycles, I might as well start now."

He certainly could not accuse her of shirking her duties, and he felt a grudging admiration for her courage in a situation that must seem very alien. Initially, he had given no thought to the fact she would have no understanding of Leor ways, or of what he personally demanded from her; that she might be confused or frightened and have no ally to whom she could turn. Unfamiliar possessive and protective feelings surged through him, startling both in their occurrence and their intensity.

His. She was his. She would turn to *him.* No others would assume that responsibility. It galled him that she sought solace in that android, a *machine,* wanting it present at the merging. He had no patience with emotional matters, no softness or ability to comfort. He'd lived a harsh and disciplined life, with no room for anything but logic, facts, and survival. But he could offer concise, objective information. That was all Jenna needed. He was confident she would adapt as she learned their ways, especially since she was taking the initiative.

He gestured sharply toward the entry. "Amyan, you may go. I will not need you further tonight."

The server darted away, her head down. Jenna watched her leave, obviously concerned. "Where will she go now?"

"To her barracks. The unmated servers live in several large domes, and each has his or her own chamber."

Jenna considered that. "Then you have mated slaves? Entire families?"

"There are a few." He could almost see the thoughts processing in her mind, and headed her off. "I do not care to discuss this issue now, or in the future."

She bit her lip, lowered her gaze. "I'm sure I couldn't change your opinion anyway."

"No, you could not. There are many things you do not understand." He snapped the dryer off. "I am ready for the oil."

The Leors' goddess had blessed them with solid, muscular bodies and incredible strength and stamina. Yet they faced a serious reproductive dilemma, and they had to deal with maintaining body heat and skin moisture on a daily basis. Which they did, in the usual methodical way of their people.

Arion indicated the gold metal bowl sitting on an electronic warmer. "The oil is there. Coat your hands with it and rub it into my skin."

She nodded, with another quick glance at his body. She turned and dipped her hands into the bowl, scooping the warmed oil into her palms. As she faced him, he noticed the rapid rise and fall of her chest. "Where . . . where should I begin?"

"My back." He turned away from her, waited. He sensed her silent movement behind him, picked up the sound of her quick breathing. She radiated reluctance. Unyielding, he continued to wait. If she wanted the status of a Leor mate, then she must perform the duties of one.

He almost jumped when her hands made contact with him, at waist level, then tentatively slid upward. Her touch was whisper-soft, an odd sensation. "Use more pressure," he ordered. "You must rub in the oil well."

He felt her move closer, felt her hands press more firmly as she spread the oil up over his shoulder blades. He could feel the heat of her slight body, smell her unique scent, so different from that of Leor females. Remaining silent, she scooped more oil, returning to smooth it over his shoulders. Her fingers slipped over his shoulders, then down his upper arms. The heated oil soaked into his skin, warming it and easing stiff muscles. It felt so good, he almost groaned.

She dipped out more oil and started rubbing down his back. He closed his eyes, dragging more air into his lungs, taking with it more of her scent. With an acute sense of smell in both his nose and his tongue, he could almost taste her—sweet, like warm homa. Her hands swept along his lower back, lingered there, her fingers curling around his waist. She moved away to get more oil, and he felt the loss of her touch. Strange, but he never felt that when Amyan rubbed in the oil. But then, he never consciously opened his senses to his server. He appeared to be more attuned to Jenna.

Her hands returned to the small of his back, finished there. "Do you need the oil ... everywhere?" Her voice was low, slightly shaky, and the timbre of it resonated in his head, seemed to heighten every sensation more.

He did apply the oil all over; however, usually Amyan only did his back, the one part he could not reach. But he was not ready for Jenna to stop. Normally, he did not like others to touch him, although the impersonal ministrations of a server had never bothered him.

As a rule, Leors were not demonstrative. His parents had never displayed any physical affection, not that he had spent much time with them. Most of his early years had been spent in a communal camp, where the strongest and smartest Leors trained for battle and leadership. The only touch he'd known there had been the harsh stroke of an electrolyzer rod when he didn't perform perfectly.

Yet he did not find contact with Jenna repulsive at all. Her fingers left a tingling warmth wherever they stroked, something he had never before experienced. Not only did he want her to continue, but a part of him wanted to test her resolve, to see if she would follow through. They were to be mated in less than two days, so this small intimacy was not out of line.

"The oil must be rubbed in everywhere," he said.

She hesitated and he heard her indrawn breath. Another pause, and then her hands cupped his rear, kneading in the oil. The tingling feeling intensified, sending an odd tension through his body, and his breathing speeded up. Adrenaline surged, as if he were getting ready to go into battle. Taken aback, he struggled to regain his normal magnasteel-clad control over his body. Jenna's hands left him, and he exhaled slowly.

She scooped up more oil, returned to spread it down the back of his thighs. This time his heart jolted, feeling as though it had slammed into his chest, and his breathing again accelerated. He had never experienced such a thing from a female's touch, but knew it must be part of the physical reaction between mates. Determined to see this through and maintain control, he widened his stance to give her better access to his legs.

Her breath hitched again, and she ran her fingers along the inside of his thighs. They brushed dangerously close to his most sensitive parts, and the breath froze in his lungs. He was totally unprepared for the sensation that arced through him, like a solar flare, spreading outward to the rest of his body. The reaction was immediate and intense, his male member responding in a heated, painful rush.

A wave of need crashed over him, and every muscle in his body clenched. Any more of this, and his control would be lost. "That is enough," he managed to growl, at the same time stepping out of her reach. "I will do the rest."

"Are you sure?" she ventured.

He pivoted. "I will finish. You may go."

Her face was flushed even more. "Did I do something . . . ?" Her gaze dropped to his aroused state, and her eyes widened. "Oh."

"Go."

She turned and fled, without a backward glance. More shaken than he cared to admit, Arion strode to the oil and began slathering it on his chest and arms. He had never lost control over his body like that. Never. At least, not before Jenna came into his life. He had reacted the same way on Shamara, when they had sealed their mating agreement with the blood-sharing ritual.

It was hard to accept, because spans of rigorous training had disciplined and honed him until he could command every muscle, every physical response at will. Having honored his race's strict code of abstinence before taking a mate, he had never experienced sex. He could only assume his body's reaction was an instinctive, primal response; a basic urge to propagate the species, for survival. He just had not expected the reaction to be so strong, so over-whelming.

He hoped he did not lose total control when he and Jenna actually came together. He was big, massive, like all Leors, and she was so small. What was the word the android had used? *Delicate.* Lani's words came back to him as well: *"It will be rape if she's frightened. . . . You could hurt her if you're not careful, and she's not ready."* He wanted to curse them for their interference, but at the same time he accepted that there might be truth to their words.

One mate for life. He had only one opportunity, and the Goddess had decreed that Jenna would be his mate. He could not risk hurting her. He had thought it would be a simple matter of performing a basic act that was as old as the universe. But none of this had been simple. His mate was human, and apparently human women needed to be handled more carefully than Leor females.

He did not need, or want, this complication. Yet he had given his word he would stand for this fragile human. And he would, to the best of his ability—but he knew their life together would not be easy.

He hoped that Jenna was up to the challenge.

Chapter Six

Jenna woke up stiff and sore, once again on the hard floor, her tunic damp with sweat. Sunlight flooded the chamber, so brilliant it hurt her eyes. Disoriented, she squinted up at Arion towering above her. It took a moment for the fog of sleep to clear; then the events in the bathing chamber rushed back with mortifying clarity. She felt her face heat.

"The floor is not a designated sleeping place," he informed her, no sign of emotion on his formidable face.

She pushed up on her arms, trying to avoid the smooth, muscled legs so close to her. She also tried not to see the patterned golden skin; and most especially, she tried not to think about what he looked like without the loincloth—or how big certain parts of him were. She wasn't sure she would survive mating with him. She certainly didn't expect him to be gentle about it, and her fears intensified.

Wearily, she rolled to a sitting position and pushed back her hair. "I wasn't aware of moving to the floor. I think the heat from the bed makes me restless and I'm just trying to get away from it."

His black-hole eyes glittered. "You will have to get used to it. It is a necessity for us."

She was struggling to adapt to a lot of things, but she made no comment, instead rising shakily to her feet. She looked around hopefully for the cool tumbler of homa he'd been bringing her, and was disappointed not to see it. She'd managed to beg off leaving the dome yesterday, pleading exhaustion, although her shock at discovering the fact that the Leors kept slaves had been the real reason she'd wanted more time.

As if reading her thoughts, he said, "Today you will eat in the communal dining hall. Then you will go to Shaman Morven."

Oh, yes. To prepare for the merging ceremony. Her stomach clenched, and she didn't think she'd be able to eat anything. *Time to begin your new life,* she told herself. *You have to see this through.* She glanced down at her sweat-stained tunic. "Let me freshen up, and I'll be ready to go."

"You must make special preparations first." He stepped back and gestured to Amyan, who stood just inside the doorway with a cloth bundle in her arms. The slave shuffled forward in her fast, nervous way, refusing to meet Jenna's gaze. "Amyan has clothing for you," Arion said. "It is very similar to what she is wearing. The fabric reflects the suns' rays, but allows airflow. It will help you stay cool. You will also have to wear a special lotion on all exposed areas of skin to protect you from our fierce suns."

So the Leors had experience with how non-Leors fared under the harsh meteorological conditions of the desert planets they favored. Of course they did—from their slaves. Jenna forced her thoughts away from that topic. She had no objection to protective clothing and lotions, especially if they would help her stay cooler in the terrible heat.

"However," Arion continued, "if you are insistent on behaving as a Leor female, you can wear our traditional garment instead. I believe the lotion will protect your skin sufficiently."

"I don't think I could wear just a loincloth," she said, shaken by the suggestion. It hadn't occurred to her she might be expected to dress like the Leors. "It would be immodest."

He stood there, calm and implacable, his stance wide, his arms crossed over his powerful chest. His eyes were challenging. "We do not concern ourselves with false modesty."

"I understand that, and I respect it." She took a deep breath, not yet willing to rise to this particular challenge, despite the need to hold her own. "You know my culture is very different from yours, Your Lordship—Arion. We cover more of our bodies. I'm just not ready to expose myself in that way."

He shrugged. "It does not matter to me." He turned toward the computer station, and breathing a silent sigh of relief, Jenna headed for the bathing chamber.

She donned the long-sleeved top and the loose pants, amazed how lightweight they were. They were identical to what Amyan wore, except they were a pale orange color instead of white. They fit her so well, she could only assume they had been replicated specifically for her.

She fixed her hair in a neat twist; then she rubbed on the thick green lotion the server gave her, surprised that it immediately became clear and was absorbed into her skin. Slipping on the simple pair of sandals Amyan also provided completed her preparations.

She left the bathing chamber to find Arion working at the computer. He glanced at her, his gaze sweeping over her. Without comment, he rose and led the way to the main entry. They left Amyan behind to clean the dome and await their return, and headed for the dining hall. It was the first time Jenna had ventured very far from the dome since her arrival, when she'd been suffering the aftereffects of sleep stasis, and had noted little of her surroundings.

They were in an area of small individual domes, most likely living quarters. As they walked farther, she saw that the settlement appeared to be laid out in an orderly and practical fashion. It was immaculate, with precise walkways and skimmer lanes. It also appeared to be much larger than she had realized, stretching at least ten kilometers toward the towering mesas. She saw a number of large, flat-topped structures and walled-in compounds, and a small airstrip with at least a dozen modest-sized spacecraft resting on pads.

She didn't see many Leors, and assumed they were already about the cycle's business, but she saw a number of slaves, all dressed in flowing white tops and loose pants, all wearing the silver bands noting their status, and all working industriously at various tasks. Jenna again reminded herself it was something she would have to get used to.

The communal dining hall was a large, rectangular building, made of the same textured stonelike material as the domes. As they stepped inside, Jenna felt the wave of heat, probably generated by the fireboxes lining the two long sides of the building. The pungent smell of cooking food assailed her next, and she fought down a wave of nausea. What was that odor?

Looking beyond Arion, she saw rows of tables and benches filled the enormous chamber, running the building's length, and most had Leors occupying them. Slaves scurried up and down those rows, serving platters of food and beverages. A gradual hush spread through the dining hall as she followed Arion inside. The atmosphere in the chamber seemed to change, to become heavier, more ominous, as numerous midnight eyes focused on her. Arion strode rapidly down an aisle between two rows of tables, acknowledging the half bows and respectful greetings as he went. Jenna hurried to keep up, trying to focus on just getting wherever they were headed, which was a single table, set perpendicular to the rows, at the far end of the chamber.

Three men and two women sat at the table, and they rose when Arion approached, arms crossing their chests as they bowed. Jenna assumed they were his chief officers, but since the Leors only wore loincloths, there was no indication of their rank. She recognized one of the women as Lanka, who eyed her with the usual disdain. The others stared at her with expressions that appeared more curious than hostile—although it was hard to tell, with their granite, immobile faces. Arion didn't introduce her, merely waved Jenna to a chair.

She sank into it, feeling like a baby krat that had wandered into a den of Oderian vipers. Arion took the seat to her left, and then everyone else sat. Immediately two servers approached the table with plates of food. One of them, a blond-haired boy who looked no older than fourteen or fifteen seasons, placed a plate before Jenna. She nodded her thanks, but his eyes remained downcast as he backed away. She looked down at her plate and tried not to gag. It contained meat, very rare, with red juices pooling beneath. It had a distinct odor, the same she'd smelled when they entered.

In the Dark Quadrant, there had been virtually no meat in the Shielder diet, because they'd been forced to live on barren planets that could not support livestock. Now, on Shamara, some Shielders raised animals and ate meat, but Jenna had never been able. The thought of killing when there were many other food sources appalled her. As she stared at the plate, bile rose to her throat, and what little appetite she had dissipated. She inched the plate away, and folded her hands in her lap.

Around her the Leors were conversing in their guttural voices, and she heard one of the men say, "Controller threat." That caught her attention as nothing else could, as the Controllers had attempted to systematically hunt and destroy every Shielder in the old quadrant. Then, with a shock, she remembered she was back in the Dark Quadrant, from which the majority of Shielders had fled almost four seasons ago.

Arion shifted beside her, tapping his eating utensil on her plate. "Eat."

"I can't," she told him, keeping her voice low.

"You will." He moved the plate back in front of her.

"Arion . . ." She looked up to see the others at the table staring at her. "I mean, Your Lordship. I don't eat meat."

His eyes grew icy. "I will only compromise on so many things. Your health is not one of them." He speared a piece on his utensil and thrust it toward her. "Eat. Now."

The odor hit her, and her stomach roiled. She pressed a hand against her midriff. "I won't be able to keep it down."

"Do not defy me on this," he warned.

She leaned close to him, so she could talk quietly. "It is not my intent to defy you, especially with others present. But if I eat that meat, I will be sick right here, in front of everyone. It's your decision."

His breath hissed out. "You are more challenging than the entire Controller starfleet."

She closed her eyes so she wouldn't have to look at the meat. "I could say the same for you."

"This discussion is not over," he growled.

She felt him pull back and opened her eyes to see the utensil gone and him signaling the blond server. The boy hurried over and bowed his head. "Bring her some homa," Arion ordered. "Then go get some bread and tarini fruit from the kitchen."

Jenna felt a curious softening toward her future mate. At least he was making some allowances for her. He was letting her dress modestly and he wasn't going to force her to eat meat, despite her own insistence that she be treated like any Leor female. Maybe they would be able to find a middle ground.

Just then, the server returned with a mug of homa—heated, much to her disappointment—and as he placed the mug before her, she saw his neck. An ugly scar slashed down the side of it, brutal evidence that his vocal cords had been severed, just like Amyan's.

Any warmth she'd been feeling vanished like vapor, replaced by the harsh reminder of what the Leors were, and the extent of their atrocities.

They left the dining hall and headed to the shaman. Arion kept his usual silence, and Jenna was grateful. She wasn't sure she could have conversed civilly with him. The turmoil and the fears had returned. He was a Leor, a member of a race that was known for its violence and cruelty.

There was nothing they could talk about. So they walked in silence. Although it was still early in the cycle, the heat was already oppressive, and the two suns beat down mercilessly. Her new clothing kept her cooler, but still Jenna felt the drag of the heat, felt the moisture at her hairline.

Arion turned down a pathway leading to a solitary dome about forty meters away. A Leor man came to the entry as they approached the dome. Somehow, Jenna had been expecting an ancient wise man, similar to Janaye, the matriarch of a group who had befriended the Shielders when they lived in the Dark Quadrant. But the male stepping forward appeared young and in the prime of life. He was as tall as Arion, but not quite as broad and muscular, although he moved with the peculiar physical grace the Leors displayed, despite their size. He wore a white loincloth, a stark contrast against his dusky skin. Arion acknowledged him with a nod. "Shaman."

The shaman crossed his arm diagonally across his chest and bowed to Arion. "Greetings, Comdar." He turned his midnight gaze to Jenna, but did not acknowledge her. He wore the same harsh expression Arion always had, and she wondered if Leors ever smiled. Without a word, Morven stepped back and gestured toward the dome's interior, obviously expecting her to enter.

She turned to see if Arion was following and saw him striding off, already quite a distance away. He hadn't even given her his customary grunt. She'd have to get used to the abrupt Leor ways. Feeling strangely deserted, she followed Morven inside.

The shaman's dome was a surprise. It had a skylight, and large portals ringed the perimeter, allowing the blazing sunlight to stream in, just as Arion's dome did. But instead of a bare floor, there were several brightly colored rugs scattered about. Six large cushions and several low tables were the only furnishings.

The usual orange and red colors were present, but there were also shades of indigo, green, and gold, creating mosaic patterns in the rugs. The cushions were solid-colored, matching the hues in the rugs. A brazier sat in the center of the chamber, white smoke drifting from it. The scent of burning, aromatic herbs filled the chamber.

She took it all in, wondering which was the Leor standard—Arion's dome or this one. She had only seen the exteriors of other domes, but suspected Morven's dome was the exception. He grasped her shoulders firmly and turned her to face him. At his touch, a jolt of power surged through her. All Leors emanated power, raw and physical, but this was different, more like the potent energy of a strong electrical shock.

He didn't seem to notice either the power surge or her startled gasp. Taking her left arm, he turned her palm toward him. He slid his finger along the scar from her blood pact with Arion. Then he shoved up her sleeve and examined her arm closely, running his rough fingers over her skin. The energy from his touch continued to course through her, but the initial intensity had lessened, so it was only a mild tingling sensation.

"Your touch feels different," she said, growing uncomfortable with his silence. He had yet to utter a single word to her. "It's like you're generating electricity."

He grunted, but didn't look up. She sighed, wondering if perhaps there was a secret Leor language composed of grunts. So much for the idea of a warm and nurturing spiritual leader. Resigned to his perusal, she stood quietly, assuming her skin was as fascinating to him as the patterned, rough Leor skin was to her. After a few moments, he moved to her face, tracing the bone structure with his long, broad fingers.

He also traced each eyebrow, raised each eyelid to stare at her eyes. He even lifted her upper lip to look at her teeth, as if she were an animal being purchased at a market. She fisted her hands, ready to protest, but stopped herself. His actions weren't hurting anything but her pride, and it might be a good idea to pick her battles carefully. She knew there would be many.

So she endured while he turned her head from side to side, studying her ears; and while his hands slid to her shoulders, squeezing as if he were testing the strength of her bones. Resignation turned to shock, however, when he jerked open the seam of her top and looked at her breasts.

"Stop that!" She backed away hurriedly, glad he wasn't holding on to her. Whirling, she resealed the seam, trying to calm her racing heart. "*That* is off-limits to you," she said, hoping he understood Contran. "I know your race thinks nothing of nudity, but I do. I am *not* baring my body for you. Don't do that again." Dead silence met her tirade, and she glanced over her shoulder to see his reaction.

Stone-faced, of course. With an impatient motion, he gestured her back to him. Seeing no immediate way out of the situation, she turned around. "All right, but leave my clothing alone. No more body exposure."

He simply stood there, arms crossed over his chest—a common Leor mannerism, she was beginning to believe—his mesmerizing stare commanding her compliance. Very reluctantly, she took the two steps back to him. He reached toward her, but she pulled away, raising her hand in warning. "I mean it. Leave my clothes and my body alone."

"Your modesty is foolish," he growled. "Be still."

She tensed when he reached out, but his hands went to her hair, tugging at the twist and releasing it. Her hair clasps clinked on the floor and lay there, glittering gold against the beige clay. She felt the heavy weight of her hair falling over her shoulders and down her back as he shook it loose. She forced herself to stand still while he stroked and studied it for the longest time.

The feel of his fingers running along her hair was almost hypnotic, and she found her eyes drifting shut, found herself swaying on her feet. She felt his sudden movement, and her eyes snapped open, wariness and distrust bringing her alert. He had raised a long section of her hair to his mouth and was running his tongue over it.

"What are you doing?" she asked, more amazed than offended.

His gaze flashed to her. "I am observing the scent of your hair."

"With your tongue?" She stared back, a new realization dawning on her as she got her first real look at his face. He had the massive, square head of a Leor, and the chiseled features and high cheekbones, but his eyes were a deep blue—so dark, they could almost pass for the regulation obsidian Leor eyes. "Your eyes aren't black!"

"No." He returned his gaze to her hair, again ran his tongue over it.

This was too strange. "I need some answers," she said. "There is so much I don't understand. I was under the impression you would explain things to me."

He dropped her hair. "Be careful what you seek, off-worlder. Do not ask until you are ready to hear the wisdom of the Goddess."

"Knowledge is better than stumbling around blindly," she said. But then she thought of Amyan, and wondered if that was really true. Maybe ignorance was preferable in some instances.

Morven gestured to the pillows. "Sit."

Jenna looked around, chose the indigo pillow, and walked over to it. She sank down, immediately feeling calmer.

"The color of the crown," Morven murmured. "And that of your own energy."

"What is the color of the crown?"

"The indigo color of the cushion you chose." He added some dried leaves to the brazier before he settled himself, cross-legged, on a rug rather than a cushion. "It is the color of the crown chakra, that which connects us to the Goddess. It is also the color of the energy that surrounds you. You are attuned to your gods, have the gift of the sight."

Jenna thought of the horrendous visions she had endured, including those of her parents' deaths, and of the censure her ability had brought. "It's more of a curse."

"It is what you make of it."

"I would make it go away if I could," she said in all honesty. "I've never had a vision that would help anyone. I either see something that has already come to pass, or is happening as I see it, or I see things that I can't possibly do anything about."

He said nothing to that, just stared at her. The smoke from the brazier thickened, began snaking around them. It had an odd scent, both sweet and acrid at the same time.

"Tell me about your tongue picking up scents. And why your eyes are blue," she requested. "I want to understand."

"We can smell as well as taste with our tongues."

"Then you don't smell through your nose?"

"We use our noses also. The Goddess has blessed us with very strong senses. We can pick up the faintest of scents, hear sounds great distances away, and see very clearly, even on a moonless night."

Somehow, Jenna wasn't surprised by this. She had already realized Leors were extraordinary beings, at least physically. "What about the color of your eyes? Are you a full-blooded Leor?"

"I am of full Leor blood," he answered haughtily. "As Comdar Arion was born with the mark of the clan, declaring his heritage as our leader, I was born with the mark of the shaman—blue eyes, the color of the Goddess energy."

Jenna was fascinated with the concept of physical attributes signifying rank. "Will your children also have blue eyes?"

"I will not take a mate, or have offspring."

"Why?"

"The path of a shaman is one of solitude. My life is dedicated to the Goddess." He raised his hand before she could speak again. "Enough. I am to prepare you for the merging ceremony." He looked her over again. "You have not been eating."

"I've been eating some," Jenna said defensively.

"Not enough. I feel your weakness."

"I won't eat meat. I find it repulsive."

Morven's eyes narrowed. "You must have sustenance. I will speak to the Comdar about it."

Great. All Leors were overbearing. It appeared to be an intrinsic part of their nature. "I like the homa. I'll drink more of that. Tell me about the ceremony."

93

"Tomorrow, at the moment of the Mystic Trine, you and the Comdar will perform the ceremony that will merge your souls."

Jenna felt a sudden rush of dizziness, and wondered if it was from the smoke pouring from the brazier. "Merge our souls? What does that mean?"

"The two of you will be as one."

"And what does *that* mean, exactly?"

"He will know all that you are, and you will know all that he is."

An ominous chill swept through Jenna. The merging sounded invasive, and implied far more intimacy than she was ready to undergo. She had agreed to live her remaining years as Arion's mate, but she wasn't willing to lose herself in the process. "That tells me nothing," she pointed out, forcing her voice to remain steady. "What happens when our souls merge?"

"Your soul will belong to the Comdar, for the rest of your existence."

She clenched her hands in her lap. "And his soul?"

"Will belong to you."

She closed her eyes, took a deep breath, then regretted it. The smoke she sucked into her lungs sent her into a spasm of coughing and made her feel extremely light-headed.

"Breathe deeply. Do not fight it." Morven's voice was calm, hypnotic.

She found herself inhaling again. The odor was sweet now, without any of the previous bitterness. *Do not fight what?* she wondered. *The merging?* It was a ceremony, she reminded herself. The natural mind barrier that all Shielders possessed protected them from invasive psionic brain waves, and from other forms of mind probes. Not even the Controllers or the Leors could penetrate that barrier.

What was it she had wanted to ask? Oh, now she remembered. "What is the Mystic Trine?"

"When our two suns are each aligned with Saura in a perfect trine. It is the holy day of the Goddess. Our Comdar is always joined with his mate on that sacred day."

She began to feel as if she were floating, her body detached from her mind. It was a pleasant sensation, making it difficult to remember what they were discussing. She felt Morven's strong hands on her arms as he pulled her to her feet.

"Come," he told her. "The Goddess will soon begin speaking to you. But first, you must prepare yourself."

She went with him readily, too light-headed and unfocused to protest. She didn't mind soaking in the large sunken tub to which he took her. Didn't even care about his presence as she undressed—why had she ever worried about nudity?—and slid into the herb-scented water. Nor did she care that the water was far warmer than she preferred. She really liked the soothing, low-pitched chanting that drifted across the chamber as she lay in the tub, and the feel of the herbs in the water drawing the toxins from her body.

She didn't mind that Morven—that *was* his name, wasn't it?—helped her to dry off and dress in a flowing white robe, to honor her purity, he said. Somehow, she didn't seem to have the coordination or the strength to do it herself, but she just didn't care. It was wonderful not to care, not to fear. It didn't matter that he told her she couldn't eat or drink until after the ceremony. And it didn't matter that she was so hot, a scorching heat searing through her, leaving a fine sheen of perspiration on her body. No, nothing mattered, nothing at all.

Until the visions started.

Her mother, screaming as first one, then another Antek raped her. Until the disrupter blast stilled her voice for-

ever, but not before she suffered horrible, painful convulsions.

No! Jenna thrashed, trying to escape the vision, one she'd already experienced when her mother's scouting ship had been captured by Anteks over fourteen seasons ago.

"Do not fight it," came a calm masculine voice.

Gasping, Jenna opened her eyes, vaguely aware she was on a hard mat on the floor. Morven sat beside her. She stared at him, tried to speak but couldn't. "Trust in the Goddess," he told her. She couldn't keep her eyes open, her heavy lids closing as she drifted, drifted, again surrounded by his chanting.

Her father, being tortured in a Controller prison, suffering horribly before he was finally executed in a barbaric and painful manner.

No, no! She wrenched her eyes open, searching out Morven. He was still beside her, his mysterious eyes watchful. "Make it stop," she whispered. "Please, make it stop."

"You are strong," he answered. "The Goddess is with you."

She felt herself drifting once more. "No, please no," she begged. But he was chanting again, and she was sucked back into the vortex. A kaleidoscope of visions flashed past her: *a young Shielder blown up in his ship, his last thoughts of his wife and son; Jenna receiving the horrifying vision of her mating with Arion; the death of Captain Ranul san Mars, the great Shielder leader; then the disconcerting hallucination of a shimmering pink moon.* The visions flashed by, inexorable, the darkest moments of her life. Had there been nothing good? No joy, no happiness?

Feeling an inconsolable sadness, Jenna again became aware of lying on the mat. Her face was wet with tears, her body drenched in sweat. She could still smell the faint, sweet odor of the smoke. Morven's voice came from nearby. "You have shared your burdens with the Goddess. Now she will share her wisdom with you."

This time, it was more like a dream, without the emotional pain. Jenna saw images, but more as an objective observer. She saw the great multicolored mesas of Saura rising up as a backdrop, while she and Arion stood facing one another; then suddenly she was in a large chamber filled with people, staring at the bloodied carcass of an animal. Next she was beside the base of a mesa, staring at the broken form of a young Leor boy. None of it frightened her because a comforting voice whispered to her throughout the dream, telling her that all would be well, that she was a beloved daughter and would be guided to her rightful destiny.

The scene shifted, and she was inside a cavern with Arion, lying on a blanket. Did Saura have caves? She stared up at him as he leaned down and kissed her, a surprise because to the best of her knowledge, Leors did not kiss. He spread her legs and settled between them, and oddly she felt no fear. Then the scene shifted again. She stared down at her rounded belly. *"You will present Arion with a daughter,"* whispered the voice, and for the first time, Jenna felt real hope. Then dark clouds drifted around her. When they cleared, she stood on the edge of a deep pit. Below her, Arion was chained to a wall. Covered with dirt and blood, he stared up at her. *"He will need your faith in him, and your love,"* came the voice. *"It will be his salvation."*

The voice began to fade, as did the images. Jenna tried to ask what was going to happen, to plead for more information, but received only silence. Her body suddenly felt very heavy.

"Your journey is done," came Morven's deep, raspy voice. "You will rest now."

And she sank into a soft, welcoming darkness.

Chapter Seven

She awoke on the floor, staring down at a bright rug. She looked at the mat to her right and groaned. She was still in Morven's dome, and she was in a long white robe, which meant it hadn't been a dream after all. She sat up and pushed her tangled hair from her face. Her head throbbed and she was very thirsty. She vaguely remembered soaking in a large tub, while she clearly remembered reliving her worst visions.

Then it got vague again, although it seemed she had seen new—most likely future—events, had heard a voice whispering to her. But she couldn't recall what the voice had said, wasn't sure she wanted to remember. Maybe *that* part had been a dream. Or maybe the first part had been the dream, and the second part real. Or maybe all of it had been a terrible nightmare. Did it really matter? she thought wearily. It would probably be best if she could forget all of it.

"You seem to prefer the floor to the mat," came Morven's voice. "I placed you on the mat three times, but you insisted on moving off it."

Jenna squinted up at the shaman, her eyes even more sensitive than usual to the bright sunlight. "It's the heat coils beneath the mat," she croaked, startled by the hoarseness of her voice. She cleared her throat. "The heat bothers me."

His expression clearly said, *Get used to it.* But Morven merely squatted beside her, his massive presence overwhelming. He stared at her a long moment, then nodded. "Your energy is violet. There is also some green."

She was too tired to care what any of that meant, so she merely drew up her legs and dropped her face against her knees.

"What? No questions?"

"No," she said hoarsely, ignoring the challenge. "Wait. There is one. Did you tell me I can't have anything to drink today?" She'd really like some cool homa right now.

"You cannot eat or drink until after the ceremony."

Since her memory had been accurate about that, it probably also meant she hadn't imagined soaking in the tub as he watched and chanted, or him helping her dry off and dress. Great.

He grasped her elbow. "Come. You will bathe now. It will revive you, and then you must prepare for the ceremony."

"Oh, no. I can't go through that again. I don't know why I did it the first time. I don't suppose you're going to tell me?"

He ignored her question. "All you will do is bathe and dress."

"Only if it's by myself," she insisted, appalled at how shaky she was. She made it to her feet, but it was a moment before she felt she wouldn't crumble to the floor.

"Foolish modesty."

She lifted her chin and tried to look as stern as possible. "We did it your way last night. It's my way today."

He stared back with the typical Leor nonreaction. "You

may bathe alone. Then your comrades are coming to help you dress."

Comrades? Jenna couldn't imagine whom he might be talking about. She had no friends here. She rubbed her aching forehead. She'd worry about it after she washed. Maybe her mind would be clearer by then.

"All right." She stumbled toward the bathing chamber.

"Lady Jenna."

That brought her up. He hadn't used her name the entire time she'd been there, at least not that she could recall. She turned carefully. "Yes?"

"The violet energy around you indicates you achieved purification and transmutation. It is a very powerful energy, the second color of the Goddess."

Surely she was imagining the approval in his voice. "And the green color?"

"Ah, finally a question." His eyes gleamed. "The green energy is growth and healing."

"I'm guessing that's good."

"You are very strong. I thought you would do well."

"Thank you. I think." She went into the bathing chamber and firmly closed the panel.

The bath did refresh her, especially since she was able to adjust the water to a cooler temperature. She had just finished drying off when there was a light rapping on the panel.

"Jenna?" came a very feminine voice. "Are you in there?"

Not a voice she knew, but certainly not the voice of a female Leor. Bemused, she called out, "Just a minute," and located her clothing from yesterday. She slipped it on and opened the panel.

"There you are!" A dainty woman tripped into the chamber, balancing on very high spike heels. Maxine followed.

Jenna had never seen anything like this tiny woman. She

100

had blue hair flowing down to her hips, blue eyebrows, blue eyes, blue lips, blue finger- and toenails. And blue feathers. Lots and lots of blue feathers, in the elaborate headdress perched on her head and the loincloth she wore. Jenna had never met her, but she knew immediately who the woman was. She'd heard quite a bit about her escapades.

"You must be Lani."

"Oh!" Lani let out a high-pitched squeal of delight, and launched herself at Jenna, wrapping her in a tight hug. "You are such a clever girl. How did you know? Did Morven tell you?"

Jenna managed to extricate herself. "Actually, I guessed."

"Well, aren't you something! I told Gunnar that no human female should have to go through an MC—that's what I call these silly merging ceremonies—alone. I insisted that he bring me to Saura so I could help you get through it."

"Get through it?"

"Don't worry about it," Lani said cheerfully. "It doesn't hurt much. And it's over quickly."

Doesn't hurt much? Jenna felt the stirring of real panic. "How bad is this ceremony?"

"Oh, not that bad." Lani waved a blue-tipped hand. "Is it, Maxi?"

"I do not know," Maxine replied. "It is a highly secret ritual. I could not locate any files on the subject."

"Morven didn't tell me very much about it. He said a lot of things, but nothing that made any sense." Jenna's stomach was starting to knot.

"That's a man for you," Lani declared. "Especially if it's a Leor male. They either don't say anything at all, or when they do, it's so cryptic you still don't have any information."

She was quite a character, but she hadn't offered any

information, either. Jenna took a deep, steadying breath and suddenly realized what the android was wearing—or wasn't wearing, actually. "That's an interesting outfit you have on, Maxine."

"It is, is it not?" Maxine smoothed her green-feathered loincloth. "I thought it would be appropriate to dress like the natives. I do not want to stand out too much."

Right. The six-foot female android with dark brown-and-gold-streaked hair and a magnificent pair of breasts, wearing green feathers, didn't want to stand out. Not that the android had anything on Lani. Komissar Gunnar's infamous mate might be small, but she had some impressive assets. Next to Lani and Maxine, Jenna knew she looked flat-chested.

"Lani was kind enough to have a loincloth replicated for me," Maxine continued. "While the idea of feathers sounded very intriguing and very high fashion, I opted for green. It goes well with my coloring, do you not agree?"

"Well—"

"Maxi and I are going to help you get ready for the MC," Lani interrupted. "I even brought the dress."

"You brought me a dress?" Jenna stared at her, a new misgiving added to her already existing concerns. "I'm not sure I would look good in feathers."

Lani laughed, a high musical tinkling. "Oh, you are too much! I think you would look *divine* in feathers. Don't you think so, Maxi?"

"With proper draping and shading," Maxine conceded, studying Jenna intently.

"I'll be right back," Lani trilled, hustling out the entry.

Jenna rubbed her forehead, which was throbbing again, and wondered if she was still dreaming. "Are you all right?" Maxine asked. "You look pale. Have you been mistreated in any way?"

That was a good question. Jenna thought about it, but outside of having sleep stasis forced upon her, and the total loss of her dignity at the hands of an uncommunicative shaman, she couldn't claim true mistreatment. "Not really. I think the worst of it is the culture shock."

"That is understandable. Outside of the lack of data on the merging ceremony, I have very comprehensive files on the Leor culture. Please let me know if you have any questions or any problems. Also, I will be glad to give you instruction for tonight, should you have need."

"Tonight?"

"You know." Maxine raised her eyebrows roguishly. "The wedding night. The horizontal docking procedure. Although it can certainly be done vertically."

Jenna had almost forgotten about what would happen after the merging. Now she could worry about it, too, along with everything else. "Oh. *That*."

"It is the entire purpose of this exercise, is it not?"

"I guess it is." Her legs suddenly shaking, Jenna leaned against the sink enclosure. "I don't think I need any instruction for that. I have a basic idea how it's done." And not much confidence that she would fare very well, given Arion's nature and his size.

"But there are many variations," Maxine supplied helpfully. "I am well versed in all of them."

"Yes, well, thank you anyway, but—"

"Ta da!" Lani tripped back in, holding up a dress. "What do you think?"

The dress was long, cut in simple, flowing lines, not a feather anywhere on it. The fabric was a shimmering silver color, and lightweight, despite the satiny finish. The long sleeves were made in a sheer silvery fabric, cuffed at the wrists.

Silver, just like it had been in her vision. Jenna wondered how a vision that was four seasons old could manifest so accurately. "It's beautiful," she said sincerely, breathing a sigh of relief that it was modest and feather-free.

103

Lani beamed. "Isn't it, though? I found out your size and designed it myself. I figured you wouldn't be ready for a loincloth yet, so I chose a dress instead. I insisted on the silver fabric. These Leors are so fixated on all that harsh red and black, and even gold—although gold certainly has its value, I must say. But they're such masculine and warlike colors. Now, silver, that's the color of the moons. It's the female energy, and very strong. Females hold all the power, Jenna. Don't ever forget that. We're the ones who bring life into the world. These men think the planets revolve around them, but they don't have a clue."

Jenna wasn't so sure. She doubted she would ever hold much power in this world dominated by the fierce Leors. But there was nothing she could do about it now. Her fate was sealed. She reached for the dress. "Let's get this over with."

Morven was nowhere in sight when the three of them left his dome. Jenna didn't see any Leors in the common areas, either, just slaves doing their work. They took an enclosed skimmer toward the mesas, with Maxine piloting. Jenna stared at the delicate silver sandals on her feet, identical to those in her vision. She didn't remember seeing the silver nail polish that Lani had insisted on applying to her fingernails and toenails, though. She patted her upswept hair, a small—and possibly the only—victory she would have today.

"Arion requested that you wear your hair down," Lani had told Jenna after she was dressed. "Which is typical. Leor men are fascinated by our hair."

Jenna thought about the awful heat, and how much worse it would be with her hair down. It wasn't Arion's place to tell her how to wear her hair, she decided in a flash of rebellion. She was already giving up enough without relinquishing personal choices. "I'm wearing it up," she stated firmly.

Lani had nodded approvingly. "Good for you. If you give these big oafs a millimeter, they'll take a kilometer. You have to let them know you won't be intimidated."

But she was intimidated, Jenna realized now, standing at the base of the mesa, with Lani and Maxine beside her. The women were at the pathway leading to the sacred altar of the Goddess. Maxine had located it with the precise directions she'd downloaded from the skimmer's computer, but Jenna would have recognized the path regardless, because it matched that in her vision, down to the carpet of scarlet starflowers flanking each side of the entry. This was it. The end of the existence she'd always known, and the beginning of a strange and frightening life among the Leors.

"Well, then," Lani murmured. "I guess it's time. These guys get really upset if the MC doesn't start right at the moment of the Mystic Trine. They are positively fixated on certain things. Maxine and I will go on ahead. We don't want to spoil your grand entrance." She gave Jenna a tight hug. "May Spirit be with you. I wish you joy and long life."

Jenna clung to her, panic descending. "You still haven't told me what happens during the ceremony."

"I really can't tell you." Lani drew back, the concern in her deep blue eyes far from reassuring. "Everyone who goes through a merging ceremony has a different experience. It depends entirely on the two people who are merging. I can tell you it doesn't last very long. Just hold tight to Arion. He'll anchor you."

Not at all soothed, Jenna turned and gave Maxine a hug. "Thank you both. I'm glad you're here."

"I look forward to recording your account of the ceremony," Maxine said. "My best wishes to you and Arion for a long and productive life."

"Thank you." Jenna watched the two of them walk down the path, where the others would be waiting. Lani had instructed her on the protocol, although she already knew what to do, based on the vision. She glanced up at the two suns, noticing they were positioned over Saura so that the three bodies formed a perfect V-shape. It was time.

She started along the path, unsurprised to see it had been strewn with scarlet starflower petals. The oppressive heat surrounded her, and she found it hard to draw a full breath in the stifling air.

One silver-sandaled foot in front of the other, a step toward her fate. Then another, and another. *Don't think of what lies ahead, don't let the fears close in.* Just one step closer. Closer. Her heart began to pound, and her throat felt like it was closing off. She couldn't breathe.

Be calm, beloved daughter, came a feminine voice inside her head, a hauntingly familiar voice . . . yet one she couldn't place. *I will be with you as you meet your destiny. I will always be with you. All will be well.*

Was the voice a hallucination, the aftereffects of last night, perhaps? Jenna didn't know, but she did feel calmer, and she found she was able to breathe again. It was senseless to let her fears incapacitate her. She was committed to mating with Arion, and there was nowhere else she could go, except to the end of the path. She kept walking.

She came to a bend in the path, heard the murmur of voices. Up ahead, she saw the large gathering of Leors, saw the blazing shades of orange and red loincloths, just like in her vision. She slowed her steps, praying to Spirit for the courage to continue. It seemed as if a relentless force took over her muscles, a powerful undertow that made her feet move and drew her inexorably toward the group.

They stared at her as she approached, their eyes like black holes, no emotion reflected in those frightening ebony pits. Her feet continued to move, and the Leors parted as she walked among them, towering above her, overwhelmingly big and vital. They remained silent as she moved forward.

Then she saw Arion. Standing at the head of the path, he cut a magnificent figure. He wore a shimmering gold cape and matching loincloth. He also wore some ornately carved gold wrist cuffs. He stood calmly, majestically, his regal presence setting him apart from the others. His unblinking midnight gaze was fixed upon her. The familiar terror of her vision descended, and her heart pounded even more fiercely.

"My bride is here," Arion said, his deep voice shattering the silence. He held out his hand. "Come. Let the ceremony begin."

In her vision, this was where Jenna resisted, tried to pull away. But she held fast to her resolve and refused to shame either Arion or herself. Amazed to discover that free will could overcome at least part of the vision, she stepped up to him and, taking a deep breath, placed her hand in his.

The contact was electric, a current of energy that sparked between them. She didn't realize that she'd placed her left hand in his until she felt the throbbing of the scar from their blood pact, felt the connection of that shared blood, and the power of the ancient rite binding them.

She stared up at Arion, unable to look away from the probing blackness of his eyes. She saw his determination to see this through, and knew nothing would turn the man from a course once he had committed to it. She drew on his solid strength, amazed at the renewed calmness flowing through her, at the slowing of her heart.

"The Mystic Trine has commenced," came Morven's voice. "The Goddess is with us."

Startled, Jenna noticed the shaman for the first time. He was dressed in a loincloth and cloak similar to Arion's, but in white, trimmed with gold. Arion had commanded her attention so completely that she hadn't seen Morven, or noticed the stone altar behind him. It was cut directly from a large reddish rock formation that was part of the base of the mesa. A large crystal pyramid, about half a meter high, stood on the altar.

Behind it rose the carved form of a woman. Of a paler red hue, she almost blended with the towering span of mesa beyond. Her head was bald, and there were no features on her face, only smooth, oblong stone. One hand was raised, palm up, toward the sky, while the other hand was extended forward over the pyramid, also palm up. Intricately carved suns rested on each palm. Shafts of sunlight reflected off the pyramid, their beams eerily hitting both carvings and illuminating them.

"The time of your merging is upon you." Morven stepped to the side, gesturing to the altar.

Arion moved forward, taking Jenna with him. As they approached, the pyramid seemed to glow. Surely that was a trick of the light, Jenna thought. He drew her to one end of the altar and took both her hands, placing them on two of the pyramid's sides. The crystal was surprisingly cool, despite the heat of the day and the blazing suns overhead. The platform holding the pyramid wasn't very long, and Arion moved to the opposite end, placing his hands over hers.

Jenna found her gaze on the pyramid, was mesmerized by its glow. The light intensified and the pyramid grew warm, tingling beneath her palms. A mist began flowing through the translucent crystal, growing darker and darker, until the entire pyramid was glittering black. A sudden wave of dizziness hit her, and she felt the same strange disembodied sensation she'd experienced at Morven's dome. She couldn't move, couldn't react, couldn't do anything but watch the pyramid, caught up in its power.

The black began to lighten, a new mist swirling through the crystal, changing and shifting, until the pyramid was a deep magenta color. The crystal was vibrating beneath her hands now, energy flowing up her arms and into her chest, filling it with heat. Arion pressed his hands more firmly against hers, keeping her there. Not that she was going anywhere.

More swirling mist, as the color shifted and deepened to indigo. *The color of the crown chakra,* Morven had said. *That which connects us to the Goddess.* The heat in Jenna's chest intensified, surrounding her heart like a tight band. She experienced a momentary panic that she was suffocating. Arion took her head in his hands and pulled her toward him. Before she could react, he leaned down, pressed his forehead to hers.

Energy exploded inside her brain like a supernova, spiraling outward in waves. She tried to jerk back, but she was bound physically by the strength of Arion's hands holding her in place. Yet it was the power, flowing from him into her, back into him, that truly fused them.

Jenna, hear me. Arion's voice was like a detonation inside her head. She felt his presence within her, flowing around her, and through her. She felt him in every millimeter, every pore, of her being. She didn't want this invasion, this terrifying spiritual intimacy.

No! Stop! She desperately tried to tune him out.

The Goddess has acknowledged her blessing by facilitating our mind link. Come, join with me. Merge your soul with mine.

She resisted, certain she'd be lost for all time. Trying to wrench free, she stumbled against the altar. Arion caught her and pulled her against him. He kept their foreheads pressed together. *Merge with me. Now.* Even as he issued the sharp mental command, their bodies seemed to flow and meld together.

She knew the instant his soul touched hers. Heat flared through her in a fusion of energy and light. A sparking, violet glow materialized and drifted around them, growing brighter. Scenes flashed through her mind, a startling collage of Arion's life experiences. Years of brutal training;

harsh, solitary living conditions; even harsher discipline; war and weapons; blood and death. Violence, so much violence. Honor and courage; dedication to the survival of his clan; the honing of his body and his mind, day in, day out, so that he could—*would*—hold fast to every tenet of his heritage. Nothing but training and duty, span after endless span. . . .

As she absorbed the essence of her mate, Jenna felt her own essence being sucked from her into Arion, every detail of her insignificant life. It terrified her. She was losing her identity, becoming enmeshed in another entity. She fought and resisted, trying to wrench her forehead away. She wouldn't give in! She wouldn't, she wouldn't, she wouldn't—

"Jenna!" Strong hands grabbed her upper arms, stilled her. Gasping, she opened her eyes. Arion stared at her, his face set in harsh lines. "Calm yourself. It is done."

He appeared totally in control, unaffected by what had just transpired. Had she imagined the emotional maelstrom—another hallucination? She looked at the pyramid. The indigo was dissolving away, leaving a glimmering white. And the Goddess . . . the face of the Goddess was glowing! But the light radiating from the blank stone visage of the statue faded quickly, returning the stone to its dusty red color.

Jenna felt the residual tremors in her body and suspected Arion's strength was the only thing keeping her from crumbling to the ground. She also knew she was completely awake, and not dreaming, despite her desire for it to be otherwise. She had truly gone through some sort of merging with Arion. Her soul had somehow connected with his.

More of the shaman's words came back to her, his answer when she'd asked what happened during the merging ceremony: *He will know all that you are, and you will know all that he is.* She felt violated somehow, as if her most personal secrets had been torn from her and displayed for all to see, even though Arion was the only one who had witnessed them. At least she hoped that was the case, but that was bad enough.

Even more unsettling had been Morven's answer to her next question about the merging: *Your soul will belong to the Comdar, for the rest of your existence.*

It was done now. What kind of beings traded souls when they took a mate? She couldn't help wondering if she hadn't just made a pact with the Dark Spirit of Hades . . . and lost herself for all eternity.

Chapter Eight

Arion led Jenna to a seat beneath the special awning that was kept in readiness for visits from the Komissar and his mate. Lani couldn't endure long hours in the sun, and often took advantage of the awning.

Knowing his fellow Leors would celebrate his taking a mate throughout the lengthy day and into the night with demonstrations of strength and prowess in weapons, hand-to-hand combat, and other physical challenges, Arion had ordered the awning set up at the far end of the arena, away from the blazing heat of the fire pits and the animals roasting over them. He suspected the odor of the cooking meat would bother Jenna as much as the sun and the heat. While she would have to accept the Leor way of life sooner or later, he was willing to allow some latitude.

She had been so pale and shaky after the merging, he had immediately escorted her to a skimmer and taken her directly to the arena. A second skimmer had been provided for Gunnar and Lani, while the android Maxine had run the distance to the arena with the rest of the clan.

Jenna hadn't said a single word since the ceremony, and

she was still alarmingly pale, which emphasized the dark circles beneath her eyes. She took the seat Arion offered, not meeting his gaze. She looked small and fragile, like a piece of the highly valued Elysian sand china. Concern nagged at Arion, and he motioned a server over.

"Bring Lady Jenna a large mug of homa, and get it from the cold store, so it will be cool. Bring her some fruit, too." The young girl bobbed her head and ran to do his bidding.

He squatted next to Jenna, placed his hand on her arm. Her skin was clammy, an impossibility in this heat. Shock, he decided, his alarm increasing. He had been more shaken by the merging ceremony than he cared to admit, and he had known what to expect. Even then, the intensity of the energy, the invasion of another mind into his, and the vivid scenes from Jenna's life had been startling. It would be even more daunting for her.

"How are you doing?" he asked.

"I'm fine." Her voice was just a thread of sound, barely discernable.

"You will talk to me. Or I will take you to Lanka and have her examine you."

Her head snapped up and she looked at him, rebellion sparking in her eyes. "No."

"*No?*" He was incredulous that she was defying him.

"*No,*" she said, her voice stronger. "I am fine. Just a little . . . shaken up. I don't need to be examined by that woman."

"I will decide if you need to see the healer or not," he informed her, filing away the knowledge of her apparent dislike of Lanka. He gestured toward the slave arriving with a tray of homa and fruit. "I want you to drink and eat; then I will evaluate how you are doing."

Her expression mutinous, Jenna took the homa from the proffered tray and sipped it. Noting her color was already better, Arion stood. Lani was strutting toward them in

113

those ridiculous shoes and that ludicrous headdress, with Komissar Gunnar behind her. Beyond them, Arion saw the other Leors arriving, running into the arena. "I must take care of some business," he told Jenna. "I will be back later."

She dropped her gaze. "That's fine." He turned and strode past Lani to Gunnar, stopping to talk briefly with the Komissar and arranging to meet with him after the festivities were under way.

Then he sought out the shaman, who had just entered the arena. Morven bowed to him. "Greetings, Comdar. Your merging was one of the most powerful I have witnessed. I am not surprised."

"That is what I wish to discuss. Jenna is very pale and weak. Is there a possibility that the merging harmed her?"

"I do not think so. She is very strong. She withstood the saktar ritual well."

"You let her go through saktar?" Arion demanded, appalled. There were several different saktar rituals, and they could all be brutal, even for a highly disciplined and well-conditioned Leor. Some Leors even died during the rituals. Saktar was used for each of the five sacred rites of passage, to purify the body and spirit, and prepare the participant to ascend to the next level of being. The rituals were also used in preparation for demanding or perilous challenges, such as going into battle.

His own saktar to prepare for the merging ceremony had been draining. It would be much more difficult for an inexperienced human, especially one as small and delicate as Jenna. For her, saktar could be very dangerous, quite possibly fatal. Yet the shaman had allowed—intentionally induced—her entry into the trance state, opening her chakras to the potent Goddess energy.

Morven nodded. "She is surrounded with the color of the Goddess. I could sense her power, very strong for a human. I knew she had the strength to endure saktar, and

I remained with her the entire time. She did well. You have a mate who is worthy of you."

Arion felt a rush of pride at the shaman's words, intermingled with renewed concern for Jenna's. welfare. He trusted Morven, knew the shaman was guided by the Goddess, yet he worried how the stress might affect Jenna. No wonder she looked pale and exhausted. She had endured saktar, which was physically and mentally debilitating. It also meant she had maintained a total fast, including no liquids—this in heat to which she was unaccustomed—and gotten very little sleep. Add to that the shock and force of a merging ceremony, and it was a wonder she was still functioning at all.

Morven was right. Jenna was unusually strong for a human, but the strain of the past cycle had to be enormous. Arion resolved to leave the festivities as soon as he could get away, and get his mate back to their dome. She could rest then, but more importantly, there were other matters they needed to . . . discuss. His body reacted at the thought, newly discovered desire and need slamming through him, tightening every muscle and speeding up his heart.

He was amazed at the force of his reaction, that the mere thought of his human mate could cause such a response, and he fought for control. Perhaps it was the merging ceremony affecting his libido—or simply the knowledge that he could allow his carnal nature to surface. Regardless of the reason, Jenna was his. He would soon claim her in every way a male claimed a female.

Right now, however, he must meet with Komissar Gunnar. They did not often have the opportunity to get together in person, to talk of highly confidential matters. Arion turned back toward the awning, saw Lani and the android seated with Jenna. Gunnar was nearby, speaking with three of Arion's officers, and Arion strode in their direction.

As he approached, Gunnar looked up, caught his discreet signal, and nodded. Arion continued on to the opposite entry of the arena, stopping to accept well-wishes. He turned down an offering of kashni, the potent drink the Leors favored for celebrations, opting instead for homa to break his fast. He would indulge in the kashni after his business with Gunnar was concluded. Finally clear of his fellow Leors, he strode through the exit. The Komissar followed.

Arion started to bow to the powerful male who held dominion over all Leors, but Gunnar stopped him, offering his arm. "Long life, Arion."

"Long life, Gunnar," Arion responded, following the Komissar's lead. They had grown up together, each taken away from his parents at a young age to train at the same communal camp. They usually dispensed with formalities when they were alone. He had great respect for Gunnar, despite the male's serious lack of judgment when it came to his choice of mate, as well as his unprecedented leniency for her antics. Arion clasped Gunnar's forearm, felt the reciprocal grip.

"And long life for your new mate," Gunnar said. "A most unusual merging ceremony."

"How so?"

"The energy around you and your mate was clearly visible, and a vivid color—that of a Dukkair sunset merging with the clouds."

He must be talking about the violet glow that had surrounded Arion and Jenna. Arion knew the energy had been intense, although he was not certain what that indicated. He grunted, having nothing to reply.

In unspoken accord, both males broke into a steady run, heading toward Saura's command center, which lay five kilometers east of the settlement. Distances meant nothing in the sprawling desert, not when Leors could rapidly run fifty kilometers or more without tiring. Whenever Gunnar visited the settlements under his jurisdiction, he inspected the military facilities and the tracking and defense systems.

It was even more crucial now, with the encroaching Controller threat.

"Carain was attacked by Anteks five cycles ago," Gunnar said, anger vibrating beneath his calm words. "Someone turned off their tracking system, and they were unaware of the approaching ships."

Shocked, Arion almost stumbled. "Why did I not hear about this?"

"Because you were just returning to Saura with your mate, and there was nothing you could do. I knew we would have the opportunity to discuss this face-to-face. As you are well aware, I no longer trust the secured transmissions of data."

A few short spans ago, that would not have been a concern, as most Leors were loyal to the death. But lately, there had been startling incidences of treachery, as evidenced by what had just occurred on Carain. Gunnar's expression grew murderous, as he allowed his fury to show. "We have traitors among us, our own people."

Arion felt his own rage roaring up. He vowed that all traitors would be caught and executed without mercy or remorse. It was the way of the Leors, set in ancient laws that were immutable. "What happened to our comrades on Carain?"

"They rallied and fought back, but they lost half of their number."

Arion's rage subsided to a cold, hard insistence on revenge. He spoke his thoughts. "The traitors will be hunted down. And they will pay."

"They will," Gunnar agreed. "But the grasp of the Controllers is insidious, reaching out like the greedy tentacles of a Jaccian. They offer great wealth and power to those who help them. Our people are not immune to such inducements, especially as it grows more difficult to maintain our way of life. You must be vigilant, Arion. Like Carain, Saura is isolated, and as such, faces a greater threat of attack than Dukkair. You can no longer trust anyone."

Arion knew Gunnar was right. The Leors maintained quite a few outposts away from their home planet of Dukkair, used both as points for observing activities in the quadrant and as supply stations for Leor ships on intergalactic missions. These outposts were crucial to ongoing Leor operations, and would be prime targets for Leor enemies.

"I will watch all my people closely," he told the Komissar. "And I will increase security at the command center."

They ran in silence for a few moments, and then Gunnar asked, "How many Shielder settlers did you transport to Shamara?"

The news was not good. "Only two hundred and eighty. The first settlement we traveled to had been discovered and destroyed. There were no survivors."

"More treachery," Gunnar hissed.

"A certainty," Arion agreed. The Controllers offered substantial rewards to anyone who led them to a Shielder settlement, and an additional allotment of gold for every Shielder killed. Shadowers, Anteks, pirates, and renegade Shielders had all participated in the methodical genocide of the Shielders. Someone had reported the settlement to the authorities and received a generous reward.

"You did not tell your mate." Gunnar said it as a statement rather than a question.

"No. There was no need to give her such news." Arion had been glad that Jenna was in sleep stasis when they discovered the carnage; and while he reported the news to Captain san Ranul. He did not want her upset, and he did not want her to feel her sacrifice in agreeing to mate with him was diminished by the fact that only one settlement could be saved. She was resistant enough without further cause.

He and Gunnar discussed a number of matters during the run to the command center. Once there, they did a walk-through of the center, checking the state-of-the-art tracking system and the defense system, and Gunnar spoke with the Leors on duty. The Leors took their defenses very seriously, and their arsenal of weapons guaranteed deadly retribution to anyone foolhardy enough to threaten their settlements. Their star-class battleships were just as deadly, and no one challenged them openly. But without advanced warning systems, they were not indestructible—as recent events were beginning to show.

Business concluded, Arion and Gunnar returned to the arena to join in the celebration. The combat and endurance competitions were well under way, and the kashni was flowing freely. Their comrades hailed them when they entered the arena, offering them each a large mug of the potent beverage. Arion accepted his and raised it in a salute. "To the Komissar. May he live long, and may his deeds become legend." Loud roars greeted that, and the mugs were raised to Gunnar.

Arion downed his drink, his gaze seeking out his mate. Jenna was still beneath the awning with Lani and the android, but it appeared she had replaced the homa with kashni. Lani was talking rapidly (did the woman ever cease?), and when she saw Gunnar, she squealed— *squealed,* like a lanrax—and waved wildly. "Gunnar, sweetie, you're back! I missed you!"

The Komissar's entire demeanor changed, his expression going from a cold detachment to glowing warmth in the span of a millisecond. She blew him a kiss, and he raised his mug in a salute to her.

Barely repressing his disgust, Arion refilled his own drink. He turned back, catching Jenna's gaze on him. They stared at each other a long moment; then she looked away and hastily finished the rest of her kashni and held out the mug to the android. It replenished her drink from a pitcher on the table next to them. Apparently, his mate was seeking a diversion from the night to come.

Arion shrugged. He did not begrudge her the oblivion kashni could bring. It would not change his decision in any way, and it might offer the illusion of comfort, however briefly. She would pay for it at the twin suns' rising, though.

What irritated him, however, was the conversation Lani and the android were having with Jenna. Whatever they were discussing, it was obviously upsetting her, because she would listen for a moment, glance at him, and gulp more kashni. He could just imagine what heresy they were spouting: *sexual liberation*—whatever the Hades that was—or planting unrealistic expectations about *courtship* and *bonding*; or worse, terrifying her with grim tales of what she could expect when he mated with her.

He started forward to put an end to their conversation, but Gunnar intercepted him, stepping close and lowering his voice. "Since taking a mate, comrade, I have come to some interesting conclusions."

Arion did not want to hear another word on this unsettling subject, but this was the Komissar speaking, friend or not. He remained silent.

"I have learned that human females are far more complex and more resilient than I would have thought possible," Gunnar said.

Arion relaxed slightly. He had learned the same thing himself, but although his respect for Jenna was increasing, so was his level of frustration. He was beginning to think the two things were directly and proportionally related. Of course, the frustration was due in part to interference from a female in blue feathers and an android.

"I have also discovered that the relationship between mates is much like any other endeavor," Gunnar said. "The more you learn about it, and the more effort you put into it, the greater its strength and the greater the return. You only have one mate, comrade. One mate for life. I urge you to treat her well."

The Komissar might as well cross the ranks and go stand with Lani and the android, Arion thought. Mating did not have to be as complicated as they were making it. He would not accept that. It was like any other contract: a mutual agreement where the terms and conditions were clearly laid out, the end result specified.

Granted, there might be some considerations not present in most business agreements. And granted, this was a very long term contract. Arion resigned himself to the fact that he might have to navigate this arrangement with more care than he would normally take, to get these three off his back, if nothing else.

"I will take care with my mate," he told Gunnar. "She will come to no harm with me. I have given her my word on this, and I also give it to you."

Gunnar nodded. "That is good. You must bring Jenna to Dukkair for a visit."

Only if he could minimize the exposure to Lani. "Of course, Komissar." Arion finished his drink. "It has been a long day. I am going to take Jenna to our dome."

Gunnar looked like he wanted to say more, but held his silence. Relieved that the conversation was over, Arion strode over to his mate. She looked up as he approached, her eyes widening. He could feel the fear radiating off her like radar waves, and wondered if the merging ceremony would make them more sensitive with each other's emotions.

He also wondered how Jenna would react when she found out the merging forged telepathic links between mates. But right now, his main focus was the night ahead.

"Come," he said. "It is time to go."

She wasn't totally inebriated, but she wasn't very steady either. She stumbled as they walked to the skimmer, forcing Arion to grasp her upper arm to steady her. "I think perhaps you overindulged in the kashni," he commented.

"Not enough," she muttered. "I'm still conscious."

"You will think it more than enough in the morning."

Rather than depend on her compromised coordination, he simply lifted her into the skimmer, then went around to the other side. The merging ceremony had taken place in the afternoon, and now darkness was descending. They made the ride to the dome in silence. Jenna was leaned back in her seat, her eyes closed, but he knew she wasn't asleep. There was too much tension radiating from her.

When they reached the dome, he helped her from the skimmer, this time taking her arm before she could stumble. The dome was empty and dim, Amyan having been dismissed from her duties for the cycle. The only illumination came from the firebox, which operated continuously. Arion could easily see in the dimness, but he knew his mate couldn't. "Lights on," he commanded, and they blinked on.

Jenna stood in the middle of the chamber, the folded fabric she'd carried from the arena clutched against her chest.

He had been wondering about it. "What is that you have there?"

"Oh, this." She placed her other hand over the fabric, as if she could hide it. "It's nothing, just something Lani gave me."

Anything involving the echobird could not be good. "What is it?"

A faint flush tinged her cheeks, a sign he now recognized as embarrassment or discomfort. "Something to . . . wear."

He stared at the visible part, trying to determine if it had any feathers. He absolutely would not allow his mate to wear feathers. "Let me see it."

"There's not much to see. Really."

Her reluctance only piqued his interest. "I wish to see it. Now."

She considered a long moment, her eyes slightly unfocused. "Am I allowed to defy you on this?"

The fact that she was asking indicated how much the kashni was affecting her. "No."

She released a loud, wavering sigh and held up what appeared to be a crumpled tunic. It was black, and completely sheer.

"Why would you wear that?" he asked. "It covers nothing."

She balled it up in her hand. "I told Lani I needed something solid, with a high neck and long sleeves and a *lot* of coverage, but she insisted this would help with . . ." Her voice trailed off.

"With what?" he prompted.

She heaved another sigh. "Tonight."

Sudden understanding dawned on him. The garment was meant to be an enticement. To enhance a female's appeal to a male. The echobird was still trying to manipulate his mating with Jenna. The most intriguing thing about it was his mate's embarrassment and her continued adherence to her foolish modesty. He had already seen all of her, when he examined her so intimately on his ship. He fully expected to see all of her again. He did not intend to conduct their mating partially dressed, or in total darkness, or beneath sleeping covers.

He took the opportunity to let her know she would not be allowed to hide from him. "Then you will have to wear it for me, so I can see if it has the desired effect."

Her eyes were huge in her flushed face. "I don't think— I'm not . . . quite ready to wear this."

She wasn't ready for any of this, including mating with him. He accepted that, just as he accepted the fact that Lani and Maxine had valid points about the hardships with which Jenna was dealing. He hated to admit they were right, but he was a ruthless and skilled tactician.

He knew the greatest likelihood of victory occurred when nothing was left to chance, when even the smallest details were taken into consideration. He was aware fear could be detrimental, that a continuous flow of adrenaline was unhealthy, and tensed muscles would not give as readily as relaxed ones. He had made his decision accordingly.

Right now, Jenna's fear was so tangible he could almost reach out and touch it. Yet he knew if he attempted mating with her, she would not resist him in any way, at least not intentionally. He sensed her determined resolve to hold to her end of the bargain. She was exhausted and frightened, physically and emotionally battered from the cycle's events, under the influence of the kashni, and still she suffered in quiet dignity. He admired that, saw no reason to draw out her apprehension.

"We will not mate tonight," he said.

It took a moment for his words to sink in—probably the muddling effect of the kashni—then she pivoted toward him, staggering slightly. "Ohhh," she groaned, raising one hand to her head. "I shouldn't have moved so fast. What did you say?" She was swaying on her feet.

"Come," he said. "We will finish this discussion in the sleeping chamber." He strode into the other chamber, and ordered the lights on. Turning, he looked imperiously at her. "Come. Now."

She followed slowly. "I don't think I heard you right."

He gestured toward her dress. "You cannot sleep in that."

Her hand automatically went to the front of the dress, fumbled to find the seam. "What did you just say?"

"You cannot sleep in that dress."

"No! You know what I mean. What did you say about mating?"

"We will not mate tonight."

She stared at him, looking confused. "Why not?"

He considered how he could explain without her thinking he was compromising, which he wasn't. He merely wanted to give himself the best tactical advantage, and he did not want to subject her to anything stressful in her current state. "You are in no condition to do anything tonight. You are weakened from the saktar and the merging."

"The what?"

He patiently repeated, "The saktar and the merging—"

"What is saktar?"

Morven had not told her? Frustration roared through Arion. It appeared it would be his duty to explain everything to his mate. He was not used to giving explanations, only orders. But Jenna was looking at him expectantly.

"Saktar is a ritual Leors undergo to prepare for certain rites, such as the merging ceremony. We purify ourselves, then enter a trance state, and open ourselves to the Goddess."

"So *that's* what Morven did to me." She shuddered. "I don't want to do that again any time soon."

He brought the subject back around. "Because of the saktar and your exhaustion, as well as your . . . apprehension, as you prefer to call it, we will delay our mating until the full moon alignment. That will give you a little more time to get used to your new situation."

"When does the moon alignment occur?" She swayed again and reached out to steady herself against the wall, reminding him of her unstable state.

"Get out of your dress and into bed," he ordered gruffly. "Then we will talk."

"I need something else to put on." Rubbing her forehead, she looked around the chamber. "Can't seem to find my satchel."

"You do not need anything. Leors sleep without clothing."

"Why am I not surprised?" she muttered in a low voice. He wondered if she knew how acute Leor hearing was. "I've got tunics in my satchel, and it's somewhere around here."

Maybe the kashni was affecting him as well, but he

couldn't resist the opportunity to shake her up, which was surprising, since he was rarely playful. "You could put on the garment Lani gave you," he suggested.

She gave him a squinty-eyed glare. "I might as well sleep without anything on."

"My point exactly," he said, stone-faced, although he was smiling inside, an oddity for him. He felt the rightness of his decision. The full moon alignment was seven cycles away. That would give Jenna time to get used to her new life and to recover her strength. Then they would see to this mating business.

She looked at him suspiciously. "You've been drinking that kashma—no, that's not it—kosh . . . Blazing hells! Whatever it is, you've been drinking it, too."

"Kashni. I have had some. But *I* am not inebriated."

She had to think about his words for a moment. Definitely slowed reactions. "I am not drunk. Just . . . a little tipsy." She looked around the chamber again. "Where is that satchel?"

"Will finding your clothing speed this up?"

"Spirit willing."

He walked over to a panel and pushed the pad. The panel slid open, revealing a recessed closet. "Amyan put your things in here."

She stepped past him, fumbled around in the closet for a moment, reappearing with one of her tunics. She went into the bathing chamber, and the panel whispered shut behind her.

Arion stretched his tired muscles, and moved to the recessed dresser to put away the gold cuffs that had been in his clan for generations. The bathing chamber panel opened, and Jenna leaned out, losing her balance and almost falling. She grabbed the frame to catch herself.

"Son of an Antek. I shouldn't have done that," she muttered, the influence of the kashni revealing an intriguing side of her personality. "I can't . . ." She tightened her grip on the frame and pulled herself upright. "I can't get out of this cursed dress. The seam is in the back, and I can't reach it. Would you . . . um, would you undo it for me?"

He strode to the entryway and gestured for her to turn around. She did, presenting her back. Her upswept hair revealed a graceful neck so slender he could almost encircle it with the fingers of one hand. He grasped the top of the dress. The satiny fabric caught on the rough pads of his fingertips as he slid open the seam.

The silver material gaped, revealing the sleek line of Jenna's back, and an expanse of smooth, pale skin. He remembered how amazingly soft that flesh had been when he'd examined her on his ship. He had the sudden, powerful urge to touch her skin again, to run his tongue over it, to experience the taste, texture, and smell of his mate.

"Thank you." She shifted, stepped away.

"Wait," he ordered.

She froze. "What?"

He stepped forward and pulled the pins from her hair, running his fingers through it to shake it out. The strands flowed over his hands, silky and glowing, a rich, burnished color. It felt oddly sensual, and he wondered what it would feel like against his body. "You did not wear your hair down, as I specifically requested," he said gruffly.

She turned to face him, almost bumping into his chest. She took a wobbly step back to look up at him. "I felt that was my decision to make."

"You are still defying me."

"Not on the important things," she said softly.

"We will see," he replied, stepping away. She closed the panel, and he went to his computer. Merging ceremony day or not, his duties could never be neglected.

He glanced up when she came out of the bathing chamber a few moments later, in a tunic that showed a generous expanse of legs. She must have brushed her hair, as it flowed down her back as smooth as Saija silk. She looked at the bed with obvious distaste. "I suppose I have to sleep on *that*."

He leaned back in his chair. "That is where I sleep, and you sleep with me."

"Fine." She climbed shakily onto the bed and sank down with a deep sigh.

"You are to sleep on the other side."

Her eyelids fluttered open. "Hmmm?"

"You are on my side. Move over."

She scooted over, flopped back down with another sigh. He waited to see if she would notice. She wiggled a little, settled into the mat, and closed her eyes. "Arion?"

"Yes?"

"When is the moon maligning?"

"Aligning. The full moon alignment, when both moons are full and in conjunction with each other. It is another sacred time, when the Goddess blesses us with fertility. It is in seven cycles."

"I'll try to remember that."

"I will remind you."

"Oh. Yeah. I'm sure you will." She snuggled back into the mat. He waited.

"This is strange." She raised her head. "It's different."

"What is different?"

"The bed." She rolled onto her back, bounced a few times. "It's not as hard. It's not hot, either."

"It should not be. I had the heat coils removed from that section."

"You did?" She rolled to her side, eyes wide in amazement. "Did you do that for me?"

"I grew tired of finding you asleep on the floor. Your place is in my bed."

"I don't know what to say." She continued to stare at him, her hair cascading wildly about her. "I can't believe you did that for me."

Oddly pleased with her reaction, he stood. "It is nothing. Sleep now. I will join you soon."

"I *am* really tired," she murmured, lying down. She rolled back up before he reached the bathing chamber panel. "Oh! Your skin. I need to put the oil on your back."

He seriously doubted she had the coordination or the visual focus to handle that task right now. "We will not worry about it tonight."

"But it's my responsibility, now that I'm your . . . mate."

He liked hearing her say that, and he felt a strong surge of possessiveness. She *was* his. "You are too tired to handle that duty." And drunk, and they did not need oil all over the bathing chamber. "I can go one dark cycle without the oil."

"If you're sure . . ." Her eyes were already closing as she slid down.

She appeared to be asleep when he finally left the bathing chamber and ordered the lights off. He slid into the bed beside her. Lying on his back, he savored the heat of the coils.

"Arion?" Her voice was a sleepy whisper.

He turned his head. "What?"

She rolled toward him, her eyes opening. "Thank you." She reached out, touched his face. Her hand was warm, soft. "Thank you for altering the bed, and for giving me more time."

He watched as she leaned closer. Then she pressed her lips against his, gently, briefly, but the effect reverberated through his body. He felt a sense of loss when she sank back with a breathy sigh. He lay there a long time, mulling over her amazing action.

She had kissed him. Kissing was not inherent to the Leor culture, so it was a unique experience for him. He realized he liked it, as brief as it had been. It occurred to him it was a skill he might want to cultivate. A noise interrupted his musings, and he looked over at his petite mate.

Jenna was snoring.

Chapter Nine

Jenna wiped at the sweat streaming down her face and into her eyes, and wished fervently for even the slightest breeze to dissipate some of the stifling heat. The immense kitchen felt like an inferno, and she wondered how the servers working so silently around her stood it cycle after cycle— and how she herself would survive.

Much earlier today, Arion had taken her to Shela, the Leor female responsible for assigning work details to all the nonmilitary Leors and to the servers; then he left for the command center. Shela was older than Jenna had expected, although it was difficult to truly tell age on Leors. They had no hair to turn gray, and they didn't appear to get many lines or wrinkles. Their faces softened, though, the flesh a little puffier and fuller. Shela questioned Jenna briefly and gruffly, and upon hearing that Jenna had worked in the horticulture center, had immediately assigned her to the kitchen.

Jenna had no idea how Shela had linked growing crops with cooking, but intuitively guessed it was a not-so-subtle insult and possibly a challenge. Brona, another older Leor female, oversaw the kitchen operations. Aside from Brona and Jenna, the only other workers in the kitchen were servers—another indication of Jenna's lowly status in the settlement. She told herself she didn't care. There was nothing shameful about hard work, as long as it was honest.

And it was backbreaking labor, the most difficult Jenna had ever done. The kitchens were amazingly state-of-the-art, with highly advanced equipment and fast-cooking ovens. However, the Leors disdained replicators. They wanted their food prepared directly from its natural source, on a daily basis. This meant fresh meat went into the mammoth roasting ovens in the morning, to be served at the three main meals of the day. Fortunately, Jenna was assigned to another area of the kitchen, although the smell of the meat cooking still found her.

The Leors did eat other things besides meat. Newly harvested grains were ground and made into bread and a thick, hot cereal called *raizel*. Fruits brought in from the hydroponics centers were washed and some were peeled, seeded, and cut. Homa was made from a combination of kerani milk, tarini fruit, and homan—broad, spiky plant stalks that had a thick clear liquid inside.

Jenna was put to work making the homa, and her hands already sported numerous cuts, incurred while she struggled to slice the razor-pronged stalks into uniform pieces and feed them into a peeling machine, before putting them into the giant magnasteel mixers; all under Brona's contemptuous gaze and terse criticisms.

When the homa was mixed and automatically poured into large containers, Jenna dragged those containers onto wide, low air carts and took them to one of four walk-in coolers called cold stores, each larger than her old quarters in Shamara. On this load, she paused inside the cooler as long as she dared, finding momentary relief from the debilitating heat. It didn't help that she still had a nagging headache—it had been raging yesterday, compliments of kashni—or that she was still fatigued. Saura's heat and different atmosphere dragged at her.

"You there!" came Brona's sharp command. "You are taking far too long in the cold store. You are here to work, not stand idle all cycle."

Sighing, Jenna stumbled from the cooler and started slicing more homan stalks. The servers working around her must be used to the grueling pace, because they never slowed or let up. She wondered if they feared retribution should they lapse in their duties. She didn't want to think about that. It was difficult enough dealing with what she did know about the Leors. She sliced another stalk into three sections, wincing when a particularly sharp barb stabbed the palm of her left hand, very near the scar from her pact with Arion. Frustrated, she stared at the blood welling from the wound.

A sudden dizziness had her grasping the edge of the work surface, wondering if heat and fatigue were making her faint. But that quickly shifted into the rocking motion she often experienced before a vision. *Oh, no, not now.* She battled the encroaching vision, trying to keep her focus on the servers moving around the kitchen, but found herself hurtled with heart-stopping speed to another place.

She was staring at an unusual face . . . It was the Goddess statue. Strange, but she always saw people first in her visions, not objects. A pair of hands came into view, masculine and strong, the thick wrists encased in carved gold bands.

She'd seen those bands before . . . oh, on Arion, at the merging ceremony. How weird that she was seeing only hands, like they were extensions of her. She felt a sensation of vertigo, as if she were standing on a high cliff, looking down.

The hands lowered, and with them, her line of vision. The body of some sort of wild boar lay there, blood seep-

ing from the slash across the width of its neck, its lifeless eyes open and glazed. She did not want to see this. Yet, as always, she was held inexorably in the vision. The hands rested lightly on the boar's body, oddly reverent, as if blessing rather than condemning the animal. But the animal was already dead, had already been condemned and slaughtered. The hands shifted and moved, the line of vision changing again.

It was then Jenna realized what was happening. She was seeing through someone else's eyes. In all her countless visions, she had never done that before. She'd always seen through her own eyes, as if she were present, standing on the sideline and observing the events. But this was very different, as if she were locked inside someone else, watching through that person.

One of the masculine hands moved to a golden chalice lying beside the boar. The chalice was half full with a black-red liquid—blood, she realized. Her stomach clenched. Both of those powerful hands framed the chalice and raised it toward the Goddess, and a deep, familiar voice began a melodious chant. It was difficult for Jenna to pick out the words, but she got the main part of the intonation: "Our offering to you, Goddess, in gratitude for your blessings of gracious abundance. Grant us strength and fortitude, make us strong in spirit, and give us victory over our enemies."

She realized the voice was not Morven's, as she would have expected. It was Arion's voice. Somehow she was seeing through his eyes. How was that possible? She had never done that, and she absolutely didn't want it to continue. *Please, Spirit, spare me!* she prayed. But the vision continued. *The chalice of blood drew toward her, closer, closer, as if to touch her face.* "Arion!" she practically screamed. "Stop!"

The chalice froze in midair. There was a pause, and then Arion said, *Jenna?* She knew it wasn't part of the vision.

The voices in her visions were always outside her. This voice—Arion's voice—was as clear as if he were standing in the kitchen with her, only it was inside her head. His voice was in her mind!

Jenna, he said again, clearly projecting to her somehow. *Answer me. I know you can hear me.*

I don't want to talk to you this way.

Communicating like this is a natural occurrence between mates. I must see to other duties before I can come to you. Then I will explain what is happening.

She didn't want any explanations. She only wanted to be free of the horrifying scene and for the excruciating invasion of his voice in her mind to end. *I don't want to hear any more. Just make the vision stop.*

You can see what I am doing?

Yes! And it's horrible. Make it stop.

There was a brief pause. *I cannot control what you see. I will come to you as soon as I am free.*

He was talking to her telepathically. She was seeing through his eyes. Both events were shocking enough, but she was also witnessing a scene—the slaughtered animal and the blood-filled chalice—that threatened to make her stomach revolt. She felt as if she were spinning out of control, and panic swept her. She whirled blindly, only vaguely aware of the clatter of utensils onto the floor.

"You! What are you doing?" Brona bellowed.

Thankfully, the woman's voice broke the hold the vision had on Jenna, and it faded away. Gasping, she braced herself against the worktable.

Brona strode over, towering above Jenna, her black eyes flashing. "I will not tolerate disruptions in this kitchen. If you defy me and continue to behave out of line, you will be disciplined. It will not matter that you are mated with the Comdar. Is that clear?"

Jenna drew a deep breath. "Yes. Very clear."

"Pick up the items you knocked on the floor. You will

NAME:_____

ADDRESS:_____

_____

_____

TELEPHONE:_____

E-MAIL:_____

_____ I want to pay by credit card.

__ Visa   __ MasterCard   __ Discover

Account Number:_____

Expiration date:_____

SIGNATURE:_____

Send this form, along with $2.00 shipping and handling for your FREE books, to:

Love Spell Romance Book Club
20 Academy Street
Norwalk, CT 06850-4032

Or fax (must include credit card information!) to: **610.995.9274.**
You can also sign up on the Web at <u>www.dorchesterpub.com</u>.

Offer open to residents of the U.S. and Canada only. Canadian residents, please call 1.800.481.9191 for pricing information.

If under 18, a parent or guardian must sign. Terms, prices and conditions subject to change. Subscription subject to acceptance. Dorchester Publishing reserves the right to reject any order or cancel any subscription.

take them to the sterilizer and clean them. Then you will finish making the homa. You will stay until it is done, even if you miss the evening meal."

That didn't matter to Jenna. She knew she wouldn't be able to eat anyway. She refused to be cowed by Brona, or to be accused of shirking her duty. She was exhausted, but if she had to crawl to the mixers, then the cold stores, to get the homa made and put way, then by the Spirit, she would. She met the other woman's gaze evenly. "I will complete my assigned chores."

"You will indeed. Now clean this up." Brona's lip curled in disgust, and she swept away.

Jenna scooped up the knives and the bowl she'd dropped on the floor. She took them over to the sterilizers, stepping through the wall of steam issuing from the units. It was even hotter over here, and very humid. Swiping at the moisture on her face, she helped the two servers working the sterilizers to empty one of the units. She loaded her items into it, and then one of the servers had to show her how to start it. When sterilization was completed, she retrieved her utensils and went back to making homa.

She finally finished the last batch of homa and wheeled it into the cold store. Stepping back into the wall of heat in the kitchen, she wondered wearily what she would be asked to do next. She'd been on her feet for hours, with only two breaks for meals; and those at tables on one side of the kitchen, rather than the main dining hall, which suited her just fine.

Two Leor men entered the kitchen from the outside entry, lugging the body of a large boar between them. She didn't need a closer look to know immediately it was the one she'd seen in her vision. It made sense. At least the Leors ate the animals they killed; they weren't wasteful. Brona directed the men to a large worktable near the cold store where the meat was kept. They slung the body onto the table and left.

"Taron," Brona called, her rough voice booming across the kitchen. "Prepare this beast for cooking."

A middle-aged male server with graying hair stepped forward at her order. Her cold, obsidian gaze continued sweeping the kitchen, coming to rest on Jenna and gleaming with malice. Jenna knew what Brona was going to say before she growled, "You there. Come assist this server."

Apprehension twisting inside her, Jenna moved forward slowly. "You will help Taron clean and skin this animal," Brona ordered. She stared hard at Jenna, issuing a silent challenge. "He will show you how it is done. When that is finished, your duties will be completed this cycle." She turned and stalked away.

Jenna stood there, unable to believe the assignment she'd just received. Taron moved beside her, touched her arm hesitantly, and pointed to a nearby table where glinting, sharp knives lay in a neat row. *You can do this,* she told herself. *You have to do it.* She'd asked for this. She'd wanted, and demanded, equal rights from Arion. She had to live here the remainder of her life. She'd expected to have to prove herself, although she'd never imagined she would face such a situation.

Taron tugged on her sleeve again. Wiping her damp hands on her pants, she moved slowly to the table, the server beside her. He picked up a huge, wicked-looking knife and offered it to her. Reluctantly, she took it. He made a slicing motion across his neck, indicating she was to start by cutting off the animal's head. Then he picked up another knife for himself. She turned back toward the boar, her feet like lead, her stomach churning.

Taron moved more quickly, stepping around her to get to the table. He began sawing at the animal's thick neck. She approached the table slowly, reminding herself that many races, the Shielders included, ate meat. It was a part of the natural food chain. She couldn't pass judgment on the Leors for being carnivorous. She refused to think about who had killed this boar, or any possible part Arion could have had. Yet all she could do was stare at the bloody slash across the poor creature's throat. Her stomach roiled, and bile rose swiftly. The room suddenly seemed to spin.

Clutching the knife, she clapped her free hand over her mouth. She felt the wild flux in her stomach, whirled, and ran for the exit, praying she'd make it outside in time. She got through the entry, then gasped as she careened into Arion, who was headed in. Fortunately, she was holding the knife at her side, so it didn't go into him. He grabbed at her arm, but she wrenched sideways and made it just off the path, where she dropped to her hands and knees and was violently ill.

When the heaving stopped, she remained where she was, too weak to move. "Are you done?" came her mate's voice from nearby.

She turned her head enough to see his powerful legs squatting next to her. Blazing hells. Her humiliation was complete. "Just go away."

"Can you stand?" His voice was calm.

She closed her eyes and drew a trembling breath, knowing full well he wouldn't leave. She scooted back, realizing she still had the knife in her hand, then pushed herself up, sitting back on her heels. "I'm not sure if my legs are working right now," she said wearily.

"I will have this." His fingers closed around her wrist, and he pried her hand open and commandeered the knife. "Take it," he said to someone, and Jenna looked around to see him handing the knife to Brona. The woman flashed her a contemptuous look, her eyes narrowed and her lips compressed in a thin line. Jenna was too drained to care.

Arion kept his grip on her wrist as he studied the cuts on her palm and fingers. She stared at his big hands, at the ornate gold cuffs covering a third of each forearm, and déjà vu swept through her, the vision flashing back in a dizzying rush: the animal sacrifice he had made to the

Goddess, the blood offering, the likelihood he had even drunk the blood.

Barbaric. Merciless. Inhuman. Her mate was a member of a race that was all those things. She fought down a renewed wave of nausea, although she didn't think there was anything left to heave up.

"What were you doing with that knife?" he asked, taking her other hand and checking it as well, ignoring her wince of pain when he uncurled her fingers for a better look.

"I was getting ready to cut off the hea—" She stopped, the very thought threatening her tenuous control over her stomach. "I was going to help skin and clean a wild boar."

Arion flashed a sharp look from her to Brona. "Is that how you injured your hands?"

"No." She tried to tug free from his grasp, but he wouldn't release her wrist. "That was from cutting up the homan to make homa."

"Why did you not wear the gloves that are used when handling homan?"

"Gloves?" Jenna raised her gaze to Brona, who wore a self-satisfied smirk. "I didn't know about them."

"She did not ask, Comdar. I was not aware of her injuries, and I had forgotten how frail human skin is," Brona said. She wasn't quite insolent, but Jenna sensed she wasn't showing the full respect due to Arion.

His expression hardened. "Stand up," he ordered Jenna, but he assisted her, grasping her upper arms and pulling her to her feet. Her legs buckled, forcing her to cling to him, her fingers digging into his bulging biceps. He supported her easily. She hated that she was so weak, especially in front of Brona, but figured Arion holding her up was better than her falling on her face.

"Lady Jenna will not be working in the kitchen again," he told Brona, a magnasteel edge in his voice. "There is another position where we can better utilize her skills."

Jenna leaned into him gratefully. A part of her was mortified she hadn't been able to see the cycle through and complete her duties with a semblance of dignity. But another part of her felt only relief that she wouldn't be working under such grueling conditions, or anywhere near Brona.

Brona's grunt might as well have been "good riddance," but if Arion noticed, he didn't react. "Come," he told Jenna. "We will take a skimmer."

Since they walked from their dome to the dining hall every day, she knew the skimmer was for her benefit, but right now her pride was too shredded and her legs too shaky for her to protest. He turned her toward the path, taking her arm and linking it through his. "Hold on to me," he ordered.

Surprised by his action, she gripped his forearm, leaning against his big body for support. He was incredibly hard all over, not an ounce of fat on him. His patterned skin felt cool and odd beneath her fingertips. With all she knew about the Leors, about their savageness and their lack of humanity, she should have found touching him repulsive, yet she didn't. At this moment, she felt only relief that he had extricated her from a nightmare situation. He kept the pace slow and steady as they moved to the skimmer pads.

Neither of them spoke, and when they reached the skimmer he simply slid his arm under her legs, lifting her as if she were no more than a tiny infant and placing her in the craft. He exercised his great strength casually, obviously used to it, but she found it nothing short of amazing. She leaned back against the seat, every muscle in her body aching, the dull throbbing of the kashi hangover still in her head. The skimmer jounced as Arion got behind the controls; then the engines roared to life. The vehicle lifted from the pad, did a sharp cut around, and headed toward the open desert.

The top was down, and the air rushed against Jenna, taking the edge off the heat, while wisps of her hair came lose from its twist and whipped around her face. It took a moment for her to realize they were headed away from the settlement. "Where are we going?" she asked, raising her voice to be heard over the engines and the wind.

"Just over there." Arion gestured to a clump of tall, pointed plants near an outcropping of rocks. He guided the skimmer close to the rocks, lowered it to the ground, and cut the engines.

Jenna looked around. The settlement lay behind them, and the wall of mesas was about five kilometers directly ahead. Quite a ways off to her right lay the arena, where her merging with Arion had been so wildly celebrated. She had learned that distances meant nothing to the Leors, not with their nonhuman speed and endurance. But right now, they weren't near *anything*.

"What are we doing here?" she asked.

He turned his fathomless gaze on her. "Do you wish for Lanka to treat your cuts?"

That would be an awful ending to a terrible day. "No," she said emphatically. "I'll wash them good with soap."

"This is better. Wait here." He jumped gracefully to the sand and strode to the plants, pulling his knife from its sheath. He grabbed one of the thick stalks and cut it off, then flipped the cut end upright and carried it back to the skimmer. He got into the craft and turned toward her. "Hold out your hands, palms up."

She wondered what he had planned, but realized with a jolt that she trusted him. When had that happened? Too worn out to analyze her discovery, she gave in and held out her hands. He tipped the stalk—which looked very similar to homan, but didn't have spikes on it—over her palms, and a pink gel oozed out. It was warm, and it created a tingling on her skin. Arion propped the stalk on the floor and took first one hand, then another, rubbing the gel into the cuts. His fingers were long and broad, powerful, like the rest of him, but his touch was surprisingly gentle.

The gel didn't sting at all, and immediately the pain of the cuts began easing.

"There," he said, releasing the second hand. "The kayaan sap will speed up the healing and will prevent infection."

"That's amazing." She stared at the cuts, noticed the red was fading.

He held out the stalk. "Keep the cut end upright until we reach the dome. We will apply more after you bathe."

She took the plant, slipped it between her knees to keep it vertical. "It looks a lot like homan."

"They are closely related, and they both have beneficial sap. One is edible, the other is medicinal."

Jenna nodded, then leaned back into her seat, fatigue seeping through her. Her gaze settled on the mesas. The second sun was setting over them, sending a stain of red and rose and gold across the orange sky. "Arion, look." She pointed toward the sunset. "That's so beautiful."

"The beauty of our surroundings is one of the many blessings our Goddess bestows upon us."

The deep reverence in his voice seemed at odds with the Leor persona. How could Leors be so savage, so cruel, and yet possess such a profound spiritual nature? They took innocent people as slaves and cut their vocal cords so they couldn't speak. They sacrificed helpless animals to a Goddess exemplified by a cold, harsh statue. They were infamous for their barbarous treatment of their enemies, rivaled only by that of the Anteks and the Controllers. Yet they raised their voices in prayer and praise to a supreme being, and honored ancient spiritual rites.

Then there was the incongruity between the Leors' advanced technology and their primitive lifestyle, as well as their outdated values and insistence on virgin mates, while at the same time they were highly educated. It didn't make sense. She was too exhausted to ponder these issues, and suspected Arion wouldn't be forthcoming with information anyway. Neither would Morven. She knew whom to ask. Maxine. The android was a walking, talking conglomerate of information. She would have answers.

Jenna watched the stunning sunset as Arion started the skimmer and headed back toward the settlement. When he turned in a direction where she couldn't see it anymore, she closed her eyes. But the images of Amyan's ruined throat and the dead boar replaced those of the scenery. It seemed they were branded in her mind, and she couldn't chase them away.

Despite Arion's surprising gentleness, despite the fact he was giving her some time before asserting his mating rights, nothing could negate the facts about the true Leor nature. They were barbarians, in every sense of the word.

Coldly furious, Arion seethed all the way back to their dome. Jenna might not recognize the malice Shela and Brona had displayed toward her, but he did. He glanced over at his mate. Her eyes were closed, her body in an exhausted slump. Her clothing was filthy, stained with sweat and the natural green dye in the outer homan husk, and with blood—her own blood, from the multiple cuts on both of her hands.

Her face wasn't much better, her skin abnormally pale and smeared with dirt and grease. Beneath the filth, he could see lines of fatigue, and there were dark circles under her eyes. Fiery strands of her hair had escaped its severe twist and formed a riotous halo around her head. She was a mess, although not of her own doing.

It was indefensible. She should have been given protective gloves, should have been treated with the respect due a Comdar's mate. Servers received better treatment than she had this cycle. At least, they were supposed to. He made a mental note to check on Brona, to ensure that the servers working under her command were treated fairly and humanely. The Leors had been blessed with enormous strength, and the fierceness and battle skills necessary to maintain their freedom. Arion felt that made them morally obligated to protect those who were weaker and under their care.

He couldn't believe Jenna had been asked to skin and clean a wild hog—the same one he had hunted this morning, as an offering to the Goddess in honor of his taking a mate, and to thank the Goddess for the successful merging of his and Jenna's souls. There were servers who were specially trained in butchering and preparing the meat the Leors ate. Some of that meat came from herd animals raised in one of the agricultural centers, while some came from the wild boars that roamed the plains of Saura.

It was traditional for Leors to commemorate special life events, such as the merging of mates, the birth of a child, or victory over an enemy, by hunting and capturing wild game, and making a sacrifice to the Goddess, at her altar. The sharing of the animal's blood was part of the bond with the Goddess, and the blood pact ritual had come from that tradition. A blood pact wasn't only between the parties involved, but formed a sacred circle with the Goddess, evoking her blessing.

Arion was amazed that Jenna had "seen" him at the altar. Although he knew the merging of mates created telepathic links between them, he had not known how such a link would work between a Leor and a human, and a Shielder at that. He'd had no idea the ceremony would link Jenna's visions to him, or that she would witness his sacrifice to the Goddess. He could see how it would be abhorrent, especially since she did not eat meat, for her to see the slaughtered boar and the blood offering.

Then, after an obviously difficult day in the kitchens, Brona had ordered her to clean the animal, a task that would be just as upsetting to her as witnessing the sacrifice. Her distress over that had caused the disturbances in her body, and the resultant scene outside the kitchen. She should not have been subjected to that, not with ample servers trained in preparing meat. He felt certain it had been a spiteful act on Brona's part, and he intended to make sure it never happened again.

He knew most Leors disdained humans in general, and acceptance of Jenna as his mate would be slow. He would have to take a strong stance to ensure she received the respect that was due her. Already, she was commanding his grudging respect. He could see the truth of Gunnar's words. Humans were more complex and had more spiritual strength than was generally realized among Leors.

Arion would deal with some of this cycle's issues tomorrow. Right now, he needed to see to Jenna. He maneuvered the skimmer onto the pad and cut the engines. He looked at her, his anger flaring again. The protective and possessive feelings she seemed to evoke in him surged to the surface. She belonged to him, and her welfare was his responsibility. So far, she had not fared very well while under his care:

She'd been traumatized by sleep stasis, and it had left her cold and weak. The heat bothered her, and the servers and the animal sacrifices had disturbed her—just as Lani had predicted. She'd eaten very little and lost weight, as evidenced by the hollows in her cheeks. She had endured saktar, then a merging ceremony, suffered a raging hangover, then been subjected to Brona's vindictive nature and a debilitating cycle in the kitchens.

Yet she had complained very little, instead displaying an amazingly strong inner core. Morven was right: For a human, she was a worthy mate. And she deserved better than she had gotten thus far. Arion was glad he had given her the time until the lunar conjunction before he claimed his mating rights, just as he was determined her life on Saura would be less traumatic from now on. He would shield her from the darker side of Leor life as much as he could, and demand that she receive the proper respect from the clan.

She stirred, her eyes opening and her gray gaze settling on him. "Why are you staring at me?" Jenna's hand went to her head, tried to smooth her wild hair. "Do I look that bad?"

She looked as if she'd been fighting the fires of Hades. Not being a master of tact, he chose to say nothing.

"Really bad, huh?" She sighed, leaned her head back. "I don't even care right now."

His heart did a funny little skip at her desolate tone. Disregarding it, he dismounted and strode around the skimmer and offered his hand. "Come."

She picked up the kayaan stalk and took his hand, flinching when his fingers closed around hers. Cursing her cuts, he released her hand and leaned over, grasping her waist and lifting her out. Instead of setting her down, he slid his arm beneath her legs and carried her to the dome.

"I can walk," she protested breathlessly.

Ignoring her, he took her inside. He'd always thought it was a weakness to be carried for any reason, but found he enjoyed holding her in his arms. Her weight was insubstantial, and her small body fit well against his chest, as if it belonged there. Usually she had a sweet, enticing scent, although not tonight. A bath was the first order of business. It would also help with muscle soreness and the cuts on her hands. He spoke briefly to Amyan, then carried Jenna to the bathing chamber before setting her down.

"What are you doing?" Jenna asked, her eyes wide as he turned on the water in the large tub that was sunk into the floor.

"You are going to have a long soak." He picked up a bottle of special bathing oil that his people used, debated what it might do to human skin, and decided not to risk it. She would have to use the milder soap, and tomorrow he would try to locate oil that she could safely use. He adjusted the water temperature to a little cooler than he liked it.

"A bath sounds wonderful." Jenna sighed.

He walked back to her, took the kayaan stalk, and propped it carefully in the sink. "Turn around."

Her eyes narrowed with suspicion. "I can get myself into the tub."

Back to the ridiculous modesty issue. "Turn around," he repeated. "I will take your hair down for you."

"I can do that."

"I will do it." He took her shoulders and turned her to give him access to her hair. She took one look in the mirror and gasped. "Oh, Spirit! I look awful." She whirled back around. "I don't want to see. And I don't want you looking at me, either. Get out." She shoved at his chest, wincing as her sore hands made contact.

He stepped around her, moving her forward enough that he could stand behind her. "I have already seen how you look." Reaching up, he pulled the pins from her hair, placing them on the counter. He loosened the twist, slid his fingers through it, shaking out the heavy mass. He liked his mate's hair, liked watching it uncoil into strands of fire that glowed in the bright bathing chamber light.

"Ummm." She sighed, tilting her head back slightly. "That feels good."

He combed his fingers through the thick waves. "This gives you pleasure?"

"Oh, yes. Especially after it's been up all day. It's like taking off your boots after wearing them for hours, and being able to wiggle your toes."

He could relate, to an extent. Leors wore boots when they visited other cultures, but went barefoot the rest of the time. He disliked the constriction of footwear. He leaned forward, whispered by his mate's ear, "Leors do not wiggle their toes."

"That's because you're way too serious," she said. Her

head was still tilted, her eyes closed. "I'll bet you never have any fun."

"We celebrate merging ceremonies," he pointed out. "And some of us overindulge in kashni."

She groaned. "Please don't remind me. My head still hurts."

"You brought that on yourself." Even as he reprimanded her, he brought his hands up and rubbed her temples. He had lived most of his life alone, and now he found he liked touching this woman, liked the bantering of words. For many spans, his evenings had been spent in silence, with the computer his only companion. "Have you eaten today?"

"Not much. I haven't been very hungry."

And she had lost what little she'd had. "You will eat," he said firmly. "I will send Amyan to bring food from the dining hall, so we will not have to return there tonight."

"That would be great."

The gratitude in her voice caused another tug on his heart. "I will leave you to bathe then." Allowing her the privacy she valued so highly, he went to the living area and sent Amyan to get their evening meal.

When the server returned from the dining hall some time later, he dismissed her for the evening and strode to the bathing chamber. He rapped on the panel. "Jenna. You have soaked long enough. The food is here." Only silence met his words.

Concerned, he went in. Jenna was leaned against the back of the huge sunken tub, her head tilted to the side, her eyes closed. One arm lay limply on the tile floor next to the tub. Her hair floated on the water, blurring the form of her body beneath the surface. For a moment, he thought something was seriously wrong, and his heart jolted in alarm, but then she let out a small breath and moved slightly, her hair flowing with the rippling water.

Relief rolled through him. She had merely fallen asleep.

He strode over to the tub and squatted down. "Wake up, Jenna." She stirred, then stilled again. The motion moved her hair, and he could see the outline of her breasts. He splashed water on her face, watched her grimace, and said, "Wake up, *charina*."

It was a Leor endearment, a word he had never uttered in his forty spans, yet it rolled off his tongue with surprising ease. Startled at how right it seemed to call his mate his "cherished one," he leaned forward and shook her shoulder. "Jenna. Wake up."

Her eyes fluttered open, soothing pools of gray. Until realization of where she was hit. Her eyes widened, and she sank into the water, up to her chin. "I must have fallen asleep," she murmured.

"You did." He offered his hand. "Time to get out."

She crossed her arms over her chest. "If you'll give me a few moments, I'll dry off and join you."

He was through with this foolishness. "There is no need for modesty in a Leor community, much less between mates. I am not leaving, Jenna. Get out. Now."

Chapter Ten

Staring into Arion's resolute eyes, Jenna knew he would not yield this time. She also knew, on an intellectual level, that he was right. Nudity was natural and normal to the Leors, and there was no valid reason for shyness between mates. She had entered into a blood pact with Arion, had merged her soul with his. Those two things were probably more intimate than baring her body could ever be. But emotionally, she felt terribly vulnerable. Her clothing was one of the few barriers she had against the Leors and their savageness; perhaps it was even a defense against Arion's inexorable claim to her. But she couldn't hide behind barriers forever. Her life was now irrevocably entwined with his.

Keeping her gaze locked with his, she took the hand he offered and rose, the water swirling around her. He wrapped his fingers around her wrist, rising as she moved up the two steps set within the tub. When she was standing on the heated floor tiles, he drew her beneath the dryer and activated it. Hot air blasted down on them, sent her wet hair fluttering. They stared at each other a long, timeless moment, a current of awareness running between them. His gaze shifted, moved down the length of her body. She kept her hands by her side, resisting the strong urge to cover herself, even though she felt a flush spread through her face and chest.

His perusal swept back up, his obsidian gaze trapping her, stealing her breath. There was blatant male possessiveness in his midnight eyes, in the satisfied set of his sensual mouth. Her own mouth went dry, and her mind blanked out any rational thought. All she could do was stand there, like a kerani caught in a trap, while he reached out and snagged a folded drying cloth from a nearby shelf, snapping it open in one smooth move.

He took a step forward, began blotting her hair with the cloth. It felt wonderful, and for a moment she luxuriated in the pleasure of having her hair dried, in the comfort of being cared for. That faded, however, as an odd tension began coiling low in her body. She sensed the same tension in Arion. He wasn't one to converse, and she was used to the quiet lulls, but the silence between them now seemed evocative, erotic. She became acutely aware of his close proximity, the masculine scent of him. Her heart rate increased to a dull pounding, and she knew it wasn't from fear. She felt the chemistry pulsing between them, primal, elemental, a lure as old as the universe.

Arion dropped the drying cloth to the floor, then framed her face between his big hands. His gaze locked with hers again as he slowly leaned toward her. He dipped his head and ran his tongue along her cheeks. With a jolt, she realized it was rough rather than smooth, and she remembered that he could smell as well as taste with it. The sensation of him licking her was startling, sent heat spiraling through her. He stroked his way to her lips, then hovered just above them.

"Your people like kissing." His breath whispered across her mouth.

"Yes." Her low answer was only from vicarious knowledge, as no Shielder man had ever attempted to kiss her.

"Then we shall work on it," he murmured, tracing her lips with his tongue. She swayed and caught his arms to steady herself. He emitted a low growl, pressed his mouth to hers, firm, demanding, an initial claiming of her. The tip of his tongue teased the seam of her lips. She'd never felt anything so sensual. Oh, Spirit, she was burning up inside. With a gasp, she pulled back.

He allowed her retreat, but kept his grip on her, moving his hands from her face to her shoulders. He slid his hands slowly down her arms, and she felt the roughness of his fingers, very much like his tongue, and a tremor ran through her.

"Your skin is so smooth, like the finest Saija silk," he murmured, sliding his hands back up, stroking her shoulders. His gaze moved to her breasts, and the breath stuttered in her chest. Very slowly, he ran a finger from her collarbone, down along the slope of her left breast, stopping just above the nipple. The sensation was electric, and both her nipples hardened in a tingling rush. Her lungs froze completely. His eyes flared, darkened, then flashed back to hers.

She saw intense hunger in those ebony depths, pure sexual desire, and she felt the force of his need—and her need—right down to her toes and everywhere in between. He dropped his hand and stepped away, leaving her bereft from the sudden loss of contact. His chest was heaving. Good. Her own body was screaming with newly awakened desire. She was glad he was just as affected.

His face hardened, and she sensed his battle for control. "I have given you my word that we will not mate until the full moon alignment. Five more cycles, Jenna."

He turned and strode to the panel. It whispered open, and he looked back at her. "Finish here and join me in the living area. There are matters we need to discuss."

She nodded, not trusting her voice, and he left the chamber. Her heart was still pounding, and her legs trembled. Turning off the dryer, she pressed a hand against the wall to steady herself. She wasn't sleepy anymore. The electrifying exchange with Arion had sent every nerve ending in her body into full alert.

She touched her fingers to her lips, thought about how his tongue had stroked there; how his touch had burned her skin. One thing appeared certain: Despite their cultural differences, they definitely had a strong sexual chemistry.

Five cycles, and counting.

Jenna toyed with a piece of tarini fruit. "You talked to me in my mind today."

Arion set aside his empty plate and picked up his warmed homa. "Yes."

She stared down at the fruit in her hand. She was at the settee's far end, her legs curled beneath her. He didn't miss that she was as far away from him as she could get on the settee, or that her posture was defensive. "Is this normal for Leors?" she asked.

"You are aware we have some unusual mental abilities. We can read the thoughts of most humans, or at least sense their emotions and intentions. But both Shielders and Leors have natural mind shields that prevent us from doing this with each other. So, no—it is not normal, except with mated couples."

Her head jerked up, and her startled gaze swung to his. "What do you mean?"

"Eat your fruit," he ordered, then waited until she took a small bite. "When a couple goes through the merging ceremony, a telepathic bond is formed between them. They can then communicate mentally. Apparently, Shielders and Leors can also form such a bond."

Her gaze was reproachful. "Why didn't anyone tell me this?"

"It was my belief Morven would explain. It appears he did not."

"He said a lot of things, but none of it made any sense. Leors don't seem to be much on explaining."

"We are warriors, not politicians. We live by action, not words."

Jenna considered a moment, and he could feel her increasing tension. "Can you read my thoughts now?"

It might be a good thing if he could. Perhaps that would enable him to understand how to better handle her. Thus far, his attempts at dealing with a human female had not been very successful. But he sensed his mate was a private person, just as he was. She would not like such an invasion into her privacy.

"No," he answered honestly. "I have not been able to read your mind. We can communicate mentally, but only if we intentionally send our thoughts to one another."

"I wasn't trying to contact you today. I didn't even know I could," she said. "Yet all at once, I was inside your mind. It was like I was looking through your eyes, and I was seeing whatever you saw. I didn't like it."

He did not like it, either. First because he could not control it; secondly, because there were many things she was not ready to see. Yet the Goddess had facilitated the merging and the end result. He must honor and accept Her wisdom in all things. "What happened today is not a normal occurrence between mates," he replied. "I can only assume it is because of your special ability, and that somehow I became a channel for your vision, allowing you to see through me."

"It's not a 'special ability.' It's a curse." She set down her half-eaten fruit. "I'm sorry. My visions are not your problem."

She was wrong about that, and she must learn to trust him. "You are my mate. Anything that concerns you also concerns me."

"You do not own my soul," she muttered. "No matter what Morven says."

She belonged to him, whether or not she accepted it. "What did you say?" he challenged.

"I have another question," she said.

He allowed her evasion, for now. "And that is?"

"The mating act . . ." She cleared her throat, then plunged on. "Is Leor mating different from that of humans?"

The question gave him pause. He had been educated in the mechanics of the act, but only as it pertained to Leors. He had assumed it would be the same with a human, but he did not know for a fact. A nagging doubt, fed by the previous concern he might inadvertently hurt Jenna, rose inside him. It appeared he would have to do some research on the matter after all.

"I do not think the differences could be very great," he said. "I believe we will be able to figure it out. The attraction is already there." That was an understatement, given the way need and lust had blazed through his body in the bathing chamber earlier. He knew Jenna had reacted just as strongly, and not just from the external signs. Her taste and scent had changed, becoming musky and even more alluring.

She ducked her head, smoothed her tunic. "Yes, it is."

"We will deal with any differences when the time comes." He watched her try to hide a yawn. "You need to get some rest."

"I know." She rubbed her forehead. "I don't think I'll have any trouble sleeping tonight." She was silent a moment. "I won't be returning to work in the kitchens, will I?"

The anger that had been simmering all night flared. He would be talking with Brona on the new cycle. "No. You will not."

"Then, what will I do?"

"That is a good question, one we must discuss." He knew she had no real understanding of how she would fit into Leor society. "As my mate, you will be accorded a certain amount of respect. You should not have been treated as you were this cycle. Brona was out of line, and I will deal with her. You are to let me know if you ever receive such treatment again."

"I don't mind hard work, Arion. I've always had to work."

"Your attitude is commendable. All adults on Saura are expected to work. But you should not work harder than a server would, or be treated disrespectfully."

She nodded in understanding. "It might be difficult for your people to accept me. I am different."

"They *will* accept you. You are my mate."

"Perhaps. But even the Shielders . . ." She paused. "It's hard to accept those who are different."

He suspected she was talking about herself. "You were shunned by your people, because of your ability to see the future?" he asked, although he'd already seen how she'd been treated, gleaned from the images during their merging ceremony.

"They were afraid of me." She shrugged as if it didn't bother her. "I got used to being alone."

But it had bothered her, as he already knew from the merging. He could sense the hurt and loneliness radiating from her. He felt anger on her behalf, anger that she had been penalized for an ability her god had given her, and rebuffed by her own people. And now, she was facing the same thing on Saura. But he could, and would, do something about that.

"So, you worked in horticulture in Shamara?" he asked.

"In the hydroponics unit. We produced a lot of our crops in water."

"You told Shela?"

"Yes. I explained exactly what my duties were."

There was a large hydroponics center on Saura. Yet Shela had decided to assign Jenna to the kitchens, even though they were not understaffed. Shela was also placed on Arion's list for a visit. "Did you enjoy working in crop production?" he asked.

Jenna picked up her homa, fingering the mug's handle. "It was all right. I didn't mind."

"But you did not really like it."

She shrugged again. "It wasn't bad. There are worse jobs."

"Look at me, Jenna." He waited until she turned her gaze to him. "What did you really want to do?"

"Well . . . I wanted to work in the nursery."

He felt a flash of surprise. "Taking care of the young ones?"

"The infants, the toddlers, or even the older children. It wouldn't have mattered."

"You like children?"

Her face lit up, with the first real excitement he had seen her show. "Oh, yes. They're so innocent and loving. So accepting."

"Leor offspring are very active," he warned. "And stronger than human children. You would probably be able to handle only the infants."

"You'd let me be around the children?"

"Is there any reason I should not?"

"No." Her voice was level, but he saw that her hand tightly gripped her mug. "Unless you're worried about my visions."

"Your visions are a spiritual gift, Jenna. They do not concern me. You will need to understand that Leor offspring are raised differently from those of most humans. They begin military training as soon as they can walk. If you can accept that, and agree to abide by nursery regulations, then I will see that you are assigned there."

"I can accept that, and I agree to follow the nursery

156

rules." She set down her homa. "Thank you."

There was an odd catch to her voice, and he looked at her sharply, noting the moisture in her eyes before she wiped at them. Were those tears? The android had said humans produced them when they were upset or sad. He could not see how assigning Jenna to the nursery, where she wished to be, would produce those emotions.

"What is wrong?" he asked.

Sniffing, she stood and turned away from him. "Nothing." Her voice still had that catch.

He stood as well. "You are not upset or sad?"

"No." She looked at him over her shoulder and he saw telltale streaks on her face. "You've given me a great gift. I . . . I think I'd better get ready for bed now. Then I'll put the oil on your back."

She was gone, slipping into the sleeping chamber before he could question her further. He stared at the closed panel a long time, pondered her baffling reaction. It had been obvious she really wanted to work in the nursery, and he had granted her that. She should have been pleased. So, why had her eyes leaked tears? Apparently, he still had a lot to learn about human females, a fact that reminded he needed to study mating between Leors and humans.

Tears. He shook his head. He had thought she might kiss him again. Instead, he had gotten tears.

Arion stared at Jenna. She was curled on her side, with her hands tucked beneath her face. In sleep, she looked incredibly young, almost childlike. But he knew very well she had the body of a full-grown female. Granted, not the statuesque figure of a Leor female, but a feminine and softly curving body, all the same. He thought of how she had looked earlier that evening, standing beneath the bathing chamber dryer, her skin glistening with moisture, her fiery hair cascading over her shoulders and breasts.

His body reacted to the memory, heating and tightening

with an urgency he'd never before experienced. It was not just her hair and her body, but her exotic scent, and the taste and feel of her skin. It had been more of the same torment when she rubbed the warm oil on his back. Her mere touch sparked heat and need. Perhaps the merging ceremony had heightened his awareness of her, but he felt the increasing need to touch her in return, to claim her.

Now, as he watched her sleep, he was determined there would be no more mishaps. He would not allow ignorance—his or that of anyone else—to cause her further distress. To that end, he was making a tremendous concession. He was going to watch the blue echobird's cursed holovideo. He would rather face ten consecutive saktar rituals or an entire Antek army than view the HV, but when he looked at Jenna he felt a curious wrench inside. He did not want to hurt her any more than necessary.

At least Lani was human, and familiar with the mating habits of Leors—and numerous other races, if the rumors were true. Surely the HV would expound the differences between human and Leor. That was all he needed to learn, nothing more. Arion told himself no one would ever know.

Reluctantly, he went to his computer and put in the disc. Glancing at Jenna, he turned the screen away from the bed and donned his headset. Even if she awoke, she would not see or hear what he was watching. Taking a deep breath, he started the HV.

The scene opened on a startling expanse of deep red Sarnai satin, bunched in what he supposed was considered a creative, suggestive manner. Credits flashed across the bottom of the screen in white. Curious, he froze the frame and magnified the words, then converted them to his native language. *Property of Saron Pleasure Domes, Ltd. For training purposes only. Not for sale or public distribution. Violators will be prosecuted.*

Well, that verified the rumors about Lani's previous occupation. Goddess above! This was a training video for professional courtesans. Arion let out a grunt of disgust, but he released the frame. Next came Lani, adorned with blue feathers twined in her hair and her usual loincloth—obviously this HV had been altered or adapted after she mated with Gunnar. That theory was confirmed when Lani began to speak in her grating, high-pitched voice.

"Hello!" she trilled. "If you've gotten this far, then you're probably a Leor. You're most certainly a seeker. A seeker on the path to true sexuality and sexual pleasure, both for you and your mate, or—if you're ready to challenge a highly archaic and outmoded system—your lover. You have come to the right place for information about sex. I can promise that after you view every section of this holo, you will know how to properly woo and romance your mate or partner, and how to make love with such expertise, he or she will keep dragging you back to bed for more."

Gritting his teeth, Arion resisted the urge to beat his head against the screen.

"Now, then," Lani continued. "This holo has been revised with the special mating needs of Leors in mind. So before you begin, read over the contents frame, and you can pick which specific topic you wish to review." She smiled brightly, her blue lips garish against her white teeth. "And don't forget to practice, practice, practice! You'll find it very *uplifting* and highly rewarding!"

Arion had never been sick a cycle in his life, but now he felt nauseous. He experienced the intense urge to yank out the disc and smash it into microscopic pieces. But he glanced at Jenna sleeping so soundly, and was reminded of his purpose. He was a warrior. He could endure—barely.

He moved on to the contents frame, surprised at how much information was on the disc. The topics included: *Sex Basics, Intermediate Lovemaking, Advanced Positions, Variations, Leor Anatomy, Human Anatomy, Aliens*—

Slimy, *Aliens—Non-Slimy*, *Kissing Techniques*, and quite a few more.

While Arion was primarily interested in the anatomy information, he found himself drawn to the section on kissing. He had enjoyed the small amount he had experienced, and he knew Shielders put great importance on it. So he chose that topic. Lani appeared on the screen and cooed, "So you want to learn to kiss. Good for you. Let me begin by saying that it is positively *criminal* that Leors do not incorporate kissing in their standard sexual practices. The Leor tongue is far more sensitive and sensual than a human tongue, can feel and taste and smell far more acutely. Kissing is very stimulating for humans; for Leors, it is even more arousing. Let's start by discussing . . ."

Arion grimaced. Too much information. Not only that, but watching Lani, all he could think about was her and Gunnar together, and that did not bear consideration. He had already discovered it was highly arousing to run his tongue along his mate's silky skin and soft lips. That was sufficient. He exited the section on kissing and went to human anatomy.

He watched this section all the way through. When he reached the end, he was satisfied that humans and Leors were biologically close enough to mate without problems. He had also gleaned some knowledge that should be helpful in ensuring the mating went successfully. He exited the disc without watching anything else. He did not want information overload clouding something that should be natural and basic.

Males and females had been mating since the beginning of the universe, and without a holovideo for reference. At this point, if there was something he did not know, he was confident that instinct and the blazing chemistry between him and Jenna, along with the blessing of the Goddess, would be more than sufficient to guide them through the process.

Which would be soon. Very soon.

Chapter Eleven

Arion had been right about Leor children, Jenna thought, chasing after one especially determined baby and peeling him from the wall for the third time in a few minutes. They were balls of energy. Even the infants, to whom she was assigned, crawled and walked much sooner than humans, and were very strong. And they climbed amazingly well. Their fingers and toes had special pads that enabled them to scale straight up the walls. She now knew the roughness on Arion's fingertips was more than the calluses she had first believed.

The floors of the nursery were padded to cushion any small Leor who lost his or her grip and tumbled from the walls. Even so, Jenna tried to pluck them off before they got out of her reach and attempted to navigate the steep slope of the dome. Under those conditions, even special pads couldn't withstand the demands of gravity. But it didn't seem to upset the little ones when they fell. Oh, they roared out their displeasure in powerful voices, but she quickly learned it was more from frustration than physical discomfort.

They didn't take naps, and they were on the go constantly. They spent about half their time outside, in a walled compound that had a special, thick sod that cushioned their falls. There they practiced numerous drills orchestrated by the head of the nursery, along with the assistance of some of the servers. The infants didn't seem to mind the regimentation in the least; in fact, they seemed to thrive on it. They had all sorts of equipment for climbing, swinging, balancing, and testing their strength. They wore special little helmets, which she assumed were to protect their heads. They tried to lick *everything,* probably because of the sensory receptors in their tongues.

Keeping up with them was a challenge, but Jenna loved every moment of it. Even though they acted like wild little keranis, the babies responded to voice and to touch. They allowed her to hold them—briefly—and they hugged her back . . . before they would squirm from her arms and take off again. They explored their environment with an intense, serious manner. Their occasional smiles were totally unaffected, and like bursts of sunlight.

The children apparently had very high metabolisms and ate frequently. They drank milk, but their main diet was meat, processed into a cereal-like consistency. Since they already had most of their teeth, they didn't have any trouble ingesting it.

The head of the nursery was an older Leor male named Kerem. As with the kitchens, he was the only Leor staffing the nursery, with servers doing the brunt of the work. Having asked Arion, Jenna now knew that virtually all young and able-bodied Leors did military duty, leaving the older Leors to do the supervisory jobs. A lot of things were different on Saura, she realized. She received another surprise when she realized that some of the servers in the nursery could talk. Their vocal cords had not been severed.

During a lull when the children were eating, shoveling their meat mixture into their mouths, either with the assistance of the servers or their own quick hands, she took a break and sat down with Kerem. She ate a piece of fruit, while he downed a large serving of meat and bread. "May I ask you a few questions?" she ventured after a few moments of silence.

He grunted, which she assumed was assent, so she asked, "Why are the children wearing helmets?"

"We have a special sensory receptor in our heads, similar to those in our tongues. The skull over that area does not close and harden completely until four spans of age."

She filed that information away for future research, then gestured toward the tables. "Are these all the children on Saura?" She had been surprised to see only fifty or so infants and toddlers in the nursery.

"These are all the offspring through their third span," Kerem replied. "Those through their sixth span are in another dome."

"Surely there are many more of those children?"

He popped a large chunk of meat in his mouth, chewed for a moment. "About the same number."

Jenna found that baffling. It was her understanding that the Leor population was shrinking, and they were trying to increase their numbers. "Lord Arion told me there are over six hundred mated couples on Saura. Surely there should be more children."

"Our females' fertile period is short," Kerem said bluntly. "And many offspring are born dead or die quickly."

No wonder the Leors were seeking human brides, especially if those females were able to produce viable babies! Jenna mulled this over, asked her next question. "Why do the servers in the nursery still have their voices?"

"They are from a group whose vocal cords were not severed," came the laconic reply. "So those servers can work in the nursery. The offspring can hear voices to emulate, and the servers can warn of problems." He pointed to the band on his beefy wrist. "Can call for assistance if need be."

Earlier that cycle, Arion had given Jenna a comm unit to wear on her wrist, in case she had any problems. He always wore one; even his ceremonial armbands had a comm embedded within one of them. She saw now that the servers also wore them. So the Leors didn't destroy the vocal cords on all their slaves; just the ones who didn't need to communicate. Somehow that selectivity made the custom seem even more barbaric. She steered herself away from that avenue of thought.

"Where are the children over six?" she asked, remembering Kerem's comment about the other dome.

"Most of them have been sent to training communes. To learn advanced battle skills."

"To communes? Where?"

"Usually Dukkair."

The breath froze in Jenna's chest. *Leor children were taken from their parents at age six? Sent away?* No. She couldn't imagine giving up her child, watching him or her go away at such a young, vulnerable age, to learn how to fight . . . and how to kill. Granted, Shielder children learned how to use weapons at a very early age, but mainly for self-defense and survival, not to wage warfare. And they continued to live with their parents—as long as they had them.

Sharp pain swept through her, partly grief for her parents, a grief that was never far from the surface, even after fourteen seasons; and partly the anguish of realizing that everything she had hoped to gain by coming to Saura with Arion had been negated by the barbarous traditions of the Leors.

It appeared that even the promise of children, something she badly wanted, was tainted by the fact that they would be taken from her. And she seriously doubted she'd ever be accepted by the Leor people. She was every bit as alone as she had been in Shamara, and possibly worse off.

Leaving Kerem, she returned to the children. The earlier joy she'd experienced at being with the infants had dissipated; not even the toothy grins or crushing hugs, or the musty smell of faintly patterned skin could lift her spirits. She continued fulfilling her duties, all the while wondering how she could bring children into the world only to see them shipped off to a training camp at the age of six. She didn't think she could do it. The cycle passed in a numbing blur.

Some time later, she was sitting outside, watching the infants demonstrate amazing climbing and acrobatic abilities, when she heard her name. *Jenna?* came Arion's voice, inside her head. *Jenna, can you hear me? I tried to contact you on the comm, but you did not reply.*

She'd heard a faint beeping, but hadn't realized it was from the band on her wrist. Hesitantly, reluctantly, she attempted a reply, directing her thoughts toward him. *I'm here. I guess I don't know how to use a comm properly.*

I will show you this evening. How is the situation in the nursery?

It was an eerie sensation to hear him in her mind. It was strangely intimate, every bit as unsettling as standing beneath an air dryer with his intense perusal sweeping her nude body. It probably bothered her more because of her internal turmoil, and since she was a solitary person she retreated when she was upset. Right now, she wanted badly to close her mind to Arion.

Jenna? What is wrong?

She was no longer alone, and although it seemed her prayers for companionship had been answered, she wasn't sure she liked the answer. But she couldn't change it now. *Nothing's wrong. I like the nursery. Kerem has treated me well.*

I think you have been there long enough this cycle. The past cycles have been draining for you, and I want you to

165

get sufficient rest. I will send an escort to take you to our dome.

She didn't want to return to the dome, to Amyan's mute presence, or to be alone with her fears. She wanted the company of someone who came from her world, or at least a world that was similar. And she wanted information, answers to her questions. *I would really like to visit Maxine before I go to the dome.*

You mean the android. There was a pause. *You consider it a friend.* He said that every time Jenna mentioned Maxine, his tone one of bafflement. It was difficult for him to understand Jenna's attachment.

Yes, I do. I want to see her. Please.

Very well. She is at the research laboratory. I will tell Kerem to get a server to drive you there. When you are ready to leave the lab, let me know, and I will send someone to take you to our dome.

She felt his energy receding, knew the conversation had ended. The telepathic contact between them left her feeling uncomfortable—not violated really, but with the sense she no longer had any privacy, not even the sanctuary of her own thoughts.

Arion contacted Kerem on his comm, and the older man gestured one of the male servers over and ordered him to take Jenna to the research lab. The skimmer ride there was quick and silent. The lab was a long, low building, made from the same textured clay used for most of the structures on Saura, except it was white instead of sand-colored. Jenna thanked the server and entered the lab.

She stepped into a foyer. To her left was a regular entry panel. Straight ahead lay double clear plexishield panels, and beyond them was a long corridor. The entire wall running along the right side of the corridor was plexishield, revealing a row of chambers, although she couldn't see inside them from here.

She heard a low hum and saw the red beam of light

flash up her body and into her eyes. "Greetings, Jenna, mate of Arion," came a stilted, unisex computer voice. "State the purpose of your visit."

"I want to see Maxine, the android."

"The android is currently in a nonsterile section of the lab. I will notify her of your presence." There were more beeps and hums; then the computer said, "You are granted access to the complex. However, much of the laboratory is a sterile field, so first you will enter the chamber on your immediate left for decontamination."

Amazing, thought Jenna, standing in the enclosed chamber, with the heat of the decontamination rays enveloping her. Going from the basic Leor lifestyle to the ultrasophisticated technology of the lab was just another reminder of how little she understood the Leor culture. The rays shut off, and the doors slid open.

"Decontamination is completed. You may now enter the laboratory area. You will locate the android Maxine in the specimen collection unit, which is the second panel on the left," the computer informed her.

The clear panels leading into the corridor opened, and Jenna started down it. The first thing she noticed was the temperature, significantly cooler than outside or in any Sauran structure she had entered. It felt wonderful. She looked along the plexishield wall to her right, and saw there were quite a few chambers running along its other side, separated by more plexishield.

Each chamber contained various pieces of equipment, and both Leors and servers were working within the chambers. They were all clad in white jumpsuits and wore gloves and masks. Jenna was somewhat surprised to see Leors working here, but thought of Lanka, and figured not all the younger Leors went into military endeavors.

Still staring at the equipment and the bustle of people within each unit, Jenna walked to the second panel on her left, and it opened for her. She entered, stopping when she saw five brawny Leor males, standing awkwardly in what appeared to be a line. They shifted uncomfortably when they saw her, and each of them nodded stiffly. Maxine was nowhere in sight.

A counter ran along the left wall of the chamber, with a sink at one end and an upright cold store at the other end. In between was an array of unfamiliar equipment. Then there was a panel in the wall straight ahead, and she noticed all five Leors had returned their attention to that panel, watching it with what could only be termed trepidation. That couldn't be right. There was very little that could shake up a Leor.

The panel opened and Maxine sauntered out, straightening her white jumpsuit and smoothing her hair, which appeared to be mussed. She was followed by a young male holding a small container. He was flushed, an oddity for a Leor, especially in this cool environment. Maxine patted his shoulder; then her hand slid down and rested on his impressive biceps. "Thank you, Jael," she practically cooed. "You did very well. Put your container in the cold store, and then you are free to go."

Jael's chest puffed out and he hitched up his loincloth and strode to the cold store. He paused by Maxine on his way out. "Let me know if you need any more samples," he said gruffly. "I know the research is of great importance."

"Oh, it is, Jael," Maxine assured him. "Thank you for your full cooperation."

Jael practically strutted from the chamber. "Jenna," Maxine called, striding toward her. "I am glad you came for a visit." She turned and flashed an appreciative look at the group of waiting males. "If you men do not mind, we will stop for the cycle. Report back at eight hundred hours. I will clear your absence from your duties with the Comdar."

They all grunted in unison and quickly made a group

exodus that reminded Jenna of a stampeding herd of tri-horned bulls. Maxine stared after them, a smile on her face. "What exceptional male specimens." She turned to Jenna. "It is good to see you."

"It's good to see you, too." Jenna couldn't contain her curiosity. "What were you doing when I got here?"

"Collecting semen." Maxine smoothed her jumpsuit again. "I randomly selected a group of males in the prime age range for fertility and virility from the Sauran data-base, and asked Commander Arion to send them here so I could get samples. I plan to analyze the semen for sperm count and motility. The mated males do not have much trouble providing samples, as they have more experience in the procedure. But the unmated ones . . ." Her eyebrows arched suggestively. "Seem to need a little help. Lani is working on a holovideo to demonstrate the proper way to procure a sample, but until it arrives I must provide assistance." Her smile widened, twisted sideways. "The process is very 'hands on,' you might say."

"By the Spirit!" Jenna started laughing. "Oh, I wish I could see that." She paused, thought. "I mean that figuratively. But I can just imagine the reaction of these big, macho males when you hand them a container and tell them what you want."

"It is quite an experience," Maxine said smugly. "I would say the collection aspect has been the highlight of my work thus far."

Jenna couldn't help herself—she laughed again, and felt as though a weight had lifted from her chest. "Oh, Maxine, it really is good to see you."

The android preened. "I know." She gestured toward a small table and two chairs against the exterior wall. "Sit down, and we will talk. I have some homa in the cold store, if you would like some. I keep it on hand because some of these males get *light-headed,* so to speak, after providing their specimens." She looked very proud of her humor, and Jenna smiled again.

"I would love some homa." She took one of the chairs. "And please don't warm it."

"The heat still bothers you?" Maxine guessed, pouring the thick liquid into a tumbler.

"I'm a little more used to it, but I don't like it. Does it bother you?"

"I can easily adjust my temperature." Maxine handed the cup to Jenna, then sat down.

"Stupid question. I wasn't thinking. You seem so human to me."

"I was intended to appear human." The android leaned forward. "Now you must tell me everything that has happened since the merging ceremony. I tried to contact you, but the computer blocked me."

"You couldn't reach me?" Jenna felt a jab of disappointment. Arion knew how important Maxine was to her, so why had he kept the android away?

"The main computer would not grant me access to the Comdar's personal computer," Maxine explained. "That is probably standard operating procedure to protect his privacy. But I see you have a comm unit now. Give it to me and I will program it so you can easily contact me." She took Jenna's band and deftly punched in a sequence. "There. All you need do is press the preprogrammed pad number one. You can contact me at any time."

"Thank you." Jenna slipped the comm back on, feeling better knowing that Maxine was only a pad push away.

"Now, then, tell me all that has happened. I especially want to know how the horizontal docking procedure went."

"Actually, we haven't . . . done it yet."

"No?" Maxine tilted her head. "That is odd. Why not?"

"Arion gave me more time to get used to things, and I guess, to him." Jenna felt a curious warming inside her.

Arion could have forced the issue. She had been intoxi-cated and determined to fulfill her end of the bargain, and would have seen it through had he insisted. Instead, he had given her time.

"That is very interesting. I wonder if he sensed your nervousness and thought you would be more receptive dur-ing the full moon alignment. You are aware the union must be consummated by then? And that it is exactly four Sauran cycles, two hours, twenty-one minutes, and 38.2 seconds from now?"

"I am very aware of the mating requirement." Jenna's heart did a little skip, started beating faster. "Why do the Leors keep such rigid timetables? I think the mating act should occur when people are ready, not when the moon is full. You can't command passion or emotions by the calendar."

"They believe that they are most fertile when the moons are full and in conjunction. They also believe their pas-sions are at a peak during that time. It is a part of their law, and adherence to their laws is of major importance to them. If the union is not consummated by the full align-ment, then it is null."

"How can that be?" Jenna demanded. "I can't imagine how the merging ceremony could be undone, or how the telepathic link between the mates could be severed."

"You have a valid point. Tell me about the telepathic link. I was unable to find any information on the merging ceremony. Leors do not talk about it outside of their clans."

"They don't talk about it *inside* their clans, either. I didn't know anything until I was suddenly linked to Arion." Jenna filled Maxine in on seeing the sacrificed boar through his eyes. She also told the android about her day in the kitchens, and how Arion had reassigned her to the nursery.

They discussed the amazing traits that the infants could

manifest from a very early age, but Maxine already knew that information, having drawn on her extensive data banks. "Tell me something else then," Jenna said. "How is it that the Leors have this advanced technology, especially in their ships and with their weapons, but they live in such primitive conditions?"

"It is all related to their religion and their worship of their Goddess," Maxine explained. "They are not opposed to technology, and they are very aggressive in developing it for their ground and ship weapon systems, and for space travel. They are also very advanced in medicine and science, as you can see by this laboratory.

"Yet as physical and combative as the Leors are," she continued, "they are also highly spiritual. They believe that living in a simple manner keeps them closer to the land, and in closer attunement to their Goddess. They want their focus to be on how they live their lives, and not material possessions. They are also very practical. Since they do better in a hot climate, they reside in desert areas. The domes they build are very well suited to that climate, and structurally very strong. Considering how many beings cheat and kill for material wealth, I must commend them on this aspect of their culture."

When put that way, Jenna had to admit it seemed admirable. Yet the Leor devotion to their Goddess had not curtailed their fierceness toward their enemies, if the stories were true, or the fact they kept slaves whose vocal cords they severed. They seemed a dichotomy of good and evil.

A sudden, odd feeling of regret shot through her, followed by an unpleasant foreboding. Jenna set the homa down, looked around the chamber. Nothing there. She swung her gaze to Maxine, focused on the android's calm face. A rhythmic thumping sound started inside her head. Startled, she realized it was a slow, steady heartbeat.

"Jenna? Are you all right?" Maxine's voice sounded distant. The chamber faded, receded . . .

A Leor male stood in the middle of a high, open structure. He was tall and powerful, even with shackles on his wrists, and the oddly glowing magnasteel band around his bare head. His ebony eyes showed no emotion, but his rigid stance and tensed muscles gave evidence to his state of mind. The heart was still beating, relentless, pulsing, inside Jenna's head. Not her heart, but that of another.

She stirred, resisted, saw a momentary flash of the lab chamber and Maxine's golden eyes, before they faded again. The shackled man was still there. The heartbeat was still inside her mind, but somehow she knew it wasn't his. It felt strangely familiar.

"Clavon of Saura, have you anything to say to these charges?" came Arion's voice, clear and calm.

The shackled Leor clenched his hands into fists. "It was an accident. I regret the suffering I have brought upon the family of Raiden."

The visual changed from the accused to a sweep of the surrounding structure, very similar to that of the arena, only smaller, and round rather than oval. Seats circled the perimeter, rising upward toward the orange sky. Leors occupied about half.

"All here have heard the testimony of the witnesses," Arion said, his voice as terrifyingly clear in Jenna's mind as if they were talking face-to-face. "Clavon has freely admitted he drank too much kashni three cycles past, then fought with Raiden, who later died as a result of the injuries inflicted by Clavon. Does anyone wish to come forward to dispute these facts?"

A murmur ran through the assembled Leors, a low rumbling that grew and swelled. A chorus of "nays": none in disagreement with the stated facts. Another visual sweep of the stands, one last chance for another consideration. The heart beating, never changing its cadence. Regret, re-

solve, finality, weighing upon that steady heart.

"Then, in accordance with our laws, I sentence you, Clavon of Saura, to death—"

"No!" Galvanized to action by his shocking pronouncement, Jenna jolted back from the table, shoving so hard that her chair went over backward. She hardly felt the jarring of her head, as the relentless hold of the vision sucked her back to the horrifying scene, like debris into a black hole. "No!"

She felt Arion's pause, sensed his awareness of her, as well as his resolve to continue. "You are sentenced to death, at the hands of Raiden's family, in the manner of their choosing."

Clavon lowered his head and his big body trembled. Oh, Spirit, she couldn't handle this.

"Tomorrow, at the setting of the first sun, your sentence will be carried out. You may have the time remaining to give your farewells to your family and to prepare yourself. The shaman will be available to assist in the final saktar, should you wish his presence."

The prisoner held himself still, didn't respond, didn't protest, an aura of acceptance and utter sorrow radiating from him. He had a family, a mate and two sons, one of them an infant in Jenna's nursery. That thought came to her, surely from Arion. She didn't want to know any more. Spirit, no. I want out of this. Now, she prayed frantically.

She must have unintentionally projected to Arion, because he responded. *I am sorry you had to witness this. I do not know how to end your vision. I must remain until the final details of this situation are settled. I will try to block as much of it as possible.*

How could you sentence that poor man to death? She knew she was overstepping her bounds, but she couldn't stop herself. She kept seeing Clavon, the dejected slump of his shoulders. *He said it was an accident. He has a family, for Spirit's sake.*

Jenna, I will not discuss this with you now. Are you still at the laboratory? I will come for you when I am done here.

No. I don't want you anywhere near me. You're a barbarian.

I will not argue with you about this. I will be there soon. She felt his withdrawal, realized he had successfully broken the link, and the vision mercifully faded away.

"Jenna, are you all right?" Maxine crouched next to her, easily lifting both her and the chair upright. "What happened?"

"Another vision," Jenna said wearily. She felt inundated with pain, from her throbbing head to the heaviness in her chest. She winced when Maxine probed the back of her head.

"When you fell, you hit the edge of this cable housing, which should have been run beneath the floor, instead of where it was." Maxine got a square of gauze and pressed it to Jenna's scalp. "There is a fair amount of bleeding. I believe you will need sutures."

She needed a lot more than that, Jenna thought, panic thrumming through her. She needed to get away from this nightmare, and from a mate who was more beast than man.

But there wasn't anyplace to go, or anywhere to hide.

Chapter Twelve

Jenna had been through this discussion with herself every cycle since she'd arrived on Saura, and she was going to have it again. She had put herself in this situation. She had agreed to come here. Not only that, but it was the will of Spirit, as evidenced by the vision of four seasons ago. Jenna had given her word to become Arion's mate and bear his children, and to honor the Leor laws. She'd had no idea what those laws entailed, or that the Leors were so primitive and cruel, but the fact remained that she had agreed.

Even if her children would be sent away when they were six seasons old—which she would fight with every breath in her body. Even if Leors executed people, and for something that was an accident. Even if they kept slaves and removed their vocal cords so they were forever mute, or slashed the throats of innocent animals to appease their Goddess.

She had to stop doing this to herself. She must pull herself up and go on. Nothing she could say or do would change the Leor ways. And nothing, short of rescinding her word and shaming both herself and her people, would alter her circumstances. Besides, what sort of life would she have had if she'd remained in Shamara? She mentally surrendered to the inevitable, but it didn't ease the terrible anguish she felt inside.

"It is almost done," Maxine said from somewhere above.

Jenna's head throbbed painfully, despite the numbing agent the suturing unit was injecting as it hummed over her scalp, closing the gash. Her increasing light-headedness and a slight floating sensation made her suspect she was getting a narcotic as well.

It was a good thing Maxine had accompanied her to the medical unit, or Lanka would likely have sutured her wound manually, without any benefit of deadening or pain-killing drugs. She would probably have shaved Jenna's entire head, too, instead of the small patch required for the stitches. Maxine had been insistent on being present for the procedure, and a terse conversation with Arion via comm unit had verified his consent.

"How are you feeling?" Maxine asked.

"I'm all right." Jenna gave in to the lure of the narcotic, let herself drift. "I do seem to have ongoing problems with my head, though." She thought about that a moment, maybe several moments—she couldn't be sure. "You know, I've had a headache every cycle since I've been here. The first two cycles, it was from sleep stasis. The one the next cycle was from the saktar—"

"You did not undergo saktar, human," Lanka interjected disdainfully. "You could not have survived it."

"Did so," Jenna muttered. "Not that I wanted to. Morven burned some leaves in that metal thing in the middle of his dome and put me into some sort of trance. It gave me an awful headache." She ignored Lanka's derisive snort and tried to refocus her train of thought. "Where was I? Oh, yes, my head. Then the merging ceremony made the saktar headache worse. Then, the next two cycles—"

"Were due to overindulgence in kashni. Entirely her own doing." Arion's voice startled her, and she jumped.

So did the suture unit, and a sharp pain stabbed through her head, wrenching a moan from her. "Be still!" Lanka ordered, grasping Jenna's shoulder and pressing her back down on the table none too gently.

"She did undergo saktar," Arion said, his voice much closer. Jenna was facedown on a special table with a breathing space for her face, so she couldn't see him. But she could sense him, the force of his presence, near her head. "Morven said she was worthy of the Goddess."

"I am not surprised," Maxine said. Lanka just grunted.

Jenna no longer felt so relaxed with Arion there. She wasn't ready to face him yet, to deal with what he'd done today. "What damage has she suffered?" he asked.

"A cut approximately five centimeters in length," Lanka replied. "It will take at least thirty sutures to close."

She felt him lean closer. "Jenna, how did this happen?"

"I was talking with Maxine in the lab, when . . . when my chair fell backward and I hit my head." She fervently hoped he wouldn't connect the accident to her linking with him, at least not here. She didn't want to discuss her visions in front of Lanka.

"I see." There was a pause. "Lanka, what is the prognosis?" His voice seemed to be moving away.

"She will be fine. There are no signs of concussion, but she will probably have head pain for another cycle or so. I will provide something for the discomfort."

"See that you do. I do not want her suffering needlessly. I have some communications coming in. I will be back soon."

Lanka must have given her more narcotic then, because Jenna found herself drifting again. Gratefully, she allowed herself to forget for a little while. That ended all too soon, when Arion returned for her. The suture unit had been removed, and along with it the continuous flow of oblivion. She felt a little woozy, but she was fairly clear-headed and able to sit in a chair. Lanka had gone to attend other patients, and Maxine returned to the lab as soon as Arion appeared, leaving Jenna alone with him.

He squatted next to her, his dark gaze probing. This man was her mate—and judge, jury, and executioner for his people. She refused to think about that. "I have a skimmer outside," he said. "Can you walk?"

"I think so. I might even be able to float, if there's still enough pain meds in my system."

He didn't smile at her weak attempt at humor, but then he never smiled. His gaze remained on her, serious and brooding, but if he wanted to say anything, he held his words. He rose and offered his hand, and for the second cycle in a row, supported her as they walked to the skimmer. It occurred to her that living on Saura was definitely perilous to her well-being.

She wondered if she would even survive until she and Arion actually mated. Surely her inane musings were the result of the drugs; yet beneath the narcotic-induced haze lay enough negative events to lend her fears credibility. She could tell she would have to give herself "the talk" again, when she was more coherent and rational.

They made the trip to Arion's dome in silence. Jenna escaped immediately to the bathing chamber, ignoring his disapproval and assuring him she was steady enough to function on her own. She took off her bloodstained clothing, the second set she'd ruined in as many cycles, and stuffed them into the refuse bin. Then she took a bath, careful to keep her sutures dry, per Lanka's brief instructions. She tried to keep her thoughts focused on the children in the nursery, rather than the other horrendous events of the cycle. She'd deal with them at another time, when her head wasn't throbbing so fiercely or her spirit so wounded.

When she came out of the bathing chamber, she saw that Amyan had brought their evening meal to the dome again. Arion was waiting on her, polishing his ceremonial gold cuffs. He would probably wear them for the execution tomorrow. She locked that away with all the other disturbing thoughts, sinking onto the far end of the settee and reaching for her homa. Arion set the cuffs aside, took his plate heaped with meat and bread.

They ate in silence, the tension coiled between them like an Oderian viper preparing to strike. She found she could only manage a few bites of fruit and a few sips of homa. Arion didn't seem to have any problem with his food, and readily devoured everything on his plate. Apparently, condemning a man to die didn't mar his appetite.

Jenna stopped herself. On one level, she knew she wasn't being completely fair. Shielders had put people to death—innocent people, whose only crime was that they were too sick or too old to work. But that had been under dire circumstances, when there wasn't enough food or medicine for the able-bodied, and they were fighting for the survival of an entire race. And it had been euthanasia rather than execution, a peaceful painless ending of life.

She wasn't sure she was qualified to judge, given the history of her people. But that didn't make the Leor practices right, or any less horrifying.

Arion finally broke the silence. "How did you like working in the nursery?"

So they would be civil, act as if everything were normal, at least as normal as life could be among Leors. "I liked it very much," she replied quietly. "I want to keep working there."

"Kerem said that you worked hard, that the infants bonded with you."

"I enjoyed being with them."

"We need to talk about what happened today," he said, ending the pretense.

Jenna's breath caught in her chest. "Will it change anything?"

"No. But ignoring the issue will not make it go away. It will only come up again."

She was sure he was right, but she wasn't ready to talk. "I can't discuss this right now, and maybe never." She rose, clenching her hands by her side. "We're too different. I don't think we can ever agree on things like this." She turned away from him. "I need some rest."

She started for the sleeping chamber, but he moved with his peculiar grace and speed, standing and trapping her wrist in his large hand. He could crush her bones with one powerful squeeze, but he merely exerted enough pressure to keep her immobile. His other hand grasped her chin, forcing her to look at him.

"You agreed to abide by our laws before you came here. You are struggling needlessly against things you cannot change." He stared at her intently a long moment; then his hand slid up, rested lightly over her sutures. "I do not want you suffering any more injuries."

So he had connected her chair falling with her linking to him during the trial, if it could be called that. She could never accuse him of lacking in intelligence or astuteness. Compassion and mercy were another matter entirely.

"What I suffered today is nothing, especially compared to what Clavon and his family are facing right now," she told him. "Your laws are barbaric. So are you."

His grip on her wrist tightened. "I may be the savage you claim. But that changes nothing between us. We *will* mate in four cycles."

It always came back to that. Her ultimate challenge was not only accepting the fact she had agreed to be a breeding machine for this man, but to disconnect her emotions from the process. The sooner she did that, the better off she'd be.

"I'm sure we will, Comdar," she replied, deliberately

using his title to maintain the emotional distance between them. "But let me tell you this: You may possess my body, but you will never own my heart."

Something flickered in the black expanse of his eyes, but his expression remained frozen. Without another word, he released her. Feeling oddly bereft, she fled to the relative safety of the sleeping chamber. Huddled on her side of the massive bed, she tried to shut off her thoughts.

She was able to block most of the trial, but she couldn't forget what she had said to Arion. She'd accused him of being a monster, claimed she'd never have any feelings for him, and he hadn't even reacted. Maybe he wasn't capable of feeling.

Yet saying those things left *her* feeling empty and dispirited. And more alone than ever.

The next morning found her back in the nursery. While the babies were whirlwinds of activity, demanding her constant attention, she couldn't stop thinking about the drama that would be playing out later in the cycle, when the first sun set, and a man's life was taken from him. She wondered if Clavon was with his family now, if he was holding his young sons tightly one last time, and telling his mate he loved her. Jenna didn't even know if Leors expressed such emotions, but she knew there was genuine affection between mated Leors, having witnessed it on several occasions. How hard it would be to leave children and a mate, to face death, in the prime of life! A great sadness weighed on her heart.

Resolutely, she forced herself to pay attention to her duties, trying to keep her focus on the infants, who represented the future and life, not death. Yet the morning dragged by with an aura of despair. Nothing could negate the reality of what was about to happen.

At one point, she stepped outside and saw the red sun had begun its descent over the horizon. Then she saw groups of Leors jogging toward the distant tribunal, which was the circular structure she'd seen in her vision yesterday. Kerem had explained that the tribunal was .where all judgments were passed down, and all punishments meted out, in a public forum. Jenna wondered if such an event was considered sport or entertainment, and prayed that wasn't the case. Sickened, she returned to the nursery.

About an hour later, she saw Leors returning en masse from the tribunal. It was over. Clavon was dead.

And she felt as if a part of her had also died.

Arion came for her later in the cycle, when glare of the sunlight had become muted, about an hour before the evening meal. She sensed his presence, even before she heard him greet Kerem and heard the older Leor's respectful reply. Balancing a fussy infant on her hip, Jenna turned and faced her mate. He seemed to take up the entire chamber, towering over the infants rapidly racing toward this new diversion. He was wearing his shimmering gold loincloth, with the gold ceremonial bands on his forearms. She didn't need to be told why he was dressed the way he was. Apparently, he wore the same ceremonial clothing to executions that he wore to his own merging ceremony.

His inscrutable gaze fixed on her, and he said a few brief words to Kerem, then strode toward her, carefully maneuvering around small bodies. Priman, the baby in her arms who had been howling ever since he'd been brought back inside, found a lock of her hair that had come loose and busied himself chewing voraciously on it.

She watched Arion approach, his powerful muscles bunching beneath an impressive expanse of golden skin. He was so assured, so masculine, he took her breath away. He affected her on a level so basic, so primal, it almost negated his actions, almost negated the fact he was a barbarian. She was aware she was a mess, with her hair falling down, and stains on her sweat-dampened tunic. Despite her differences with this man, a startling feminine side of her was dismayed he always managed to see her at her worst.

He halted before her, his gaze sweeping over her, taking in the baby chewing on her hair. "That young warrior must not be getting enough to eat."

"All the babies like my hair," she said, trying to retrieve said hair from Priman without losing any fingers in the process.

"Here. Let me." Arion reached out, his fingers cupping the infant's cheek and sliding between Priman's mouth and Jenna's hair, neatly extricating it. Priman burst into a new storm of fussing. Arion leaned down to eye level with the infant. "Hush, young warrior. You must not protest over something so trivial as not always getting your way."

This from the most domineering male she'd ever met? Jenna rolled her eyes, ignoring the stern look Arion shot her. He returned his attention to the squirming baby. "You are strong, little one. I will be proud to see you taking your place on Saura some spans from now."

Priman stopped crying, appearing totally entranced with this male watching him, and with the deep voice. He even offered a toothy grin. Arion seemed taken aback. "He smiled at me."

"They do that sometimes," Jenna retorted. "They don't know yet that Leors don't believe in smiling."

Arion shot her another look, then turned toward a nearby server and gestured to Priman. "Take this young warrior and find him something to eat." The server bobbed her head and came over, reaching for Priman. The child went to her and was happily stuffing her blond hair into his mouth as she carried him away.

Arion turned back to Jenna. "You are through here for this cycle. Come."

She might have objected at his high-handedness, but she was exhausted, both from the rigorous challenge of working in the nursery all cycle, and the emotional drain of the execution. She would save her protests for more important issues, and for a time when she had the strength to argue. So she followed as he led the way to a side entry that faced a skimmer lane.

Surprised, she climbed into the waiting skimmer and watched Arion stride to the other side. Their dome wasn't that far, and she had expected they would resume walking. Again, too tired to question his actions, she leaned back in the seat. He steered away from the nursery, but instead of heading for their dome, he nosed the skimmer toward the open desert.

"Where are we going?"

"Into the desert."

Well, anyone could see *that*. But, in typical Leor fashion, he didn't explain further, so she contented herself with watching the color-streaked horizon. The second sun, a large orange orb, had dropped low in the sky, scattering rays of light and creating stunning swirls of rose and orange and gold. The diffused light haloed the tall, majestic mesas, giving them the appearance of giant solar lanterns. The air rushing against Jenna's face as the skimmer accelerated was no longer hot; merely warm, with a hint of coolness that the night over the desert would bring.

If there were anything to be said for life among Leors, the wild desert scenery and the breathtaking sunsets would definitely be on the list. The untamed beauty even helped ease the pain of today's events. They reached, then skirted, the first group of mesas, barreling farther into the wilderness, and leaving the Goddess and her shrine far behind.

Jenna turned her head and stared at Arion. He remained silent, his tense body indicating he was anything but relaxed. She wondered if racing across Saura's open plains was one of the ways he dealt with tension. She didn't want to harbor such strong negative feelings about him, yet she couldn't forget the ruthlessness of his decision yesterday.

Who was the real Arion? Her sworn mate, a man who

had treated her cut hands, and dried her off so gently, and who showed her a surprising measure of respect; or the fierce, indifferent warrior who owned a slave with severed vocal cords and ordered executions?

She knew that somehow she'd have to come to terms with this man, and with their relationship. She had committed the rest of her life to him, and she couldn't change that fact. She looked back out at the desert. They rode on in silence, reaching a second grouping of mesas, this one wider and higher than the first. He appeared to be heading straight toward the towering monoliths, with no sign of slowing or turning.

"What are you doing?" she asked, watching in horrified fascination as the stone walls loomed straight ahead.

He glanced at her. "Is your harness secure?"

She tugged on the straps. "Yes, it is, but— Oh, Spirit!" The sudden incline and ascension of the skimmer flattened her against the seat and halted further words. Her chest felt as if a rocket coil had dropped on it, and she managed only a frightened squeal as they flew straight up the face of a mesa.

Unable to watch, Jenna closed her eyes and gripped the sides of her seat, the vehicle's swift velocity evident from the force of the air against her face. Then they were slowing and leveling out, and finally, coming to rest. She heard the engines cut off.

"You can open your eyes now."

Reluctantly, she did so. "Where are we?"

"On top of the mesa." He unhooked his harness and jumped from the skimmer. Striding around, he released her harness and tugged her toward him. "Come."

"If you don't mind, I think I'll just stay here."

"Little coward."

That sent a rush of fortifying anger through her. She certainly had her faults, but after her experiences on Saura, she figured she'd displayed her share of courage. Tilting her chin at him, she ignored his outstretched hand and climbed out of the skimmer on her own. She took a step away from the craft, then saw they were only about three meters from the edge of the mesa top on which they had landed. She couldn't tell for sure without getting closer to the edge to look down, but it appeared they were quite high up. She backed up quickly, slamming into Arion.

"You have a thing for heights?" she managed to gasp, partially distracted by the feel of the rock-hard body she was pressed against.

"Does this make you nervous?"

Was that laughter she heard in his voice? Arrogant Leor. "No, of course not," she lied.

"Then come." He moved around her and toward some large rock formations closer to the edge. Her heart pounding, Jenna grabbed his arm with both hands and held on tight, staying behind him and taking small steps—as if that could prevent them from going over the cliff.

He settled on a flat rock, sitting cross-legged and looking completely comfortable, despite the close proximity of a hundred-plus-meter drop. Warily, Jenna settled next to him, keeping a magnasteel grip on his arm and reminding herself to breathe.

The silence stretched out, and her heart finally settled back inside her chest. "Do you come here a lot?" she ventured.

He scanned the panorama before them. "I find the beauty of the Sauran desert soothing when I am weary or need to make peace with myself or the Goddess."

What a strange and unusual statement that was, coming from him. For the first time, Jenna considered how difficult being the leader of a Leor clan must be. She respected the strength and sense of duty Arion displayed, but she still couldn't accept the harshness of his judgment at the tribunal.

"Why?" she asked. "Why did Clavon have to die?"

He stared out at the desert a long moment. "Our laws decreed Clavon's fate. These laws are sacred to us. Without them, we would not have order. We could not have survived as we have." He turned his head, his dark gaze locking with Jenna's. "I do not create these laws, but as the Comdar, it is my duty to enforce them. Such was the case with Clavon. Sometimes it is a responsibility that weighs heavily, but it must be carried out."

"Don't you ever regret the decisions you're forced to make?"

"At times," he admitted. The sincerity in his voice, the fact he would even make such an admission, surprised her. "But I have to believe I am doing the right thing," he continued. "The welfare of all must come before that of one individual."

That's what the Shielders had faced, in their desperate bid for survival. They had euthanized their own people for the good of the whole colony. Jenna understood that laws were essential to civilization, for order and for balance. The lawlessness of the Controllers in the Dark Quadrant was proof enough of the necessity for rules and regulations, adhered to by all. As much as she hated Clavon's execution, she reluctantly accepted that it was not decreed out of anger or hatred, but out of that considered necessity to maintain the integrity of the Leor race.

She looked at her hands gripping his arm. More than just Clavon's death was weighing on her. She'd been bombarded by so many things since she'd arrived on Saura, she wondered if the barrage would ever let up. "Is it true that children over six seasons of age are separated from their parents and sent to training camps?"

"Yes. Most of our offspring are sent to the planet Dukkair when they reach six spans of age."

His confirmation sent a soul-deep pain through her. "Arion, I don't want my children taken away from me."

"Leor parents do not like being separated from their offspring, either. There has been discussion about starting a training camp on Saura."

"But what if that doesn't happen? Why would I bring a child into the world only to send him or her away?" Jenna tried to keep her voice level, but it broke as she blinked back a sudden rush of tears.

He was silent a few moments. "Do not worry about such things until they are a real possibility," he finally replied. "When the Goddess blesses us with offspring, then we will deal with the issue of any children being sent to Dukkair. For now, we have other challenges to face and overcome. Do you not agree?"

She knew he was right. If she tried to think about everything at once, she wouldn't be able to function. But she couldn't banish the marauding thoughts, or the profound sadness that suddenly shadowed her heart. She'd never been one to feel sorry for herself; nor was she one to cry. But now she felt entirely adrift, with nothing or no one to cling to.

In Shamara, she'd at least had the familiarity and safety of her world, and the friendship of Eirene and Jarek. But here on Saura, her one friend was an android, and her only other relationship was with a man who threatened her on one level, yet fiercely attracted her on another. Theirs was a tenuous bond at best, fraught with cultural differences and uncertainty.

Studying Arion's stiff, perfect posture, Jenna slipped her hand from his arm. She drew up her knees, wrapping her arms around them, and resting her chin on them. "I must seem weak to you. Maybe you were right in calling me a coward. But I'm trying to adjust, Arion. I really am."

"I am aware of that. You do not appear weak, Jenna. Nor are you a coward, except when it comes to heights."

"Oh!" She drew back, trying to decide whether or not to punch him, but he effectively circumvented any action by grabbing both her wrists. He tugged her forward, forcing her up on her knees and pulling her toward him until they were face-to-face.

"There is only one thing you must focus on," he said softly, strange lights glittering in his exotic eyes.

She watched, absolutely mesmerized, as he released one of her wrists and raised his hand to grasp her chin and hold her captive. He lowered his head and traced her lips with his tongue; then his thumb applied enough pressure on her chin that her mouth opened to him.

She jolted at the touch of his rough tongue against her smooth one, but he easily held her still for his invasion. His tongue stroked hers in a slow, thorough dance, as though he had all the time in the universe, yet there was a ruthless demand in his kiss, a primitive, masculine statement of ownership.

He drew back, and she was grateful for his tight grip on her, because she felt utterly boneless. "The full moon alignment is less than three cycles away," he said, his voice unusually harsh. "*That* is our next challenge, *charina*. *That* is what you need to be thinking about."

She stared at him, her heart pounding and her body completely alive with sensation. Whether or not he was man or beast, friend or enemy, one thing was certain: The sexual attraction between them could rival a supernova.

Jenna scooped up Mirel and carried the laughing infant girl to the sink to wash off her meat-stained hands. This was her fifth cycle in the nursery, and she had settled in and felt comfortable here, and the babies seemed to accept her. Working in the nursery was demanding and tiring, but she loved it.

It was also the seventh cycle since the merging ceremony with Arion—and the cycle of the full moon alignment.

Just thinking about the alignment set her heart to pounding. Arion had not mentioned it since they had been on the mesa, but she knew he hadn't forgotten. They had discussed very little since that night. It was as if they'd declared an unspoken truce. She'd given herself "the talk" every cycle, had tried to focus on the fact that Arion was her mate, and not think about the darker aspects of the Leor culture.

He'd been working longer hours the past two cycles, and was even quieter than usual when he did return to the dome. She sensed he was worried about something, but he didn't volunteer any information, and she didn't ask.

For the past two cycles they had been more like polite strangers than mates. They had walked to the dining hall, eaten, and walked back, all in virtual silence. She rubbed oil on his back, trying to ignore his magnificent body; then they went to bed, and she fell asleep immediately, too tired for her overactive imagination to keep her awake. With no more incidents to throw her off-kilter during the past two cycles, she had at least begun to feel rested, to feel a little bit in control.

But she knew the lull had simply been a time of waiting, and now it was over. This was the cycle they would mate. She wondered how it would come about. Would Arion return to the dome as he did every night, taking off his weapons and his comm unit before he did anything else? Then throw her down on the bed and claim her? Or would they eat first? Panic edged around her, constricted her breathing. Yet at the same time, a tingling warmth flowed through her body, bringing with it a sense of anticipation, amplified by the memory of Arion touching her in the bathing chamber.

Mirel's splashing and delighted giggles pulled Jenna's attention back to the nursery. She drew a deep breath, forcing her turbulent feelings into a tiny mental compartment. It would be what it would be. And it would happen soon. The red sun had already set, and the orange sun was halfway to the horizon. She turned on the wall dryer and held

Mirel's hands beneath it. The infant shrieked with glee and kicked her chubby feet against Jenna's midriff.

"You're a wild little kerani," Jenna told the girl, leaning forward to put her down.

A sudden wave of dizziness rushed over her, and she staggered. She squatted quickly and tried to set Mirel onto the floor. The girl roared a protest, her arms tightening around Jenna's neck. Breathe . . . Jenna couldn't breathe. . . . She fell sideways to the floor. Mirel scrambled free, ready to wrestle. But it was no longer her mischievous face Jenna saw.

The boy was intent on a large Branuka bug flitting through the clear air. It was a beautiful day, the lure of the suns and the mesas calling to him. He had slipped away from his watcher, Leelan, who was very old and often fell asleep. It had been easy to sneak off and get his net. He liked catching bugs and examining them.

When he was younger, his father had often taken him to the mesas. They talked to the woman of stone and collected unusual rocks and insects for the boy's collection. He liked collecting things, liked it when his father took him to the mesas. But more and more, his father was too busy to take him into the desert, and the boy got tired of asking, of waiting. He'd decided to go exploring on his own. He was old enough. He knew what to do.

This boy was different, Jenna realized, drifting out of the vision. Something was not quite right about his mind. He was approaching adolescence, as evidenced by his height, but his muscles were not fully developed and he was slight for a Leor. He had the usual well-shaped bald head and dark eyes, but those eyes lacked the intelligence that most Leors displayed.

The fact he was on Saura well past six seasons of age further proved something was wrong. He was childlike, didn't have normal thought processes for his age. He shouldn't be out in the desert alone. A cold, insidious premonition swept through Jenna, carrying her back into the boy's reality:

He wanted that Branuka bug. It was the largest and most colorful he had ever seen. He scaled straight up the side of the rock wall, following its erratic course, then pulled himself onto a wide ledge. The bug slowed, fluttering in the slight breeze. Just a little closer, and he could ensnare it in his net. It drifted lazily across the stone shelf, and the boy followed, stepping near the edge ...

"No!" Jenna thrashed, trying to reach out to the boy to warn him. "No! Don't go any further. Stop!"

He felt the sudden loss of rock beneath his foot. The rush of fear at knowing there was nothing but air beneath him, that he was too far off balance to catch himself. Then he was falling, falling, screaming for his mother.

"No!" Jenna cried again. "Oh, Spirit, no!"

The boy's broken body lay motionless at the base of the mesa.

"Lady Jenna! What is wrong?" Kerem's voice came from above her.

She knew intuitively that she'd just witnessed the boy's fall in real time. Maybe he was still alive. Arion. She must tell Arion. She struggled to sit up, trying to find the right pad on her comm unit, and ended up mashing several at once. Blazing hells. *Arion!* In sheer desperation, she mentally reached for her mate. *Arion, something terrible has happened.*

Jenna? What is it?

A boy has fallen from one of the mesas. I just saw it happen in a vision. I think he might be ... She broke off, unable to finish the thought.

Can you describe this boy?

He was thirteen or fourteen seasons of age, not fully grown. Something was wrong with his mind.

I need you to tell me exactly where this happened. Which mesa is it?

She scrambled to her feet. *I'm not sure. I think it's the closest group of mesas, because it's near the statue of the Goddess.* She closed her eyes, forced herself to see the scene again. *The mesa on the far left, I believe. I'll go with you.*

I will take care of it. You do not need to be there.

I do, she insisted. *I'll be able to find the exact spot if I can see the mesa up close.*

There was a pause, and Jenna suspected Arion was debating the wisdom of allowing her near such a tragic scene, but she'd already seen it happen. *Arion, he might still be alive. I need to be there. And we need to go now.*

All right. I will have Kerem assign you a server to drive you out. I will summon Lanka and we will be there quickly.

The rest happened in a blur. She and a young male server took a skimmer and raced to the first grouping of mesas. As they approached, a feeling of dread weighed on Jenna. She stared at the mesa on the left end of the group, taller and narrower than the other three, and she knew it was the one. "Over there," she directed her driver. He banked sharply, slowing as they approached the base of the mesa, and the small mass that she knew, even from this distance, wasn't a rock.

Arion, it's the mesa to the far left. The tallest one.

We are almost there.

She leaped from the skimmer before it was fully stopped, running to the still form of the boy. She halted a meter away, suddenly terrified to go any closer. She could see no spark of life in the child. His body was bent at unnatural angles, seemingly broken beyond repair.

Oh, Spirit! Forcing back rising hysteria, knowing she had to stay coherent, she dropped to her knees by the battered body, touched her fingers gently to his neck. He was still warm, and maybe, just maybe, she felt a faint pulse. She couldn't be sure. She saw that the net handle was still clutched in his fingers, a bright orange-and-black bug buzzing angrily inside the netting.

"What in Hades are you doing?" came a strident female voice. "Erek! Goddess, Erek!"

Jenna looked up just as a female Leor shoved her hard, knocking her sideways. Then the woman lunged past, hunching over the boy. "Erek!" she cried.

Jenna struggled to rise, finding a strong hand beneath her elbow. She looked up at Arion as he pulled her to her feet. Behind him came Lanka, Morven, and two male Leors. She saw three skimmers resting on the sand by the one she'd arrived in. Arion moved her aside as Lanka knelt by the distraught female. "Let me see him, Nona," Lanka said firmly. "You must let me examine him."

Morven leaned down and took Nona's arm. "Come." He pulled the woman to her feet as Lanka went to work on the boy.

But Jenna feared it was too late. Even if the boy was alive, there was little chance he could survive such a brutal fall. Sick inside, she turned and walked a few meters away. What use were her visions when they were never—*never*—in time to be of any use? Either that, or they were of future events she couldn't possibly control.

Outside the merging ceremony, this was the first time she'd ever seen up close the horrifying verification of the accuracy of her visions. *Oh, Spirit, why have you given me this ability?* She wanted to believe there was a valid reason, but so far it had only been a curse.

Behind her, she heard the mother's cries of denial and grief, and she wrapped her arms around herself. Tears filled her eyes. Was there anything good in this Spirit-forsaken place?

"You," came a guttural voice from behind Jenna. "You, human."

Startled, she turned to see Nona advancing, her face ravaged with emotion. "What did you do to him?" the woman growled, her voice escalating. *"What did you do to him?"*

"I wasn't even here," Jenna tried to explain, wiping at the tears overflowing her eyes. "I saw him fall in a vision, and I told Arion immediately. I'm so sorry."

"You saw it?" Nona shrieked. "And you did not stop it! This is your fault!" She lunged at Jenna, knocking her to the ground.

Stunned, Jenna didn't have time to fully react, or to dodge the woman's fist. She saw it coming, though, and managed to move her head. The blow glanced off her cheek, whipping her head sideways into the hard sand. It left her dazed and disoriented, but she struggled to heave the woman off of her. She braced for another strike, which never came.

Arion grabbed Nona's shoulders and hauled her up. "You will cease this immediately," he ordered.

"My Erek is dead!" she screamed, trying to break free of his grip. "And this human knew it was happening! She is spawn of the Demon."

"He is still alive," Lanka said, stepping beside them. "Your behavior is dishonorable and is wasting crucial time in getting him treatment." At a sign from Arion, the healer pressed a hypochamber against Nona's neck and hit the release. Nona staggered, almost collapsed, but Arion held her up. He looked toward the Leor warriors, jerked his head, and they strode over.

"Take her back to her dome and notify her mate," he instructed. "Inform him of his son's condition, and let him know Lanka will take Erek to the medical facility. Also tell him that Nona must appear in the tribune in three cycles' time to receive judgment for breaking our laws."

"What?" Jenna gasped. "Why would she be judged?"

"She attacked you," Arion said. "Assaulting any member of the settlement is forbidden, self-defense being the only acceptable reason for striking another Leor. Nona struck you and will be punished."

"But she didn't know what she was doing," Jenna protested, appalled. "By the Spirit! She thought she had lost her child. She was crazy from grief."

"It is the law."

Something inside her snapped, releasing a flood of pent-up emotions. "I can't believe you would allow this woman to stand trial when she didn't know what she was doing," she hissed. "Damn your laws, and damn you!"

Arion moved toward her, but Jenna stepped back. "Don't touch me. I don't want you anywhere near me."

"You are upset," he said quietly.

"No." She struggled to draw air into her constricted chest. "I am beyond upset. I am shocked and disgusted. With you—with all of you Leors. I wish to Spirit I had never come to this hellhole."

"We will discuss this later."

"There's nothing to discuss." She turned and stumbled toward the skimmer, tears blurring her vision. Arion would never soften. Everything was black and white to him. Life had so much gray, gray he would never see.

She reached the skimmer and looked for the server who had driven, then saw he was helping Lanka and Morven load the boy onto a stretcher. Not willing to wait, desperately needing to get away from the near-tragedy and from Arion, Jenna heaved herself into the driver's seat. She had driven skimmers in Shamara, and this one couldn't be too different. It appeared basically the same, and she got it started without any problem. She accelerated, spinning away from the other skimmers, and headed for the settlement.

Her stomach clenched at the thought of returning to the colony. She didn't want to go back there. There was nothing there but cruelty and rigid mentality and the so-called Leor justice. And a soul-deep pain she couldn't bear right now. She looked toward the open desert, and the groupings

197

of mesas in the distance. It looked fresh and clean . . . and free.

She cut around and headed the opposite direction of the settlement, away from the merciless Goddess, and away from the pain.

Chapter Thirteen

Arion waited until Nona was en route to her dome, and Erek had been carefully loaded onto a skimmer before he went after his mate. He gave Lanka a few instructions and sent the server back to the settlement with Morven and Lanka. Then he took the remaining skimmer and followed the dust trail into the desert. He did not blame Jenna for being shaken up, but she could not shut him out or run away every time she was upset.

Goddess, what a cycle this had been. He thought of poor Erek, and his spirit felt heavy. The boy had been born with a mind that could not progress beyond that of a child, but he was a good boy, beloved by his parents, and he brought joy to those around him. He should never have been out on his own, but it was difficult to place blame.

Leelan had probably fallen asleep again, but she was an old woman, with growing medical problems, and there had been discussion of finding other ways to care for Erek. Now the boy faced a battle for his life and, if he survived, he would likely be permanently crippled. Leelan would blame herself, and Nona would have to face the justice of the tribunal. There were cycles when his responsibilities weighed very heavily upon Arion, and this was one of them.

He studied the dust trail he was following, concerned that he could not see Jenna's skimmer yet. She must be driving very fast. She had surprised him again; he'd had no idea she could pilot a skimmer. He thought about communicating with her mentally, but decided it might only spur her away from him. It would be best just to track her down. He locked his computer's tracker onto her craft, in case he lost the visual trail, and increased his own speed.

Added to everything else, this was the cycle of the full lunar conjunction, and he must claim his mate by moonrise or forfeit his right to her. He had no intention of that happening. They would mate tonight, whether or not Jenna was ready. He feared what had happened with Erek—not to mention the events of the previous cycles—had upset her to the point that she would be resistant to any overtures from him.

Again, he thought of Lani's words on his ship, and vehemently refuted them. Jenna was his mate, and her welfare his responsibility. He was determined mating with her would not be rape, and just as determined he would not hurt her. It might be a battle, but he was a master at finesse and strategic maneuvers when it came to combat. He only hoped he could apply those same principles in his dealings with this small human female. Thus far, she had been more challenging than a major military assault.

He slowed as he approached a slight rise he knew to be dangerously deceptive, as it hid a grouping of large rocks that jutted out just beyond it. As he came over the rise, he steered sharply to the left in order to clear the boulders. The breath froze in his chest when he saw that Jenna had not made the correction in time, and had crashed the skimmer nose-first into the massive stones.

It was lying at a sharp angle on the driver's side, and

the front end was crumpled. Jenna! Fear pounded through him as he leaped from his craft and raced to the wrecked skimmer. He had to step carefully, because the craft was resting in a patch of gargan, a desert plant with nasty, painful spines.

But there was no sign of her in the skimmer, just large chunks of crash foam. He whirled around, his nostrils flaring and his tongue projected, in order to pick up her scent. With his acute vision and olfactory senses, he could readily track her in light or darkness. He scented her immediately. She was headed toward the mesas about three kilometers away. He started after her, but had only gone ten meters when he rounded the end of the rock formation and almost stumbled over her.

She was sitting on a low rock, her left leg stretched out before her. Her head was down, and most of her hair had fallen from its twist.

"Jenna." He squatted next to her, grasping her shoulders.

She lifted her face, and he saw she had a cut across her forehead, and a large bruise on her cheek—the injury from Nona. Her gray eyes were huge, and her skin was ashen. "I figured you would come for me sooner or later," she said. "I wasn't sure how to get you on the comm. I decided I'd wait awhile to see if you showed up, then contact Maxine if I had to. She's pad one."

"It is all right. I am here now," he told her. She was in shock, he decided. But before he did anything else, he needed to be sure she was not seriously injured. "Be still and let me look at you."

"I crashed the skimmer. I'm sorry." Her voice was shaky.

"I am not concerned about that right now." He ran his hands down her arms. It was then he saw the four long gargan spines embedded in her left thigh. He knew they were very painful and could cause infection.

She winced when he ran his hands lightly along her left

calf and part of her thigh, moving around the spines. "I fell when I was getting out of the skimmer, right into these things. When I tried to walk, it hurt too much, so I sat down and waited for you. I didn't know if I should pull them out or not."

"You did the right thing. I will take them out and treat the leg."

She started shivering. Although the second sun had almost set and the desert was cooling, it was not yet cold, so he suspected her reaction was shock. But he could not take her to his skimmer until he knew it was safe to move her. He continued running his hands over her until he was certain nothing was broken.

Then he picked her up, being careful of the gargan spines, and carried her to the skimmer. She rested against him without a protest. He eased her into the seat and took a blanket from the storage bin and wrapped it around her.

After getting in and starting the engine, he raised the top and turned the heat on full force. He stared at the mesas ahead and came to a decision. There was a cave in the base of one of those mesas. He had performed several saktars in that cave, and knew it was level and dry and free of animals. He would take Jenna there.

The skimmer's medical supplies contained what he needed to treat her leg, and there was also food and water, blankets, solar lanterns, and even a portable generator—standard supplies kept on every skimmer for emergency situations.

The twin moons were rapidly rising and would soon be in conjunction. He did not want to take the time to return to the settlement; not only that, out here there would be no distractions or interruptions. It would be just Jenna and him, in a primal setting for the most basic act between a male and a female. So decided, he headed the skimmer toward the mesa.

If Jenna noticed they were moving away from the settlement, she made no comment. Nor did she seem aware of his communication to the control center, informing them of his location and instructing them to contact him through his comm if he was needed. She stared straight ahead, and did not utter a single word.

When he reached the cave, he left her in the skimmer (after securing the ignition so she could not start it) while he took in lanterns and blankets and made up a bed of sorts. Then he carried her in, depositing her on the blankets. He was glad to see she was no longer shivering. Another trip out, and he got the medical pack and cut a stalk of kayaan growing by the cave entrance.

He went inside, and found that Jenna had pulled into a sitting position, propping herself against the stone wall behind the blankets. "What are we doing here?" she asked, staring around the cave. The solar lamps cast a golden glow on the walls, but did not illuminate the upper reaches of the cave, which remained dark and shadowy.

"This is closer than the settlement. I have what I need to treat your injuries, so there is no need to return yet." He did not add he intended to claim her here. She would know it soon enough.

She rubbed the outside of her injured thigh, carefully skirting the spines. "These things sting like Hades."

He noted her color was a little better and decided the shock had not been too severe. "They are painful, but not poisonous. The only concern is infection. I need to get a few more things from the skimmer. Try not to move too much."

He brought in a few more supplies and the generator. "What is that?" Jenna asked, watching him set up and activate the generator at the mouth of the cave.

"It is a generator. It will create a protective electric screen and it will heat the cave."

"Heat. Of course." Her eyes widened as he knelt beside

her, drawing his knife from its sheath. "Are you going to dig these things out?"

"That will not be necessary." He began slitting her loose pants up the side. "But I must be able to access the area."

"Oh." She sank back, watched him slice the fabric.

"This would be much simpler if you did not insist on clinging to your modesty and wore a loincloth."

"I guess it would," she admitted. "But I can only deal with so many new and strange situations at a time. I haven't coped very well with anything so far."

Several images flashed through his mind: Jenna cutting his palm with his knife and raising his hand to her mouth; the morning after their arrival on Saura, with her demanding that he grant her the same respect he would a Leor female; her enduring of saktar, the merging ceremony, and Brona's intentional mistreatment.

"I think you have shown exceptional courage and fortitude," he said. "You are a worthy mate, Jenna dan Aron."

She lowered her gaze and shook her head, and he knew she wasn't convinced. He cut her pants up to her hip, parting the fabric and lifting it over the four spines jutting from her leg. Her thigh was red and swollen around the entry points of the spines. He sheathed the knife.

"This will hurt," he warned, pressing one hand down on her thigh and quickly yanking out a spine with the other.

She flinched, but did not cry out. She remained silent while he removed the other three spines and cleaned the area with antiseptic, her balled-up hands and tense body the only indication of the pain.

"That was fun," she finally said, when he finished cleaning the wounds and began applying the kayaan sap. Some of the tension left her body, and he knew the kayaan was working its healing and soothing magic. But she was still very pale, and there were dark circles beneath her eyes.

"I would prefer that you find a different form of entertainment," he chided, pressing a bandage over her leg. "We have had this discussion about injuries. We agreed there would be no more."

"Easier said than done. I can't seem to avoid getting hurt around here." She leaned her head back and closed her eyes. "It must be your fault, Comdar. I never had any accidents or injuries until I met you."

Guilt twinged through him. Jenna was under his protection. He felt responsible for all she had suffered since arriving on Saura. While she was struggling to adjust to her new life and to him, so was he striving to adjust to a human mate, and to thinking for two instead of one.

It was a challenging transition, after being alone for forty spans. He did not even count his first six spans as being part of a family, as his parents had been emotionally distant and nondemonstrative.

"Then you should listen to your mate, and obey all his instructions," he said, grasping her chin and turning her face toward him so he could treat the cut on her forehead.

"I was under the impression that female Leors have equal rights, and you promised me those same rights," she reminded him, opening her eyes and meeting his gaze.

He grunted at that and began cleaning the gash. Fortunately, it did not appear deep enough to require sutures. She clenched her jaw as he applied antiseptic, relaxing when he put kayaan sap on it, and on her bruised cheek as well.

"I am finished." He gave her a stern look. "From here on, I do not expect to treat any more injuries."

He put the kayaan stalk aside and repacked the medical kit. Then, not quite sure how to approach this mating business, he sat beside Jenna, leaning against the wall, which felt cool beneath his bare skin. While his instincts were to lay her down and claim her without any further preliminaries, just as Lani had suggested they would be—and he hated to admit the echobird might have been right—he knew this first mating would lay the foundation for his relationship with Jenna, for the remainder of their lives, and that foundation needed to be strong. To that end, he would call on all of his patience and self-discipline to see that the mating proceeded as smoothly as possible.

Seemingly unaware of the direction of his thoughts, Jenna said, "I'm sorry that I overreacted earlier. I shouldn't have said what I did, especially in front of the others. We did agree to keep our differences private. I wasn't thinking clearly. I'm sorry about the skimmer, too."

That was one thing Arion was learning about humans. They liked to talk, needed to talk, as a way of bonding with others. If Jenna needed this conversation to feel more comfortable with him, then they would talk—but not for long.

He also knew she was still struggling to come to terms with their cultural differences, and he was willing to give her some leeway. "I accept your apologies."

"Does Nona really have to be punished? She was very upset, and with good reason. She overreacted, just as I did, and I'm not going to be disciplined." She looked askance at him. "Am I?"

"No. But outside of your disrespect toward me, you did not break our laws."

"But—"

He shushed her with a finger to her lips. "I am not willing to discuss this now."

She sighed, and he could sense her inner battle. "All right," she conceded. "We won't discuss Nona right now. But will you please tell me about Erek? How is he?"

"Lanka thought he would survive, although she did not know the extent of the damage."

A tremor ran through her. "That poor boy. Why is life so unfair?"

Touching others was something Arion, or any Leor, rarely initiated. It was foreign to him, but Lani's holovideo section on human anatomy had stressed that touch was very important to humans. He had to admit that the times he'd run his fingers along Jenna's skin, it had been very pleasurable and alluring. Now, sensing her distress, knowing his touch might soothe her, he reached out, sliding his hand over her shoulder.

"Oh, Arion." She turned, curling into him and catching him completely off guard. He hesitated, then brought his arm around her. She burrowed even closer. "It was terrible," she whispered against his chest. "I saw it happening and there was nothing I could do about it."

He felt warm moisture on his skin, and realized it must be tears. She had kept her composure as long as necessity dictated, and now the barriers were down. More importantly, she had turned to *him* for comfort. Possessive and protective emotions surged through him, and he brought his other arm up, tightening both arms around her. "You did do something, Jenna. You got help. You saved Erek's life."

"I hate being able to see things happen. They're always bad things, like my parents dying, or animal sacrifices, and Clavon . . . and Erek."

He reached up to tug her hair the rest of the way down, and shook it out with his fingers. "You foresaw our union. Was that such a bad thing?"

She was silent a moment. "I don't know."

Well, he had asked. And he had told her from the beginning that he expected honesty between them. "I do not think our merging is bad," he said. "I believe it is the will of the Goddess, and that She will bless our union."

"Maybe," Jenna conceded, her voice muffled because she was still pressed against him. "But I'm not so sure I can handle the Leor lifestyle. I might never fit in."

"It is overwhelming right now. You will adapt in time."

She did not appear to believe him. She radiated misery, and he felt the slow slide of her tears down his chest. He slid his fingers through her hair, knowing it gave her pleasure, and maybe a measure of comfort. "Your sadness unsettles me."

"Nothing shakes you up or affects you," she denied. "I've never seen you react to anything."

"You are wrong," he murmured. "My mate has a very unsettling effect on me." He slipped his fingers beneath her chin and raised her face toward his. Leaning down, he traced the path of her tears with his tongue, then moved to the other cheek. Her cheeks tasted salty, but when he moved to her lips, he found the tantalizing taste of sweet innocence and a beckoning softness that could tempt even a hardened warrior. He dipped his tongue into the moist warmth of her mouth.

Her tongue tentatively touched his, and a jolt of desire sizzled through him, stimulated by the sensory receptors in his tongue. He felt the effects all the way down to his lower extremities, where his body hardened painfully. Now that he was not exerting any control over his body's reactions, he was discovering it took very little to ready a male for the mating act. Human females, however, were very different, if the holovideo was correct.

He slid down on the blankets, taking Jenna with him, partially covering her body with his. She stiffened and pushed against him. "Arion, stop!" The panic in her voice cut through his rising passion, and he shifted off her.

She pushed upright and brushed her hair from her face. "What are you doing?"

"You know what I am doing. We are going to mate."

Her eyes widened. "We're mating *now? Here?*"

He sat up, watching her steadily. "You knew this was inevitable, Jenna. And you agreed to it. You also knew when it would happen."

"I know. I guess I thought it would be different. Like in a bed instead of a cave."

"Where it happens is not important. But when it happens is crucial. The moons are now in conjunction. It is time."

She moved away from him and drew her knees up to her chest in a protective posture. "I thought I'd be used to the idea by now. And I was, until . . . I didn't expect to be upset so badly right before it occurred." She looked down at her knees, and her voice dropped. "I didn't think I was such a coward, either."

They were going to mate, and it was going to be in the next few moments. Arion prayed to the Goddess to guide him through Jenna's resistance. "There is no need for your fear. You know me by now. I will try not to hurt you."

"Sometimes I think I know you," she said softly. "But every time I start to believe you might have a heart, you do something to prove me wrong. I don't know what to think anymore."

Her words bothered him more than he would ever have imagined. Yet he knew they were spoken from the wounds, both physical and emotional, she had endured since coming to Saura. He moved beside her, capturing her wrist so she could not slide away. "Listen to me, *charina*. As Comdar, I can have no heart. I must uphold our laws, and put the welfare of all before that of any individual. But as a man, as your mate, I do have a heart."

He took her clenched hand, gently uncurled it, and pressed it against his chest. "See? Feel my heart pounding? With need, for you." He pulled her hand down to his lap, pressed it against the bulge beneath his loincloth. "Feel my need."

Her breath caught, and her fingers flexed against him. Sensation shot from his groin into his bloodstream in a heated rush. He almost groaned aloud. Calling upon every ounce of self-control he possessed, he eased her hand away from him. "Trust me in this, *charina*. We will see to your fears. We will make this work."

Her gaze searched his face. "*Charina*. You've called me that several times. What does it mean?"

"It means 'cherished one.' You are my mate, Jenna. I

will always protect you and stand for you. Come." He offered his hand, and hoped she would come to him. He could not give her any more time.

She turned, moving onto her knees to face him, her gaze locking with his. "If I think about things too much, then I start to doubt you," she said. "But if I listen to my heart, then, despite everything that's happened, I feel safe with you. Only Spirit knows why, because I can't explain it, even to myself." Slowly, she placed her left hand in his. "But I do trust you."

His soul felt as if it had just been set free from invisible chains and now soared high above Saura's mesas. "Listen to your heart." He raised her hand, ran his tongue over their blood pact scar. Then he rose, pulling her upright with him.

She stood quietly as he undid her top and slid it off. He tossed it aside, then hooked his fingers in the waist of her pants and knelt as he tugged them down. She helped by kicking them off, and he tossed them as well.

He stared at the perfection of her satiny skin, her slender, firm legs, and the fascinating triangle of fiery curls between her thighs. He inhaled deeply, taking in the scent of feminine heat. Grasping her waist, he leaned forward and trailed his tongue from the top of those curls up her abdomen and midriff, between her breasts.

He absorbed the taste and scent of her, imprinting it upon his soul, and his body responded with primal need. Rising, he tore off his loincloth with an impatient flick of his hand. Then he stroked his hands over her shoulders, down over her breasts. The response was immediate, with her breasts swelling beneath his hands, the nipples contracting into tight nubs. Fascinated, he stroked his thumbs over those nubs, and Jenna gave a little gasp.

"Good or bad?" he growled. "You have to tell me what gives you pleasure."

"Good," she said breathlessly. She brought her hands up

and rubbed them over his chest, tracing the swells of muscle, and brushing against his flat nipples. Her touch was electrifying, and he felt his nipples harden, pulse against her touch. "Your body is beautiful," she said. "It's so hard and so perfect."

He pulled her against him, letting her feel just how hard he was. Her eyes widened, but he did not give her a chance to think, instead lifting her face to his and tracing his tongue over her eyes, cheeks, and lips. He found using his tongue incredibly stimulating, and decided he would taste all of her before they were through.

For now he contented himself with probing her mouth again, savoring the sweet softness. She responded more boldly this time, thrusting her tongue against his. Heat roared through him like a brushfire, stoking a savage need.

With a growl, he took her down to the blankets. Fisting his hands in her hair, he explored her with his tongue, mapping the curve of her breasts, sampling the texture of her nipples, lingering there when she arched against him with a little cry and gripped his shoulders.

He knew from the holovideo that touching was an essential part of preparing a human female for the actual act of mating, and he discovered he had no trouble at all with that. Jenna was so soft, her scent and taste so heady, he found he was ravenous for her. He moved his hands down her body, sliding them over her slightly rounded stomach, tangling his fingers in the curls there. Then he dipped his hand between her legs. She was even warmer there, and wet, like heated homa. He stroked the soft flesh, and she gasped again. He raised his head, looked at her. "Good?"

"Yes." The cadence of her voice was lower, huskier.

Watching her face, he slipped a finger inside her. Liquid heat surrounded it. He knew that was good, a natural lubrication that would allow him entry. He stroked his finger in and out, hoping to heighten her readiness. She moaned softly, shifted her legs restlessly. He could smell the scent of her arousal now, a musky essence that stirred his blood and swelled his erection even more. Nature had ensured that their physical reactions would attract one to the other.

He withdrew his finger and settled between her thighs, moved over her body. He paused to run his tongue over each of her nipples and again over her lips for a lingering taste of her mouth. "Now. We do it now," he grated out.

"Yes," she whispered, her own obvious need a blessing from the Goddess.

He pressed into the center of her heat. She was incredibly tight. He rocked his hips, meeting the resistance of her virgin sheath. This was not going to be easy or painless. He withdrew a little, pushed back in. He gained some ground, but felt her muscles tensing and fighting his entry.

He held himself still. "You must relax."

"You're too big," she gasped, panicked.

"It is your virgin state, *charina*," he soothed. "We will make it work. Relax and breathe." He rocked farther in, calling on all his control to keep from plunging into her, as his raging libido demanded he do.

She clenched her eyes shut, tears seeping from beneath her lids. Her fingers dug into his shoulders. He pulled back a little, lowered his head near hers. "Feel the energy, Jenna. I have performed many saktars here, in this cave. The energy still lingers. The Goddess is with us. Relax, and let Her help you."

She took a deep breath. Her eyes opened and her gaze locked with his. He stared down into luminous gray orbs, and pressed forward, feeling her muscles give around him. He sank all the way in and stilled, giving her time to adjust to his invasion of her body. He did not ask if this was good or bad, as he suspected it burned like the fires of Hades. He had told her he would try not to hurt her and had not been able to keep his word. "Are you all right?"

She nodded slowly. "I think so. It's almost as fun as pulling out gargan spines."

He could not appreciate her attempt at humor because a wild, primitive need was upon him. The clasp of her muscles around him only inflamed him further, and he battled the powerful urge to thrust long and hard, instead of moving in the slow, shallow strokes that her innocent state necessitated. He moved as slowly as he could, sliding gently in and out.

The friction of being inside her created the most compelling, pleasurable sensation he had ever experienced. It was headier than the trance brought on by burning zarra leaves, more potent than communion with the Goddess. It was all-consuming and held a compulsion he could not withstand.

He fought the savage demands of his body, but it was futile. "I cannot hold off any longer," he said, his breath ragged. "Give yourself to me."

He could not wait for her consent, could not control the urges of his body as nature took over, and he rocked in a hard and fast cadence. Despite the frenzy of his need, he was aware of his mate on some deep level; was aware of her hands gripping his shoulders, of her harsh breathing against his chest.

He retained enough presence of mind to keep his weight off her, to try to control the force of his strokes. Then all awareness ceased, except for the building storm in his body and the final explosion of light and color and waves of pure pleasure. A supernova of incredible sensation and magnitude. Never had he experienced anything like it.

As sanity gradually returned, he again became aware of the solar lights reflecting off the cave walls, of the fragile human woman beneath him. Jenna. His mate. She had taken him into her body, and he had given her his seed, maybe even the first stirring of life. If not this time, soon.

And now that all mating restrictions had been lifted, and he knew just how incredible sex was, he looked forward to many long and pleasurable sessions of creating offspring with her. He knew her first experience had been painful, and he regretted causing that pain, but he could not regret claiming her. She was bound to him completely now. The mating ritual had been completed. She was his, for the remainder of their lives.

His breathing heavy and uneven, Arion rolled off Jenna and settled beside her, his chest rising and falling rapidly. She lay there, bombarded by so many things that it was difficult to sort them out. Physically, she felt sore and battered. Both her face and her wounded thigh were throbbing, her backside felt bruised from the hard stone floor, and she ached between her legs where Arion had claimed her so thoroughly.

He had been rough at the end, but she had sensed his struggle to keep from hurting her, knew he had not taken her with the full force of which he was capable. Until the point where he appeared to lose his control, he had been careful and gentle, showing a consideration she had not expected.

And the ways he had touched her . . . Her breath caught in her throat as she thought of his mouth on her breasts, his finger stroking deep inside her, creating a maelstrom of need. Her entire body had come alive with the stroke of his tongue and the sweep of his rough fingers across her skin. It had been wonderful until his penetration. She had known it might hurt, but she hadn't been prepared for such burning agony.

Pain so sharp it had taken her breath away, making it nearly impossible not to clench her muscles and fight his intimate invasion. Until he had urged her to feel the energy of the cave.

Then a strange force had swirled around her, and she'd heard the now-familiar, feminine voice whispering to her: *Relax, beloved daughter. This is natural and right. Arion is your mate, your destiny. Trust in him, and give yourself freely to him. All will be well.* Then Arion had begun moving inside her and the pain had eased, although it hadn't disappeared entirely. She certainly hadn't received any pleasure from the act itself.

The emotional barrage had been almost as bad, an overwhelming rush of thoughts and feelings, a jumbled collage of memories flashing through her mind. Sadness, happiness, joy, grief, along with inexplicable feelings of tenderness and caring toward Arion. All caused by the awakening of her physical senses and her body's hormones, she supposed, which were contributing to the tears still seeping from her eyes, even though the worst of the pain was gone.

Arion rolled to his side and leaned over her, his ebony gaze probing and seeing more than she wanted him to see. "I hurt you," he said, his strong fingers wiping away her tears. "I was not able to avoid it. I am sorry."

"It wasn't your fault," she answered, trying to draw her tattered emotions together. "I understand most virgins have to endure some discomfort."

"You are no longer a virgin. The next mating should not be so painful." His fingers trailed from her face down over her breast. He stroked the nipple, watching it harden in response. A sensual shiver swept through Jenna, despite her exhaustion. His fingers moved lower, drifting over her abdomen. "We will work at creating offspring, and at giving you pleasure in the process."

Her heart speeded up, as did her breathing. She was amazed he could raise such a reaction, after what she'd just been through. He froze, staring intently at some lower point on her body. She glanced down, saw the smear of blood on her thigh. Not from the gargan wounds; those were on the other leg. This was the lingering proof of her virginity, taken by her mate.

Arion reached down, swabbed up her blood with his finger. He raised his left hand and smeared the blood on his palm, right along the scar of their pact. Taking her left hand, he pressed his palm against hers. "The pact is now complete, in accordance with our ancient and sacred laws," he intoned, his voice holding a reverence that wrapped around Jenna's heart. "I ask for the blessing of the Goddess upon this union. I ask that our blood one day run through our offspring, and that we be granted many children."

He lowered their hands to the blanket. "That was beautiful," Jenna said quietly. "Your dedication to your Goddess is very special."

"She has granted us many blessings."

Jenna thought about the Leors' reproductive problems. "What if you're sterile?" she asked. "Isn't that a possibility?"

"No, *charina*. The Goddess has revealed, during *saktar*, that I am not."

She loved the way he said *charina*, how his deep voice slowed and softened. Maybe he was beginning to care for her, at least a little. She didn't know if Leors were capable of strong feelings of love, or if their culture conditioned them away from such emotions. Yet Nona's reaction today when she thought Erek was dead would indicate otherwise.

Mating with Arion had strengthened the bond the merging had created between them, but their relationship was still tenuous. She did have feelings for him, though. He had stood for her, on more than one occasion, and he had given her as much time to adjust to her new life as he could before they mated. She looked down at their hands, still pressed together, and knew she and Arion were bound in many ways: an ancient pact, a merging of minds and souls, the blood of her virginity. The two of them were irrevocably linked, regardless of her feelings on the matter.

They lay there in silence a few moments; then he stirred, releasing her hand. Rolling gracefully to his feet, he went to one of the packs he'd brought in, squatting to open it. He appeared totally unconcerned with his nudity, and she had to admit she enjoyed watching how he moved, how the light played over his magnificent body. Removing a bottle of water and a cloth, he returned and knelt beside her. "Open your legs."

"Why?"

"I am going to take care of any damage I might have inflicted."

Realizing his intent, she tried to sit up. "I can do that. There's no need—"

"For your modesty," he interjected, pressing her back down. "Or your defiance." He gripped her knees and slid her legs apart, then wet the cloth and pressed it against her feminine flesh. She closed her eyes, torn between acute embarrassment and how wonderful the cool cloth felt.

"There is not much bleeding," he said, very matter-of-fact, as he washed away the residue of their mating.

There wasn't much left of her dignity, either. She breathed a sigh of relief when he finished and turned to put the cloth and water away. Feeling uncomfortable lying there exposed, she drew the side of the blanket over her. He turned back with the kayaan stalk in his hand. "We are not finished yet."

"I beg to differ. I think you've done enough."

He shook his head as he squeezed kayaan sap into his finger. "I am responsible for your welfare, and there is no reason for you to suffer needlessly." He yanked the blanket from her grasp and firmly parted her legs a second time, despite her resistance.

He was determined to have his way, and it was a battle she could not win. She lay back and closed her eyes again, wincing as his finger slid deep inside her, depositing the soothing sap. She *was* very sore, and she felt the relief almost instantly, but she wasn't sure the benefit outweighed the absolute mortification she was experiencing.

On the other hand, Arion appeared perfectly at ease and unaffected. She supposed it was only a matter of practicality to him, taking care of her the same way he would one of his weapons or a piece of equipment, but she wasn't yet used to the casual attitude Leors had toward their bodies.

"That should help," he said finally, moving away to dispose of the kayaan stalk. He glanced back at her. "You are flushed. I have told you there is no need for embarrassment. We are mates."

"I know, but I'm till trying to adjust to it."

"Try harder," he suggested.

She narrowed her eyes, wrapped herself in the blanket, and sat up. She watched as he closed the packs. "Are we getting ready to leave?"

"Unless you prefer to stay here for the night." He turned toward her. "I assumed you would want the opportunity to bathe and sleep on a bed, but I have slept here many times and there is food in the packs. It does not matter to me."

"Going back to the dome sounds wonderful." And it did. In the past few cycles, the dome had become her haven against the alien Leor world. She felt safe there. She suddenly realized she was beginning to think of the dome as home. *Her* home.

Arion retrieved his loincloth and put it on. Jenna was also becoming used to him, and their daily routines. While he might be merciless in his dealings with others, he had been surprisingly tolerant with her. Oh, he sometimes imposed his will on her with ruthless authority, but he had never been cruel, and he kept his word.

If she were completely honest with herself, she would have to admit he wasn't the monster she had first believed. They might even be able to find a middle ground. It was a start, and she was willing to go forward from here.

"I want to go back," she said. "The sooner, the better."

Chapter Fourteen

The next cycle found Jenna moving a little slower than usual as she tried to keep up with the infants. The kayaan sap had reduced the swelling and the pain of her external injuries, but her leg was stiff and sore, as was her backside, and the bruise and cut on her face. Other, more intimate parts of her were also sore, although Arion's ministrations and a hot bath had helped. It seemed every movement only served to remind her that she had been claimed, quite thoroughly, by her mate.

When she'd first entered the nursery this morning, Kerem had taken one look at her and actually grinned. That was the first shock of the cycle. She'd stared at him, debating whether or not to ask him why he was smiling. Surely it wasn't because of her battered face. But then he'd returned to his work with his customary grunt, so she went about her own duties.

The next surprise came later in the morning, when Morven made an appearance. Although she had her back to the entryway, Jenna felt the change in the air the minute he entered the nursery. It was strange, but she could sense the energy that seemed to crackle around him. She put the infant she was holding on the floor and turned to see the shaman striding toward her, his expression inscrutable as always.

He halted before her, staring at her with unsettling intensity, but she wasn't about to let him know how much he unnerved her. As long as he wasn't burning those strange leaves, she figured she could stand up to him. Putting her hands on her hips, she said, "Well, good morning to you, too, Shaman. It's always interesting to converse with you."

He gave her what she was beginning to think of as "the look," which Arion often employed as well. It was a combined expression of incredulity, Leor arrogance, and a clear warning that she was trespassing past acceptable boundaries. It ranked only second behind the grunt, with crossed arms coming in a close third, as the most common Leor mannerisms she encountered.

Now Morven's gaze returned to some point either just above or behind her. She turned to see what he might be staring at, saw nothing but a wall. She turned back, tired of this game. "*What?* What are you looking at?"

His midnight-blue eyes glittered. "You."

"Me?" She looked down, made sure her tunic seam was sealed, patted her hair twist to see if it was coming down, wished she had a mirror. Then she remembered her injured face, and her irritation increased. "You find my face interesting?"

He waved his hand in a dismissive gesture. "That is nothing." He looked satisfied. "But you are red."

"*What?*" she demanded.

He turned and strode toward the entry.

No. He was *not* going to play his little mind games with her this morning. "Wait just a minute, Shaman." She followed him and grabbed his arm. "You're not leaving without an explanation."

He turned, glanced down at her hand on his arm, and gave her another one of his looks, but she refused to be intimidated. "What do you mean, I'm red?"

"It is your energy that is red. Actually, rose." He removed her hand from his arm. "It is good." He gave another satisfied nod and strode out.

Bemused, Jenna stared after him, then turned to find Kerem watching her. The older Leor raised his mug of homa as if toasting her. A nagging suspicion stirring inside her, she walked over to him. "Kerem, can I ask you something?"

"You always ask, with or without permission, do you not?"

She supposed she did. Persistence was necessary when trying to pry information from the reticent Leors. "Is my energy red?"

"Would appear so." With that laconic reply, he lumbered off to check the play and exercise equipment.

Jenna got an uneasy feeling inside, as her suspicion came closer to being confirmed. Although she wasn't sure she really wanted to know, a part of her felt compelled to discover the truth. She couldn't go see Maxine until her work shift was finished, and she was reluctant to ask her questions via a comm link, so there was only one other way for quick answers. She reached out mentally. *Arion, can you hear me?*

I am here. What do you need?

What does it mean that my energy is red?

Where did you hear that?

The shaman came to see me, and he told me my energy is red. What does that mean?

We can discuss this tonight. I will explain fully.

She didn't want to wait until tonight; plus she suspected he was putting her off, a sure sign she wouldn't like the answer. *I want to know now. I can always ask Maxine if you're too busy.* She knew that would get a reaction.

She could almost feel his disapproval, as if emotion could also traverse their link. *You do not need to go to the android for answers.* Pause. *Certain shades of red, usually tinged with dark pink, denote sexual energy. If those shades are present in someone's energy field, it means he or she has either been sexually active or is having strong sexual thoughts.*

So the shaman knows now that we—feeling the heat rise to her face, Jenna took a deep breath, then continued—*mated during the moon alignment?*

Disapproval was replaced by blatant male satisfaction. *Yes. It is his duty to ensure that we meet our obligations to the Goddess.*

It didn't bother her so much that Morven could see her energy. But her other suspicion was more alarming. *Arion, can other Leors besides Morven see auras?*

Yes.

Can you?

Yes.

She took another breath. *Who else?*

All adult Leors can see the energy fields that surround every living thing.

Great, just great. Jenna had thought Arion's ministrations last night were embarrassing, but this was far worse. Every Leor in the settlement could look at her, could look at him . . . *I'm assuming you've got red, or rose, around you, too?*

Yes.

So everyone knew what had transpired between her and Arion. Not that they wouldn't have expected it, at least by the moon alignment. But the fact they would know exactly when it happened was highly disconcerting. That explained Kerem's reaction and his cryptic words. She wondered if there was anywhere to hide. *Could you just take me back to the cave and leave me there?*

My little coward. You will stay right there in the nursery and complete your shift. Now, if you have no more questions, I will return to my duties.

No, no more questions.

I will see you tonight then.

She went to pick up Priman, who was sitting in the middle of the floor, roaring his unhappiness. He was a chunky baby, large even by Leor standards, and he was always hungry. Soothing him, she got a bowl of the meat mash.

As she fed him, her thoughts returned to the issue of the rose energy. The fact that every Leor who saw her or Arion would know they'd mated bothered her. It felt invasive, a violation of her privacy, which was hard enough to maintain as it was. But, like everything else, she didn't see that there was much she could do about it. Maybe Maxine would have some ideas.

Heartened by the thought of a visit with the android, Jenna washed off Priman and took him outside. Then she went to the next infant, and the next, forcing herself to focus on her duties. Finally her shift was over, and she wasted no time heading for the research laboratory.

She didn't ask Arion's permission, nor did she ask Kerem to assign a server to drive her there; she simply took one of the communal skimmers and drove herself. She was tired of being dependent on others, and decided it was time she demanded the same rights as Leor females. In her mind, mating with Arion had completed the initial terms of their agreement, and she was determined to gain a foothold in her new life.

She parked in the skimmer lane and entered the laboratory, going through decontamination before entering the corridor and walking to Maxine's area. The android's lab was crowded, this time with five female Leors. They stood around Maxine, all taller than the android's six feet. She was solid and fairly muscular, but appeared dainty next to the female warriors. She was handing them small plexishield containers.

"I want each of you to collect your saliva samples at precisely seven hundred hours tomorrow. Don't eat or drink anything before you get the saliva. Then bring them to me before you report for your duties." She glanced over and saw Jenna just outside the entry. "Jenna! Come in."

The Leors all looked in her direction; then each of them did a double take, turning and staring intently at her. Maxine stared at her, too, but Jenna didn't know if androids could see auras. "I didn't mean to interrupt anything." She entered reluctantly.

One Leor woman grinned—another smile, which made two in one day—and elbowed the female on her right. A third Leor just grunted and turned back to Maxine. "Is that all, android?" she asked in her guttural voice.

"Yes." A bemused expression on her face, Maxine looked from the smiling Leor to Jenna. "I might run some more tests when you bring your samples tomorrow. Thank you for your cooperation."

All five women filed out silently, although they stared at Jenna as they walked past her. "Interesting reaction," Maxine commented. She moved to Jenna, her expression hardening. "What happened to your face?"

Jenna thought back to yesterday's traumatic events. "An altercation and an accident."

Maxine's mouth firmed to a thin line. "Did Arion do this?"

"Oh, no!" It hadn't occurred to Jenna that anyone would assume Arion responsible. "I got the bruise on my cheek when a Leor named Nona hit me. She was upset because her son fell off one of the mesas and was badly injured."

"She must be young Erek's mother," Maxine said. "I heard of his accident. He is in the medical center under Lanka's care."

"What can you tell me? I've been worried about him."

"There is not much to tell. His legs were broken and his spinal column was crushed. His condition is very serious. They do not yet know what the outcome will be."

"Will he live?"

"That is also uncertain."

"That poor boy," Jenna said, feeling a deep sense of sorrow. "I saw it happen. I had one of those cursed visions, and I saw him fall from the mesa. It was horrible."

"I am sorry. I know the visions upset you." Maxine gestured toward the table. "Sit down, and I will get you some homa." She poured the chilled homa and brought the tumbler to the table, sitting across from Jenna. "How did you cut your forehead?"

Jenna sighed and sipped the homa. "I got that when I wrecked the skimmer yesterday."

Maxine's eyebrows rose. "You wrecked a skimmer? That is most interesting. How did it happen?"

Jenna filled her in on the events of the past cycle, stopping just short of Arion claiming her in the cave.

"Four gargan spines in your thigh?" Maxine shook her head. "Captain san Ranul entrusted me with your care. Thus far, I have not performed anywhere close to one hundred percent efficiency. Perhaps not even fifty percent." She considered a moment. "Last night was the full moon alignment. Knowing the Comdar, I assume the mating mission was successfully completed." The android raised her brows again. "How did the docking go?"

"It hurt like Hades."

"Not unexpected. The loss of virginity can be quite painful. In fact, studies show that 95.65 percent of virgins suffer some degree of pain on their maiden sexual voyage."

"Tell me about it." Jenna sank back in her chair.

"Well, although the hymen ruptures naturally in physically active women 78.52 percent of the time—"

"No more." Jenna raised a hand. "That was another expression."

"Oh. I see."

"And now I'm red, or rose," Jenna said glumly. "All adult Leors can see it, so they know Arion and I mated last night."

"Explain this red rose."

Jenna told Maxine about the color of sexual energies and how they appeared in auras, and that adult Leors could see those auras. "That is fascinating," Maxine said. "I knew Leors could see the life force around living beings, but I never considered what the ramifications of such an ability might be. I will have to do further research on the matter. However, back to the mating. Aside from the pain, was it what you expected?"

Jenna felt a flare of heat as she thought about Arion's tongue and hands on her body. She had not realized that the pleasure from his touch would be so startling, or the craving to take him fully inside her would be so intense. Yet she didn't want to discuss those aspects with Maxine, preferring to hold them close to her as intimate, personal memories.

"I didn't notice anything unusual," she said neutrally.

"The pleasure will increase with future matings," Maxine said. "It will be even more enhanced by the fact that Leor males have approximately double the endurance of human males. As Lani would say, they have 'incredible stud potential.' "

"I guess that's good," Jenna commented, although she didn't really know what it meant.

A lopsided grin appeared on the android's face. "It is *very* good. Many cultures place a high value on sexual endurance in their males. I do not anticipate that you will be disappointed with the quality or the quantity of the Comdar's mating abilities."

Jenna was feeling unusually warm again, a state she'd experienced off and on since last night. She took a sip of the cool homa, just as Arion's voice flowed into her mind. *Jenna, can you hear me?*

She was amazed at how easy this form of communication was becoming, and that it no longer seemed so invasive to have Arion speaking inside her head. *I can hear you.*

You are at the laboratory, with the android?

She wondered if someone had reported her location, or he'd just guessed. *Yes, I'm with Maxine.*

You did not apprise me of your whereabouts.

Is that something Leor males normally require of their mates?

She sensed his disapproval, but she knew his honor was too ingrained for him to lie. *No, it is not.*

She saw this as an opportunity to begin asserting her independence. *I didn't see the need to tell you.*

I am heading for the dome, he projected. *Do you wish for me to come by the laboratory?*

Jenna sighed, recognizing the underlying command in his question. *No. I can get home on my own.*

Then I will see you there.

Realizing independence would be hard won, and acquired in small chunks, she decided she'd pushed as far as she dared for one cycle. So she said good-bye to Maxine and left the lab. As she got into the skimmer, it occurred to her she'd used that word again, this time in a conversation. *Home.*

Amazed, she realized not only had she begun to think of the dome as her home, but she had vocalized it. Another milestone, perhaps even real progress toward a new life.

Arion was already at the dome when she got there. He stood in the entryway, watching as Jenna parked the skimmer and walked toward the structure. His massive shoulders and broad chest crowded the entry, and the late afternoon sun reflecting off his body made his skin appear even more golden. With his gleaming, powerful head and black-hole eyes, he looked wild and primitive.

At the sight of him, Jenna's heart speeded up. She stopped at the entry, her irregular heartbeat making her jittery. Her gaze locked with his, and she found herself sucked into the dark whirlpools of his eyes. Without a word, he moved back to let her enter. Forcing a breath into her constricted chest, she stepped inside. He stared at her, still silent, as she walked to the settee. "Did you have a good cycle?" she asked.

He grunted. She stopped before the settee, looked over her shoulder to see he had not moved. Sensing his displeasure, she decided to deal with it now. She turned and faced him. "Is there something you want to say?"

"You always create the need for many words," he said. "Right now, it is the issue of your defiance."

They were back to his desire to dominate. "I was not aware I had defied you."

"You did not keep me updated on your whereabouts. Your well-being is my concern and responsibility. When I do not know where you are, I cannot ensure your safety."

"I thought I would have the same freedom as other females."

"You are not completely acclimated to our culture," he pointed out. "Nor are you as strong as a Leor female, or as capable of protecting yourself."

She hated that he was right, but she wasn't going to put herself at risk just to challenge him. "I have no intention of compromising my safety," she told him. "But I need my personal freedom. It's important to me. I think I should be able to move around the main settlement without restrictions—unless you believe I'm in danger from other Leors."

His eyes narrowed. "No one would dare harm you," he growled.

"Then let me have *some* freedom," she urged. "I won't

leave the settlement without telling you, or go out into the desert on my own. I give you my word."

He considered, and she could sense his internal struggle; his need to control and protect battling with the intellectual part of him that knew he had promised her certain concessions. "All right," he finally agreed. "I am giving you my trust on this, Jenna. I expect you to remain in the main settlement at all times, and to inform me immediately if you plan otherwise."

Another step forward, she thought. "I will. Thank you."

He continued to stand there, staring at her, much like Morven had earlier in the cycle.

"What is it?" she asked.

"I find the rose color around you very pleasing."

"Oh, that. Surely it's not so obvious anymore."

"It is there. But it is beginning to dim. I believe it will be necessary to replenish it often." He moved toward her, radiating a masculine possessiveness.

Her heart resumed its racing, and Jenna took a step back. "I'm not sure I like everyone knowing when we mate."

"It is normal for Leors." He continued advancing on her, a graceful predator. "Most mated couples continually project red or rose colors."

Her mouth went dry as he reached her, the settee stopping any further retreat. "That must take a lot of effort to maintain," she managed.

His heated gaze swept down her body. "Repetition is a crucial part of any discipline." One hand grasped her arm and pulled her against him. The other hand lifted her chin, forcing her to look into his glowing eyes. "We are just learning about this mating business; therefore I am certain we will require a *lot* of repetition."

The breath froze in her chest. He leaned down, sliding his tongue over her cheeks, then claimed her lips. She required no coaxing to open her mouth, welcoming the demanding stroke of his tongue against hers. Need pulsed through her, coiling low in her belly. She stretched up on her toes to fully kiss him back.

With a low growl, he pulled back. She protested the loss of his mouth as he set her away from him. "Your movements are stiff," he said. "Are you sore?"

"A little," she admitted.

"Perhaps you need more kayaan."

"No," she said quickly. "That won't be necessary."

"Foolish modesty." A small smile flirted with his lips as he stepped away. "You need time to heal. We will not mate this cycle." She heard the regret in his voice, and his concern warmed her. She *was* sore, and felt certain mating again so soon would be very uncomfortable.

He had surprised her once more with his thoughtfulness. It occurred to her that the physical act wasn't necessary to strengthen the bond between mates. She already felt a strong tie with Arion, and his consideration was wrapping around her heart and drawing her closer to him.

It was enough—for now.

Arion walked into the dining hall, Jenna beside him. He looked around and found what he sought. The android was at a table halfway up the left side, surrounded by four male warriors. Of course, it did not have to eat, but it often came to the hall during meals and conversed with his warriors.

"I need to speak with the android a moment," he told Jenna. "Go to our table and I will join you soon."

She nodded and moved toward the front of the hall, but he sensed her reluctance. He knew she was still uncomfortable with his officers, and he suspected she was self-conscious about her newly acquired rose aura. Masculine satisfaction swelled inside him, but diminished somewhat when he reminded himself of what he wished to discuss with the android.

He strode toward its table, tensing with disapproval when he saw that all four warriors with the android emanated clear, red auras. Their red was not tinged with the pink generated by mated lovers; besides, none of the four were mated. They did not appear angry, so that left only one possibility: lust. They were staring at the android with lustful gazes and generating unmistakable sexual energies.

It was highly inappropriate for unmated Leors to even be thinking about sexual matters, much less be lusting after a machine. Arion reached the table, his cold, condemning glare moving over each of his warriors. "The four of you will vacate this table so I may speak with the android. And you will all report to me at six hundred hours tomorrow."

The warriors apparently read his displeasure, and quickly stood and bowed before departing. They wisely opted to leave the hall entirely rather than relocate to another table. Arion watched them go, a low growl in his throat.

"Is something wrong, Comdar?" the android asked.

"Discipline is slipping among my warriors," he hissed. "It will not be tolerated."

The android looked toward the departing Leors, a puzzled expression on its face. "I sense your animosity toward those males, yet they have been most cooperative in my research efforts. As a matter of fact, I had asked them to return tomorrow to give more specimens."

"They will not be able to assist you tomorrow. They will be completing extensive work duties."

"I see. Then I will have to check the data banks for other suitable candidates for further testing. Did you need me for some reason, Comdar?"

Forcing his displeasure into a mental compartment, he took a deep breath and got to the business at hand. "How can I ensure that mating will not be painful for Jenna?"

The android considered a moment. "You have only mated the one time, during the full moon alignment?"

He hated discussing any of this with a machine. But he knew he'd hurt Jenna badly last night, that he had lost

231

control—unheard of for him—and been too rough. "Yes, just once," he admitted. "I believe it was very stressful for her. I do not wish for that to happen again."

"Stress." A lopsided grin appeared on the android's face. "Ah, yes. You do not want your mate to suffer stress."

His irritation grew. "Can you advise me on this situation or not?"

It nodded, looking annoyingly smug. "Of course. Some sexual responses are not automatic. You will need to help create these responses in Jenna. There are also different positions that will allow her to control movement and penetration. Do you still have the holovideo that Lani gave you?"

Outrage roared through Arion. "How did you know about that?"

"Lani told me she had given it to you."

That cursed echobird had a big mouth and was far too meddlesome. Now Arion wondered how many others knew about the HV.

"I would advise you to consult the holovideo," the android continued blithely. "I believe *Intermediate Lovemaking* is the section you need."

"I will consider your advice," he gritted out.

"Getting Jenna to relax will also reduce the level of discomfort. Alcoholic beverages are often helpful in inducing a relaxed state. You might try offering her kashni." The android's lopsided smile returned. "She seems to have a taste for it."

Yes, his little mate appeared willing to imbibe large amounts of kashni, even though she did not handle it well. While Arion's pride demanded that he be able to give his mate sexual pleasure without the aid of alcohol, he did not want her suffering any more pain or stress than necessary.

"If kashni does not help, and the holovideo does not provide the information you seek, let me know," the android told him. "I will be glad to advise you further."

"There will be no need," he muttered, turning away. It

appeared he would spend some time at his computer tonight, after Jenna was asleep.

He was the head of the Sauran clan and commanded almost a thousand warriors. He could wield innumerable types of combat weapons with deadly skill, and kill with his bare hands. He could pilot a star-class spaceship, could strategize and orchestrate precise, successful space battles.

There was no reason he could not handle a single human female; no reason he could not find a way to perform the mating act successfully and satisfy said female without hurting her. Even if he had to watch the echobird's video, he would prevail. One way or another, he would get this mating business right.

The next cycle passed without incident, although Kerem looked at Jenna and snickered several times throughout the cycle. She pointedly ignored him. As the end of her shift approached, she thought about the night ahead and about Arion, and felt a nervous fluttering in the pit of her stomach.

She wondered if their next mating would occur tonight. A part of her was apprehensive, while another part of her felt a heated rush of anticipation, and tendrils of desire curled through her. She admitted to herself she was very much affected by Arion's raw animal magnetism, and wanted to explore the newly awakened cravings inundating her body.

She wondered if more than concern for her welfare had kept him from mating with her last night. After she'd gone to bed, he'd spent a long time at his computer, intently watching something on the screen. She couldn't see what it was, as he had the monitor turned away from her. When he finally came to bed, there was an expression of ruthless determination on his face.

Yet tonight, when she returned to the dome after her shift in the nursery, Arion acted as if he had no unusual concerns. They walked to the dining hall and ate the evening meal, then returned to the dome. He settled on the settee as he did every evening, and cleaned his weapons. He trained almost every cycle, and was fastidious in the care of his equipment. He didn't attempt to kiss her, or initiate anything sexual in nature.

Somewhat disappointed, Jenna sat next to him, reading a file about Leor infant development on a handheld scanner. Maxine had accessed and downloaded several files on Leor offspring, and Jenna found the data informative and fascinating. She and Arion spent a long time in companionable silence.

She decided he must be giving her another cycle to recover from their mating, and since she was still a little sore, she didn't challenge his decision. She also decided that if he tried to give her any more time after tonight, she would take matters into her own hands. She was ready for their relationship to move to the next, more intimate level, despite her nervousness.

"I wish to have a drink," Arion announced suddenly and rose from the settee. "Join me in some kashni." He strode to the large console that contained a small cold store where fruit and homa were available for quick snacks, as well as a cabinet where kashni and glasses were stored.

His request seemed very odd, since he had teased her several times about her overindulgence in kashni on their merging day. Her own experience with a two-cycle headache made her reluctant to imbibe again. "I don't think so," she hedged.

He looked at her over his shoulder. "Afraid to try it again, little coward?"

She found the knowing smirk on his face annoying. "Let's just say I'm a fast learner."

He turned back and poured two glasses before returning to the settee. "It will not harm you to drink a moderate amount," he said, handing her a tumbler that was only half-full. "It can be very . . . relaxing."

Perplexed, she took the drink. "I don't have any trouble sleeping, especially since you had the heat coils removed on my side of the bed."

He sat beside her. "You do appear to sleep well. In fact, your snoring can be quite loud."

"I do *not* snore!" she insisted, then fretted silently a moment. "Do I?"

He gave her one of his rare smiles, and her heart skittered. He was very attractive, in a rugged, savage way, and when he smiled he was downright sexy. "Only when you are very drunk," he said.

She opened her mouth to protest, closed it abruptly. She had lived alone for the past fourteen seasons, and had no way of disproving his claim. Not only that, she knew her denial would only encourage his outrageous behavior.

He returned his attention to his tasks. Bemused, she picked up the scanner. She sipped the kashni slowly as she read, and had to admit the warmth seeping through her was soothing.

After a while, Arion stood and put the cleaning supplies and his weapons away. He also took her empty glass. "I'm going to bathe," he announced.

Jenna's heart rate kicked up a notch as she thought about the hot oil she would soon be rubbing on his bare skin—and what might happen after that. But it wasn't the nervous fluttering she'd experienced earlier. The kashni had mellowed her just enough to take the edge off her jitters.

"All right," she murmured. "Call me when you're ready for the oil." She tried to concentrate on the scanner after he left, but all she could think of was his magnificent, nude body in the shower, glistening in the water.

She jumped when his voice slipped into her mind. *Jenna, come to the bathing chamber. I require your assistance.*

I'll be right there.

Wondering if he might have somehow picked up on her thoughts, she put away the scanner and went to the bathing chamber. She paused in the entry, surprised. Arion wasn't in the shower, his usual preference for bathing; nor was he drying beneath the overhead blower. He was reclining in the huge sunken tub, steaming water lapping at his impressive pectorals.

Her mouth suddenly dry, Jenna cleared her throat. "Yes?"

Arion's dark, searing gaze swept over her, as potent as a physical touch. "Come scrub my back."

She moved forward slowly, feeling like a kerani held in thrall by the mesmerizing gaze of a sleek viper. Wetting her lips, she knelt by the tub, her attention drawn to Arion's impressive maleness, his state of arousal evident even through the rippling water.

"You are getting distracted, wife. You were going to scrub my back."

Her gaze jerked up to meet his glittering, knowing stare. He slid over to the steps on the side of the tub, presenting his back. Any woman in her right mind would be distracted by his body, she thought. He handed her the washing cloth over his shoulder and leaned forward expectantly. She could see though the clear water, down to his nice, tight rear.

"I am waiting."

Blazing hells. She began scrubbing with a vengeance, starting with his broad shoulders and working her way to the middle of his back.

"That feels good. Lower."

Lower? She wasn't sure she could go much farther down and keep her balance, or her wits. Bracing herself on her left hand, she leaned down, her chest resting on the warm tiles, and ran the cloth to his waist and below. In the next moment, he turned sideways, his strong fingers wrapping around her wrist and yanking her forward. With a startled cry, she slid headfirst into the water.

She went under right where Arion's body should have blocked her entry, bumping down the two steps into the tub. She came up sputtering, and found herself face-to-face with her mate.

His eyes gleamed with amusement. "I believe you fell into the tub, *charina*. That is odd. You are usually very graceful."

She spat out a mouthful of water. "*What?* I did *not* fall in! You pulled me in."

"Such an accusation." He slipped a powerful arm around her waist and maneuvered her against his rock-hard body, settling back on the steps so that she straddled his legs. She could feel his hardness pressing intimately against her, and heat curled through her blood. "Now your hair is wet." He tugged at the twist, and the sodden mass plopped against her back.

"Arion—"

"And your face is wet." Framing her face in his hands, he leaned down and licked her eyes and cheeks.

The words died in her throat. Automatically she slanted her face toward him. His tongue on her skin was a touch that was rapidly becoming familiar and very . . . stimulating. His hands slid down over her breasts to her waist. He lifted her easily, as if she weighed no more than a feather, dragging her along his chest, until she was above him.

"Arion, what are you—"

Her question ended in a gasp as his mouth closed over her nipple, his tongue teasing it through the wet material. The sensation was electrifying, and she arched against him with a small cry. *Good, charina?* His voice filled her mind, low, sultry, knowing.

"Umm . . . yes," she managed, as liquid warmth rushed to her lower extremities.

He sucked her nipple, pulling it deeper into his mouth.

At the same time, he deftly eased her pants down her thighs. Then his fingers were between her legs, finding her sensitized flesh and stroking. One long finger slid up inside her, and all the breath left her lungs.

We are going to ensure your pleasure tonight, he told her mentally. *Whatever it takes.*

Oh, my. She didn't think it would take much. His mouth on her breast, his fingers touching her so intimately, the personal invasion of his voice in her mind, all surrounded by the kashni's warm glow, threatened to send her body into meltdown.

He withdrew his hand, but before she could protest, he gripped her waist again and lifted her from the tub. She found herself sitting on the heated tiles that edged the tub, with him rising onto his knees on the top step, water sluicing off him.

"What . . ." she started to say, ending with another gasp as he pushed her back onto the tiles. He stripped off her pants fully, then moved over her, taking her mouth in a savage, ruthless possession. All protests fled the feel of his tongue dueling with hers. She gave a little moan of satisfaction, running her hands along his arms.

He shifted, lifting away. She tried to drag him back, but he rose above her and ripped open her soaking tunic. He moved back down, bracing both hands on each side of her, and lowered his mouth to her breasts. She moaned again as his tongue circled each of her nipples. *Lie still and feel what I am doing to you,* he murmured inside her head. She was too stunned to argue—not that she wanted to.

His tongue rasped across her breasts, lapping the water from each before he moved lower, exploring her midriff. Then lower still, making her shiver as his tongue trailed over her abdomen, dipping into her belly button before continuing even lower. He reached the auburn curls and she stiffened, surprise jolting her from the sensuous stupor. He parted her legs.

I can smell your arousal, charina. His words went through her like a jolt of electricity. Then she felt the shocking slide of his tongue against her most intimate flesh. Her brain ceased functioning completely, over-whelmed by an onslaught of pleasure.

He was merciless, tasting and teasing, then delving deeply, the rough texture of his tongue wildly exciting. Tension coiled deep inside her, a building craving for more . . . for something she couldn't name. Just more.

He growled deep in his chest, and she could sense the wildness in him, the implacable resolve that she reach the same peak he had in their first mating. The same wildness was growing in her, fueled by the shocking things he was doing to her, by the relentless stroking of his tongue. She moaned, feeling the flames searing her, the tension build-ing higher and higher.

Then the explosion hit, with the force of a supernova. *Arion!* she screamed mentally, her lungs too constricted to allow her voice to function properly. She grabbed his smooth head, and twisted beneath him, mindless in the throes of the detonation.

As her senses slowly returned, she lay there breathing raggedly, unable to utter a word. She stared up at her mate, who stared back, triumph in his eyes. "We are not through," he muttered roughly, lifting her and pulling her back into the tub.

He brought her against him, spreading her legs so that she again straddled him, her knees on the step. Her senses still reeling, she grabbed his shoulders to steady herself. She felt his erection probing between her legs, and then he was inside her, filling her in one smooth stroke. There was a moment of discomfort, but her muscles gave way around him until she felt only a pulsing fullness.

"Look at me," he commanded, lifting her chin so that she was forced to comply. Dazed, she stared up into his smoldering eyes. "Does it hurt?"

"No," she whispered.

"Good." His hands cupped her hips, lifted her up, lowered her down.

The friction was stunning and she forgot to breathe, or to think, or do anything but move, his hands guiding her. Her body took over instinctively, setting its own pace when he relaxed his grasp. She was again seized with a spiraling tension, a need that drove her until her movements became frenzied. She gripped Arion's shoulders, and he became her anchor in the maelstrom of sensation. She heard his harsh breathing mingled with hers, felt his heart pounding as fiercely.

Another explosion, more powerful than the first, rocketed through her, and she cried out. The waves of sensation seemed to go on forever until she finally collapsed against him, feeling as if she'd just been shot from a rocket projector. He shifted and stood, keeping them joined, and she realized he was still fully aroused. She hadn't even collected her wits before he carried her, dripping wet, to the bed.

He settled her there, the length of his body pressing her down. He stretched her arms over her head on the mat, and his hands circled her wrists and pinned them. Bracing against her wrists, he lifted himself enough to stare down at her. "Again," he growled.

She tried to shake her head, tried to tell him she wouldn't survive another climax. But then he was moving inside her, slow, and so deep that she could feel him against her womb. He stroked over and over, with no sign of reaching his own completion.

Incredibly, the tension began building inside her once more, the insatiable craving, the burning need for a relief only he could give. Everything faded but the plunge and retreat of his powerful body, filling her physically and spiritually, as his midnight eyes held her prisoner.

Again, charina. You will find pleasure again.

Helpless against his physical mastery and his compelling voice inside her head, she did just that, tumbling once more into a vortex of intense pleasure. He found his own release with a mighty groan, his massive body shuddering. She held him tightly, amazed by the intense, primal feelings his physical surrender roused within her. She sensed they were both equally vulnerable during the explosive moment of climax; that giving oneself fully during mating was an act of ultimate trust. The power of the union awed her.

Arion rolled off and collapsed beside her, his chest rising and falling rapidly. He didn't speak for a long time, although he reached over and cupped her cheek. He wasn't normally demonstrative, and his gesture spoke louder than any flowery words ever could.

When he finally did speak, he said, "I am certain I will gain more control with repetition."

More control? Spirit help her! Jenna began to understand what Maxine had meant about the sexual endurance of Leor males, and it was almost beyond her comprehension. At first, she'd been concerned she wouldn't survive mating with Arion because of his fierceness and his size. Now she wondered if she could survive this planet-shattering pleasure in such great quantities, and on a regular basis—and she had no doubt it would be frequently. She didn't know if her heart could hold out, or her body escape incineration. Not that she had any choice; she had committed to mating with Arion.

It would certainly be a challenge . . . and she intended to give it her best shot.

Chapter Fifteen

Jenna entered the medical center, a small plexishield container in her hand. The center was very similar to the laboratory, with an entry lobby and a decontamination unit. Although Leors rarely became ill, they apparently adhered to standard medical practices concerning bacteria and contagious diseases. Jenna knew they all underwent routine inoculations against any diseases they might encounter in their travels and possibly bring back to their settlements. With their grueling physical lifestyle, Leors were more likely to become injured than sick, so the medical center had advanced surgical and physical therapy facilities.

Not advanced enough, however, to help young Erek. Jenna knew, through regular updates from Maxine, that the boy's condition had stabilized; but Lanka did not have the necessary technology at her disposal to repair his damaged spinal cord or to reconstruct his shattered legs. Jenna hadn't been able to stop thinking about Erek, and when she'd seen the huge Branuka bug buzzing around the starflowers near the Goddess mesa the previous cycle, she'd cajoled Arion into capturing it for her.

She smiled now, thinking of his incredulity when she asked him to get it, and then how her heart had warmed at the sight of her massive mate chasing a Branuka bug across the sand. Of course, it had cost her: a kiss, followed by more extensive sensual activity, right at the base of the Goddess altar.

Apparently, the Goddess was not offended by the lusty appetite of her worshippers. Voracious might be more accurate, since Arion seemed insatiable. He was very demanding, but he was also a thorough, considerate lover— and Maxine had certainly been right about his stamina. Just thinking about their intense mating, especially at the mesa yesterday, Jenna felt a flare of desire low in her belly. The Goddess obviously approved, because Jenna could have sworn she saw the statue's face glowing afterward.

Now she stood impatiently in the decontamination chamber, hoping the process wouldn't hurt the bug, which buzzed angrily every time the plexishield container was disturbed. The rays shut off, and the panel slid open, and the bug protested loudly as Jenna shifted the case and entered the actual center.

Unlike the lab, the center was sectioned into two main areas, one on the left, where Leors received immunizations or waited to see Lanka, and one on the right, composed of examining tables and an array of sophisticated medical equipment. The entire area was brightly lit by overhead halogen lights, and extremely warm, as were the majority of the public facilities on Saura. At first glance, the center appeared deserted, the only sounds the hum of machines.

Then Jenna saw Lanka treating a Leor male on one of the examining tables. There was a suture unit on his thigh, and the healer was cleaning some cuts across his chest. Training injuries, most likely. Even Arion, as skilled at combat and weapons as he was, sometimes returned to the dome at night with minor injuries.

Lanka looked up as Jenna approached, her expression

none too friendly. "I'm here to see Erek," Jenna said, knowing formalities were a wasted effort.

Lanka's eyes narrowed, and Jenna thought for a moment the healer would deny her access to the boy. But the healer grunted and jerked her head toward a panel at the end of the examining area. Jenna walked to the entry, and drawing a deep breath, pushed the pad. The panel slid open and she stepped through, into what must be an intensive care area. There were four flotation beds, each with its own impressive bank of equipment. Three huge floor-to-ceiling portals lined the far wall, and blinding sunlight streamed in, in addition to the halogen lights recessed in the high ceiling.

Three of the beds were empty. Erek was in the fourth, on the far left, near a portal. Jenna recognized the Leor woman by the bed as Nona, although she didn't know the older Leor female wearing the green loincloth signifying a healer, and who was taking readings from the equipment. Both women turned at the sound of the panel and stared at Jenna.

"*You*," Nona hissed, her eyes narrowing. "What do you want?"

"I'd like to see your son," Jenna said, walking forward. She knew Nona had been punished with two shocks from an electrolyzer rod, despite Jenna's vehement protests to Arion. Since there had been five other witnesses to Nona striking her—amazingly, the server counted as a witness—Arion had not been able to circumvent disciplinary action, although he had imposed only the minimum punishment. Jenna was hoping Nona would be reluctant to hit her again.

"I do not want you here," Nona growled. "Get out."

Jenna looked at the boy on the flotation bed. He was awake and watching her. "I don't intend to stay long. I just want to see how Erek is doing, and I brought him something." She held up the plexishield container, and the bug buzzed loudly.

Erek's eyes lit up. "Branuka," he said.

Jenna moved around Nona and to the bed. "Do you like it? The Comdar himself caught it for you." She hoped he could understand Contran, since she had only learned a few words of the harsh, guttural Leor language. Most of the Leors on Saura either could speak Contran or had neural translators.

Erek's eyes grew wide, and a shock went through Jenna. His eyes were a deep blue—the sign of a shaman. She stared, wondering if shamans were born at random, and how rare was their occurrence. The boy gestured imperiously, then held out his hand, and she could almost visualize him as a future Morven. She placed the container in his grip, and he studied the bug, satisfaction gleaming in his startling eyes. "*My* Branuka."

Her gaze dropped to his legs. They were encased in bulky castlike units, the indicators on them probably monitoring healing electrical currents and readouts on the bone and muscle. They were totally motionless, a stark reminder that this boy might never walk again. Surely there was something that could be done, the necessary technology to heal him available *somewhere* in this quadrant, or perhaps the Verante Quadrant. A possibility occurred to Jenna, but Erek distracted her. "Head," he said, pointing to her.

Confused, she lifted her hand to her head, then realized what had caught his attention. "Do you mean my hair?" she asked, smoothing her fingers over the twist. "This?"

He nodded. "Hay-er," he said, drawing out and exaggerating the word. Apparently he understood Contran, surprising in view of his childlike mind, or he had a translator implanted. He stretched out his free hand. "I want to see."

"All right." She stepped closer and leaned down so he could run his fingers over it.

"It is red brown." He gave a curious tug on the twist.

"Yes, it has some red color. Here, I'll let you see all of it." She loosened the twist and shook out the tresses.

He gave a delighted shout, and a smile split his face. Setting the plexishield container beside him, he grabbed her hair with both hands and ran his fingers up and down it. He was surprisingly gentle, only pulling a little. "Hay-er, hay-er, hay-er," he said, practically beaming. Then he ran his tongue along it as well.

Jenna remained bent down, patiently letting him examine her hair to his content. His injuries were so grievous, it was a small thing she could offer. He finally drew back, gave her a calculating look. "Mine. My hay-er."

Behind her, Nona grunted.

"Actually, it's attached to my head," Jenna said. She gave a little jerk. "See? I can't give it to you." The boy's expression fell, so she added, "I'll cut off a little and bring it back tomorrow. All right?"

He considered. "You bring some hay-er tomorrow?"

"Yes."

"That is good."

He sounded so much like a miniature Morven, or just about any Leor male, that she had to smile. "I'm glad you like that solution. I'll leave you with your Branuka bug now."

He scowled, his lip thrusting out. "Do not go. I like you here."

"Well, Erek, my mate is the Comdar, and he will be displeased if I don't return to our dome so we can have our evening meal."

"The Comdar," the boy said, awe in his young voice. "Very strong and brave."

"Yes, he is. And he's waiting for me, so I have to go. But I'll come back tomorrow."

He picked up the plexishield container and stared at the noisy bug, then finally nodded. "You come tomorrow."

Jenna left the medical center, deep in thought. She had an idea that might help Erek, but she needed more information. She pushed pad one on her comm and contacted Maxine.

"You will not cut your hair," Arion said. "I will not allow it."

Jenna threw up her hands in frustration. "You're going to cut it, not me. And it's my hair, so I can do whatever I want with it."

His expression grew ominous. "You belong to me, and so does your hair. If you cut it without my consent, you will experience my hand on your rear—and it will not be a mating touch."

He was so primitive. "What happened to your promise that you would never hit me?"

"Putting you over my knee and warming your backside is not the same thing as striking you."

She rolled her eyes but decided not to point out that Leor females would never tolerate such an action. "Look, Mr. Macho, I only want you to cut off a little, about five centimeters. You won't even notice the difference. Besides, hair has to be trimmed from time to time. Look at these ends—they're split and uneven."

He scowled at the strands she held up for his perusal. But he didn't say no again, so she pressed her case. "My hair grows very fast, and it's good to trim it. It will benefit my hair and, at the same time, I can give some to Erek. I told him I would."

"I do not know about cutting hair," he protested.

"Then I'll have Maxine do it, and you'll hardly be able to tell the difference. All right?"

"She had better not cut too much."

"Or you'll put her over your knee?" she retorted.

He gave her a squinty-eyed glare. Then he grunted and headed for the bathing chamber. Jenna debated whether to voice her other request now or later, and opted for now. Later she would be putting the heated oil on his skin, and that generally distracted them both and led to other, highly sensual pursuits.

"Arion, I want to speak to you about another matter."

He stopped and turned. "What is it?"

"It's about Erek. Maxine thinks the technology that might repair his spine and legs isn't available on Saura."

His expression grew grim. "No, it is not. Lanka has informed me that she cannot help the boy."

"And he's destined to be a shaman, right?"

Arion nodded. "Yes."

"How can he possibly perform the duties of a shaman, or participate in saktars, if he's crippled?"

"I do not know. But it is obviously the will of the Goddess that Erek face this challenge."

"Maxine and I both know one person who might be able to help Erek to walk again."

"Who would that be?"

"Dr. Chase McKnight. He's a renowned healer in both the Dark and the Verante Quadrants. He has a spaceship that is outfitted with the most advanced medical equipment in the galaxy."

"I have heard of him. He is the one who formulated the cure for the Orana virus that was destroying the Shielders about eight seasons ago. His mate is a Shielder, I believe."

"That's right. He's married to Nessa dan Ranul, who is Captain san Ranul's sister."

"I remember now." Arion said. "However, with the exception of servers or human mates, we do not allow non-Leors to visit our settlements."

"But this is a special situation," Jenna argued. "Erek's quality of life will be horrible if he remains the way he is—especially since Leors put so much value on physical ability. Not only that, he might not be able to fulfill his destiny as a shaman. Dr. McKnight is highly respected and very honorable."

She paused, then used the one point Maxine had said

would guarantee Arion's cooperation. "He might even be able to do some research on Leor fertility problems."

Arion considered a moment. "I will discuss the matter with my officers. If a majority of them are in favor of allowing Dr. McKnight to come to Saura, then I will agree to it."

"That would be great. Thank you."

He took her hand and pulled her toward the bathing chamber. "You can express your gratitude by scrubbing my back."

Jenna went readily, anticipating a pleasurable mating session in the big tub. She was not disappointed.

Chase McKnight arrived six cycles later, in the middle of sleep shift. The dome's comm roused them. Jenna lifted her head in sleepy confusion as Arion rolled out of bed and went to the console to respond to the command center's hail. She snuggled back down, closing her eyes and drifting away to the murmuring of her mate's voice, until he said, "Jenna, wake up."

"What is it?" She struggled to sit up, pushing her hair from her face.

"Dr. McKnight has arrived, but he is not alone."

She yawned. "Who's with him?"

"For one thing, his mate and a son."

"I know Nessa always travels with him and assists him. I also know some of their children travel with them from time to time. Is that a problem?"

"No," Arion said slowly. "That is acceptable. However, another ship is accompanying them."

"Really?" Jenna settled back on the bed. "I thought McKnight took only family on his travels. Who else is with him?"

"A male who claims he is your brother."

"*What?*" Fully awake now, she came to her knees. "My brother?"

"Zerahm says he has identified himself as Damon san Aron, and he states he wishes to see his sister."

Her brother? Wanting to see her? It was beyond Jenna's comprehension, even more so because of her current muddled state. "Damon," she said wonderingly. "I haven't heard from him in almost . . . fourteen seasons."

"Do you wish to speak to him?"

"Oh, yes." Anticipation thrumming through her, she slid from the bed and padded to the console.

"Patch me through to san Aron's ship," Arion instructed Zerahm, then vacated the chair for Jenna.

She sank into it, her heartbeat rapid, as the view screen blanked, then flickered, then came into focus to reveal the face of a man. It was older, had more lines, but the face she remembered well. "Damon," she breathed, unable to think of anything else.

"Jen-Jen," he answered, the nickname hurling her back to the distant past, when they'd shared a camaraderie of sorts, before her visions and the death of their parents had driven a wedge between them.

A yearning stirred inside her, a need for the family she'd long been without, had yet to find, even on Saura. Her relationship with Arion was still too new, too uncertain, and the other Leors had not given any indication of accepting her. Now Damon, her brother, her only living kin, was here.

"What are you doing at Saura?" she asked.

"When I arrived on Shamara twenty cycles ago, I was hoping to see you. I learned you had been mated to a Leor and had relocated to Saura." He paused and stared at her. "I've missed you, Jen. I didn't realize how much until I got to Shamara and found you weren't there."

A thrill shot through her at his words. She and Damon were related by blood, and by shared experiences and memory. He was not only family but he was her own kind, and she saw acceptance and caring in his green eyes.

"I've missed you, too," she replied. "I didn't know where you were these past fourteen seasons, or if you were alive."

"I know." Regret filled his gaze. "There is so much to explain. When I heard Dr. McKnight was traveling here, I requested that I be allowed to travel with him, so I could see you. I'd like to spend a few days on Saura with you, to try to catch up on everything that's happened."

"That would be wonderful. But . . ." She glanced askance at Arion. "I don't know if you can."

Her mate squatted next to her, his narrow-eyed gaze on Damon. "We do not allow non-Leors to visit our settlements. Dr. McKnight is authorized because of extenuating circumstances."

"I understand that, Comdar," Damon said with quiet respect. "But perhaps you would consider me a relation, since you are mated with my sister. I will only stay a few cycles, and leave when McKnight departs."

Muting the speaker, Arion turned to Jenna. She looked at him, silently pleading. "He's my only family."

"*I* am your family," her mate growled.

"He is my only blood relation," she amended, laying her hand on his arm, touched by his vehement proclamation. "You're right. You are my mate, and together we'll create our own family. But he is my brother."

Arion's breath hissed out. "I will allow it this one time, *charina*." His gaze snapped back to the view screen, and he reactivated the speaker. "San Aron, you have permission to land, and to remain on Saura until Dr. McKnight departs. During that time, you will be restricted to the residential part of the settlement, and you will be accompanied by a Leor warrior at all times. Do you agree to these conditions?"

Damon nodded. "Absolutely, Your Lordship. I only want to see my sister, and I agree to honor your wishes."

"So be it. Prepare to receive landing coordinates." Arion

hit the screen pad and reconnected with the command center. "Zerahm, allow both McKnight and san Aron to land their ships. Instruct them to remain on board their craft until first sunrise, when I will personally greet them. Station guards nearby to ensure that they follow those orders. I also want you to assign warriors to accompany both males at all times."

Zerahm, some seasons older than Arion, and his second in command, did not look happy. "Sir, may I remind you that it is against our laws to allow non-Leors to visit Saura?"

"And I will remind you that I am the Comdar, and I give the orders. You were present, as were all officers, when we discussed Dr. McKnight coming here. A vote was taken, and it was agreed that McKnight would be allowed to treat Erek."

"I voted against it, because it goes against the intent of our laws, and I also wish to go on record as opposing Damon san Aron's presence on Saura."

"Your opposition is so noted. Now I expect you to follow orders."

Zerahm nodded, but his eyes sparked with anger. "Yes, sir." The view screen blanked, and Arion rose.

Jenna leaped from the chair and threw herself against him, wrapping her arms around his waist. "Oh, Arion, thank you!" She felt a low rumble in his chest, and looked up at him, amazed. He rarely laughed. "What's so funny?"

"You, *charina*. Look at yourself. Do you realize that you just greeted your brother wearing no clothing?"

She automatically looked down, although she knew she was nude. At Arion's adamant insistence, she hadn't worn anything to bed since they had first mated, and she was getting used to moving around the dome without any clothing. A hot flush spread upward from her chest to her face. Most likely, only the upper half of her chest had been visible on the view screen, and much of that had been covered by the wild jumble of her hair. But still, her state of undress had probably been obvious.

"Perhaps some of your foolish modesty has worn off," Arion suggested. "Would you like me to order a loincloth replicated for you?"

"Very funny," she muttered, tempted to punch his chest. Instead, she found herself stroking the textured skin that stretched over swells of muscle. Unable to resist, she leaned forward and ran her tongue over a flat nipple, savoring the shudder that ran through her powerful, fierce mate. It continually amazed her that she had such sensual power over him.

Smiling to herself, she pulled back and sauntered toward the bed, faking a yawn. "I'm going back to sleep."

"I do not think so," Arion growled, fisting his hand in her hair and tugging her back to him. "You cannot rouse a raging beast and then walk away from combat." He pressed her against him, letting her feel how very roused the beast was.

"Combat, is it?" she whispered, a now-familiar heat running through her body like molten lava.

"It is." He slid his hand between them, down her abdomen to the heart of her need. He was learning just how to touch and stroke her until she couldn't think of anything other than the intense pleasure he gave her. "I intend to use every weapon at my disposal," he promised in a husky voice.

Her knees went weak. "I see." She did a little reconnaissance of her own, discovering the impressive length and width of his main weapon. "It should be quite a battle."

With another growl, he swept her up in his arms and carried her back to bed, where he proceeded to prove he had just as much sensual power over her as she had over him.

Chapter Sixteen

Jenna went with Arion to greet the visitors at first sunrise. She was surprised at the quality of her brother's ship. A sleek, private, star-class cruiser, it appeared relatively new and in good condition. She wondered how Damon had come by such a nice ship, as she waited anxiously for him to disembark, both nervous and excited at the same time. It had been so long since she'd seen him, she didn't know what to expect.

Stepping from his craft, he looked good in the pale sunlight. His hair, the same auburn color as hers, waved gently back from a high forehead, and was long enough to brush the tops of his shoulders. His eyes were greener than she remembered, his face a little more weathered, but he still had the boyish good looks and the broad-shouldered, slim-hipped build that had attracted his share of women.

She felt the unique tingling sensation that signaled the presence of another Shielder. It was an energy all Shielders radiated and could sense in each other. Fortunately, few other races could detect it. Damon came down the ramp and stood there, staring at her. She moved forward, uncertainty restraining her.

"Jenna," he said, his voice also uncertain.

"Damon." She took the last step, grasped his arms.

"Jen-Jen." He hugged her awkwardly.

It was enough to loosen her reserve, and she hugged him back with a shaky laugh. He pulled away and they both smiled. His gaze roved over her. "You're looking great, Jen."

"You look pretty good yourself," she said, fighting back a rush of emotion. "It's been a long time."

"Yeah. Too long." He looked past her to Arion and nodded respectfully.

"Greetings," Arion said.

"Greetings. May a thousand suns shine favorably upon Your Lordship," Damon responded formally and appropriately. He obviously knew the protocol for dealing with Leors.

"We extend our hospitality and expect that you will honor our ways," Arion said, a clear warning behind his words.

"Of course." Damon returned his attention to Jenna. "It's good to see you, Jen. We have a lot to talk about."

"We do," she agreed. "Hopefully, we can start catching up at the morning meal. Getting Dr. McKnight to Erek is the first priority."

"I understand." Damon stepped back as Dr. McKnight and his family disembarked from their ship, which was twice the size of Damon's, and very impressive.

Chase McKnight was a big man, almost as large as Arion, and he dwarfed his mate, Nessa. Their son, Brand, walked down the ramp behind them. He'd grown significantly in the two seasons since Jenna had last seen him, making a transition from boy to young man. He towered over Nessa now, and his frame had filled out and taken on sleek muscle. He was good-looking, with dark hair and dark eyes, and the energetic glow of youth.

As Leor protocol dictated, Chase waited for Arion to speak first, then presented his wife and son before turning to Jenna with a warm greeting. "Lady Jenna, it's good to see you again."

"Please, just Jenna. Thank you so much for coming, Dr. McKnight."

"Please, just Chase," he said, a smile lighting his eyes.

"All right, Chase." Jenna turned and accepted Nessa's embrace. The two of them were close in age and both had grown up on Liron. But while Nessa had been an outcast from the entire colony, including her own parents, at an early age, Jenna had merely been shunned by the other colonists. Even so, she felt a true affinity with Nessa, and had enjoyed her company the times they'd crossed paths on Shamara.

"Nessa, how are you?" Jenna drew back, studied the other Shielder. "You look like life has been good to you."

"Life is very good." Nessa smiled warmly. "How about you?" She glanced at Arion, then leaned close and whispered, "Your mate is most impressive. Is he treating you well?"

"Yes, very well," Jenna answered, realizing it was true. Arion might be overbearing and stubborn at times, but he'd never been unfair or cruel, and for the most part he granted her the respect she'd insisted upon. She was beginning to feel comfortable with him.

"Good." Nessa patted her arm. "We'll have to talk more later."

"I'd like that. And is this Brand? I can't believe how much he's grown!"

"Hasn't he though?" Nessa smiled proudly at her son, who shifted uncomfortably under her regard.

"How old are you now, Brand?" Jenna asked.

"I'm seventeen, Lady Jenna," he replied in a deep, masculine voice.

He certainly had grown from a gangling youth into a fine young man. Jenna wondered if Erek would ever have that chance. "Do you mind if we go directly to the medical center?" she asked Arion. "I want Chase to see Erek as soon as possible."

"We will go when Dr. McKnight is ready. We can break our fast after that." Arion gestured to the two male Leors standing a respectful distance away. "Dr. McKnight, san Aron, a warrior is being assigned to each of you for the duration of your stay here."

Damon frowned, but nodded in understanding.

"I have no problem with that," Chase replied. "Let me get my case, and we'll go to the boy."

Lanka was already at the medical center when the group arrived. She regarded Chase with narrowed eyes and merely grunted when introductions were made. She unbent enough, however, to answer Chase's questions. Jenna had only heard Lanka speak in curt monosyllables, so it was interesting to hear her discuss complex medical matters in surprising detail. Chase seemed adept at drawing out Lanka's answers, without threatening her position as Arion's chief medical officer.

Damon shifted restlessly during the discussion. "I think I will excuse myself, since I can't understand any of this," he finally said, turning to Arion. "I'd like to look around, if I may?"

Arion's expression hardened. "You must stay within the boundaries of the settlement, and be accompanied by Marok at all times."

"Of course." Damon turned, obviously eager to leave the center, and one of the Leor warriors strode after him.

"I must also attend my duties," Arion said. "Dr. McKnight, I would like a full report after you finish your examination."

"Of course, Comdar." Chase looked at Lanka. "Shall we see the patient now?" She turned and led the way, as their odd group traipsed to the acute-care chamber, trailed by the remaining warrior.

Nona was waiting with Erek, who smiled broadly when he saw Jenna. Since her initial visit, she had come to see him every cycle, and she had grown very fond of the mischievous boy. She brought him something new each time. He had his Branuka bug, a small bundle of her hair, some colorful rocks from the desert, some hologames and holopuzzles, which Maxine had created, and some advanced toys sneaked from the nursery housing the five-year-olds.

"What you bring me?" Erek asked now, holding out his hand.

"I don't have any gifts today," Jenna said. "But I brought some people who might be able to help you get better. This is Dr. McKnight and his mate, Nessa, and their son, Brand."

Erek eyed them, his gaze lingering on Brand. "How many spans are you?" he demanded.

"I'm seventeen seasons," Brand responded. "What is your age?"

"Thirteen spans." Erek spoke proudly, his chest puffing out. "You like Branuka bugs?" He held up the case with the buzzing bug, kept alive with pieces of homan plant, and Brand was suitably impressed. He kept Erek occupied while Chase completed his exam.

Erek insisted on touching and tasting everyone's hair before he allowed them to leave. At Chase's request, Nona followed them out. He discussed his findings with Lanka and Nona: "The damage is extensive, but I believe I might be able to reconstruct the spinal column. I know I can repair the legs." His gaze moved to Nessa, and his expression softened. "I've had some experience with that."

Jenna remembered how badly Nessa had limped, due to a serious childhood injury that had never been properly treated—until Chase had repaired the leg. Now she walked normally.

"Will you allow me to work on your son?" Chase asked.

Nona nodded. "Yes. I do not want him to remain as he is."

"I am optimistic about his chances." Chase turned to Lanka. "Your facility is very impressive, but I have the specialized equipment that I'll need on my ship. It would be best to move the boy there. I'll start reconstructing the spine today. It will take several sessions and at least two days. Then we'll let him rest a day or so before we start on the legs. If this is acceptable to you, Healer Lanka, I would really appreciate your assistance during the procedures."

Lanka simply grunted and nodded, but she seemed pleased that Chase had included her. They arranged to begin right after the morning meal.

Damon, trailed by Marok, joined them at the dining hall. Jenna felt a jolt of happiness as her brother settled next to her at a table near the rear of the hall. Arion sat with his officers at the head table, leaving her free to talk openly with their visitors. Damon and Chase and Brand all accepted the meat the servers presented, while Jenna and Nessa declined. "I never could get used to the thought of eating animals," Nessa murmured to Jenna.

"Me either," Jenna replied, delighted to find a kindred spirit.

Chase eyed the scarred throats of the two servers attending them, and his mouth compressed into a grim line. "Damned barbaric practice," he muttered.

Although surprised that he would openly criticize the Leors, Jenna had to agree. "It really bothers me."

Chase's eyes had cooled to a magnasteel gray. "As much as I've been around the galaxy, it always surprises me what beings do to each other. Cursed Jaccians."

"Jaccians?" Jenna remembered they were horrible,

multitentacled aliens who survived as merchants, although they were known for cheating their customers.

"Yes. It's a common Jaccian practice to sever the vocal cords of those they capture or get from the Anteks to sell as slaves."

Damon leaned forward, nodding his agreement. "Chase is right. The Jaccians don't like their victims to get word out to family members, or to tell others about their cruelty."

"You think the Jaccians did this to the servers on Saura?" Jenna asked, stunned. "But I always thought . . ." She stopped herself. She didn't have any business voicing criticisms of her mate's people to outsiders.

"That the Leors did it?" Understanding softened Chase's gaze. "While it's certainly foolhardy to cross a Leor or break their laws, they're also known for their sense of honor and justice. They do not mistreat those under their care, nor do they punish the innocent. I would bet a hundred miterons that the scars on these servers were inflicted by Jaccians."

Jenna sat back, her thoughts whirling at this revelation. It made sense, she realized, because it explained why some of the servers on Saura still had their vocal cords—they hadn't been purchased from the Jaccians. She felt a huge sense of relief, although she was already discovering the Leors were not as vicious as she had originally believed.

"So, Jen, how did you end up mated with a Leor?" Damon asked.

Chase and Nessa and Brand all looked interested as well, and Jenna told them how she'd foreseen her mating with Arion four seasons past, and about the events leading up to the merging ceremony. She didn't reveal the details of the ceremony itself, knowing it was a sacred ritual, one that the Leors did not wish to share with the outside world.

"That was a very brave thing you did," Nessa said

softly, when Jenna finished. "Your unselfishness saved two Shielder colonies."

"No," Damon interjected. "Only one colony was saved."

"What?" Jenna turned to look at him. "Arion was supposed to transport two settlements in return for a bride."

"One of those settlements was massacred by Anteks before his ship reached them," Damon said. "I was still in the Dark Quadrant at the time, and that's what I heard."

"Oh, Spirit." Feeling sick, she shoved her homa away. Why hadn't Arion told her? No, she knew why. It would only have upset her further, and she'd been struggling to adapt to the Leor lifestyle as it was.

Nessa went utterly pale, her dark eyes glistening with unshed tears. Chase reached over and placed his massive hand over her tightly laced hands. "The bastards," he hissed, his eyes sparking with fury.

"Yeah," Damon agreed.

"Well, then, on that unpleasant note, let's see if we can accomplish something positive." Chase stood and helped Nessa to her feet, then wrapped a protective arm around her. "Time to start on Erek's recovery. Brand, do you want to assist us?"

"Yes, sir." The boy rose, and Jenna was again amazed at how much he had grown.

"Brand is fascinated with medical procedures," Nessa said proudly. "He wants to follow in Chase's footsteps."

"That's a very impressive path," Jenna said. "But you're an impressive young man, Brand. I look forward to hearing about your accomplishments."

"Thank you, Lady Jenna." Brand turned and followed Chase and Nessa from the dining hall, their Leor guard right behind.

Damon scooted his chair closer. "Are you really doing all right, Jen?" He looked around, dropped his voice. "I've heard these Leors are barbarians, not much better than Anteks."

"Oh, no, that's not true," Jenna protested, feeling compelled to defend the race who were now her people. "They're fierce, and I've seen them do some violent things, but they live by a code of honor. Arion has treated me well. I swear to Spirit."

"Good." He stared at her, his gaze earnest. "I know I haven't been much of a brother, especially these past fourteen seasons, but I've thought of you often."

"You have?" She was absurdly touched by his statement. "I've thought of you, too."

"I'm sorry I wasn't there for you after our parents died." He leaned back with a sigh. "I was young, and I couldn't deal with their deaths, with what those murdering Anteks did to them. And the fact that you had actually seen them die, in those visions of yours . . . I couldn't handle it. I let you down."

The rush of emotion she'd felt earlier swept over her again. Damon cared about her. He was her brother, and he cared, and he'd traveled a long way to reestablish their relationship. Joy swelled inside her heart. "It's all right," she told him. "I understand. We went through some awful times, but that's behind us. I'm so glad you're here."

He reached over and squeezed her hand. "I'm glad, too."

"What have you been doing for the past fourteen seasons?"

He shrugged. "Oh, a little of this, a little of that. I became an expert in weapon systems, both air and ground. I worked at developing better defenses against Anteks and attacks on settlements. I was also involved in the fight for our freedom, and I had a price on my head. I didn't dare risk returning to Liron for fear of leading shadowers or Anteks there, which was another reason I didn't try to contact you."

"A bounty on your head? How awful." Jenna sent a silent prayer of thanks to Spirit that her brother hadn't been captured by Controller agents. "You need to get away from this quadrant. You'll never be safe here. After you leave Saura, I want you to return to Shamara."

"I plan to. I'm going to help develop their defense system."

"Surely Shamara doesn't need a complex defense system," Jenna argued. "There is no warfare in the Verante Quadrant.

"The Dark Quadrant was also peaceful a hundred seasons ago, until the Controllers took all the power. We can't afford to become complacent. On Shamara, our people still learn how to fight and how to use weapons, don't they?"

"Yes, they do," Jenna admitted. Her brother was right. Shielders could never take their rights and freedoms for granted.

"That's why I'd like to tour the control center here on Saura, and see their weapon systems," Damon said. "I know they're very advanced, and it might give me some ideas on how to set up a ground defense for Shamara."

"I don't think you'll be allowed anywhere near the control center," Jenna replied, remembering Arion's reluctance to allow non-Leors on Saura. "But I suppose you could ask."

"Maybe you would ask Arion for me."

"Why wouldn't you ask him yourself?"

Damon shrugged again. "He's your mate. He'd be more likely to grant permission if you ask him." He leaned forward. "It would be great to see how the Leors have successfully defended themselves against the Controllers these many seasons. We could use such a defense on Shamara."

Seriously considering Damon's request, Jenna jumped when Arion's voice swept into her mind. *Are you enjoying your time with your brother?*

She glanced up to see him watching her from across the dining hall. *Very much. Thank you for letting him come to the settlement.*

Would you like to spend more time with him this cycle?

Yes, I really would.

Then I will excuse you from your duties today and inform Kerem you will be absent.

Touched by her mate's generosity, Jenna smiled at him. *Thank you.* He gave a brief nod before turning back to his officers.

"I'm free of my duties this cycle," she told Damon, deciding not to tell him about the telepathic link she shared with Arion. That was private, a special bond she had with her mate. "Why don't we spend it catching up on all that's happened the past fourteen seasons?"

"I'd like that." Damon grinned, revealing a flash of the boyish charm, of the brother she'd known so long ago. "I'd like that a lot.

"Chase said the procedure on Erek went very well this cycle," Jenna commented as she spread oil over Arion's broad back. He'd worked extra hours, well past second sunset, and hadn't returned to their dome until a short while ago. She had shared the evening meal with Damon and the McKnights.

"Lanka reported the same." Arion flexed his muscles and rolled his head.

"Sore?" she asked, sliding her hands lower.

A grunt was all she got, but she knew he'd been working out hard, had been on his feet many grueling hours. She moved to his beautifully sculpted rear, her breath catching at the perfection of him. "I enjoyed my time with Damon today."

"Good." He moved to allow her better access.

"I'd like to ask you something." She turned to scoop up more oil.

"What?"

"Damon is a weapons specialist, and he's working on a more sophisticated ground protection system for Shamara. He'd like to visit the Sauran control center and to look at your defense system." She slid her hands down the inside of his thighs.

"No."

"But he says the Leors have some of the most sophisticated weapons in the galaxy. He thinks your technology would benefit Shamara. I'm sure they would be willing to purchase it, or work out some sort of trade."

"I said no." Arion turned, grasping her wrists, and placing her oiled hands on his chest. Automatically, she smoothed the remaining oil over his pectoral muscles. "None except Leors cleared for the highest security are allowed access to the command center," he continued.

Jenna knew that was a good policy, but she had told Damon she would ask, and she had fulfilled that promise. "I understand." She ran her hands down his rippled abs.

With a harsh growl, Arion picked her up and carried her to the bed. "I haven't finished with the oil," she protested, as he laid her down and stripped off her tunic and pants.

"Later." He lowered himself over her, circling his tongue around her breast.

She sighed and stroked her fingers over his scalp. "Would you mind if I give Damon a tour outside the settlement tomorrow? I'd like to show him the mesas and the arena."

Arion raised his head and his glittering eyes captured her gaze. "You may take him out in a skimmer as long as a warrior accompanies you. You may not take him to the statue of our Goddess, or to the command or weapon centers."

"All right. I know he'll enjoy seeing the desert."

"Now," her mate rasped, sliding down and running his tongue over her belly. "No more talk." He parted her legs and lowered his head between them. Jenna gasped, arching back as his intimate kiss sent incredible pleasure roaring through her. He didn't have to worry about further conversation, because at the moment she was utterly incapable of coherent speech.

The next morning, Damon was moving a little slowly and his eyes were bloodshot. "What happened to you?" Jenna asked.

"A little too much kashni, sis," he said sheepishly.

"Kashni? Where did you get that?"

"Marok took me to the barracks of the unmated warriors last night." Damon squinted at the bright sunlight and shuddered. "Let's get to the dining hall. This light is making my headache worse."

"Homa will help," Jenna offered, having learned that fact from personal experience. "I thought the barracks would be off-limits to you."

"Apparently not. They're right on the edge of the settlement." With a grateful groan, Damon stepped inside the dining hall. "The light is better in here, but this damned heat is bothersome."

"You get used to it after a while." Taking his arm, Jenna guided him to the table where the McKnights were already eating. "So you drank kashni with the Leor warriors last night?"

"And played a little Fool's Quest," he admitted. "Fortunately, I didn't have many miterons to lose."

"But you lost what you had," she deduced. "You always liked gaming."

"Yeah. I guess some things never change."

"I'm grateful to have you here, just as you are." She nodded at the McKnights. "Good morning, Chase, Nessa. Where is Brand?"

"He caught another one of those orange and black bugs earlier this morning," Nessa said. "He took it to Erek, thinking it might cheer him up."

"It will. Erek loves Branuka bugs. That's very considerate of Brand." Jenna took a seat and leaned toward

Chase. "Tell me about Erek. Will he be able to walk again?"

"I think so. I'll finish working on the spinal cord today, and then we'll apply light and electricity for a cycle and see how the nerves and muscles respond. Once we see a regenerative response, we'll start on the legs. Those will be easier to repair. It will take time for full rejuvenation, but I'll leave the necessary equipment and instruct Healer Lanka in applying the treatments. Erek should be able to start physical therapy in about twenty-one cycles. I won't be able to stay much longer, but I'll take the data Maxine has collected on the Leor reproduction problems with me and review it to see if I can come up with any solutions."

"That's amazing," Jenna said, excited and hopeful. "I can't thank you enough for doing this for Erek, for all the Leors."

"It is my pleasure," Chase replied. "I'm fortunate that the Creator has blessed me with this ability and with the opportunity to help others."

They chatted for a while longer; then Chase and Nessa left to start the second part of the procedure on Erek. Damon drank some homa and his color improved. His eyes seemed clearer, too, and he said his headache was gone. Since Arion had granted Jenna another day away from the nursery, she and Damon and Marok—who also had suspiciously red eyes—took a skimmer out to the mesas.

They spent a wonderful cycle together, exploring the landscape, and the arena and the tribunal. Damon had smeared the sunblock lotion on his skin, so he was protected from the rays of the suns, but he complained several times about the heat. It dawned on Jenna that the high temperature didn't bother her nearly as much as it first had. Surprised, she realized she was beginning to adjust to life on Saura. It really was her home now.

The next few cycles rolled along comfortably. Erek continued to respond amazingly well to Chase's treatments.

Damon continued to enjoy his evenings at the Leor barracks, although Jenna was concerned he might be drinking too much kashni. But he was attentive during the hours they spent together, and she gloried in having her brother back, in being accepted and part of a family again. She also spent time with Nessa, expanding a casual acquaintance into a true friendship. Her relationship with Arion was going well, and her work in the nursery was fulfilling. Her life was better than it had been in over fourteen seasons.

As Chase completed the complex surgical procedures and declared Erek should eventually have a full recovery, Jenna knew her time with Damon was coming to an end. He would not be allowed to stay on Saura, and would depart when Chase did. She would miss him, and she would also miss Nessa.

The cycle came soon enough when Arion and Nessa and Brand said their good-byes and departed for Shamara in the morning. Damon planned on leaving shortly after midday, and Jenna felt a great heaviness in her heart, although she knew they would continue to communicate regularly and visit occasionally.

Now she was back in the nursery, and glad to be in her normal routine, despite her sadness that her newfound friend, Nessa, was gone, and her brother would soon be leaving. But she'd already told Damon good-bye, and it was time to get back to work. Priman started fussing the moment he saw her, holding out his arms, an imperious demand that she pick him up. He calmed immediately, tugging at her hair until he freed a lock to stuff into his mouth. She hugged him close, finding comfort in his sturdy body and musky baby scent.

She had just put him down and was getting him some homa when the dizziness hit her. She swayed, fortunately close enough to a wall to steady herself with one hand.

She saw a panel, about the size of a normal entry. A

hand, encased in second-skin gloves, reached for the control pad by the panel. The hand carefully punched a series of strange symbols, and the panel slid open to reveal a large console containing a complex array of circuit panels, switches, and blinking green lights.

A faint sound reverberated in her head, at first barely audible, then growing stronger. A heart beating. An irregular beat that seemed to be increasing in pace and raggedness. Loud breathing also became audible, speeding up as the heart rate did. Nervousness, or perhaps anticipation, hung in the air, like a tangible presence.

The focus returned to the console. There were more control pads on this console, at least four visible. The hand began punching sequences on the pad to the far left. One green light flashed off. The hand moved to the next pad.

The dizziness became more pronounced, and Jenna was vaguely aware of sliding along the wall, down to the floor. Was she seeing this through Arion? It seemed the most likely possibility, since she'd never seen a vision through anyone else's eyes. However, the angle of the hand she saw wasn't right—as if that hand belonged to a second individual, who must be standing beside Arion. Why was this individual wearing gloves, and where was this console? But her questions were forgotten as the vision again claimed her.

A second green light flashed off. The hand moved to the third pad. More strange symbols were punched, and a third green light flashed off. The movement to the fourth pad revealed the arm attached to the hand. A faint crisscrossing pattern on golden skin confirmed it was a Leor deactivating the components on the panel. The powerful muscles indicated a male rather than a female.

The heartbeat was practically pounding now, very fast, as was the breathing. Something was wrong. Arion was always calm, always controlled, as were most Leors. Why would he be nervous? Why did she sense stealth and excitement? Unless he was doing something illegal or forbidden . . .

The fourth green light flashed off. Then she was moving along a white metal wall, to a second panel that was identical to the first. The hand reached out again, entered the sequence to open this panel. It slid open, revealing another console, more flashing lights. The heart continued pounding, the excitement reaching a fever pitch. The hand touched the first pad, the fingers moving confidently. Just then, a harsh Leor voice intruded. "You there! What are you doing?"

The pounding heart was almost deafening now, and the focus shifted like a careening skimmer to the face of a familiar-looking Leor officer. The loud discharge of a blaster roared, and an expression of disbelief flashed across the officer's face as he crumpled. No! It couldn't be Arion holding the blaster. He would never kill one of his own men without just cause, nor allow anyone else to do so.

The vision began to blur. Spurred by an inner sense that something was terribly wrong, Jenna battled to see more, prayed the vision would return again, as it had a moment ago. But it faded completely, like a dissipating mist. For the first time in her life, she wanted a vision to continue, wanted more information.

She *knew* something terrible was happening, although she wouldn't accept that Arion was behind it. True, she was bound to him through the merging ceremony and their telepathic connection, and although she'd never linked into a vision through any other mind than his, she knew he wouldn't be involved in underhanded activities or killing one of his officers. There had to be some other explanation. She didn't know whose eyes she was seeing through, but it wasn't Arion.

"Lady Jenna? What is wrong?" Kerem's strong, meaty

hand grasped her shoulder, and she looked up into his weathered face.

"I don't know," she said, still trying to orient herself. "Where is there a panel that opens to a big console that takes up the full space behind the panel, and has control pads and flashing green lights on it?"

His eyes narrowed, "How would you know of such a thing?"

"I saw it in a vision, just now. Please tell me."

He considered her a long moment. "It sounds like the ground protection system in the main command center."

"The protection system?" Jenna grabbed his forearm and scrambled to her feet. "What is that?"

"It is the tracking system that warns of approaching spacecraft."

"Is that all it does? I saw two separate panels in my vision." He hesitated, and she grabbed his arm again. "Tell me! Please. My visions are always accurate, and I need to understand what I saw."

"There is a second console that controls the ground-to-air weapons. What exactly did you see?"

"I'm not sure." Suddenly cold despite the heat and humidity in the nursery, she rubbed her arms.

"Lady Jenna, what did you see?" Kerem persisted.

She whirled towards the entry, not bothering to waste time with a comm. *Arion? Where are you? Please answer me.*

His response came almost immediately. *I am training at the arena. What do you need?*

You have to go to the command center now. I had a vision, and something is terribly wrong.

What is it?

I think one of your officers has been killed. And I think the tracking and defenses have been disabled.

Chapter Seventeen

Arion took a skimmer to the command center because it could travel at twice his running speed. He issued rapid-fire commands over the comm as he raced across the desert. "First priority is to get the weapon systems back online, and get the neutron cannons fully charged. Assign warriors to man the weapon banks, and dispatch half of our fighter craft. Have the other half on standby. Make certain only authorized craft take off. I do not want the traitor who did this to get away. Shoot down any fighters that have not been cleared."

"Already working on it, sir," Zerahm replied.

"Second priority is to get the tracking back up."

"Yes, Comdar. I will see to it." Despite the urgency of the situation, Zerahm was calm.

"I will be there quickly." Arion knew he could count on his second-in-command to remain in total and rational control. He cursed his distance from the center, wanting to push the skimmer harder, but he was already at maximum throttle. His mouth thinned to a grim line. *There was a traitor in their midst.*

When Jenna had contacted him with details of her vision, his first thought had been of their visitors. But Chase McKnight and his family had departed hours ago, and all systems had been online when Arion did his customary walk-through only two hours past. The brother, Damon, was a possibility, but not likely. There was no way he could get past the security at the command center, much less access the complex codes and disable sequences necessary to bring the systems to a complete halt. Not only that, but Jenna insisted it had been a Leor male entering the codes, although she had only seen his arm.

She also said the perpetrator wore second-skin gloves, so there would be no traces of DNA to identify him. But he would not escape. A furious growl tore from Arion's throat. He *would* find the traitor, would search out the dishonorable bastard, no matter how long it took. And he would ensure certain and merciless punishment—death, slow and painful.

An earth-shattering boom reverberated through the air, drawing his attention toward the airfield, which lay about two kilometers to the west of the command center. A large metal bolt had entrenched itself just off center of the field, plowing up huge mounds of concrete and sand and destroyed aircraft. Since pilots had been dispatched to fighters, there would probably be loss of life. With another boom, two more bolts embedded themselves, one in the airfield, and one perilously close to the command center. Kinetic weapons like these metal rods could only have been discharged from a full-sized battleship, and only from orbit around Saura.

Before he could react with new orders to Zerahm, another series of booms drew his attention to the sky, as six alien fighter crafts broke the sound barrier. They hurtled over the desert, splitting into three groups. Two crafts headed for the command center, another two for the airfield. The last two headed for the arena, where hundreds of Leors had been training earlier, and could not have fully evacuated yet. Almost simultaneously, the fighters fired missiles, streaking beacons of destruction.

Saura was under full attack.

Some time later, Arion stood by the ruins of the command center, staring at the devastation around him. About three-fourths of the airfield was gone, and the dome housing the command center had been completely decimated. Fortunately, most of the center was belowground, so the equipment controlling tracking and weapons had not been seriously damaged. The actual ground-to-air weapons were in underground vaults placed strategically around Saura, with platforms that raised them to the surface when they were activated, so they were unscathed.

By the time the alien fighters had released their first round of missiles, most of the neutron cannons and ground missiles were again operational. Some of the Sauran aircraft had also managed to get airborne, and the enemy craft had been dispatched. The main spaceship responsible for deploying both the fighters and the huge metal bolts had moved out of striking range. With the tracking and weapons back up, if it orbited back over the settlement again, not a strong likelihood, it would be destroyed. Thanks to Jenna, possible annihilation had been averted, and the attack successfully halted. But not without great cost.

In addition to the airfield and the command center, the arena had suffered heavy damage. Over a hundred lives had been lost, although the actual count was not yet known. Lanka and all medical personnel were treating the casualties. The android was also helping, and Dr. McKnight had been contacted and was returning to give assistance.

There would be much to do this cycle, and many cycles to come. First and foremost would be ensuring that the systems safeguarding Saura were returned to maximum capacity and extra security measures implemented. Second would be caring for the wounded and preparing the dead for final saktar. And then, the traitor or traitors behind this atrocity would be hunted down.

"Comdar, respond," came Zerahm's voice over Arion's comm.

"Go ahead."

"A few moments ago, we shot down one of our ships, which was not authorized to take off. Marok and Naraam were aboard. Naraam is dead, Marok is dying. But we have been able to get a confession from Marok about his part in the treachery. He has some information that leads to another traitor."

"Where is Marok?"

"He has been taken to the arena, but he will not survive much longer."

"Instruct Lanka to keep him alive until I get there."

"Yes, sir."

Arion headed for the arena, a fierce fury burning inside him. All traitors would be found, and retribution would be forthcoming.

Sick at heart, Jenna stood at the edge of the semideserted settlement, staring at the destruction, which was overwhelming, even from this distance. She blamed herself in part for this. Maybe if she'd reacted more quickly, hadn't been so disoriented coming out of the vision, the attack could have been averted entirely. She would go to her grave with guilt and the blood of innocent Leors staining her soul.

Who could have done such a thing to Saura? She couldn't begin to comprehend who could betray their own people like this, or who would be so foolish as to attack the Leors. None of it made any sense. Unable to look at the carnage any longer, she started back to the nursery, where she would be in charge while Kerem and every available adult Leor and server worked to clear debris and find survivors. Only enough servers remained in the colony to take care of the children and anyone in the medical center.

A movement to the side caught Jenna's eye, and she turned to see Damon heaving a duffel bag into a skimmer. She'd been so caught up in the attack and its aftermath, she had forgotten all about her brother. She hurried toward him. "Damon!"

He turned with a start, looking surprised to see her. "Jen."

"What are you doing?" she asked as she reached him.

He was pale, and the hand he ran through his hair was shaking. "This wasn't supposed to happen so fast."

"What?"

"The attack on Saura was horrible," he said quickly. "I wish I could stay and help, but I need to get going." He shifted uncomfortably and waved a hand toward the desert. "There's not much I could do anyway. It's best if I leave."

He could probably do a lot to help, but she didn't blame him for wanting to leave such a terrible scene of death and destruction. "I hope the civilian landing bay is still intact," she said, wondering if his ship might have been damaged.

His eyes widened. "It's supposed to be. At least, I don't think they had time to attack it. The Leors must have had some sort of warning to mobilize as quickly as they did."

"*I* warned them," Jenna told him. "I had a vision this morning, and I saw someone disabling the tracking and defense systems."

He seemed to grow even paler. "You saw this in a vision? Who was behind it?"

"I didn't see the person doing it, only his hand and arm. It was a Leor male."

"Oh." He drew a deep breath. "Then I guess your having visions was good, for once."

"It appears that it was," she conceded.

"Well, I'm leaving." He opened the skimmer door, paused, and turned to look at her. "Are you sure you don't want to come with me? There's nothing for you here. And if the Controllers declare war on the Leors, you won't be safe."

"Do you think the Controllers are behind this attack?" she asked in amazement.

He shifted again. "That's the word I'm hearing around the quadrant. The Controllers are tired of the liberties the Leors take and want to either dominate them or destroy them."

"Oh, Spirit, no," Jenna murmured. "An all-out war would be terrible."

"So come with me."

She looked into his green eyes and placed her hand on his arm. "I can't. My destiny lies with Arion. Spirit go with you. May joy be your shadow."

He nodded and started to step into the skimmer.

"Halt right there!"

Jenna turned at the sound of her mate's authoritative voice. Arion strode toward them, his face set in a hard mask. "Jenna, move out of the way."

Damon swung into the skimmer, fumbled with the controls. His movement drew her attention, distracting her from Arion's order.

"Jenna, move. *Now*. San Aron, get out of the skimmer." Arion slid his laser pistol from its holster.

"What are you doing?" she asked, too surprised to think clearly. The roar of the skimmer jarred her into action, and she moved away from the clouds of sand billowing up. Arion aimed the pistol at Damon, and realization shot through her.

"No!" she cried, instinctively stepping back toward the skimmer, placing herself between the two men. "He's my brother!"

"Jenna, get out of the way," Arion ordered.

A sudden shove from Damon sent her sprawling to the ground, and rapid laser fire crackled over her. "I'm sorry, Jen," Damon yelled as the skimmer revved and roared off, leaving her in a choking sand cloud.

Coughing, she gasped for air and looked around as the dust settled. Three meters away, Arion sprawled on the sand, a red stain spreading across his chest. *No! Oh, Spirit, no!* What had she done? She scrambled to her feet and ran to him. "Arion!" She sank down next to him, saw the laser blast had hit him on the right side of his chest. How could Damon have done this? Arion appeared unconscious, his skin ashen, and blood spurted from the hideous wound. He was dying.

Her heart pounded and her lungs constricted. Grief and anguish swelled inside her with debilitating swiftness. She shoved her feelings aside. Now was not the time for emotional reaction. "Arion! Arion, don't you dare leave me," she cried, tearing off her tunic and folding it into a crude square. "Do you hear me?" She placed it over the wound and applied as much pressure as she could. "Stay with me."

There was no response. He needed help, and fast. She looked around the deserted compound. Not even a server in sight. Every available person had been sent to attend the wounded. She fumbled with her comm unit, punched the first pad. It seemed an eternity until Maxine answered, and Jenna went limp with relief.

"Maxine, I need medical assistance in the main compound immediately. Arion has been wounded with a laser."

"How serious is it?" came the calm reply.

Jenna looked at her mate, who was even grayer. Tears clogged her vision. "Very," she managed to get out. "He'll die if he doesn't get help soon."

"Hold a moment." There was static and the sound of voices talking away from the comm; then Maxine returned. "Assistance is on the way. I will guide you in the proper

278

medical procedures until the medics reach you. Get pressure on the wound."

"I've already done that."

"Good. Now I want you to do some assessments."

Numb with shock, Jenna answered Maxine's questions. While one part of her could barely process what had occurred, was reeling from the impact, another part was all too aware of the awful reality. A traitor had deactivated Saura's defenses and it had been attacked, supposedly by Antek renegades. Damon—her own brother—had shot her mate. But then Arion had been aiming a weapon at Damon, and she had absolutely no idea why. She only knew her world was crumbling around her. And much of that world revolved around the still form of her mate.

"Arion, please don't leave me." She leaned over him, stroking his familiar face, willing his exotic eyes to open, to flash with life and power. "I need you."

A startling revelation swept through her, more stunning that a supernova. She didn't just need Arion. It was far more complex than that. She had fallen in love with him.

Two cycles passed before Arion was strong enough to assert his authority and leave the medical center. It entailed a battle of wills with Lanka, McKnight, and Jenna, who all opposed his release, and it took most of his energy to overcome their objections. He was still ridiculously weak, and he cursed the fate that had put him in this position when his clan was reeling from the attack and the treachery of its own people.

Over a hundred and twenty Leors had lost their lives, and at least a hundred more had been wounded. Lanka and her medics, Dr. McKnight and his family, and every available adult Leor had worked through that first long night, tending the wounded. Morven had not slept for the past two cycles, too busy with the funeral pyres that had burned continuously since the attack.

Through it all, Arion had lain in helpless fury and frustration, unable to aid his clan. Leors healed much faster than humans, a trait inherited from their reptilian ancestors, but his wound had been nearly fatal. If Jenna hadn't intervened as quickly and knowledgeably as she had, he would be dead.

Which he would soon be, anyway. But dying later would spare Jenna's life. First he must see that the settlement's defenses were rebuilt, the injured on the road to recovery, and all traitors rooted out. He had to ensure the placement of officers to provide competent leadership to Saura after he was gone.

Out of respect for Arion, acting Comdar Zerahm had agreed to withhold judgment until Arion was on his feet. Zerahm thought the request was simply buying time for Jenna, but he would know Arion's true intent soon enough.

Walking from the medical center, with Jenna hovering by his side, Arion inhaled deeply of the arid air, savoring the warmth and the blinding brightness of the suns, the stunning panorama of the desert and the mesas. This was his world, heat and light, the reds and oranges of the desert and the sunsets, all bestowed by the Goddess. And it had been threatened.

Anger swelled and sustained him, giving him the strength to get through the cycle. After Gunnar told him about the attack on Carain, Arion had not only warned his officers of the Controller threat, but had doubled the number of soldiers on the security detail, foolishly assuming that would be sufficient additional protection. How wrong he had been, and what a costly mistake. Marok had been a trusted officer, gaining ready access to the command center. And he had been willing to murder his fellow officers in cold blood, blasting the four warriors on duty, apparently without remorse. In the time Arion had left, measures would be taken to ensure such a thing could not happen again. He crossed to the skimmer lane, already tiring. Goddess above, but he needed to be healed, to be strong *now*.

"Why do you have a warrior waiting in the skimmer?" Jenna asked suspiciously.

He turned to her. The sunlight reflected off her hair in glorious, fiery rays. Her gray eyes were clear, intelligent, her mouth soft and tempting. She looked small and fragile, but beneath that ultrafeminine frame was a core of magnasteel and determination. "Gareth will drive me to the command center," he told her. "There are many matters I must attend."

Her eyes narrowed. "You're still weak. You need to go to the dome and rest."

He could not resist touching her, sliding his hand along her smooth check, twining his fingers in her hair. He wished it was down, flowing over her bare skin like a mate's caress. "I will be there later."

"But—"

He silenced her by leaning down and pressing his mouth against hers. He sensed her surprise at his action, and his peripheral vision picked up the startled expression on Gareth's face. Leors rarely displayed such acts of affection in public, least of all the Comdar. Uncaring of his image, he dipped his tongue between Jenna's lips, absorbing her scent and taste.

She was sweeter than warmed homa in the chill desert night, and he lingered a long moment, desire roaring through him when she responded, kissing him back. Apparently, even his battered body could react to the powerful chemistry between them.

He pulled back finally, noting her increased breathing. Then he smiled, surprising both Gareth and Jenna again. "You worry too much, *charina*," he told her, smoothing her hair one more time. "Go back to your duties at the nursery, or Kerem will be complaining. I will see you at darkfall."

Opposition sparked in her eyes, but he turned and made his way around the skimmer before she challenged him. He managed to get into the vehicle without assistance. He inhaled again as Gareth steered the skimmer across the desert, and felt a deep sense of regret. So much to do, in such a small amount of time.

Sheer will got him through the rest of the cycle. At the command center, he reviewed all that had occurred in his absence. Zerahm informed him that an intensive investigation had not turned up any more traitors. It appeared Marok and Naraam had acted alone, recruited by Anteks, and motivated by greed. They'd had a large amount of gold miterons on board their craft, and Marok, threatened with retribution against his family, had provided much information before he died. He and Naraam had been approached by Anteks during an off-planet assignment, lured with the promise of gold and glory.

Damon san Aron had been their contact, synchronizing the timing of deactivating the tracking and defenses with the approach of the Antek ship. When Jenna's brother arrived on Saura, Marok offered to take the assignment of guarding him, making it ridiculously easy for Damon and Marok to get with Naraam and plan their heinous crime. Damon had escorted Marok when he disarmed the systems, after Marok temporarily disabled the retinal scans to gain the Shielder access.

Arion knew he had only himself to blame for the attack. If he had not allowed his softness for Jenna to overrule his better judgment, Damon would never have had the opportunity to give the miterons to Marok and Naraam and coordinate the strike. Arion should also have been suspicious when Damon asked Jenna if he could see the command center and the defense system. It should have alerted him to the treachery, and he should have acted then.

If that was not bad enough, Damon had then managed to get away, because he had been cleared to depart Saura before the strike hit. Arion would pay not only for the ultimate lapse in judgment, but for Damon's escape as well.

To further complicate matters, the attack had far-reaching implications. While it had been carefully structured to make it appear that the Anteks involved were renegades, both Arion and Zerahm believed the Controllers were behind the offensive—a very bad omen indeed. The Leors faced a war of galactic proportions. But first, they must deal with more immediate matters.

For now, new security procedures were implemented. The tracking and weapons consoles would be reprogrammed, and it would require the codes of two officers to change the programming in any way. Not only that, whenever the panels to the consoles were opened, even with proper codes, an automatic alert would be sent to the Comdar and his second-in-command. All officers would be required to undergo mind-scanning on a regular basis. The law prohibiting non-Leor visitors to Saura would be strictly enforced, and there would never again be exceptions to that law. Not even the Comdar would be able to override it.

Arion and his officers spent many hours putting these safeguards into place. By the time he departed for his dome, he was swaying with weakness and fatigue. Jenna met him at the door when he arrived, disapproval in her gaze.

"Look at you," she scolded, sliding one arm around his waist so he could lean on her lightly as she led him to the settee. "You're trying to kill yourself."

"You are worried about me?" he asked, sinking onto the settee and ignoring the pain from his wound. He noted gratefully that she'd had Amyan bring food from the dining hall. He did not think he had the strength to go anywhere else this evening.

"You know I am." She put her hands on her hips and

glared at him. "Leor males are far too stubborn and proud."

"Two excellent traits. Sit with me." He patted the settee, and she sat next to him, careful not to jar him.

She studied him, her eyes softening from irritation to concern. "I've never seen you look so tired before," she murmured, placing her hand against his face. "It frightens me."

"I will be fine." He reached toward the serving table, found his arm shaking.

"Here, let me." She poured warmed homa and handed the mug to him. He sipped it, enjoying the flow of warmth into his chilled body, while she put meat and bread on a plate for him.

"I like this," he said accepting the plate. "You are finally learning your duties as a Leor mate."

"Remind me to get you for that when you're fully recovered," she retorted, settling back with her homa.

He shook his head at her foolishness and ate his food slowly, savoring the simple flavors and thanking the Goddess for providing sustenance. His life had been filled with many blessings, for which he was grateful. He noticed that Jenna had not touched her food and was just holding her mug. "You need to eat, too," he informed her.

She gripped the mug, her knuckles white. "Arion, what happened on Saura, the attack, it's my fault."

He set his plate down and turned toward her. "No, it is not."

"Yes, it is." She lifted pain-filled eyes to him. "If I hadn't asked you to let Damon come to the settlement, he wouldn't have convinced those two Leors to disable the defenses."

"It was your vision and your advance warning that saved Saura," Arion pointed out.

"That vision was strange. I must have been seeing through Marok's eyes," she mused. "But I don't know why."

"I suspect you were seeing through your brother's eyes. We know he was at the command center with Marok, and you do have an emotional link with him."

"Oh. I didn't even consider that possibility. My own brother." She sounded so sad, it wrenched Arion inside.

Even worse, he suspected her brother was the one who had turned in the Shielder colony that had been decimated by Anteks before Arion's ship could reach them. San Aron was a traitor of the worst kind, betraying his own people, just like Marok and Naraam, may they burn in Hades. But Arion would never tell Jenna his suspicions. It would devastate her. Nor was there any sense in her blaming herself for her brother's actions. The attack was over and done.

He reached out and gently captured her chin, forcing her to look at him. "Listen to me. Marok and Naraam were traitors. They had already been approached by Anteks, and had already agreed to betray Saura. If Damon had not been their contact, then someone else would have facilitated the betrayal. You have no reason to blame yourself."

"You could suspect me of being part of the conspiracy and working with my brother," she pointed out, her voice shaking.

The thought had crossed his mind, but there had been no evidence of any kind to implicate her. "Were you involved?"

"No." Her sorrowful gaze remained steady. "I would never do such a thing to you, or to anyone."

"I believe you." And he did. While he placed a high value on physical prowess and precise, logical thought processes, he had long ago also learned to trust his instincts, especially if he allowed the Goddess to guide him. Every instinct he possessed, as well as the divine voice guiding him during saktars, told him his mate was a female of honor and integrity.

"Thank you," she whispered, moisture shining in her eyes. "I believe in you, too."

He found himself falling forward into those shimmering gray eyes, found himself enticed by lips that were always soft and sweet. He leaned forward for a taste of his mate, stroking his tongue over her eyes and cheeks before claiming her mouth. Their tongues dueled in a primitive mating dance, creating a heated need. The cursed echobird had been right—kissing was incredibly sensuous and stimulating, especially when the sensitive Leor tongue was involved. He felt Jenna's touch, featherlight, along his bandaged chest, and his lower body hardened even more.

He drew back regretfully and rested his forehead against hers. "I am afraid I cannot act on our mating energy tonight, *charina*. My body is still healing."

She slid her hands over his shoulders. "At least you admit you're injured. I'll let you off this once. But I expect you to make up for lost opportunity when you are recovered."

"Be careful what you ask for," he warned.

"Be careful what you promise," she teased.

He tugged at her hair, loosening it from its twist. "I always keep my word, *charina*. Never doubt it." He ran his fingers through the luxurious waves of hair, then slid his left arm around her and pulled her close. "I would like to hold you and feel you against me for a few moments."

"All right." She leaned her head on his good shoulder, her hair flowing like silk over his bandaged chest. Inhaling deeply, he dragged her scent into his lungs, memorized the warmth and satin texture of her skin. He did not know how much longer he would be with her, and he wanted to relish every moment he had.

Fatigue dragged at him, but he forced himself to remain alert, to stretch out this fleeting time with Jenna. There would be time for sleep—eternal oblivion—soon enough.

Chapter Eighteen

They came the next morning. Still somewhat weak, Arion opted to use a skimmer to drive Jenna to the nursery. As they pulled up outside the building, he saw Zerahm was waiting, flanked by two armed warriors. Arion brought the skimmer down, and Zerahm approached the craft, offering a formal bow.

"Comdar, it is my duty to inform you that during your recuperation, the tribunal convened to discuss the attack on Saura and Damon san Aron's part in the treachery." Zerahm paused, his eyes glittering and his face set in a cold mask. "Our people have demanded retribution, in accordance with our laws. If you cannot carry out this judgment, then I will act in your stead."

Even though Arion had been expecting this, it still felt like a physical blow. So soon. He stood silent, knowing what he must do next. Apparently taking his silence as denial, Zerahm motioned to the warriors, who turned toward Jenna.

"Wait!" Arion ordered, striding forward. "Do not lay a hand on her. I will offer the tribute in her stead."

Zerahm spun back, his expression one of shock. "You cannot do that."

"What is going on?" Jenna demanded, starting around the skimmer. The two warriors drew their weapons and trained them on her. She stopped, eyes wide. "Arion?"

"Put your lasers away," he ordered, then looked at Zerahm. "I *can* stand on behalf of my mate. In accordance with our laws, I claim the familial link from merging."

"You cannot mean that," Zerahm argued. "She"—he gestured toward Jenna—"is the one responsible for this. She is the one who brought her brother here. She should pay, not you."

"San Aron came on his own, without prior communication with my mate. It is my right to do this in her stead, so retribution can be met."

"What is retribution?" This time Jenna made it around the skimmer, brushing past the warriors. "What's going on?"

"Comdar—"

"Silence!" Arion cut Zerahm off with a sharp movement of his arm. He grasped the commander's shoulder and turned him away from Jenna, dropping his voice to a low murmur so she would not hear. "I hereby forfeit the title of Comdar, along with my life. You are the acting Comdar of Saura, and you will do your duty and proceed according to the letter of our laws. I do not want Jenna to know what is happening."

He stepped away from Zerahm as Jenna moved to him and grabbed his arm. "Arion, what is this?"

"*Charina*." He framed her face in his hands, took one last look to imprint in his memory for all eternity. "I must clear up some matters regarding the attack."

She stared at him. "You mean regarding my brother's actions, don't you?"

"I have to go with Zerahm now. I want you to go into the nursery and work your shift, as always."

288

"No. I want to go with you."

"That is not possible. I will take care of this. Attend your duties, while I attend mine."

Her beautiful gray eyes searched his face. "I don't understand what's going on. Why won't you tell me?"

He knew if he told her the truth, she would never willingly leave his side. "You will know soon enough. Go into the nursery and work your shift."

"Arion—"

He crushed her against him, ignoring the physical pain. He dropped his face to her hair, rubbing his cheek against the top of her head. In their short time together, she had become so special to him. "Do this for me, *charina*."

"I don't want you to go with them."

She knew something was wrong, but she did not yet comprehend the enormity of the situation. He wished he had the time to explain it, to make her understand, but he knew the sentencing and the final *saktar* would go much smoother for everyone concerned if she did not know until afterward.

"I must go." Gently, he moved her away. He wanted to say more, but didn't want to burden her with emotions he had barely begun to acknowledge within himself. He'd never had to deal with such emotions before, or consider the feelings of another. He sent an additional mental message. *It is necessary that I take care of this.* He stroked her hair one last time. *Good-bye, Jenna.*

He stepped back, imprinting one final image of her. She stood stiffly, her hands clenched, and he suspected she was exerting tremendous self-control not to protest further.

Drawing a deep breath, he turned to Zerahm, again speaking in a low voice. "I am ready to go. I would ask that you spare the shackles until we are away from here."

"I do not think shackles will be necessary," Zerahm said. "You are offering yourself voluntarily. Can you walk to the tribunal?"

He would walk, as long as his strength held out. It would be his final trek across his beloved desert. "Yes."

He strode away with Zerahm and Jael and Brulon, without a backward glance. He could not bear to look at Jenna again. His pain was already too great.

Jenna watched a long time, until Arion and the others were distant forms on the horizon. She noted that other groups of Leors were also headed toward the tribunal. Although she didn't understand what was happening, she had a horrible, sinking feeling inside her. She knew it must be some sort of trial and had something to do with her brother and the attack on Saura. It had taken every ounce of strength she possessed not to run after Arion and demand a full explanation, not to cling to him. Yet she knew he wanted—somehow *needed*—her to let him deal with it.

None of the conversation that had just occurred made any sense. She tried desperately to ignore the inner voice telling her the situation was very grave. Instead, she told herself that Arion would explain everything when he returned to their dome this evening. Then all would be well. If only she believed that.

Finally, she turned and entered the nursery. Kerem looked surprised to see her. "What are you doing here?" he demanded.

"I work here. I think I'm scheduled for a shift today."

"You were, but . . ." His forehead furrowed. "Did you not see Zerahm?"

His strange reaction only heightened her unease. "Yes. He and Arion talked about retribution, whatever that is. Arion said he would take care of it, and they went to the tribunal." She studied his expression and another thought occurred to her. "You know what's going on, don't you?" She stepped closer. "Tell me what it is."

His face froze into an inscrutable mask. "I must go see

for myself what is happening. You will be in charge until I return."

"For Spirit's sake! Why won't you tell me?" She followed him to the entry, but he was gone, sprinting across the desert with the amazing Leor speed.

Jenna turned back inside, shaken and distraught. She heard a familiar, demanding cry, and looked over to see Priman holding out his arms. She went to him, scooping him up and holding him tightly. But she found no comfort from the squirming body or the quick hands trying to jerk her hair free. Her thoughts kept returning to Arion. Something was very wrong.

She tried to busy herself with the familiar duties and routines, but she couldn't shake the feeling of dread. She made sure there was a sufficient number of servers to watch the babies, then went outside.

The suns were rising rapidly overhead, and the heat was already stifling. She saw that a few Leors were still headed for the tribunal. *A trial.* She felt certain a trial was in progress. But whom were they trying? Marok and Naraam were dead, as were all the crew of the enemy fighter craft. Damon had escaped—or so she had been told. But what if he hadn't escaped? What if he had been captured instead? For a certainty, he would be executed.

Maybe Arion wanted to spare her from that knowledge. Her stomach clenched into a knot. Damon's crime was atrocious; he had sold out an entire Leor settlement for money. But he was her brother, her only family. She had to know what was happening. She could take a skimmer to the tribunal, but she doubted she could gain admittance. She could think of only one possible way to see what was going on there.

She sank down on the ground, leaning against the building. She'd never attempted to instigate a vision through Arion, had no idea if it would work. Closing her eyes, she thought of him, focused on creating an undetected mental link. She felt a slight rocking motion and some dizziness, as if she were about to receive a vision. There were more rocking motions, wisps of white as if she were looking through a fog.

The heartbeat came first, strong, slow, and steady. Then she saw the round sweep of the tribunal, the seats rising toward the blinding suns. Leors filled about three-fourths of those seats, looking at her with cold, impassive expressions. Only it wasn't her they watched, it was someone else—

"Arion of Saura, have you anything to say to these charges?" came a voice.

The line of vision cut to the right, where Zerahm sat in the massive elevated chair that Arion usually occupied.

"I am totally responsible for the attack on Saura." Arion's voice swelled and rumbled inside her. "I allowed Damon san Aron to land on Saura, and assigned only one warrior to watch him. I did not check on him further, or take additional security measures at the command center. I also failed when I attempted to apprehend him, so the blame for his escape rests solely on me. Since I am mated with his only blood relative, I claim the right to stand for retribution in my mate's stead."

The dawning realization that it was Arion who was on trial sent terror spiraling through Jenna, but she was locked deep in the thrall of her vision, unable to react in any way.

"All here have heard Arion's testimony. He claims full responsibility for the attack on Saura and the consequent deaths of one hundred and twenty-two of our people," Zerahm's voice boomed out over the tribunal. "Does anyone wish to come forward to dispute these facts? To stand for Arion?"

A wave of voices flared from the seats, the Leors muttering among themselves. This was their Comdar; no situation quite like this had ever occurred on Saura. Some of them rose to speak.

292

"*No. Do not stand for me.*" The heart beat louder, but Arion's voice was clear and steady. "*One hundred and twenty-two lives have been senselessly lost, and the man who facilitated the strike allowed to escape. Our laws demand retribution from someone. I offer my life in the place of Damon san Aron.*"

No . . . Arion, no! Jenna stirred, vaguely aware of the hard ground beneath her.

"*Then,*" Zerahm intoned, "*in accordance with our laws, I sentence you, Arion of Saura, to death.*"

"No!" Jenna screamed, flashing momentarily from the vision, flailing against the nursery's hard stone wall.

The heartbeat stuttered before resuming, stronger. The line of vision remained on Zerahm's cold face. "Because you did not actually commit the crime, and your life is being taken in retribution, you may choose the method of death," he said.

No . . . no. Arion couldn't die. Let this be a bad dream.

"*I choose the path of the Goddess,*" Arion said, utterly calm. "*I wish to be claimed by the desert, in final saktar.*"

Zerahm nodded. "So be it. You will be taken to the pit, there to remain until your soul has joined the Goddess."

Six warriors surrounded Arion. One held a magnasteel band like Clavon had been wearing. He held it up, and Arion dropped his head. The cold metal gripped his head, the energy flowing through it ensuring his compliance until he was placed in the pit. Yet he raised his head high and moved with the warriors toward the large opening at the rear of the tribunal. He was weak, his gait unsteady, but he forced himself to keep moving.

The vision faded to gray, then dissipated entirely. Jenna found herself lying on the hard-packed sand outside the nursery. Grief and shock clawed at her. She wanted to scream in denial, to call out to Arion and plead with him to run, to save himself.

But she knew it would do no good. His fate had been

decreed, and he had been instrumental in sealing it, having blamed himself for events that were her fault, not his. She knew him well enough to realize he would not want her witnessing what had just transpired. In retrospect, he had been giving her a final farewell when he told her good-bye earlier.

No! She would *not* allow this to happen. She loved him. Hot tears pooled behind her eyes, slid down her cheeks, mingling with the red sand. She couldn't lose Arion. He had become everything to her: her mate, her lover, her confidant, her best friend. Spirit, what could she do?

One thing was certain: Lying here in the sand, giving in to tears and hopelessness, would not help Arion. She had to find some way to get him out of this. Resolute, she pushed herself up and headed for the nearest skimmer.

She stumbled getting in and realized she was trembling. She forced herself to stay calm and focus on finding a solution. Starting the skimmer, she headed toward the medical lab. A merciful numbness was setting in, taking the edge off her near hysteria. She walled off the waves of emotions inundating her, threatening her sanity, and forced her thoughts into a narrow tunnel of determination. Maxine would know what to do.

The laboratory was unusually quiet as Jenna ran down the sterile corridor to Maxine's area. The android was alone, looking through the eyepiece of the huge scanning electron microscope that took an entire corner of the chamber. She turned when Jenna burst in. "What is wrong?"

Jenna quickly told her all that had happened.

"That is not good," Maxine said, calm in the midst of Jenna's emotional storm. "But the idea of retribution is not an uncommon one. There are a number of cultures that insist on payback for any number of crimes, sometimes in the payment of currency or goods, or the taking of a life—"

"What can I do to save Arion?" Jenna interjected. She

already knew how the system worked. Now she wanted a way to circumvent it.

"I will search my data files and see what I can find on the Leor laws regarding retribution." Maxine was quiet a moment, a barely discernable hum the only indication she was checking files. She jolted, her eyes widening, and looked at Jenna. "I do not have sufficient information. I will have to investigate further. It might take some time."

Jenna studied her, sensing the android was withholding something. "Are you capable of lying?"

Maxine managed to look offended. "Why would you question my integrity?"

"You didn't answer my question."

"I am programmed to give the correct answer in accordance with the nature of the situation."

In other words, Maxine wasn't going to tell Jenna whatever she had uncovered. "Arion is scheduled to die, and I intend to fight for him with every means at my disposal. You must tell me what you know," Jenna insisted.

Maxine's expression went blank. "I do not have sufficient information at this time."

"Don't do this to me," Jenna pleaded, despair threatening to engulf her. "I can't let Arion die."

"I understand." The android's eyes seemed to soften. "I must check other data files. I will contact Max on Jardonia. I am sorry I cannot tell you more at this time."

Realizing Maxine wouldn't yield, Jenna headed for the entry.

"Where are you going?"

"I'll get my answers elsewhere. Contact me if you learn anything you're willing to share." Jenna ran back outside to the skimmer. She knew of one other person who could give her answers, even if he was usually more taciturn than Maxine.

No one answered her knock at Morven's door. Disheartened, she turned to see him loping across the desert from the direction of the tribunal. He must have been involved in the final details of Arion's trial and planned execution. *Unless Arion was already dead.* Panic surged through her, obliterating calmness and logic. No! Surely that wasn't possible. There had been discussion about a pit, about the desert claiming his life.

Gripped by fear, she ran to meet Morven. She was winded in the short distance it took to reach him, while he showed no signs of stress from his lengthy run across the desert. He stopped and stared at her, his face emotionless.

"Arion," she gasped. "Is he dead?"

"No." He stalked rapidly past her.

She followed. "Wait!" He paused and turned his cold gaze on her. "You have to help me find a way to overturn Arion's sentence."

"It is out of your hands." Morven strode toward his dome.

"No." Jenna ran after him. "I won't accept that."

He kept moving, entering the dome. She marched in behind him. "There must be some other solution. Arion didn't commit the crime. Why would he be executed for it?"

Morven went to the brazier and waved his hand over it. Flames leaped inside the metal bowl. "Our laws demand retribution for every crime. Someone must always pay. If the Leor responsible for the offense is out of reach, then another must suffer the consequences."

"That's barbaric!"

He turned glittering eyes on her. "That is *our way.*"

She searched for a means to reach him. "You know your laws far better than I do. Isn't there anything that can be done? Some other way to fix this?"

He stood there like a stone. Desperate, she placed her hand on his muscled arm. "I love him, Morven. I can't let him die without a fight. Please, *please* tell me if there is anything that can save him."

Slowly, he raised his hands just above her head, palms toward her. He moved them down along each side of her, not quite touching. She could feel heat and energy emanating from his palms. He paused at her hips, then brought his hands around to the front of her.

Aligning them side by side, he ran his palms along her abdomen and back up the front of her. She gritted her teeth and allowed it, because she knew it was futile to argue with him when he was set on one of his odd examinations. Finally he dropped his hands and turned away with a grunt.

"Damn it, Morven!" She stalked around to face him. "If there is any way, *anything at all*, that will save Arion, you must tell me. And if you won't, give me some of those strange leaves to burn. I'll perform a saktar and ask the Goddess what to do."

"No saktar at this time," he growled.

"Then I suggest you tell me what you know. Otherwise, I'll go to the desert and find some way to induce saktar on my own."

"You would do that for the Comdar?"

"I already told you, shaman. *I love him.* Without him, my life is nothing." She stared into fathomless midnight-blue eyes, then spun away with a frustrated groan. "How could you understand? You have no one close to you, no family."

"You are wrong, Lady Jenna. I have the Goddess."

The tears came then, flooding her eyes. She turned and looked at Morven through blurred vision. "Then ask your Goddess to spare him. He is far too worthy to die like this."

"There is one way," he said slowly.

"What? What is it?"

"Usually retribution is taken from someone bound to the offender by blood."

"Meaning?"

"A blood relative is the usual choice for retribution."

Catherine Spangler

It took a moment for the impact of his words to sink in. When they did, her legs almost gave out. "I should be giving up my life instead of Arion." She suddenly felt faint. Morven caught her arm in a merciless vise and kept her upright.

"They would have taken me to pay for Damon's crimes," she murmured, all the pieces falling into place as she remembered how Zerahm had been waiting for them at the nursery. How he had tried to approach her, until Arion stepped in. Her mate's words, which she hadn't understood at the time, came back to her: *It is my right to do this in her stead, so retribution can be met.*

"Arion put his life on the line in my place," she whispered. "By the Spirit." She touched Morven's arm again. "What can I do?"

He was silent a long moment. "You can go to the tribunal and offer your life for your brother's crimes. By law, a blood bond is stronger than a mating bond. Your claim of blood will take precedence over Arion's claim of relationship."

A new horror swept through Jenna. "Then *I* will be executed." She struggled for breath. She didn't want to die, especially since she now had Arion. But if she didn't step forward, she would lose him anyway.

His life was worth so much more than hers. He was a brilliant and dedicated leader of a large clan; a visionary guiding his people through treacherous times. She was nothing. Many servers could do her job in the nursery.

Even more compelling was the fact that it was totally unjust for Arion to pay for her brother's actions. She'd asked Arion to let Damon come to Saura, had even asked if Damon could visit the command center. Looking back, she couldn't believe she'd been so naive, so blind.

She had even gotten between him and Damon when he tried to bring her brother to justice. Wounded and unconscious, Arion had not been able to stop Damon's escape.

Beyond a doubt, everything was her fault. Yet, without hesitation, he'd put his life before hers.

Without question, she must step forward and offer her life for Arion's. An insidious cold crept through her, tinged with terror. What was it like to die? Did she have the courage to do this? Her mate's beloved face formed in her mind, his dark eyes and bold features, the twitch in his stern expression when he was trying not to react to her antics. The passion in those ebony eyes when his body was joined with hers; his amazing gentleness when he touched or comforted her.

Yes, she could die, for him.

She met Morven's watchful gaze. "Tell me what to do."

Even with the coordinates locked into the skimmer's navigation pod, she almost missed the pit. Although it lay approximately sixteen kilometers due west of the Goddess mesa, in the broad, sprawling expanse of desert, it was an insignificant hole.

But it was significant to her, because her mate was there, in imminent danger of dying. Morven felt Arion had been weakened by his injury and wouldn't survive the two or three cycles it would normally take for death to claim a Leor left in the pit.

Jenna was determined to keep her mate alive until the suns rose and the tribunal was called into session. Morven had agreed to contact Zerahm and arrange for a second assembly on the matter of retribution for Damon's actions. Arion had only to survive until then, when she would receive the judgment of death in his stead, and he could recover his great strength and continue to lead his clan.

The cold, which had been with her since her decision, was seeping into every cell of her body, despite the skimmer's heaters. She was also concerned about the desert's nighttime chill, a very real threat to Arion in his weakened state, since he could not produce his own body heat. But

Morven had insisted she must wait until total darkfall before going to Arion, or risk discovery.

The floodlights from the skimmer reflected the squared-off hole in the ground as she approached. Fortunately, she was moving at a slow speed, and was able to halt the skimmer a safe distance from the edge. Her heart pounding, she took a solar lantern and got out. The chilled desert air hit her like a slap, and she feared what effect it might have on Arion.

Overriding her aversion to heights, she moved to the edge of the pit. She shone the solar lantern into a hole that was about three meters wide and ten meters long, and five meters deep. The light reflected off the sagging figure of her mate, and her heart leaped in her chest.

Arion sat on the ground against the far wall of the pit, long chains attached to his wrists. He was covered with blood and dirt. Seeing him like that, filthy and chained like an animal, was almost more than she could stand. Jenna had to force herself to take a deep breath, remind herself she couldn't help him if she fell apart now.

"Arion," she called, shining the light on his face. He stirred and looked toward her, although there was no recognition in his gaze. Relief filled her. He was still alive.

A sudden sense of déjà vu hit her, a remembrance from her saktar before her merging with Arion. The Goddess had spoken to her then, in a startling kaleidoscope of visions. In one, she'd stood on the edge of a deep pit, with Arion below her, chained to a wall, dirty and bloodied as he was now.

She remembered the Goddess whispering: *"He will need your faith in him, and your love. It will be his salvation."*

Amazed at the accuracy of that revelation, Jenna prayed the Goddess had spoken the truth. She hoped she would be Arion's salvation. She shined the light around the perimeter of the pit, locating the steep stone steps Morven had said would be there. So far, so good. Returning to the skimmer, she retrieved a pack with supplies: thermal blankets, homa, medical aids. She carried the pack to the edge and dropped it in, then made her way carefully down the steps, the solar lantern guiding her.

Breathing a sigh of relief when she reached the bottom, she turned her attention to Arion. He didn't move as she approached him. In the glare of the lantern, his skin was an alarming ashen color, a darkening gray that was the Leor skin reaction to cold.

The cold wouldn't harm healthy Leors; it would merely make them sluggish, and if the temperature was very cold, it would send them into a sleep state similar to hibernation. Morven had explained that a Leor left to die in the pit would alternate between a state of semihibernation at night and wakefulness in the heat of the day. The physical extremes, along with a lack of food and water, would creative a hallucinating state and trigger a final saktar, followed by death.

Most Leors survived several cycles in the pit before death claimed them. But in Arion's case, with his wounded body and debilitated state, the cold could put him in a permanent coma from which he wouldn't awaken. Jenna was determined that would not happen. Yet it was terrifying to see him like this, slumped over and nonresponsive, with that awful gray pallor.

"Arion." She went to him, touched his face, the coolness of his skin frightening her even more. She set the lantern down, and it cast an eerie glow around them. "Arion, wake up!" She slapped him lightly and he stirred, groaned, his chest rising.

Blood seeped through the bandage over his wound; had been doing so for some time, judging from the trail down his abdomen, and the red stain spreading over his filthy loincloth. By the Spirit! Torn between the bleeding and his need for heat, Jenna ripped open a package of gauze, sinking down beside him. "Arion, listen to me. Wake up. You have to hold on a little longer." She pressed the gauze to his wound. "Are you listening?"

His chest heaved, but her mate didn't reply. Tears formed in her eyes, and Jenna blinked them back, surprised she had any liquid left in her body. She'd cried more today than in her entire lifetime. She put pressure on Arion's wound, leaning close to speak into his right ear. "I'm ordering you to hold on. Do not defy me on this, stubborn Leor." She sniffed and wiped her eyes. "You've never seen me really angry, and believe me, you don't want to."

His skin was far too cold. She took his right hand and heaved it up, his arm a dead weight, and the long chain attached to his wrist making it nearly impossible to move his arm. "Can you hold the gauze for me?" She pressed his hand against the material. "Hold it right there." But his arm sagged as soon as she released it, and she barely caught the gauze before it hit the sand. It was already stained with blood.

"Blazing hells." She tore open another packet, her cold hands clumsy. She battled with a roll of medical tape, tearing off long strips and anchoring them temporarily on the rough wall behind Arion. She kept up a steady stream of conversation as she worked, hoping to draw him back to consciousness.

"You're making this very hard on me. If I defied you like this, you'd be roaring your displeasure. That's a double standard, if you ask me." She put the new gauze over the wound, pressed the tape around the edges. "We had an agreement, husband. You're supposed to treat me as an equal, with the same rights any female Leor would have."

She sat back and withdrew a sealed heat-wave thermal blanket from the pack. When she tore open the protective wrapping, the oxygen in the air reacted with the heat disks in the blanket, generating warmth that would last for hours.

"Maxine showed me how these blankets work," she told a nonresponsive Arion. "I made her explain these medical supplies. She didn't want to, because she's trying to protect me."

When Maxine had accessed her data files earlier in the cycle, she had immediately ascertained that Jenna could offer her life in Arion's stead, and that Jenna's offer would hold precedence over his, due to her blood bond with Damon. Because Maxine's main mission on Saura was to ensure Jenna's welfare, she had withheld the information as a protective measure. But she couldn't prevent Jenna from stepping forward, especially since Morven had been by Jenna's side most of the cycle.

Now Jenna was grateful for the knowledge Maxine had imparted, albeit reluctantly. "She finally gave in because I wouldn't change my mind," she told Arion. She wrapped the thermal blanket around him, tucked it behind. "I can be very stubborn, you know."

She dragged the pack closer, then stripped off her cape, shivering in the clear, chilly air. She slid beneath the blanket, settling herself on Arion's left side. "Don't get any ideas now. I'm just adding my own heat to warm you. You're a lot of trouble. Did you know that?" She rested her cheek against his hard, cold chest. "But you're worth it," she whispered.

And she meant every word. He had become everything to her: her companion, her lover, her universe. She held him, willing him to survive, to continue on his path to lead his people.

They remained that way for some time, Jenna talking to Arion and stroking his face and chest and arms, relieved to feel his skin warming. Beneath her cheek, she felt the increased expansion of his lungs, heard his heartbeat take on a steadier rhythm. She knew when he regained consciousness, moving his legs with a groan, tensing as he became aware of his surroundings.

His left arm came around her, brushed against her chest. "I must be dreaming," he murmured hoarsely. His hand swept over her breast, settled its weight in his palm. "Or this is a most unusual saktar."

"It's not a dream or saktar." She twisted, coming to her knees to face him. "I'm very real. And I'm not leaving until the suns are up."

Confusion glazed his eyes as he stared at her. "What are you doing here?"

"I should be asking *you* how you could dare to offer your life in tribute for Damon's actions, and go off to die without even telling me what was going on." Overwhelmed by emotion, Jenna battled for control. She placed her hand against his cheek. "You didn't even give me a chance to tell you good-bye."

"I still do not understand."

"I'm here to ensure that you stay alive through the night, you thickheaded barbarian. We'll try to straighten things out tomorrow. Let me get you some homa." She slipped from beneath the blanket and retrieved the portable heat store.

"Jenna." His chest rose and fell in a shaky sigh. "I do not know how you found me, but you should not be here. You cannot delay what is inevitable."

She wasn't going to tell him she planned to offer her life for his; he might find a way to stop her. "This is giving me one last night with you, husband." She poured the homa, recapped the heat store, then slipped back under the blanket before holding the mug to his lips. "Drink."

He turned his head away. "There is no sense in prolonging my passage from this plane."

"I don't want to draw out your suffering, either," she said, struggling to keep her voice steady. "But I need this final time with you. Give us this night. Please. For me."

He stared at her a long moment, the solar light reflecting in his eyes. Then he turned toward the mug, his big hand coming up to cover hers as he sipped. "That is good." He sighed, laying his head back, his mental and physical weariness obvious.

She put the mug aside and came back to her knees. Sliding her arms around his neck, she rested lightly against him. "I love you."

He was utterly still for a long moment; then his arms came around her, the chains clinking. "The Goddess blessed me when she chose you to be my mate, *charina*," he said, still hoarse. "You are very worthy, and have made me proud."

The tears returned, and she didn't try to contain them. "No, you're the one who's worthy, Arion. I messed up everything. This situation is entirely my fault. I can't believe I trusted Damon. I should have known better, should have seen the clues to what he really was."

"We have already discussed this matter. You are not to blame."

She shook her head. "I *am* to blame. You only allowed Damon to come to Saura for me, and he got away because you didn't want to risk injuring me." She pressed her wet face against Arion's neck, remorse ripping her apart. If only she could go back in time and change the events leading up to this tragic point. "I thought Damon was my family, but I was wrong, and you were right. *You* are my family—all I could ever want or need."

"I am glad to know that," he said quietly. "I treasure your love, *charina*."

The tears were flowing hard. "I don't know why," she managed to say. "I know you would have preferred a Leor mate."

His arms tightened around her. "Not now. My mate has been far more fascinating and challenging than any Leor female, a prize well worth the effort to tame."

Despite his obvious weariness, he sounded so smug that she laughed through her tears. "You just *think* you have me in hand." She pulled back to stroke his beloved face, to commit it to eternal memory.

"Do not leak tears for me, Jenna," he said softly. "The Goddess has filled my life with many blessings. I will take special memories of you with me."

She made an effort to stop crying. "I've got some pretty special memories, too." She sniffed, swiped at her wet face. "So, is there a term of endearment for males in your language? Can I call you *charina?*"

His hand slid up to cup her damp cheek, his gaze holding hers. "The masculine version is *charine.*"

"*Charine,*" she whispered. "You are my cherished one, Arion. For all time."

She kissed him, and he pulled her close, kissing her back. Their kiss was gentle and tender at first, then deepened in passion and desperation. He thought, and rightly so, that they were sharing their final moments together. But he also thought he would be dead in a few cycles, while she knew differently.

Before the new cycle was through, her physical life would be snuffed out, her soul winging its way to Spirit. She only hoped she could face death with courage and dignity, despite the debilitating dread and terror filling her as the time grew nearer. She clung to Arion, drawing strength from his arms and his lips, trying desperately to make time stand still, to make this moment with him never end.

They held each other tightly through the night, each knowing that nothing could halt the relentless march of time, or the gradual lightening of the sky as, inexorably, the suns rose, and a new cycle began. . . .

Heralding the end.

Chapter Nineteen

Shortly after dawn, Jenna pulled away from the shelter of Arion's arms. There were no more words she could say to him; they had bared their souls to each another in the darkness during their final hours together.

He watched her slip on her cape and stuff all evidence of her presence into the pack. "*Charina,* I have instructed Zerahm to return to you to Shamara, so you can live among your own people."

She set down the pack and went to him, touching his face, drinking in his image to carry with her. It wouldn't have mattered where she lived; her life would be meaningless without him. But she wouldn't have to worry about that after this cycle.

"Long life, Jenna," he said quietly.

It was his final good-bye, and he was wishing her the blessing of life, while he believed he was at the end of his. The pain was so sharp, it took her breath away. Praying for the strength to leave him, she pressed her lips against his. He didn't try to touch her, which would have only made parting harder. Pulling away, she took the pack and struggled up the steep stairs.

At the top, she turned and looked at Arion for the last time. They stared at each other across the expanse of the pit, across an invisible, unspeakable chasm that death would soon bring. She wished they had more time; she wanted to run back down the steps and burrow in his arms, if only for a few moments, or a few hours, more.

But she knew it would be dangerous for him if anyone discovered them together, or suspected she had aided him while he was under a death sentence. *Good-bye, charine,* she mentally whispered to him. *I will love you always.*

His gaze remained steady. *Good-bye, charina. May the Goddess fill your life with many blessings.*

Jenna had to force herself to turn and leave. She drove the skimmer slowly across the desert as a magnificent sunrise burst over the horizon, the two suns making their appearance within a few moments of each other.

She knew Morven would be waiting for her, but she made one last trip to the Goddess statue. She was drawn there somehow, found an odd comfort in the featureless stone face. She and Arion had made love here, right at the base of the altar, lying in the scattered petals of starflowers, and wrapped in the wonder of sensual discovery. The Goddess had even appeared pleased by the union, her face glowing with a strange light.

She also seemed to be welcoming now, her hand extended toward Jenna. Jenna laid the starflowers she'd just picked on the stone altar and moved to the side to kneel by the statue.

"I have made a mess of things," she whispered, too drained and numb for tears. "Please watch over Arion and take good care of him." She closed her eyes, exhaustion sweeping through her. "I know this is selfish, but give me the strength to face death with dignity, and please make it fast and painless."

She knelt there a long time, feeling a curious warmth and energy twining around her. *Do not fear, beloved daughter,* came the comforting voice. *I will always be with you. Never forsake your faith. Never forget that love transcends all boundaries.*

Did that mean Jenna would remember her love for Arion, even on the other side? She hoped it did. Wearily, she pushed to her feet and trudged to the skimmer. She went to Morven's dome, as he had instructed the previous cycle. He was waiting for her, opening his entry without a word. She stepped inside, and he grabbed her cape, studying the blood on it. He parted the cape and studied her stained tunic as well.

"Arion is still alive," she said.

He gave her the look. "I am aware of that."

"I keep forgetting you know everything. So I guess we go to the tribunal now."

"Not yet. Come." He led her to the bathing chamber, where the huge tub had been filled with hot water and scented herbs.

She stared at it, exhaustion and fear dulling her wits. "Are we doing a saktar now?"

"No saktar." He gestured at the tub. "Disrobe and get in."

"Fine. Whatever." She didn't even care that he stood there while she undressed and slipped into the water. What did it matter at this point?

She sank back with a sigh, certain the specter of her upcoming death would fill her thoughts, but oddly enough she found herself drifting. A soothing, low-pitched chanting filled the chamber, lulling her further into a dreamlike state. She closed her eyes, and vague images swirled through her head, colors and blurred faces, and distant voices.

She jolted upright with a start. Morven stood over her, and he must have been the one calling her name. "Finish

309

bathing and get out," he said. "Maxine will assist you."

"Maxine?" Jenna looked around him, to see the android standing there, wearing her green-feathered loincloth.

"Yes, I will help you prepare." Maxine stepped around Morven. "While I do, I will again attempt to talk you out of this irrational, illogical, and basically insane plan."

With a grunt, Morven left the chamber. Maxine handed Jenna a container of scented cleansing oil. She took it, and after wetting her hair, began lathering.

"You cannot sacrifice your life like this—" Maxine started, but Jenna cut her off.

"Please, let's not discuss it. My course is set." She soaped her body, her gaze on the android. "I don't know if you feel emotions, but do you consider us friends?"

"Of course. I feel responsible for your welfare."

"I'm talking about friendship. I consider you a friend, Maxine, and I hope you feel the same way."

"I concede that I consider us friends."

"Then, as my friend, I ask that you respect my wishes on this." Jenna submerged to rinse off the soap, then resurfaced. "This is my fault. Arion didn't want to allow Damon to land on Saura, but I talked him into it. It was *my* brother who caused the death of all those people. Arion doesn't deserve to die for my mistakes, and I would have nothing to live for if he were executed. Can you see the logic of what I'm saying?"

The android's mouth compressed in a thin line, but she nodded. "I can comprehend your reasoning."

"Then you can also see that I'm the logical choice to take the punishment on behalf of my brother. Arion is far more important to this settlement than I am." Jenna stood and wrung the water from her hair.

Maxine handed her a drying cloth and turned on the overhead blower. "Then I conclude all I can do is see you through this."

"Thank you. I'm glad you're here with me." Jenna busied herself with drying off, her hair flying in all directions under the hot air. She looked around. "I need clothing."

"Here." Maxine handed her a folded square of white cloth.

Jenna shook it open. "It's just a loincloth."

"Yes. The shaman stated that you need to meet the tribunal as one of them, as the mate of the Comdar. He believes your claim to blood retribution will carry more weight, and I must concur with him."

Alarm slammed through Jenna. The possibility that the tribunal might not accept her claim was horrifying. "Morven said my claim would hold out over any others. I don't want Arion to die."

"The shaman has assured me he will not."

Jenna stared at the fabric she was holding. *A loincloth.* She wasn't sure she was ready for this, then almost laughed at her reluctance. Again, what did it matter? She was going to die, based on Leor law, and at the hands of Leors. She might as well go out like a Leor. It was a final way to honor Arion.

"All right, I'll wear the darned thing." She dropped the drying cloth and put on the garment.

Maxine took a brush and smoothed down Jenna's hair. Jenna closed her eyes, savoring this last touch. "Do you wish to wear your hair up?" Maxine asked.

"No." It would help cover her nakedness, and somehow, having her hair loose and flowing seemed like a final freedom.

Maxine laid down the brush. "Then there is nothing more to delay us."

"No," Jenna murmured again. No more delays. Nothing now between her and death.

She and Maxine went to the front chamber, where Morven waited. He had donned his ceremonial garb: a white loincloth trimmed in glittering gold, and gold arm cuffs. Jenna guessed one of his duties was overseeing executions.

Maxine drove the skimmer to the tribunal. They passed groups of Leors jogging the same direction, all coming to see Jenna die. As the structure loomed ahead, utter terror shot through her, and her heart pounded. *Spirit and Goddess,* she prayed, *please see me through this.*

The tribunal was just as full as it had been for Arion's trial. Flanked by Morven and Maxine, Jenna walked into the open stadium, her legs none too steady. At the far end, Zerahm sat in a massive chair on a raised dais. At their entrance, an instant, oppressive hush fell over the crowd.

Zerahm stared at Jenna a long moment, his face expressionless. "Jenna of Saura, formerly of Shamara, come forward to receive judgment."

Taking a deep breath, trying to calm her pounding heart, she walked alone to the center of the tribunal. She forced herself to meet Zerahm's cold gaze. "State your claim," he said.

Jenna had been instructed by Morven on what to say. She took another breath. "I claim the right to give my life in retribution for the crimes of Damon san Aron."

Zerahm's eyes narrowed, although he knew why she was there. "Judgment has already been passed on retribution for this matter."

"I am aware of that, Your Lordship. I am asking that the tribunal reverse that judgment and place it on me instead."

The crowd reacted to her statement, loud murmurs sweeping the tiers of seats. Zerahm raised his arm, and the crowd quieted. "Why would we reverse this judgment?"

"Because I claim blood relationship to Damon san Aron. He is my brother. In accordance with your laws, a blood bond takes precedence over other claims."

"You are aware your life will be forfeit."

"Y-yes." Her voice came out a whisper, and she cleared

312

her throat. "Yes. I ask that my life be forfeit in the place of Comdar Arion."

The crowd reacted again, a low roar of voices. Zerahm silenced them with a slash of his arm. "Have you anything else you wish to say?" he asked.

"I do." For Arion, she managed to speak out clearly. "It is my fault that Damon came to Saura, and that he succeeded in his plan. Arion claimed the fault was his, but that isn't so. He should be cleared of all blame and all charges."

"All here have heard Jenna's testimony," Zerahm said, his voice booming out over the tribunal. "She claims responsibility for the attack on Saura and the consequent deaths of one hundred and twenty-two of our people. She states Arion of Saura should be cleared of all related charges. Does anyone wish to come forward to dispute these facts? To stand for this female?"

In the utter stillness of the tribunal, Jenna's heart sounded like a sonic boom. She glanced at the faces staring at her in open hostility and accusation, knowing none of them would take her side.

"I will stand for her." Morven's voice resounded behind her, and he stepped to her side.

"I will stand for her," Maxine stated, coming forward.

More murmuring in the tiers; then Lanka came to her feet. "I will stand for Jenna of Saura," she said gruffly.

Jenna stared at the healer in stunned amazement. There was movement along the rows of seats. At least ten more Leors rose to their feet, each calling out intent to stand for her. She saw Nona, and Ormen, Erek's father; and Leelan, who took care of Erek. There was Charlon, Lanka's medical assistant, and a number of parents of the babies from the nursery. And there was Kerem, with his weathered face and stoic eyes. Even Shela, who doled out the work assignments, stood.

Leors standing for her! It was beyond Jenna's comprehension that she'd found a measure of acceptance and support on Saura, albeit from a small group. But not nearly enough to save her.

Zerahm gestured two warriors forward. "Release Arion from the pit and bring him here. He will likely need a skimmer." They ran from the tribunal, and Zerahm turned his attention to Jenna.

"Of your own free will, you have shouldered the blame for the attack on Saura and the loss of one hundred and twenty-two lives. You have invoked the blood bond as your claim to give your life in retribution, in the place of Damon san Aron. Only a few citizens have stood for you. Therefore, in accordance with our laws, I sentence you, Jenna of Saura, to death."

Her legs would have given out, but Morven grabbed her arm and steadied her. "Your Lordship, the law requires that Arion be declared free of guilt before another dies for the crime."

"I am well aware of the law, Shaman."

"Of course." Morven inclined his head respectfully. "I would make a suggestion on the method of death," he continued.

Jenna hadn't even allowed her thoughts to go that far. She could only stare at the shaman in helpless terror.

Zerahm considered him. "Your suggestion, Shaman?"

"Since Lady Jenna has voluntarily come forward to offer retribution, and since she did not actually commit these crimes, I would recommend a merciful execution," Morven answered. "By beheading." At Jenna's horrified gasp, he turned toward her. "It is very quick and painless," he murmured.

She closed her eyes. *Spirit, Goddess, be with me now.* Perhaps her prayers were heard and answered, because a merciful numbness stole through her. Everything around her became dreamlike, sounds muted. Even the stone block being dragged out, and the massive Leor warrior coming forward with an evil-looking sword in his hand, seemed surreal.

One word, however, pierced her stupor: *Arion*. Hearing his name, she turned. He entered the tribunal, followed by the two warriors. The chains were gone, and he moved with his usual powerful grace, despite the red-stained bandage on his chest.

He looked at her a moment before facing the dais. "Comdar Zerahm, why have I been returned here?"

"Your mate has stepped forward to accept retribution for Damon san Aron. She has invoked the blood bond, which our laws recognize above all other bonds. Our people"—Zerahm indicated the Leors present with a sweep of his muscular arm—"have passed the judgment from you to her. You are hereby cleared of all charges and judgments in the matter of Damon san Aron's crimes."

"You cannot do this!" Arion strode to the center of the stadium. "I have claimed responsibility for san Aron's actions, and I am prepared to accept death."

"Your wishes do not hold precedence over a blood claim." Zerahm leaned forward, his eyes like black ice. "Our laws cannot be disregarded. Let us see this matter concluded." He gestured to Jenna. "Begin the execution."

"No!" Arion roared. "You will not do this. Take me in her stead."

"I am the Comdar, until this matter is settled," Zerahm growled. "You are not to interfere." He looked at the two men flanking Arion. "Take the female to the block."

But Arion moved to intercept the warriors before they could reach her. "No! You will take me instead."

She could read the intent in his eyes, the determination that he would die for her. She moved toward him, reaching out mentally. *Arion, don't. This is my fault, and I'm prepared to die. You are much more important, and your people need you.*

His expression hardened. *No. I brought you here with*

the understanding that I would stand for you and protect you. I will not allow your death.

You can't protect me from my brother's actions, or my own poor judgment.

"Take her!" Zerahm ordered.

Arion stepped to Jenna's side. "If you will not reverse her sentence, then I will die *with* her."

She'd thought she was too numb to feel anything, but alarm reverberated through her. "Arion! You can't mean that."

He stared at her, resolve in his glittering gaze. "I do mean it, *charina*. Without you, my existence would be an empty shell, devoid of life."

Her heart turned over. "That's not true, Arion. Your life would be a blessing to your people. They need you."

"He has been pardoned," Zerahm declared. "Remove him."

The two warriors grabbed Arion. He struggled against them, but at less than full strength, he could not free himself. They dragged him toward the entrance. "No!" he roared. "Zerahm, I command you to honor my wishes in this matter."

"The law does not allow for killing a citizen who is found innocent," Zerahm said firmly. "I am the Comdar, and I determine the final outcome. Jenna of Saura will be executed in the place of her brother."

Jenna knew this had to end now, before she lost her nerve, or Arion managed to have his way. *Good-bye, my husband,* she told him mentally. *I wish you long life.* She turned and walked toward the block and the warrior wielding his deadly sword.

"Jenna, no!"

Her legs were shaking so much she could hardly move. *Just take one step after another,* she told herself. *Don't show your fear. It won't stop your fate, and it will only shame Arion.*

With each step closer to the block, images of her life flashed through her mind. She saw herself as a child, laughing in delight as her mother tossed her in the air; Damon teasing her about her shyness around boys; the shattering news that first her mother, then her father, were dead.

She saw her first meeting with Arion; the flash of his knife as it slashed her palm in the ancient blood-sharing rite, felt the heat of his mouth against the wound; saw their merging ceremony; her getting drunk on kashni; Arion shielding her from Brona's malice and taking care of her cuts. For a brief moment, she was again making love with him in the huge tub; watching him chase the Branuka bug and grinning at her triumphantly when he caught it. She remembered his vehement declaration when she'd yearned to see Damon: *"I am your family."*

And he was, everything she'd ever needed or wanted. She'd just found her place in the universe, and the man she loved, only to give it all up, for him. She was almost to the block now, almost to the massive warrior and his terrifying sword.

"Wait!" This time it was Morven who called out. "You cannot execute Lady Jenna." He was suddenly at her side.

She almost sagged to the ground. She couldn't take any more of this turmoil.

"Why would you make such a claim?" Zerahm demanded.

"Because she is with child."

The murmurs of the crowd amplified to a dull roar. Shock swept through Jenna. She stared at the shaman. *"What?"*

"What?" Zerahm echoed in disbelief.

"She bears a new life inside her," Morven replied with his infuriating calm. "Our laws do not allow a citizen to be executed while she carries another life."

A gray, swirling mist surrounded Jenna. She closed her

eyes, swaying. Morven grabbed her and shook her. "You will not faint," he hissed.

"Even if the Comdar's mate were not carrying offspring, I would not allow anyone to die this cycle," came a powerful male voice.

With another small shake, Morven forced Jenna to turn with him. Totally confused, she looked toward the entrance. Gunnar strode into the stadium, Lani by his side and a group of warriors flanking them.

"It is about time he arrived," Maxine muttered, moving to Jenna's other side.

Vaguely aware her mouth was hanging open, Jenna looked at the android. "What are you talking about?"

"As soon as I researched the Leor laws regarding retribution, I made the logical assumption your life would be at risk, since you were determined to rescue Arion," Maxine replied. "I sent a communication to Lani, asking her to intercede. As you can see, my concern was quite valid. When you left the lab, I estimated there was a 97.35 percent chance you would uncover the specific laws and offer your life for Arion's. I did not take into account the possibility you might be pregnant."

"Be quiet, android," Morven ordered. "The Komissar is speaking."

"I have called a special session of the Komiss to convene on Dukkair as soon as every clan head can get there," Gunnar announced. "Until that session is adjourned, all executions will be put on hold." He turned slowly, looking up at the Leors gathered there. Taller and broader than Arion, his large head gleaming in the bright sunlight, he was a formidable presence.

"The times grow perilous," his deep voice rang out. "The Controllers have decided they will no longer tolerate our existence and seek to eradicate us. Our numbers grow smaller, from warfare and low birth rates. We can no longer cling to our old ways. We will have to change and adapt. We will have to join with others to fight this threat from the Controllers. And we will have to reexamine our laws. No longer can we afford the loss of innocent lives, not even for retribution."

He turned to Jenna. Looking up at him made her dizzy, and she leaned against Morven. "Your brother's crime was heinous, and were he here, he would suffer a slow, excruciating death," Gunnar told her. "But you are not to blame for his actions. You are Comdar Arion's mate, and you carry a very precious life within you. I hereby absolve you of any association with your brother's crime, and revoke judgment."

Her legs did give out then, and only Morven's grip kept her upright. Gunnar turned his attention to Arion. "Arion of Saura, nor are you to blame for the actions of Damon san Aron. I hereby restore your title of Comdar, relieving Zerahm of that duty. I order you to report to Dukkair within the next five cycles, to attend the Komiss. There are many decisions to be made."

Arion placed his hand across his chest and bowed. "I thank you, Komissar."

"I would also like to meet with you privately, Comdar," Gunnar said. "However, first you will see to your injuries and to your mate." He glanced at Jenna, approval in his gaze.

She barely noticed, all her attention focused on Arion. She started toward him, desperate to touch him.

"Oh, Jenna!" Lani squealed, throwing herself against Jenna, almost knocking her over, and hugging her tightly. "I couldn't believe it when Maxine told me that first Arion, then you, were to be executed for someone else's crimes! How archaic! I've been telling Gunnar for the longest time that Leor laws are from the dark ages. I'm so glad you're all right. And a baby!" She squealed again. "Congratulations."

"Thank you," Jenna murmured automatically, still too stunned to take it all in.

"I'm glad we made it in time." Lani huffed and sent a squinty-eyed glare toward Zerahm. "That man is far too full of himself. He wanted to kill Arion and Jenna! Gunnar, sweetness, you need to demote him or something."

"All is well, *charina*," Gunnar soothed. "We will work on changing the laws."

"It's about time." With another sniff, Lani took his arm. She flashed a smile at Jenna. "Let's get together later. That white is not your best color. I'll have some brighter loincloths replicated for you. You'll appreciate the simplicity of Leor fashions, especially later in your pregnancy."

Jenna had forgotten she was dressed only in a loincloth. She felt her face heating. "Yes, later," she managed to answer.

"Rest and take care of your mate," Gunnar told Arion. "I will meet with you at six hundred hours tomorrow." He and Lani left the tribunal, Lani keeping pace with him despite her blue spiked heels.

The realization that she was truly safe began to seep into Jenna's mind, bringing a rush of elation. She wasn't going to die! Neither was Arion. Weak and shaky, she started toward him, and as he came to meet her, her legs grew stronger, her spirit welling inside her until she thought she might burst.

Suddenly she was in his arms, kissing him between bouts of talking and crying. "Arion! Arion, Arion, Arion!" She pulled back to look at him, his image blurred through the tears. *I love you.*

We will discuss this love issue after we discuss your defiance, he replied, but his eyes were filled with warmth, and he hugged her tightly.

"All is well," Morven said from behind Jenna.

"Oh!" She wiggled away from Arion and turned to glare at him. "I have a few things to say to you, Shaman. Why

320

did you let me think I was going to die all that time? I was *terrified,* and you were talking about beheading, when you knew all along I was pregnant and they wouldn't ex-ecute— Oh!" She splayed her hand over her abdomen, a new joy filling her. "Am I really pregnant?"

Morven nodded. "I am never wrong about such things. I regret prolonging your anxiety. But I had to be certain judgment had been transferred from Arion to you before I could halt the execution. Then I allowed you to walk to the execution block so that all could see your courage and your worthiness."

Jenna barely heard the last part of his statement, her attention focused on something she'd longed for all her life. "A baby . . ." She could hardly believe it. She whirled back into Arion's arms. "A baby! Arion, we're having a baby!"

"You have given me two great gifts." He held her close, and she felt the steady, powerful beat of his heart. "The love of a mate and the future of our race."

He had given her just as much, if not more. He'd given her his love, too, although he didn't vocalize it like she did. But he showed it in his tenderness when they mated, in his steadfast support, in his willingness to die for her. And he had given her acceptance—full, unconditional ac-ceptance, visions and all.

She kissed him again and felt heated desire unfurling inside her. Drawing back, she gazed into his beautiful dark eyes. "After Lanka checks your wound, let's go home."

"Yes," he replied, cupping her cheek. "We will go home." *I have big plans for the bathing tub,* he added mentally.

Laughing, she wondered if it was possible for a heart to burst from happiness.

Epilogue

She should have known Leors wouldn't have babies in a normal manner. Jenna had learned to accept a lot of things in her time on Saura, but giving birth to a baby outside in the desert, in the scorching heat, went beyond her tolerance.

She told everyone so, in no uncertain terms, and quite loudly, but it didn't do any good. First off, they ignored her vehement protests. Secondly, she quickly discovered labor was incapacitating. Staying on top of the pain demanded every ounce of strength and concentration she could rally, with nothing left over to wage a battle against five stubborn Leors, one blue-feathered human, and an android.

Actually, Lani was sympathetic to Jenna's plight, but she was outnumbered by Arion, Lanka, Morven, Erek, and Gunnar. Maxine had no sympathy at all, briskly informing Jenna that she lived among the Leors and should observe the proper protocols.

Jenna wasn't any too pleased about having such a large audience present for the birth of her child, either. But labor pains readily dispensed with all attempts at modesty or dignity, rendering her incapable of anything but focusing on surviving the process.

The need to have Lanka and Arion there was obvious, and she could understand Morven's presence, as he attended all births and deaths on Saura. She could even understand Erek's presence, since he was now Morven's apprentice, a shaman in training, although she did think he might be too young, and perhaps too simpleminded, to be witnessing a birth. Gunnar was there because Morven had foreseen this baby would bear the mark of the next Sauran clan leader, and of course Lani came with Gunnar.

Jenna had wanted Maxine present, but had quickly regretted it when the android turned traitor and sided with the others, insisting the birth occur in accordance with Leor tradition. Which meant having the baby at the base of the Goddess's altar.

The only concession that had been made on Jenna's behalf was the awning under which she labored. If Arión thought that was enough to diffuse her ire at the situation, he was seriously mistaken. Once she got thought this delivery and regained her strength, she was going to let him know exactly what she thought about Leor birthing practices.

"Jenna, push," he ordered, his breath warm on her ear. "You are being defiant."

She was sitting on a special birthing stool, with him behind her, his powerful thighs cradling her legs. One of his arms was wrapped securely around her, resting beneath her bare breasts, while his other hand massaged her swollen belly. Lanka knelt between her legs, waiting for the baby's arrival.

"*Charina,* I am ready to see my son," Arion informed Jenna.

Ha! she thought. Was he in for a surprise! It would be

her personal victory, just payment for what he had put her through.

"Push," he said again.

She did, but only because the urge was upon her, and because she was hot and thirsty and wanted the incessant pain to go away. The contraction eased, and she rested, gasping for breath in the stifling air.

"Good job!" Lani trilled, blotting the sweat from Jenna's face. "You're doing great. Show these Leors how tough human females are."

"Your progress is satisfactory," Maxine confirmed. "And you appear to be ahead of schedule. Since the average first human labor is twelve hours in length, and you have only been in labor six hours, five minutes, and thirty-three seconds—"

"Another contraction is coming," Lanka interjected.

"Push again," Arion ordered.

"Go to Hades," Jenna said sweetly, but she complied, determined to get this baby into the world. The contraction ended, and she collapsed against her mate, exhausted.

You are doing well, charina. I am very proud of you.

Don't you "charina" me, you Leor. Having babies in the desert is positively barbaric. Not that it matters, since you're never touching me again.

Arion had the good sense not to laugh, but she felt his smile against her hair. Lani fluttered around her, chattering and keeping her distracted between contractions, while Maxine spouted data Jenna would rather not know.

Nearby, Morven and Erek sat cross-legged on the sand, chanting in the ancient Leor language. She found the blend of a deep masculine voice and a higher-pitched, youthful voice soothing. White smoke issuing from the brazier between them drifted around her, and she suspected whatever was in the burning leaves had taken the edge off the pain.

Gunnar stood behind the shamans, legs splayed, arms crossed over his massive chest. He said very little, simply waited. She wished Maxine would follow his example. Just then, another contraction hit, and she turned her attention inward.

"The infant is coming," Lanka announced.

Jenna gave one last push, and suddenly the baby was there, caught by Lanka's capable hands and squalling mightily.

"It is . . . a female." Lanka sounded surprised.

"*A female?*" Arion and Gunnar said in shocked unison.

"Is she all right?" Jenna asked anxiously, and only when she was reassured that her daughter was perfectly fine, did she permit a smug smile on her face. She hadn't allowed Lanka to test for the sex of the baby, because she'd already known she carried a daughter, so informed by the Goddess.

"Yes, a female," Morven said, sounding rather smug himself. As usual, he had probably known all along.

"Baby is beautiful," came Erek's pure, high voice.

"But you said this infant was Saura's future leader," Gunnar protested.

"Look at her back," Morven replied.

The collective gasp told Jenna they'd all seen what she had already known would be there. "She has the mark of the new moon," Lani said. "Way to go!"

"But she is a female," Gunnar pointed out again.

There was a thunk as Lani hit him in middle of the chest. "Why can't a female be the leader of a clan?" she shrilled.

"I do not know, but never in our history has a female been born with the mark of the clan leader."

"I want to hold my daughter," Jenna demanded. She stared lovingly at the noisy bundle Lanka placed in her arms, and cooed to the child. Immediately the baby quieted, looking up at Jenna with dark gray eyes. She had reddish peach fuzz on her head, an indication she would have hair. Very faint lines crisscrossed her delicate skin, so her Leor heritage would also be evident. The best of both races.

Arion pressed against Jenna, placing one hand on the baby's head. "She is beautiful, *charina*. I thank you for this gift."

"You're not disappointed she is a girl?"

"I am surprised, but not disappointed. Why do I get the feeling you did this deliberately?"

"How could I control the sex of our baby? Talk to the Goddess about it." As Jenna said that, she heard faint, feminine laughter.

You did very well indeed, beloved daughter. Your own daughter will lead her clan in the war against the Controllers. She will achieve greatness.

So there would be war, Jenna thought sadly, although she'd known it was just a matter of time. She gazed down into the clear gray eyes watching her, overwhelmed by her intense love for this child. Then she saw something else— the golden light surrounding the baby. It was her daughter's aura, so brilliant and dazzling even Jenna could see it.

"Look, Arion," she whispered. "Look at her aura."

"I have never seen one like it." He turned Jenna's face toward him and kissed her. *You have my love, charina.*

And I love you. I might even let you touch me again.

With one of his rare smiles, he wrapped his arms around her. Together they gazed at their daughter, seeing the promise and the hope for a better world.